His Eighth Ride

HAMMOND FAMILY FARM ROMANCE

IVORY PEAKS ROMANCE
BOOK EIGHT

LIZ ISAACSON

feel-good fiction

LIANA JOHNSON

Copyright © 2023 by Elana Johnson, writing as Liz Isaacson

All rights reserved.

No part of this book may be reproduced in any form or by any electronic or mechanical means, including information storage and retrieval systems, without written permission from the author, except for the use of brief quotations in a book review.

ISBN-13: 978-1638763604

CHAPTER

One

OPAL HAMMOND RODE in the passenger seat of Gerty's truck, her sister-in-law silent. That suited Opal just fine, because she didn't want to talk about how she'd been wrong.

Her ribs had healed up nicely, but she had been overdoing things. The doctor had told her to slow down—again—and if there was anything Opal liked less than disgusting blue cheese dressing, it was being told to slow down.

She'd finished medical school faster than ninety percent of people who went into the profession, simply to prove she could. And she had.

And now you're burnt out at age twenty-nine, she thought.

"Mike picked up your birthday cake," Gerty said, glancing over to Opal.

She finally uncinched her arms from around her

midsection and released the breath that felt like it had been trapped inside for the past hour. "Thank you," she said. "For having him do that." She drew in a new, cleansing breath. "Thank you for driving me."

"Of course." Gerty's hands finally released their chokehold on the steering wheel too. "I know this is really hard for you, Opal. I'm—"

"If you apologize to me, I'm going to go the rest of the day without speaking to you."

Gerty clamped her lips closed and tightened her grip on the wheel again.

Opal sighed, trying to get her shoulders to go down. She couldn't believe her life had been impacted so strongly by getting kicked in the ribs. She'd seen patients like this too, but she'd never had to go home with them after they came into the ER. She never saw most of her patients again, and she simply didn't know the hours, days, weeks, and months that they had to continue to deal with their injuries.

And that was another problem—Opal didn't *feel* injured. Until she did, and then she had to sit down, gasping for breath.

"Just because I got hurt on your farm does not make you responsible," Opal said in a softer, kinder voice.

"I feel bad."

"I know, but you don't need to."

"Tag texts me about you constantly." Gerty looked over to her again, her face a perfect mask of anxiety.

They'd had heated conversations about Taggart Crow too, thank you very much. Opal didn't shy away from hard things, situations, or conversations, which made her avoidance of one gorgeous, strong, tall, handsome Taggart Crow doubly confusing.

"I am going to talk to him," Opal said. It wasn't like she'd given him the silent treatment or anything. They talked all the time, as Tag lived in a cabin on Gerty's farm, and Opal lived in the farmhouse with her, Mike, and their ten-month-old baby, West.

"You are? What are you going to say?"

Opal had plenty to say, but she simply shook her head and said, "I don't know. What time is it?" She looked at her phone, though her eyes had caught on the clock on the dashboard too. "I have time for a nap before dinner." She leaned her head back and closed her eyes now too, hoping Gerty would just let Tag drop.

She did, as Opal suspected she would, as Gerty wasn't the most eloquent woman ever. She said what had to be said, and she took care of business, voiced her opinion on things, and ran her household perfectly. But she wouldn't hound Opal about her unrequited crush on Tag, nor did she tell Opal much of what the man said to her.

He too had been apologetic to the point of annoyance over the past few months, and he'd been dancing around her with one of two expressions on his face since. He either wore a look of longing that quickly turned to something harder, or he painted guilt over his handsome features. Opal didn't want either. She wanted to be treated like she was normal, because she was.

People got kicked by horses. It wasn't anyone's fault, and if she'd stop trying to prove herself useful to someone by helping with feeding the horses or lifting West when someone else could get him, then she wouldn't be back on "slow down mode."

Gerty navigated them back to the farm, and Opal slid from the truck as normal. She automatically looked down the lane to the barn. She didn't see Tag, and she found herself searching the surrounding fields and area for him. They'd just gotten their winter wheat in the ground a couple of weeks ago, and he was probably out babysitting that.

He also did a lot of work with the horses that Gerty found and brought back to the farm. She couldn't stand the mistreatment of equines, and she spent a lot of time in rescue groups and forums, making sure horses didn't have to suffer needlessly.

When she brought them back here, she tended to them a lot, but so did Tag. Someone usually had to break the horses again, or at least teach them to be less wary, more forgiving, and how to trust people again.

Both he and Gerty were very good at it, and Opal loved watching both of them work. She didn't even understand herself, so she couldn't possibly deal with a horse, but Gerty seemed to speak their language.

Gerty also knew herself completely, and Opal's mood worsened as she entered the farmhouse ahead of her best friend in the world. She couldn't think badly of Gerty, and she didn't. She just wished she had half of the woman's wisdom.

Funny that Opal had the advanced degree, but Gerty possessed all the wisdom Opal wished she did.

"Are you going to lie down then?" Gerty asked as she shrugged out of her coat. Somewhere in the house, West squealed in delight. Gerty's daddy had come to watch him that day for Opal's appointment, and Boone's laughter filled the house, covering the baby's voice.

Opal turned back to Gerty, so many pieces inside her cracking. They broke, bent, bubbled up, and tears filled her eyes. She rushed at Gerty and hugged her. "I'm sorry I'm so mean at the appointments."

"Oh, hush," Gerty said, gripping her tightly-but-not-too-tightly. "You're not mean. You just don't want to be slowed down."

"I'm tired of being a patient," Opal admitted. "I'm sorry. Thank you for taking me." She stepped back and wiped her eyes. Thankfully, not too much water had escaped. "I'm going to go for a walk, I think. Don't worry, I won't pick anything up, and I'll go really slow."

"Okay," Gerty said airily. "It's really windy. Take my scarf if you want."

Opal nodded, though she hadn't needed a scarf in

ten years, since she'd left the wild winters of Wyoming and gone to California.

She hadn't shed her coat yet, so she simply had to reach for Gerty's scarf, and she then held it in her hands like she didn't know what to do with it. Gerty giggled and took it from her. "You just drape it like this."

She looped it around Opal's neck once, then twice, and she tucked the ends into the first drape. "Then you pull it...." She tugged it down, and the scarf snuggled up to Opal's throat, sure to keep out the pesky wind. "There."

"Thanks." Opal smiled at Gerty, hugged her again, and left the farmhouse. She left the baby behind. She left the warmth, the glow of a good family, and the safety of hiding in her bedroom.

She faced the barren world outside, and she marveled at how much Colorado looked like Wyoming in the winter. "Brown and gray," she said, the words making her lips warm for a moment, and then cold once the heat of her breath had gone.

She felt brown and gray inside too, and she drew in a long breath, held it, and then pushed all the air out of her lungs. She stretched her arms up above her head, pulling to the right easily. But when she moved left, she went slowly. Very slowly, trying to find the spot where it hurt and didn't just stretch.

It didn't take long, and she dropped her arms with a burst of air. She hadn't even realized she'd been holding her breath, but her head tingled now, and she took another deep breath. She could walk, and she went down the steps to the lane in front of the house. This road went all the way to the northern fence, and Opal could walk on the pristine, flat, packed-hard dirt for miles if she wanted to.

She didn't. She just needed to clear her head. She needed to be ready for her birthday party at the farmhouse that night. Gerty's parents were coming. So were her aunt Gloria and uncle Matt, and their kids. Keith and Britt and their significant others were coming, as Gerty had grown up with them on the family farm several miles north.

On her side of the family, all of Opal's cousins were coming, including Hunter, Molly, and their kids. Cord and Jane. Deacon, Tucker, and Tarr. Fine, the last man wasn't a cousin, but Tuck didn't seem to go anywhere without Tarr.

With Gerty's grandparents and Tag, almost thirty people would be there.

"Twenty-eight," Opal said, quickly counting and including herself. "Only one of whom is a baby."

So she couldn't talk to Tag tonight. There'd be far too much going on, in far too small of a space. Yes, Mike and Gerty had gutted the farmhouse, pushed out the back wall, and made their home big, bright, and beautiful. They had plenty of space to raise a family, house her grandparents, who lived in a separate cabin, and thrive on this farm for a long time.

But twenty-eight people for a birthday party would tax anyone.

Opal especially.

"They're coming for you," she told herself as she walked past Carrie and Kyle's house. The porch stretched along both sides of the front door, and Opal coveted a quaint, country cottage like what they had.

She hardly recognized her thoughts as she glanced further onto the farm, where Tag's cabin stood among a trio of them. He was the only employee on the farm, besides Gerty, so he lived among the cabins alone. Opal wondered if he ever got lonely, or if he craved the solitude.

She'd been so eager to leave small-town Coral Canyon and find herself in the cities of California. She hadn't quite done that, though she had built a good career and reputation for herself.

A career and reputation she cared little about these days. She couldn't believe she'd landed in another small town, this time in a different state. And this farm? It sat miles from any other civilization, in the county jurisdiction, not even any city limits.

And as Opal walked under the winter sky, she realized one profound truth: She loved this farm.

Maybe you're not as much of a city girl as you thought you were.

The thought rang true, and Opal paused when she came to the first fence. The pastures sat dormant this time of year, as Gerty and Tag had already pulled all the horses back to the stables and barns. Thanksgiving had come and gone, and Opal should be looking forward to Christmas, when her parents would come to town.

Mike had even managed to get Ethan and Allison to commit to coming for Christmas Day dinner, and Opal could admit she was looking forward to having her core family back together again.

She was not looking forward to being the only single one there. Again.

"Lord," she said. "Thou hast led me here. I listened. I came. I left behind everything in Burbank." She took a deep breath, because none of it felt like a sacrifice now. Perhaps nine months ago, it had. She'd been surprised to feel the tug of somewhere quieter in her soul. She'd resisted God when He'd first told her to leave her job, leave her friends, leave everyone and everything and come to Ivory Peaks to help Gerty with her baby.

West wasn't even that much of a baby anymore, and yet, Opal was still here.

"What am I doing here, Lord?" she asked. "I've done what Thou has wanted me to do in the past. If You'll just tell me now, I'll do it." Her voice took on an edge of desperation, but she didn't try to curb it.

The wind whistled past the fence posts, almost forming words, but not quite. Opal hunkered down into her scarf and pushed away from the rungs. She left the road and headed toward the trees, though they'd lost all their autumnal vibrancy and now only waved their bare branches angrily at the sky.

She let her thoughts wander where they may, trying to keep herself quiet should the Lord decide to talk to her. Her feet did the same, and before she knew it, the triangle of cabins loomed in front of her.

The sun went behind a cloud, and Opal paused as she looked up. Her fingers in her pockets fisted, and she looked back to Tag's house. A thin stream of smoke lifted from his chimney, and Opal could practically feel the warmth of the obvious fire inside chasing away the cold and wind out here.

Without second guessing herself, she continued toward his house and right up his steps. This was not the first time she'd come to his cabin. She'd been here for lunch before; she'd come several times since the accident to bring him food or cookies; she'd come to tell him to stop worrying over her, to stop blaming himself, to stop looking so sad.

Since then, he'd just avoided her, the same way she had him.

"No more," she murmured as she lifted her fist to knock.

"Come in!" Tag yelled from inside, but Opal hesitated. He had no doorbell cam, so he couldn't possibly know who stood on his porch. His choices were slim, but Opal was sure that if he knew it was her, he wouldn't be calling for her to simply walk in.

Still, Opal reached for the doorknob, twisted it, and did just that.

Tag twisted from where he stood at his dining room table, an enormous box in front of him. A large roll of sparkly pink wrapping paper sat atop it as Tag had been pulling it along the top of the box.

He half-yelped and half-choked, and then he spun toward her and pressed his back into the box as if he could hide it that way. He did have deliciously broad shoulders, but they narrowed into a trim waist that didn't span the width of the box.

Oh, and that roll of bright wrapping paper continued rolling and then dropped to the floor, where the cardboard tube bumped once, thumped hollowly, and slumped into a pile of loose paper, all while they stared at one another in silence.

CHAPTER

Two

TAGGART CROW GAWKED at the woman who'd been starring in his fantasies and daydreams for months now. Fine, he'd had a nightmare or two about Opal Hammond as well. They always included a bucking horse and her passed out on the ground, and Tag blinked to get that scene out of his head.

"Hey," he said, not sure why his words had failed him so spectacularly. He'd been avoiding Opal since he'd asked her out. That had happened on the same day as she'd been kicked in the chest by a horse he'd been working with.

All of that was fine. Rather, it wasn't, but it was what it was. Tag couldn't change the past, and when Opal had chewed him out for "looking sad" around her, he'd defaulted to not being around her.

And he probably did look sad, but it wasn't

because she'd been kicked. He didn't blame himself for that.

No, the idiotic thing he'd done that day had been to ask her to dinner.

She'd said yes—but she hadn't remembered the exchange. So, when Tag brought it up later, when he'd tried to schedule the date, Opal had been ultra-confused. Even now, embarrassment squished its way through all of Tag's cells.

"Are you wrapping a birthday present for me?" Opal had come inside and closed the door, but that was all. She stuck close to the door, like he might bend, swoop up the roll of pink wrapping paper, and wield it like a sword.

He couldn't hide the fact that he was, indeed, wrapping up a gift for her. She'd have seen it in a couple of hours anyway. So he said, "Yes."

"It's really big." Her eyes roamed the box behind him, and Tag inched away from it.

"How was your appointment today?" Darkness crossed Opal's already dark and brunette features. "Oh, not great," he said. "Why not? Was it that half-bale of hay you picked up when I told you not to? That I was literally five seconds away from grabbing?" He popped his eyebrows up, clearly challenging her.

Opal was so dang smart, she could use a challenge every now and then. Tag couldn't believe the way he'd just flirted with her, though. They hadn't had any exchanges like this in ages. Too long, in his opinion.

"I'm sure it wasn't that," she said. "But he did tell me I can't lift anything heavier than a loaf of bread."

"So West is out," Tag said. "Heck, you probably won't even be able to lift this gift." He did bend and pick up the fallen wrapping paper then. "You wanna come help me with this?"

"Do I want to help you wrap my own present?" She did approach him, and Tag smiled at her. "Who does that?"

"You're going to do it." He tightened up the paper again and stretched it across the top of the box. "I just need some tape right there." He nodded across to the other side of the box, and that would put Opal all the way in his house.

She picked up the roll of tape and ripped off a piece. She placed it where it went while Tag warred with himself over asking her why she'd come. He said nothing as the furnace pumped heat into the cabin, and he seized onto that. "Cold outside."

Opal looked up at him, her dark eyes blazing with plenty of heat. "Really? You're going to make me wrap my own present *and* talk to me about the weather?"

"What would you like to talk about then?" he shot back. "*You* showed up at *my* house. I was fine before you walked in."

"As compared to now?"

"Well, I can't wrap this in front of you. It would've been embarrassing enough to show up with it all mangled." He grabbed the scissors and cut all the way across the paper. "Tape there, please."

She did what he asked, and he folded in the corner. It didn't cover all of the box, and Tag had no idea how to fix it. Opal relieved him of the roll of paper and the scissors and said, "Let me."

A sigh of relief left his mouth. "I'll turn it when you need me to," he said. "I'm pretty sure it weighs more than a loaf of bread."

"What is it?" she asked.

"Nice try." He gave her a smile, glad when the corners of her mouth twitched too. So maybe they could somehow find their way back to being friends again. "Coffee? Tea?"

"Coffee would be great," she said. She worked on covering the present with the neon paper while he measured grounds and set the coffee to brew. "I need help turning."

Tag faced her and walked her way. He could've stayed over on the side of the table he'd stood on earlier, but instead, he crowded in next to her. Opal held her ground, her eyes locked on his and refusing to leave.

He could turn the box without looking at it, but he tore his gaze from hers to roll it onto its other side.

"Hmm, I didn't hear anything clink or clank," Opal said.

"Why did you come here?" he asked.

She put the roll of pink paper against his chest and edged him back. "I don't know. I...just showed up."

"Sounds mysterious."

"Let me finish the present."

He grinned at her, his heartbeat fluttering up into his throat, tickling it. "Cream? Sugar?"

"Both," Opal said, and Tag finally fell away from her.

He got out the cream and sugar and set them on the counter in his cabin, sudden panic pulling through him at the cleanliness of the place. Oh, and that fact that he'd thought the person knocking on his door would've been none other than Opal's older brother, Mike.

His boss and his best friend.

He swallowed and got down three coffee mugs, because Mike was coming over whether Tag wanted him to or not. Tag would have to go back out and do the evening feeding before the party, but Mike had wanted all of Opal's gifts in the house beforehand. Since he knew how big Opal's gift was, and how many people were coming, they'd devised a plan to have it there first.

"I need another turn," she said, and Tag wondered how long he'd lost himself inside his own mind.

He turned the box one last time for Opal, the house starting to fill with the scent of coffee. He picked up the tape this time and helped her finish the package, and then he took the nearly empty roll and the scissors from her. "Thank you."

He'd just turned around when Opal asked, "Tag, would you maybe want to go to dinner with me?"

Tag's ears had malfunctioned. Just one hundred percent gone into defect mode, rearranging the words she'd said into what he wanted to hear. Because his ears no longer worked, he lost his equilibrium, and he flung out a hand to catch himself against the counter.

Unfortunately, that hand held the scissors, and they went skidding across the surface—right into the jug of cream. He watched in horror as it wobbled, tipped, and fell.

At the same time, his other palm jammed into the counter, smashing the roll of wrapping paper. To top it off, he'd just spun back to Opal when someone knocked on the door.

Mike entered a moment later, calling, "It's just me, Tag."

Tag's pulse pinballed through his body, first shooting to his scalp, and then getting pinged down to his gut, then shooting through all twenty-four of his ribs. He tore his gaze from Opal to focus on her brother, noting that Mike had frozen too.

"Are you trying to get a sneak peek at your birthday present?" Mike strode forward and picked up the enormous pink box that took up almost the whole dining room table. "Opal, it's a *surprise*." He frowned at his sister, who gave him his attitude right back.

"I wasn't trying to get a sneak peek at anything." She swallowed, the only sign of nerves Tag could see in her, and he had no idea if that belonged to him or to her brother. Or to having both of them in the same space at the same time.

"I made coffee," he said, regaining his composure.

"Great," Mike said. "West has been a beast today."

"Oh, please," Opal said. "That baby is a saint, and Boone was here all day." She rolled her eyes at her brother and pulled out a seat at the table.

"He's slobbering everywhere," Mike said as he moved over to help Tag with the coffee. "And he's fussy. He puts everything in his mouth, and let me tell you, those baby teeth are *sharp*." He clapped Tag on the back, his eagle eyes missing nothing. "You didn't *tell* her what was in that box, did you?"

"No, sir," Tag said. He picked up the mugs and Mike grabbed the fallen cream carton and the sugar bowl. Tag took the mugs over to Opal, their eyes catching and holding every step of the way.

"Thank you," she murmured, and Tag's whole being itched. He needed to get a dinner date on the calendar with her sooner rather than later, because last time he'd only asked and didn't set everything up, it had all gone awry.

But with Mike in the house and seemingly going nowhere, Tag stuffed his questions away and returned to the kitchen for the coffee pot. This was going to be an exquisite form of torture.

A FEW HOURS LATER, Tag ducked into the farmhouse where Mike and Gerty lived, the heat welcoming him first. Then, the energy zipping through the place zoomed into his heart, and he had the distinct impression that God had led him home.

What that meant for him, as he worked someone else's farm and not his own, Tag didn't understand. But he was only thirty years old, and he'd given up trying to figure out each step before he took it. God laughed at him when he did that, besides.

Right now, Tag shook hands with Matt Whettstein, then his brother, Boone, who was Gerty's father. They had their teens standing over by the baby, who did have flushed cheeks and plenty of spittle on his face. West also had plenty of girls to take care of him, and Tag smiled at the grouping around him.

He stayed out of the way, because he wasn't family to Opal. He wasn't related to any of her family. The only reason he was here was because he worked for Mike and Gerty. Nothing else, despite the fact that *she'd* asked him to dinner mere hours ago.

"I wonder what's in that big pink box," Boone mused, and Tag once again kept his mouth shut.

"She's coming," someone yelled, and Tag's antici-pation grew. Then Opal came down the hall and into the living room, where plenty of people had crammed themselves. A cheer went up, and everyone started hollering and clapping. Tag put his hands together too, glad he could stare at Opal for as long as he wanted.

He was supposed to look at her, for crying out loud.

And what a sight she was. She wore a long black dress that somehow fit her like a glove and flowed around her in waves at the same time. He would never expect Opal to wear anything bright or flashy, though she had plenty of personality.

Her hair had been braided back, revealing her slender face with those big, beautiful eyes and those extremely kissable lips. In that moment, his hands somehow flapping together in slow motion and Opal smiling at her cousin Jane, Tag wondered how in the world he'd lived here with her for so long without being hers.

You'll fix that, he told himself. *Tonight.*

He vowed he would not be going to bed tonight without a date with Opal—one they both knew about and both remembered—on the calendar.

"Presents first," Mike yelled, lifting his hands up into the air. "Come on, Opal, you're going to open presents first." He indicated the garish pink box, and Opal's eyes roamed the crowd. Tag hoped and prayed she was looking for him, but he stayed out of the way, over by the side entrance to the house.

She didn't see him before she had to step over to the gift. "Wow," she said in an overly loud voice, plenty of mocking in her tone. "Whoever wrapped this is brilliant."

Tag burst out laughing, and he was the only one. He was aware of every eye in the place zeroing in on him—except maybe baby West's—but he didn't care. Opal saw him then, and her smile shone with a radiance he wanted to bask in every single day of his life.

In that moment, he realized how plain his life had become. How beige. How boring.

And Opal...oh, Opal sure could liven things up.

She ripped off the paper and took the knife Mike gave her so she could undo the seam of tape on the nondescript brown box. She threw Tag another flirty look before she peeled back the flaps and peered inside.

"It's...." She reached inside, but Mike said, "You can't lift that. Kyle?"

"You're going to make an old man lift it for me?" Opal glared at her brother, and Mike turned to the next closest person.

"Keith, help her with that, would you?"

"Sure thing," the other cowboy said, and Keith reached into the box with both hands and pulled out the shrink-wrapped item. It was bright purple, and the neon-ness of it assaulted Tag's eyes from across the room.

Several people said, "Wow," or "What is that?" but Opal plucked out the instruction pamphlet from the box.

"It's a blow-up couch," she said, her gaze once again magnetizing to his.

"I thought you could use it in your bedroom," he said. "You've been complaining that you don't have anywhere to sit."

"And," Mike said. "We thought you could take it outside with you too. It won't be too heavy, and you can plunk it under a tree and...do what you do."

"And what do I do, Michael?" she asked with the bite of acid in her tone.

"Read," he said. "Listen to your podcasts. Text your friends."

Tag liked how much they loved each other, but how they also knew each other well enough to banter back and forth. He wanted to get to know Opal like that, and he hoped he could.

"I'll get this blown up," Keith said. "It'll give us more seating."

"A third reason we wanted it," Mike said, throwing Tag a smile. Tag nodded at him and faded out of the spotlight again. That was just fine with him. He didn't need everyone looking at him, that was for certain.

The party progressed; he sang *Happy Birthday* to

Opal with a goofy grin on his face; he ate dinner with Kyle and Carrie, the three of them sort of minding their own business while Mike and Gerty played host and hostess to everyone who'd come to their home.

Sooner than others, Tag had had enough. He stood and took his plate, along with Gerty's grandparents' over to the big trash can that had been set up just for this. Opal currently sat on her neon purple couch, laughing with Molly Hammond and Britt Hansen about something.

She was beauty personified, and Tag told himself to get over there and say good-bye. She'd be upset if he didn't, and that alone got his boots moving in the right direction.

Opal looked up as he approached, and her smile slipped slightly. "You're leaving already?"

"Yes, ma'am," he said. "I've got an early start tomorrow." He cut a look over to Molly and Britt. "Up before the sun and all that."

She stood as he spoke, and Tag felt it only natural to lean in and tell her happy birthday, maybe skate his lips across that velvety cheek. He had no idea where to put his hands, as it had been far too long since he'd been out with a woman.

Especially one like Opal.

Somehow, he managed to cup his hand around her elbow as he leaned in. He did not kiss her, his brain misfiring mightily at him. "Happy birthday, honey," he said, really drawing on his Southern roots. He barely touched her, because he didn't trust himself to put his arms around her. "I'll see you later."

With that completely proper good-bye done, he stepped back. He nodded to the others there, turned, and left.

Outside, he let the door fall closed behind him and he paused on the small stoop that led out of the kitchen. He drew in the deepest breath the chilly night air would allow, and then blew it all out.

"You didn't set up a date," he told himself, and now he wanted to go back inside, interrupt the party, and hash it all out regardless of who overheard or who saw.

Instead, he went down the few steps to the dirt, because it was too cold to be standing around outside doing nothing. His cabin was a good ten-minute walk from the farmhouse, and Tag had had a busy day— and he had another one tomorrow.

Text her, he thought, but he didn't pull out his phone to do that until he'd reached the side of the barn. It provided some relief from the wind, and he pressed his back into the wood and started typing.

He read over the message once, then again. For some reason, he couldn't get himself to send it.

"Hey."

Tag looked up from his phone, his flight or fight response kicking in, though a woman had spoken. It took his eyes a moment or two to adjust from looking at his bright screen to the country darkness, and then another moment for his brain to tell him that voice had belonged to Opal.

He shoved his phone back in his pocket, finally seeing her as she neared. "Hey."

"You...left too fast," she said.

"I was just texting you."

"Oh?" She wore a huge coat that obviously didn't belong to her, and Tag wondered what she'd said to get away from her own party. "What did you say?" She settled only an arm's length from him, and that was too far away.

"Did you mean that earlier? About us going to dinner?"

"Yes," she murmured.

Tag reached for her and caught hold of one of her sleeves. Her hands were all bundled up inside, but he managed to pull her closer anyway. "I was asking you when we could do that. I'm really interested in that." He looked down at her, standing right there in front of him, the soft light from the moon or the house or maybe heaven itself illuminating her face enough for him to see her.

"Whenever," she said. "I'm not busy at all."

"Mm, yeah." She'd quit her job in California, but she hadn't told anyone in her family yet. She'd told Tag a couple of months ago, before the horse-kicking incident.

"Tag," she whispered, her eyes falling closed in a long blink.

"Yeah?" The whole world had fallen away, and Tag's heart labored to pump out enough blood, enough oxygen, to reach everywhere in his body.

"Thank you for the couch," she said.

"Did you like it?"

"I sure did." She looked up at him again, and Tag didn't know everything about Opal Hammond yet. He couldn't always read her expression and know exactly what she was thinking.

But right now, he somehow knew that what she really wanted for her birthday was…a kiss.

He lowered his head, about to make a complete fool of himself or hit a homerun. He honestly didn't know which. He knew Opal's fingers fisted in his collar. He knew her eyes drifted closed again. He knew she wasn't going to stop him.

So he touched his mouth to hers, expecting fire and getting it instantly. Now, all he could do was hope he didn't go down in flames.

CHAPTER

Three

OPAL HAD NOT COME OUTSIDE to kiss Tag. Or maybe she had. All she'd known was that he'd left early, before she'd had a chance to finish their conversation from his cabin. The one her brother had interrupted, and neither of them had been able to get back to.

Now, however, that she'd tasted this man's lips, she couldn't let go. She'd never been kissed so tenderly. So hesitantly and yet so absolutely surely.

She didn't know how to stop, and everything melted away. The cold. The urgency to get back inside before someone came looking for her at her own party. All of it.

The only thing that existed was Tag, and the magical way he cared for her.

In the end, she couldn't get the strength to pull back. He did it, and he took in a long breath as he continued to hold her face in his hands. Then he pulled her against his chest, and Opal had never fit so well against another person.

"I'm sorry," he whispered, and Opal's eyes fluttered open. "I shouldn't have...." He cleared his throat. "I just want to get a date on the calendar. I didn't mean to kiss you before we've even gone out."

"I don't mind," Opal murmured. "It's not like we're strangers." She lifted her head and looked at him. "Dinner tomorrow?"

"Yeah," he said, his eyes so dark in the shadows. "Dinner tomorrow sounds good. I'll, uh, call around and find somewhere nice."

"I don't care where we eat," Opal said. She had once, maybe. She'd wanted to be picked up by a man in a suit, his woodsy, crisp cologne stinging her nose. She loved fancy dresses, and wearing dark red lipstick, and eating in nice steakhouses.

But that life hadn't suited her, and Opal knew it now. "I like tacos," she said. "And those fast-casual pizzas where you can make your own, and buffalo wings." She gave him a smile, which he handsomely returned.

"I can't take a woman like you for wings on our first date," Tag said with plenty of conviction, though his voice couldn't travel more than a few feet. "I may not have been out with anyone in a while, but I know better than that."

"How long?" Opal asked.

"Opal?" someone called behind her, and it sounded dangerously like Molly. Maybe Gerty. Maybe Britt. No matter who, Opal stepped out of Tag's embrace and said, "We'll talk tomorrow night."

"Yeah," he said, and Opal turned to head back to the farmhouse. "Yep." His voice echoed behind her, and she rushed up the steps to the kitchen, where Molly held the door.

"There you are," she said. "Sorry, I hope I wasn't interrupting." She looked into the darkness where Opal had come from, but when Opal turned back and looked, she couldn't see anything. Surely Molly couldn't either.

"Nothing to interrupt," Opal said, though that wasn't quite true. Everyone seemed to know about her crush on Tag—probably because she'd told them. She didn't mind them knowing, but she didn't want to talk about Tag right now.

"Did you get a date on the calendar?" Molly asked as she pulled the door closed behind them. In the warmth of the kitchen, Opal shrugged out of her brother's coat.

She beamed at Molly. "Tomorrow night, but I'm not talking about it, okay? Can we just go back to the party and pretend I just had to run to the bathroom?" She gave Molly a bright smile. "Please?"

"Depends," Molly said as she picked up another plastic cup with celery, carrot, and cucumber sticks.

The ranch dressing had been poured inside too, and she swirled a carrot around in it.

"On?"

"On if you're going to text out how the date went," Molly said. "Gerty'll want to know, I'm sure. Jane. Maybe even Britt."

"Did you text out details of your dates with Hunter when you two started dating?"

Molly opened her mouth as if to say yes, then promptly shut it.

"Exactly," Opal said, turning her back on Molly. "I'll tell everyone I have a date with Tag tomorrow night. I will only share what I feel appropriate to share."

"Fair enough," Molly said as she came up beside her. They took in the dining room and living room, where people still milled about, chatting and laughing. The presents and birthday cake were long over, and Opal smiled at her loved ones.

"It was a great party," Opal said.

"Yes," Molly said. "The Hammonds do know how to put on a great party."

———

THE FOLLOWING MORNING, Opal practically bounced into the kitchen on her toes. "Good morning," she said to Gerty, who stood at the kitchen sink, washing out one of West's bottles.

Gerty looked over to her, her expression cool. "Is it?"

"Yes," Opal said with a smile. "It is. I'm sure you've heard, but I'm going to dinner with Tag tonight."

Gerty's eyebrows went up. "I hadn't heard that, actually."

Opal poured herself a cup of coffee and reached for the cream still sitting on the counter. "Are you upset by that?"

"Of course not," Gerty said matter-of-factly. "Both you and Tag are adults. You deserve happiness. Maybe it'll be with each other." She smiled at Opal. "Plus, you two have liked each other for months. Ain't no one— least of all me—can get in the way of that."

"Does Mike know?"

"Why did you think I did?" Gerty asked.

"I texted Jane last night," Opal said. "Molly knows." She shrugged. "I assumed it would make it around all the gossip chains."

"Which is why Mike and I live out here," Gerty said. "We're sort of out all the 'gossip chains.'" She grinned and turned back to West as the baby babbled and clapped his hands against his highchair tray. "Yeah, you're done, aren't you?"

She went to tend to him while Opal doctored up her coffee and scrambled herself a couple of eggs. Then she joined Gerty in the living room with a plate of breakfast. West cruised around the furniture, banging toys and talking to himself while Gerty simply watched and smiled at everything he did.

Opal knew the feeling, because he was simply the best little boy in the world. She ate in companionable silence, and then asked, "You're still planning on me having him today, right?"

"I was," Gerty said. "But your…ribs…."

"I'm fine," Opal said. "I can lift West."

"He weighs more than a loaf of bread."

"I can play with him on the floor. Change his diaper on the floor. Put him down for a nap on the floor. All of it. We'll be fine here." She set her empty plate aside. "Plus, Carrie can come help if I text her."

"I can come for my own child if you text me," Gerty said.

"Yes, but you're busy with the horses today," Opal said matter-of-factly. "And I know sometimes that work is hard to interrupt."

Gerty wouldn't admit that yes, sometimes it was hard to stop in the middle of a training session. Instead, she lifted her head as if Opal had never dealt with a stubborn person before. She had, including Gerty herself. "I have a call with another horse rescue ranch just after lunch. If you can keep him for three or four hours, I can have Carrie come help this afternoon."

"I'm not broken," Opal said.

"I know." Gerty grinned. "But you're going to need this afternoon to start to plan the Christmas party."

"I—what?"

Gerty gave her a grin that only she thought was funny. "Mike is way too busy to plan the party, and I'm probably going to get a few new horses between now and then."

And you don't do anything.

Gerty didn't say those words, but Opal heard them nonetheless. She'd offered to pay rent for the room she lived in here at the farmhouse, but Mike and Gerty didn't need the money. She helped with the small, simple farm chores, like feeding the barn cats and the chickens. She could muck out a stall—well, she could before the accident where she'd been kicked by a horse.

She'd mowed the lawn during the summer and tended to Gerty's neglected flowerbed. This year, she had plans to try her black thumb at a vegetable garden, because Gerty had a great location for it and had never used it.

"Can I ask for help?" Opal asked.

"I'm sure Carrie or Molly would love to help you plan the Christmas party." Gerty lifted her mug to her mouth and drained the last of her coffee.

"It's just for our branch of Hammonds, though, right?" Opal asked. "Easton and Allison are coming. My parents. Yours and your grandparents. Molly and Hunter aren't coming. Are they?"

"No," Gerty said. "You're right. Just us."

Opal started the guest list in her head. "And Tag?"

"Yes," Gerty said.

"So I could ask him to be on the Christmas party planning committee."

Gerty gave her a wary look, filled with so many words without her actually saying anything. "If I get the horses I want today, I'll probably have to hire someone else. Fill another of those cabins out there."

Opal's eyebrows went up this time. "And you're okay with that?"

Gerty grinned and lifted one bony shoulder. "Mike broke the ice with Tag. I think I could hire someone myself this time, yeah."

"How many horses are you going to get?"

"There's this horse rescue ranch up in Wyoming," she said. "One of the Youngs owns it; I found out about it through Jane, because she knows the guys from Country Quad, and I guess it's one of their sons who owns it. Bryce? Anyway, I'm talking to him today. He's got 'some horses' that he'd like to relocate." She made air quotes around "some horses," indicating she didn't even know how many.

"I can house five more here with my current arrangements," Gerty said. "But even one or two would be more than Tag and I can handle. We're full-up as it is."

"Right," Opal said. She knew Gerty and Tag both worked full-time on the farm, and there always seemed to be more to do. "Who are you thinking of hiring?"

"I don't know," Gerty said thoughtfully. "I'm going to talk to my uncle Matt. He always knows of good men who need jobs."

"True," Opal said, and she realized that she used to be connected like that too. That people used to look to her for answers. That she used to be respected and revered and capable of more than sitting on the couch and watching a baby play or planning family Christmas parties.

She wallowed there for a moment, and then she let God wash those debilitating thoughts away. *I led you here, Opal. You belong here.*

Drawing in a deep breath, Opal smiled at Gerty, then looked over to where West sat in the middle of a pile of colored blocks, trying to get them to stick together. "Go get your horse work done. We're fine here. I've already started the guest list in my head, and I can get a meal put together pretty easily. Then it's just activities, and we've always loved caroling."

She smiled again, starting to feel like perhaps she did have a use here. Gerty got up and put her coat on, then her gloves, hat and scarf. She put a cowgirl hat over that and turned back at the kitchen exit. "Thank you, Opal. I don't know what I'd do without you."

"Oh, you'd just take him with you," Opal said with a wave of her hand. "I saw you do that when he was a tiny baby."

"Yeah, but he'd break my back now." Gerty

grinned at the two of them, then swept over to West and showered him in kisses as he giggled.

"Mama, Mama, Mama," he said as she put him down.

"Mama loves you," she said. "I'll be back real soon." Then she left the farmhouse, left Opal there with West, left her praying that God would illuminate the next step she needed to take in her life.

CHAPTER
Four

TAG RAN his church belt through the loops and buckled it, pulling it right to the middle of his body. He owned slacks, but he wasn't sure a Friday night at The Golden Coop, even if he'd somehow dipped deep in the well of his memory and remembered Opal's love of chicken fingers, warranted church clothes.

So he wore blue jeans and this fancy brown belt with the shiniest buckle he owned. He'd never ridden in the rodeo or anything, so it wasn't the size of a dinner plate, but his granddaddy had given this family crest buckle to his father, who'd given it to him.

He turned away from the bed and looked into his closet. The cabin didn't have anything he could walk into, but he had plenty of room for the things he had to hang. As someone who went to work everyday, he didn't need a ton of button-up shirts or polos. He usually wore T-shirts and jeans, boots and hats, and sunscreen. Around the house, he wore more of the same, with a pair of basketball shorts or a baggy pair of sweatpants thrown in.

He did have a couple of white shirts he kept bleached for the Sabbath, and he had several nicer shirts in plaid, plain colors, and stripes he could choose from for purposes such as this. "What to pick, what to pick," he muttered.

Something his momma had once said popped into his head, and Tag reached for a pale green button-up that had white stripes across the top half. He put it on without thinking too hard about it, buttoned it up, and moved over a pace to stand in front of the mirror.

"You've always looked good in green," he said aloud, repeating what his mother had told him when he'd gone on a date in high school. He had to hope that now, sixteen years later, she hadn't been lying to him.

He left his bedroom, grabbed his keys and wallet, and stopped only in the living room to give his corgi a good scrub. "You're good, huh?" he asked the dog. He rolled onto his back, his little paws sticking up into the air, the cute white boots what had earned him his name.

Boots made Tag so happy, and he straightened as he said, "I'll be back later, buddy. Wish me luck." He left the cabin then and hurried to his truck parked out front. He had ten minutes before he needed to pick up

Opal, and that would mean his vehicle would be nice and toasty for her.

She'd once told him that she used to hate it when her dates in high school would come in freezing cold trucks, and she'd have to sit on their icy seats in her dresses. He had no idea if she'd be wearing a dress tonight, but Tag wasn't about to let her be cold. Not on his watch.

Oh, no. He had plans at one of her favorite places to eat, and because The Golden Coop would be busy and loud, he'd then called and got them tickets to the botanical exhibit at the Royal Chinese Gardens.

Indoors, heated, with a special Imperial Winter Christmas exhibit. If that didn't scream Opal's name, then Tag didn't know her at all.

"Dear Lord," he prayed as he sat in the cold truck as it warmed. "Bless us to have clear roads tonight. Good luck at the restaurant. An easy time at the botanical gardens." He took a breath and tried to relax. "I just want this to be fun for her."

He wanted to hold her hand and maybe kiss her goodnight. He wanted to laugh with her and talk with her. He wanted a lot more than just fun for her—he wanted this to be fun for him too. And the start of something good.

But "fun for her" would lead to a second date, and Tag really wanted one of those too.

With only three minutes to spare, he finally pulled out of his driveway and headed for the farmhouse.

Opal had texted that afternoon that she could meet him at his cabin for their date, but Tag had flat-out refused.

Yeah, it might be slightly awkward for him to walk up to his best friend's door and ring the bell—a place he normally just entered after knocking once or twice. And to have Mike look at him differently.

But Opal lived there, and Tag wanted to be a proper Southern gentleman. So he pulled up to the farmhouse, a place he'd loved the moment he'd done so the first time. That interview with Mike and Gerty had gone so well, and he'd been so hopeful. Then, when he'd gotten the job here, he'd never been happier.

He drew a deep breath and got out of the truck while leaving it running. A few steps up to the porch, a few more to the door. He knocked and fell back a step, his heartbeat pounding the same way his knuckles just had.

He expected Opal to open the door, but Gerty did, with West on her hip. The little boy almost always had a smile and a chubby-cheeked giggle for anyone and everyone he met, but tonight, fat tears clung to his eyelashes and he hiccupped as if he'd been crying a lot.

"Hey, Tag," Gerty said easily. "C'mon in." She stepped back as the scent of dinner filtered outside. "Opal just ran down the hall to grab something."

Tag nodded at her and entered the house. Mike

looked over from where he stood in the kitchen, and he grinned as he abandoned his chores. "Wow, cowboy, look at you."

"It's the same thing I wear all the time," Tag said, though he smiled too. He'd pulled a leather jacket over his shirt, and he tucked his hands in the pockets to keep it closed over his "fancy" shirt.

"Nice belt buckle." Mike came closer and shook his hand.

"It's my granddaddy's," Tag said. "I only wear it on special occasions."

"The jacket?" Opal said from behind him. He spun, and the most gorgeous woman in the world glided toward him. She'd somehow gotten the memo that they were getting chicken fingers for dinner, and she'd left the dresses in her closet.

She wore instead a pair of deep purple pants with wide legs that flowed around her like luxurious water. Her blouse had to have come with the pants, as they bore the same color purple, with navy blue, and the two colors made abstract watercolor flowers on a white background.

He could see through the blouse to a white tank top with tiny, spaghetti straps, and Tag's mouth went dry at the sight of her skin, even through fabric.

"I've seen the jacket before." Opal came right into his personal space as if her brother and sister-in-law weren't even there. She reached up and touched the lapel, her smile painted in dark red a memory he would not soon forget.

"I was talking about the belt buckle," he said.

Opal's gaze dropped to it, which felt a little awkward.

"It's a family crest," he said. "My family comes from horses in Alabama."

Opal smiled and looked back at him. "I see that. It's very nice, and no, I haven't seen it before." She looked over to her brother. "I'll be back later." She swept a kiss across his cheek and then moved over to Gerty and West. "You be a good boy for your mama now." She kissed the baby too, nodded at Gerty, and faced Tag again. "He's not happy I'm leaving tonight." A faint smile came to her mouth again. "I hold him while he sleeps, and his mama just puts him in his crib."

"I can see why he prefers you," Tag said with a smile. He took her coat from her after she'd picked it up from the back of the couch and helped her into it. Then he led her to the door and right out of it without looking back. For some reason, he didn't know what to say on the way to the truck, but when he opened her door for her, a flood of heat came out.

"Nice and warm," she said.

Tag closed her door and went to get behind the wheel.

"So," she said. "You're from Alabama."

"I'm pretty sure I've told you that before," he said.

"Maybe." She reached up and tucked her hair behind her ear. She'd left the majority of it down, with just a bit clipped back on either side. "I'm not sure, actually."

"A tiny town outside of Tuscaloosa," he said. "It's called Logandale. Literally a speck of a town. If you blink, you drive through it." Tag threw her a smile. "Sort of how you described Coral Canyon."

"Oh, Coral Canyon takes at least a full minute to drive through," she teased, and Tag laughed.

"Family?" she asked.

"The twins," he said. "Brothers. They both live in Texas now. Workin' a farm there."

"Like you're working one here." Opal smiled again, and he wondered how she made her lips shiny and matte at the same time. He also wondered what that lipstick would taste like, and he shoved that thought away.

"Right," he said. "Sawyer and Fletcher are twenty-five. I was six when they were born. I remember my momma bringin' 'em home from the hospital."

"Oh, wow," Opal said with a laugh. "I bet that was a shock for you. An only child for so long, and then two babies crowding your space."

"They were loud," Tag said with a laugh. He got them on the highway and driving away from the farm, and added, "No reservations at The Golden Coop, but I figured—"

"You are not taking me to The Golden Coop." Opal

wore a look of delight now, and Tag needed to make her do that every day for the rest of his life. She pealed out a string of glorious laughter. "I just told Kyle and Carrie today that I was craving some of their honey chipotle chicken fingers."

"With the ranch dressing dipping sauce."

"My mouth is watering," she said, her tone full of joy. She clapped her hands together. "I'm so excited."

Tag chuckled. "Glad the chicken fingers are a win, then."

"Chicken fingers are always a win," she said.

"So…it wasn't too weird with Mike, right?"

"My brother knows he's not the boss of me," Opal said. "He never has been."

"I know, but I still thought it might be weird. Or with Gerty? I mean, she's my boss."

"Neither of them acted too weird," Opal said, her voice pitching up a little now. Tag wasn't entirely sure she was telling the entire truth. But he, Gerty, and Mike—and Opal—were all adults, and he figured if someone didn't like how things went, they could say something.

It might be awkward, but it couldn't be worse than the past few months since Opal had been kicked by a horse he'd been training.

"Tell me a random fact about you," Opal said.

"A random fact?"

"Yeah, like, I'm double-jointed in my fingers." She held out one hand and bent down only the top knuckle. Tag stared at her fingers for a moment, then blinked to get his attention back on the road.

"Uh, wow," he said.

Opal giggled lightly and said, "Don't worry. It's not a plague or anything."

"I've just never seen that," he said.

"So, random fact." She clearly wasn't going to let this go.

Tag looked out his side window, but in December, even the first week, the sun set by five o'clock at the latest. No one drove this stretch of road, so he didn't really have a whole lot stealing his attention.

"Uh, I solved a Rubix cube in five minutes and ten seconds once," he said. "In junior high."

Opal looked over to him again, and it really was unfair that he couldn't do the same to her. But he didn't want to drive them off the road, so he only glanced at her. "Is that fast?" she asked.

"I mean, it's not the speedcube record," he said. "Those guys solve it in like five *seconds*."

"That is not true," she said. "Five *seconds*?"

"Yeah, it is," he said with a light laugh. "Look it up."

She tugged her phone out of her purse and did just that, the screen illuminating her fine features. Tag liked how everything with her existed in black and white then, except for her gorgeous mouth.

After only a few seconds, she said, "Fine. The world record is actually below four seconds."

"See?" He laughed again. "That's why five minutes isn't impressive. But for a thirteen-year-old in rural Alabama, it was." He turned onto the main highway, the road everyone drove to get into the major Denver metropolis. "You did say a random fact."

"That I did." Opal tucked her phone away, and Tag decided to be brave. He reached over and took her hand in his. Suddenly, images of a brilliant blue sky and a long, dusty road stretched in front of him.

And he and Opal walked there, hand-in-hand, enjoying the afternoon sunshine and all the goodness God and Colorado had to offer.

He blinked, and he found himself seated back in the warm cab of his truck, Opal's fingers settling nicely between his. "You were going to tell me how long it's been since you dated," she said quietly.

"Was I?"

"Yes," she said without missing a beat.

Tag sighed, sure he'd have to talk about his past more with Opal. But perhaps he could feed her just a little bit and move on. It was their first date, after all. "I dated a woman named Talina in Green River," he said. "She, uh, it didn't end super well. I wasn't interested in dating when I came here."

"Is that why you took a job at a ranch ten miles from everything, where the only female was already married?"

Tag glanced over to her. "Clearly not every female."

"That you knew of," she shot back. "I didn't come to the farm until West was born."

"I have other ways of meeting women," he said.

"Do tell," Opal teased.

Tag rolled his eyes, though she couldn't possibly see him do that. "I wasn't interested."

"But you are now?"

"Obviously," he mumbled. "What about you? You haven't dated since you've been in Ivory Peaks."

"No," she said, "I haven't."

Tag waited, but she didn't go on. "That's all I get?"

"I dated a lot in California," she said. "But I came here—remember I said I came here to find a different life?"

"Yeah," he said quietly. "I remember."

"I'm still working on that, and I figured I should probably know what I want before I bring in another person."

Tag let her words mingle in his thoughts. "So we're going out. Does that mean you've come to some conclusions?"

Opal heaved a great sigh. "I mean, kind of? I know I'm not going back to Burbank. Or emergency medicine." She turned away from him, her unhappiness a palpable mood in the truck. "I can't even imagine what my father is going to say about that."

"I've met your daddy," Tag said. "He seems pretty agreeable." Especially for Opal, his only daughter.

"I think I'm more of a country girl than I thought,"

she said. "I like it here. Mike and Gerty are here. Jane and Cord. I think my next step will be for me to find my own place to live."

"Mm."

"And I'm thinking of maybe asking Hunter about doing something at HMC. I don't know. I don't know if I want a full-time job in the city."

Tag looked over to her. He didn't know every stitch of Hammond family history, but he knew Gerty and Mike had a lot of money. A *lot*.

He didn't want to ask Opal about her savings, but she hadn't worked in almost a year—since she'd come to the farm to help with West when he was barely a month old. He'd turn a year old at the end of next month, and that was a long time for anyone to go without money coming in.

For all Tag knew, Opal had money coming in. Or maybe her living expenses at the farm were nothing. His weren't much, he knew that.

"I have some other ideas too," she said. "I'm still working through them." She offered him a quick smile then. "But I guess I felt ready enough to try a date now when I didn't before." She looked at him, and with more street lights in a more populous area, he could see her apprehension clearly.

"You know that's why I said no before, right?"

"I didn't know," Tag said roughly.

Opal frowned. "I tried to say—you're the only

person who knows I'm not on sabbatical from the ER in Burbank."

"I think you should tell them," he said. "What if I let it slip?"

"In all your talk about my life with Gerty?" She laughed lightly again. "I think it's fine."

"It's not them you're worried about anyway," he said. "Right? It's your parents."

"I'll tell them at the Christmas party, which reminds me." She turned toward him and put her other hand over his. "I need your help planning the party."

"Excuse me?" Tag stared at her for probably a couple of seconds too long. "I am no party planner, honey."

"I need a committee," she said. "And Gerty said I could ask you and Carrie."

"A committee?" He scoffed, The Golden Coop only minutes away now. "How many people are coming to this party?"

"Just our family," she said, and Tag's heart did a nosedive in his chest at the word "our."

"Your parents," he said. "And Easton?"

"I mean the farm family," she said. "My parents, yes. Gerty's parents. Her grandparents. Easton, Allison, and their daughter Violet. Mike, Gerty, and West, of course. Me and you."

She said "me and you" so casually, like they might

be a couple, but she didn't want to define such a thing yet.

"Fourteen people," he said. "Does not need a committee."

"It does," she insisted. "There's food to plan, decorations, activities, communications, invitations. I really need more than you and Carrie."

Tag grinned, because she really didn't, and they both knew it. "What would I be over? And it better not be communications, because I'm *not* texting your daddy about the Christmas party at his own son's farm."

"It's technically Gerty's farm," Opal said, never one to let him get away with something incorrect.

"Oh, excuse me," he teased as he turned into the parking lot at The Golden Coop. "I'm not texting your daddy about the Christmas party at his daughter-in-law's farm." He pulled into an available space and put the truck in park before looking at her, plenty of challenge flowing from him.

"Not communications," she said. "I'll do that. I was thinking...décor."

"Décor," he repeated. "Like, you want me to hang garland and decorate a tree?"

"And coordinate linens for dinner. Maybe get holiday napkins. Put up a wreath, and maybe some mistletoe." She grinned at him, and Tag shook his head.

"Sounds like you've got the décor department worked out."

"Taggart." She spoke with a certain level of irritation and disappointment, and Tag didn't like either.

He unbuckled and got out of the truck. Around on her side, he opened the door and crowded into the space so she couldn't get down. "I'll do the décor on your Christmas party committee."

Tag put one hand on her knee and looked at her. "Okay, honey?"

"Thank you, Tag." She put her hand on his chest, and he backed up enough to let her get out of the truck.

"Now, let's go eat as much chicken as we can. Then, I have tickets to the Imperial Christmas display at the Royal Chinese Gardens."

Opal sucked in a breath. "You do?"

Tag liked that reaction, and he had a horrible thought that perhaps he was coming out too strong on the first date. "Sure do."

"Wow, Tag," she said with plenty of flirtatious vibes in her voice. "You might really get yourself another kiss on the first date."

Without missing a beat, Tag said, "Oh, honey, I sealed that deal when I said I'd be on your Christmas party planning committee."

CHAPTER
Five

JANE BEHR PACED in the kitchen, waiting for her lunch to finish reheating in the microwave. Molly had made a sausage ziti bake over the weekend, and she'd sent a bunch home with Cord and Jane.

She had work to do at the shop that afternoon, and she planned to stop and get Cord a bag of his favorite fast food on her way in to work. She sometimes went to work with him in the morning and put in a full day, but she'd wanted to go Christmas shopping with Molly and Opal that morning, and her stomach had been sick when they'd decided to go to lunch.

So she'd come home, but as the microwave beeped and she smelled the marinara and spicy sausage, her gut did another lurch that had her nearly running for the bathroom. Instead, she leaned against the kitchen counter and pressed a hand to her stomach. "What is wrong with me?"

She'd been sleeping a lot lately too, and she did wake up with an ache in her belly almost every morning. It had started about Thanksgiving, so less than two weeks ago, and she'd thought she'd eaten a bad batch of stuffing. Maybe undercooked or something.

She hadn't said anything to Molly, who had cooked their holiday meal, but now she wondered if it was something else.

You have a pregnancy test in your bathroom, she thought. And that single thought propelled her out of the kitchen and down the hall to the master suite. She'd bought the tests a couple of months ago when she'd been late on her period, but it had come before she could use one.

Now, she got the job done, and she paced in the bedroom for a whole new reason. "What if I'm pregnant?" she asked herself. Hope and apprehension filled her in equal measure, causing tears to come to her eyes. She and Cord hadn't exactly been trying for a baby, but they hadn't exactly not been either.

He was eleven years older than her, already in his forties, and he wanted kids. Plural. But they'd only been married for nine months, and neither of them had started to get too desperate yet. How would she tell him? Her parents? When would she be due? *What a Christmas miracle!* she thought.

Jane sat down on the bed, completely overwhelmed with her thoughts. "Heavenly Father," she prayed. "I really want a baby." She covered her stomach with both arms protectively. "We would love them so, so much."

It had to have been long enough for the test to tell her if she and Cord would be parents, and she steeled herself and got up. In the bathroom, she peered at the test, then swiped it off the countertop and into her fist.

She didn't let go of it for a single second as she drove over to Cord's mechanic shop. It took about a half-hour to get there from their house, and they'd both agreed to start looking for something a little closer. This house had belonged to Hunter and Molly, and they'd lived in it while he'd worked in the city.

But Cord's shop was out in Cherry Creek, a neighboring town to Ivory Peaks, and they both wanted to be closer. Jane wanted to build, because she thought they'd get more of what they wanted that way, as there weren't many houses for sale in these small outlying towns surrounding the city.

At least not many houses where Jane wanted to raise her family. And now she and Cord were going to have a family.

Tears filled her eyes, and Jane allowed herself to weep for the last couple of miles to the shop. She was pregnant with her first baby, and she was allowed to cry about it. She suddenly had so much to do—find a doctor and make an appointment, start getting a nursery ready, making a list of names for boys or girls.

Her thoughts once again overwhelmed her, and she very nearly drove right past the shop. She jammed on the brakes and made the right turn far too fast. If Cord happened to look up and see her do that, he'd know immediately that something was wrong.

"The tears will do that, Jane," she told herself. Oh, and she'd forgotten his lunch. He'd know the moment he saw her something was wrong.

Except nothing was wrong.

Jane pulled up to the customer entrance of the shop, where she didn't usually park. But no one else had parked there, which meant Cord worked alone in the shop. A lucky break—or a gift from God.

She got out and started into the shop, ignoring the office where she usually put her purse and coat. She hadn't even put a coat on before leaving the house, a fact she only just now realized.

A bell would ring if someone came into the office, but nothing happened when Jane pushed open the door to the bays. She wanted to call for Cord, but she couldn't get her voice to work. In fact, she sniffled, her emotions all over the place.

She moved toward the second bay, where a light gray truck had been lifted up so Cord could work underneath it. He came around the front of it, a blue rag in his hands. He saw her, and his face brightened. "Hey, sugar."

As soon as he'd spoken, his face fell. "What's wrong?" He tossed away the cloth and came toward her quickly. "Your parents? An uncle?"

She shook her head, her tears thick now. "Cord."

She reached him and grabbed onto him. He easily folded her into his arms, the strength she found there beyond measure.

"Talk to me," he said.

"A baby," she whispered through a too-tight throat. "I'm going to have a baby."

Cord held very still; he didn't even seem to be breathing. "Did I hear you right? Because it sounded like you said you were going to have a baby."

She pulled back and grinned at him. She nodded, and his face broke from the stoic mask she knew so well to one of pure joy. He started to laugh, and oh, how she loved that sound. "Janey," he said, and that was all he needed to say.

He said her name like that when he was happy, like he was now. When he had something serious to talk about. When he wanted her opinion. When he was worried and needed her reassurance. When he needed her to know he loved her. For everything.

"You're in your head," he said next.

Jane blinked and looked at him. "I'm having a lot of thoughts," she admitted.

"Yeah, you've stopped talking." He grinned at her. "Let's go to lunch."

"I forgot to stop for lunch. I'm sorry."

"It's fine."

"Nothing sounds good," she said as he led her toward the big sink at the back of the shop. He started to wash up. "Everything makes me sick."

"Everything?"

"All the smells," she said.

"Here in the shop?"

"Food smells," she said. "I was just going to get you some hamburgers and fries."

"And that doesn't sound good? You love French fries."

"I can try them," she said. "I've been like this since Thanksgiving. Remember I thought the stuffing was undercooked?"

"Yeah." He grabbed a couple of paper towels and dried his hands. He faced her again, pure radiance pouring from him. "Janey, I can't believe you're gonna have my baby." He brought her close again and swayed with her. "I love you so much."

"I love you too." She touched her lips to his. "I hope it's a boy, and we can raise him to be a cowboy mechanic just like you."

"I hope it's a girl and that she looks exactly like you," he whispered back. "You're my everything, Janey."

"And you're mine," she said. "Let's go to lunch, and I want to talk about building a house."

He stepped back and lifted his eyebrows. He didn't have to say anything for her to know what ran through his head.

"For real, Cord-baby," she said, threading her fingers through his. "I know you've just glossed over it, but there's nothing in Cherry Creek or Ivory Peaks that we want. And if we build, then there will be exactly what we want."

"You never get exactly what you want," Cord said.

Jane grinned at him as they left the shop, and he turned back to lock the door. "You're wrong about that, baby. I got you, *and* we're having a baby."

CHAPTER

Six

OPAL GLANCED up as her cousin Jane sat beside her. An instant smile came to her face. "Hey." She leaned over and touched her cheek to Jane's as her husband Cord sat beside her.

"Hey," Jane whispered back. "No Gerty and Mike?" She looked down the pew where Gerty, Mike, and West usually sat.

"I know," Opal said. "I'm going to die without that baby as a distraction during the sermon."

Jane grinned at her and shook her head. "Pastor Danielson actually says really good things."

"I agree," Opal whispered. "I just like listening while showing West barnyard animals." She smiled at Jane. "But he's running a low fever." He'd been teething lately, and Opal had missed her goodnight kiss last night due to that fussy baby. They'd pulled up to the farmhouse only ten seconds before Mike had returned with West fast asleep in his carseat.

He'd taken him out for a drive to get him to go to sleep after Gerty had given him some baby Motrin to help with the teething.

"Mm," Jane said. "Do you want to come to our place for lunch?"

"Yes," Opal said.

"You didn't text about your date." Jane hit the T hard, even for a whisper.

"We got back late," Opal said, watching the pulpit and praying the choir director would give the nod and this conversation would be drowned out by Hallelujahs. "He had tickets to that Christmas botanical display at the Chinese Royal Gardens."

Opal couldn't even say that without smiling, and she ducked her head away from Jane, as if she wouldn't see. The woman saw everything.

Jane sucked in a breath that sounded a lot like a gasp. "Oh, boy. This Taggart Crow is aiming right for the heart."

Opal giggled with her, and then Jane linked her arm through hers. "I have something to tell you." She spoke in that conspirational whisper that made Opal's heartbeat skip.

"Oh? Family gossip? This close to Christmas?" She hoped it would be in Jane's branch of the family and not hers, because Opal wanted the Christmas party at the farmhouse to go without a hitch.

"You can't tell anyone."

"Who would I tell?"

"Gerty," Jane whispered. "Mike. Tag."

"I'll only tell West," Opal said with a grin. "Though asking me not to tell Mike and Gerty is pretty rough. Maybe I don't want to know."

Jane hesitated, and she looked over to Cord. He looked at her too, his usual stoic-ness fastened securely in place. He searched her face, and she leaned closer to him to whisper something in his ear. He bent his head so her mouth would be closer to him, and Opal shivered just thinking about having a man do that for her.

Someone who was so interested in what she had to say, he just had to get closer to hear. And he'd reply, which would put his soft breath on her neck, and she'd cuddle into his chest, and he'd put his arm around her to keep her there.

Her fantasies evaporated as Jane turned back to her. "You can tell Gerty and Mike, but no one else. We've only told my parents."

Opal met her eye, her brain whirring. Something Jane and Cord had only told her parents.... She sucked in the same type of breath Jane had a moment ago as Jane said, "I'm pregnant, Opal."

She glowed with happiness, and while Opal's eyes filled with tears, so did Jane's. She giggled again, and Opal leaned over and pressed her cheek to hers again. "Oh, this is great news; not gossip. Congratulations, my lovely."

Opal looked over to Cord, and she reached past Jane and squeezed his hand. "Congratulations, Cord."

"Thank you," he murmured, but his tough-cowboy façade fell as he allowed a smile to touch his mouth. "We're real excited about it." He looked at Jane. "Obviously."

"Oh, don't be like that," she whisper-hissed at him. "I'm not going to tell anyone else."

"All right," Cord whispered, plenty of disbelief in those two, soft-spoken words.

Opal simply grinned through their brief exchange, and she looked up and to her right this time as more people arrived on their row. Tag, followed by Carrie and Kyle.

"Hey," Tag said quietly as he sat beside her. In that moment, the choir director gave the cue, because the band started as the robed singers took their spots up on the stage. Opal didn't have a chance to respond, and she got to her feet to join her clapping to the music.

When they sat for the opening hymn—a much slower, more reverent song—Opal erased a couple of inches between her and Tag. They hadn't talked about sitting together at church, as Tag didn't come all the time, and when he did, he sat by Gerty and Mike and Gerty's grandparents.

She smiled at him and pulled out the hymnal so she could be ready for the congregational hymn.

When it was time, she tilted the book toward Tag, and he took the right side of it and held it. Warmth filled Opal, and not only because she loved hymns and the spirit they brought into her life.

But because she sat beside Tag, and Jane was pregnant, and everything seemed right in the world. And when all the hymnals had been put away and Pastor Danielson finally stood, Tag took her hand and threaded his fingers through hers.

And suddenly, Opal had a way better distraction than reading baby books to West: holding Taggart Crow's hand.

———

"WHAT DO you think of this one?" Opal turned her phone toward Jane while Cord slid their first pizza into the oven.

Jane picked up the phone with one hand and dusted flour off her other one. She studied it for several seconds. "You're looking at houses in Ivory Peaks?"

"Yes," Opal said.

Her cousin lifted just one eyebrow. "What about your job in Burbank?"

"I, uh, quit." Opal took her phone back. "I'm not married to Ivory Peaks. But I think I could guest lecture at the colleges here, or work on something like Uncle Colton did. He did the Human Genome Project and all that. I don't know." She pressed the power button on the side of her phone and turned it upside down.

"I've never done anything with my money," she said. "Everyone else has, and I want to be here."

"I didn't think you liked small towns."

"It's adjacent to a big town," Opal said as nonchalantly as she could. "Mikey's here. You're here. I want to be here. Plus." She met Cord's eye as he set a bagged Caesar salad on the counter and looked at her. "There are hospitals here. If I want to be a doctor, I can be a doctor."

"We're here," someone called, and Tucker led the way into the kitchen at the back of the house. "Hey, hey, hey! The pizza party can start now." He wore a grin from ear to ear, and he'd brought Deacon, Tarr, and Bobbie Jo with him.

The four of them worked at the Hammond Family Farm, and Tuck sat on the barstool next to Opal and put his arm around her. "Hey, you. I didn't know you were coming."

"Here I am," Opal said, glancing at Jane. She didn't need to specifically say not to bring up her moving here or how she'd quit, and Jane gave her a silent confirmation that she'd keep it to herself.

"Howdy, Opal," Tarr said as he sat on her other side. "You're lookin' pretty today."

Opal grinned at him. "Thank you, Tarr. How's Millie?"

He looked past her to Tucker. "Uh, she's not—she—"

Opal looked at Tuck too, and he wore a sympathetic expression that iced over pretty fast.

"She ghosted him." Tuck's jaw jumped. "Imagine that? He's a *National Rodeo Champion*, and she stopped texting him."

Opal frowned. "Is she fifteen?"

"What? No," Tucker said, glancing over to Bobbie Jo. "She's...."

"Not impressed by rodeo champions," Bobbie Jo said. "And she doesn't like nice, hardworking, good-looking men, obviously." She threw a look to Tarr, but all conversation had completely stopped.

Everyone stared at Bobbie Jo, and Opal looked over to Tarr, who'd started to blush red, and then Tuck, who had his mouth hanging open.

"I'm just saying," Bobbie Jo said with a shrug. "He's more than just a National Rodeo Champion. Millie obviously doesn't like nice guys." She picked up a piece of pepperoni and looked at Cord. "Can I make a personal one with this?"

He took an extra moment to blink, and then he flew into action. "Yep," he said. "Yeah. Everyone gets to make their own. They don't take long." He put a tray with pizza dough in front of them and added, "Come on, Tarr. Tuck. Get yours ready, and we'll put them all in at the same time."

Tucker got up and joined Bobbie Jo on the other

side of the counter. He flirted with her shamelessly, but at least he'd stopped asking her out. Opal thought they were super-cute together, but she looked over to Tarr.

"She's right, you know." She bumped him with her shoulder. "You *are* nice, hardworking, and good-looking. If this Millie girl isn't interested, that's on her, not you."

Tarr ducked his head, his smile practically made for TV. "Thanks, Opal."

"Tell us about your date, Opal," Jane said loudly, drawing everyone's attention to her.

"Oh, you had a date, Opal?" Tuck asked all innocent-like.

"Yes," she said, grinning despite wanting to throw a pinch of flour in Jane's smiling face. "Tag and I finally went out last night."

"Wow," Tuck said. "That's amazing, Ope."

"Yeah," she said. "It was pretty amazing." She felt very chickeny, like she could preen her feathers and be the prettiest bird in the yard.

"When are you going to see him again?" Bobbie Jo asked.

Opal switched her gaze to her, suddenly not so sure of herself. "I mean, we didn't set up a second date."

Bobbie Jo's eyes widened. "Shoot, I'm sorry, Opal. I didn't mean—"

"It's okay," Jane said. "They live on the same farm

together." She looked from Bobbie Jo to Opal. "She'll just text him and find out when he's free."

"He and Gerty are going to Coral Canyon to pick up some horses this week," she said.

"Opal's a good cook too," Jane said, implanting an idea in Opal's head. "She'll take him cookies or something tonight. Or those breakfast waffle sandwiches in the morning."

Opal gave her a grin, the idea of seeing Tag first thing in the morning so appealing. "Right," she said. "I'll take him breakfast in the morning. Something he can eat with one hand while he works."

"She'll flirt with him from the fences," Jane said, giggling.

"Oh, no." Opal shook her head. "I'm not doing that again." She laughed, the ache of her bruised ribs right there beneath the sound. "I'm still healing from the last time I tried to flirt with Tag."

"At least it hurts for someone else," Tuck said, and he grinned at Bobbie Jo.

She rolled her eyes and said, "Oh, you're fine. You don't even flirt with me anymore."

"I would if you weren't with that guy in Oklahoma."

"Not again, man," Tarr said. "I was just starting to like being around you two."

Tucker laughed. "I'm not flirting. I'm not asking her out." He grinned at her. "We're friends."

Bobbie Jo smiled back at him, and they both went

back to making their pizzas. Opal wanted to reach for her phone and text Tag, but she refrained. She thought Tucker and Bobbie Jo would be great together, and she reminded herself that sometimes friends could turn into something more—and she hoped maybe that could happen for her and Tag too.

————

OPAL HAD JUST FINISHED BRUSHING her teeth and had returned to her room when her phone buzzed on her nightstand. She sighed as she flopped onto the bed and reached for her device. She just wanted a half-hour before the clock struck midnight to play her mini crossword puzzle. It was going to be her cherry on top of a practically perfect day.

Church with Tag. Lunch with Jane, Cord, Deacon, Tucker, Bobbie Jo, and Tarr. An evening without wind. She'd held West for thirty minutes while he slept, and he hadn't woken since.

Now, she saw Tag's name on her phone, and she grinned up to the ceiling before she realized he should've gone to bed a couple of hours ago. At least.

She sat up, everything on high alert now. She slid on the call and said, "Tag."

"Oh, praise God," he said breathlessly. "I need you in the barn."

"The barn?"

"It's Boots," he said, and he panted, as if he'd been

running. "I couldn't find him after dinner, and I thought that was weird, right? Of course it's weird. I finally went looking for him, and he—he—he was hurt. He's hurt, and I need you in the barn."

"Okay, Tag," Opal said, jumping to her feet. "I'll be there in one sec." She tossed her phone on the bed and reached for the first sweatshirt she saw. "I'm putting you on speaker. Talk to me about where you found him and what's going on."

Tag's breath came through the line frantically, desperate. Opal had encountered parents like him, loved ones who'd brought in their spouses, sisters, brothers, friends.

"Taggart," she barked. "Talk to me. What am I going to find out there?"

"His foot was in barbed wire," Tag said, and she'd never heard his voice sound like that. High-pitched. Scared. Worried. Even when she'd been kicked by his horse, he'd spoken to her in a calm, only mildly urgent voice.

In fact, she could still hear it. *Come on, honey*, he'd said. *Wake up for me now. It's Tag, and I need you to wake up.*

"It's so bloody, and I can see the bone, and oh, Opal, he's breathing so fast. He was out there for hours before I found him." Something clanged on his end of the line, and Opal hurried out of her bedroom and down the hall.

In the kitchen, she shoved her feet into her boots

and yanked open the pantry. She had a first aid kit there, and she headed for the door now that she was equipped.

"I knew I should've gone looking right away," Tag said. "I ignored that prompting, and I'm so angry at myself."

"Tag, get the first aid kit off the wall in the barn," she said. She could deal with his regrets later. Right now, Boots needed help. "And turn the heater up."

"Okay," he said. "All right."

"I'm on the way," she said, the nearly-midnight air searing her lungs with icy fingers. "Get some blankets and get him comfortable. I'm two minutes away."

"Hurry, Opal," he said. "I don't know if he'll make it two more minutes."

Opal broke into a run, something she hadn't done since she'd worked in the ER, almost a year ago. "Dear God," she said aloud, not caring that Tag could hear her. "Bless Boots to just hang on for a few more minutes. Tag can't lose his dog, Lord. Please, don't let him lose his dog tonight."

CHAPTER
Seven

TAG STARTED to calm as he heard Opal pray for his corgi. She never panicked over anything, and to hear such goodness twinged with that hint of desperation in her voice somehow slowed him down.

He put a blanket on the floor next to Boots, and he opened the first aid kit he'd pulled from the wall. "I'm gonna turn up the heat," he said, and he darted over to the panel next to the door to do that. Max, Gerty's German shepherd, whined from his position next to the door. Then he barked, startling Tag and accelerating his heartbeat again.

Without Max, Tag was certain he'd have not found Boots in time, and he reached down to pat the dog before he turned to go back to his pup.

He hadn't taken two steps back to Boots when the door crashed open behind him. "Okay," Opal said, striding past him. "He is not going to die tonight. Not on my watch." She went straight to Boots and set down the kit in her hand.

"Yes, I see what happened." She dug into the kit while Tag went to join her on the cement.

The cold, hard surface bit at his knees, and he reached to stabilize Boots as Max joined them and practically lay on top of him. "Max," he chastised.

"It's okay," Opal said. "His body heat will help." She lifted a syringe, and Tag dang near passed out.

His vision blurred around the edges, and he forced himself to look away as Opal gave his dog some, "Pain-killers is all." She nodded to the first aid kit. "Get out the biggest gauze pad you can find. And I'm going to need something to clean away some of this blood." She spoke in a clear, even voice, absolutely no panic whatsoever.

Tag fumbled the gauze pads, but he got them out. "I'll get a cloth wet in the sink." He jumped to his feet and ran to do that, going purely on adrenaline at this point. The water came out of the sink ice-cold, but Tag plunged his hands into it anyway.

He wrung the water out of the paper towel and prepped a second one before dashing back to Opal.

"He's breathing better," she said. "Look."

Indeed, Boots wasn't panting in short, horrible gasps anymore, and if his front paw wasn't propped up on part of the blanket where Opal had bunched it, Tag would think he'd just fallen asleep.

"Wet cloth," he said, handing it to Opal.

She took it and started cleaning up the paw. "Hold his head, so he doesn't snap at me."

Tag put his arm across Boots's neck, but the corgi didn't move at all. He'd been outside for at least three hours, and Tag had no clue how long he'd been tangled in the discarded barbed wire just on the other side of the property line.

He started to breathe easier now that there wasn't so much blood, and he had to look away as Opal pulled out what looked like a rudimentary sewing kit for children.

"He just needs a couple of sutures," she said, almost to herself.

"Tell me when you're done," he said, reaching out to comfort himself by putting a hand on Max's side.

"Almost...there...." She held out her hand. "Gauze."

He picked up a pad and slapped it into her palm.

"And tape."

He gave that to her too, and only a few seconds later, she leaned back onto her heels. "Done." She looked over to Tag, who dared to raise his head then. "We should take him to the vet in the morning to get, you know, real canine stitches put in."

Tag met her eye. "We?"

Opal tossed her head slightly, as if trying to absorb his question. "Yes, we. I don't have anything to do, and I can explain my medical choices."

Tag grinned at her, feeling his mouth pull up too

far on the right side. "You babysit West in the mornings."

"West loves dogs," Opal said without missing a beat. "He has a carseat, and he won't be any trouble at the vet." She pulled out her phone. "I'm going to call him right now."

"Who?"

"The vet."

"It's midnight, Opal."

"Hmm." She lowered her phone. "I'll call Deac and ask him to call for us when he gets up in the morning." She gave him a knowing look. "I mean, I won't be up early enough to get one of the emergency appointments."

"I can call the vet in the morning." Tag suddenly had to stifle a yawn. "Should I—can I move him to my cabin?"

Opal looked down at the sleeping Boots. "No, he should just stay here. He'll be warm and comfortable, and he's got Max and this blanket."

Tag got up and retrieved another blanket. He met Opal's eye as he returned and dropped back to the ground.

"You're not sleeping out here," she said.

"Yes," he said. "I am." He bunched up the second blanket to use as a pillow and lay down next to Boots. Max whined and put his hand on Tag's shoulder.

"Tag."

"Opal, I am not leaving him out here alone. What if

he wakes up and starts tearing at his bandage?" He gave her a side-eyed look and closed his eyes.

She didn't get up and leave immediately, and then she started cleaning up the supplies she'd gotten out. "Okay," she said as she snapped the lid closed on the first aid kit. "I'll be right back with the proper human supplies needed for sleeping in a barn with a couple of dogs."

"I don't need you to do that," Tag said. "You're not supposed to carry anything heavier than a loaf of bread."

"I won't," she promised. She got to her feet and headed for the door.

"Opal," he called, and he lifted his head to look at her. She turned back, waiting. "Thank you."

"Of course." She ducked out into the cold, and Tag let that yawn come out of his mouth. The barn housed a lot of living things, and Tag closed his eyes as he listened to the horses and dogs breathe in and out.

His back ached, and he shifted his feet to try to get the pinch to go away. Then, the cement along his back side started to seep through his clothes, and Tag thought about getting another blanket.

He'd just started to doze when the door opened again. It banged against the wall, startling him. Max too, as the German shepherd jumped to his feet and started barking.

"It's just me," Opal said from somewhere still

outside, and the sight of the end of that blow-up purple couch got Tag right back to his feet.

He ran over to help her, and together, they managed to get the couch inside. Opal's cheeks were flushed, whether from wrestling with purple plastic or the cold, Tag wasn't sure. He did know it made her absolutely beautiful, and he quickly closed the door behind her.

"You can sleep on my couch," she said. He moved it over beside Max and Boots, and Opal had picked up the blanket. "Go on." She grinned. "Lay down, and I'll tuck you in."

He did, the couch bouncing with his weight. She covered him with the blanket and then went to turn down the lights in the barn. "There," she said quietly.

"Opal," he said, his mind already halfway back to sleep.

"Yeah?"

"Does he look okay?"

She came back over to the three of them and knelt down next to Boots. "I think he's going to heal up fine, Tag."

"Might have to delay my trip to Coral Canyon," he said, reaching for her hand.

Opal stood, and he tugged her closer.

"Do you think two of us could fit on this couch?" he whispered.

"We can find out."

Tag shifted to lay sideways on the couch, and Opal

sat down and then lay with her back pressed to his chest. He covered her with the blanket and looked past her dark hair to his dog. "Thank you, Opal."

He encircled her in his arms, really enjoying the way she fit, and the addition of the sound of her breathing to his life as he finally fell asleep.

————

TAG WOKE to the sound of snoring, and he thought he'd finally found a weakness of Opal's. Then he realized it was one of the dogs, and he pushed himself up onto an elbow—which wasn't that easy against the blow-up couch.

It finally held his weight, and he peered over Opal's shoulder. The canines both laid on their sides—Boots hadn't moved at all, which sent a sliver of concern through him—and it was Max making the offensive noises. His back paws twitched as he ran somewhere fun and wild in his sleep, and Tag smiled at them.

Opal groaned then, and he settled back into position against the cushy arm of the couch. She turned right into his chest, and Tag sank down a little further into the squishy air couch-that-was-a-bed.

A dog whimpered, and Tag tensed. "He's okay," Opal murmured. "I just checked on him, and he's not running a fever."

"You just checked on him?"

"Maybe a half-hour ago." She snuggled deeper into his chest. "I gave him some more pain meds, and I checked his bandages. He's not bleeding anymore."

"Mm."

"You snore," she whispered.

"That was Max," he whispered back.

"Sure it was." He could practically see her smile in her voice, and it made him smile.

The next time he woke, it still hadn't started getting light beyond the upper barn windows. But the sun didn't rise until later in the morning in the winter, and Tag's body told him he needed to get up.

That, and his phone buzzed against his thigh. Opal didn't stir even a little bit, and Tag managed to get his device out without disturbing her. Five-fifty, when his alarm usually went off at six.

Good enough for him. He had three texts from Deacon Hammond, the last one saying that the vet had an appointment at nine-ten for Boots. Relief painted through Tag's soul, and he lowered his phone and pressed his eyes closed.

"Thank you, Jesus," he said. He never wanted to go back to the feelings he'd had last night. The pure desperation still coating the very back of his throat, and he couldn't quite swallow all of it away.

Which was silly, really, because Tag had owned several dogs before. The circle of life dictated that they'd die before him, but he didn't want Boots to pass because he'd been stubborn and hadn't listened to God when he'd been told to go find his dog.

Another vibration, and Tag looked at his phone again. From Gerty: *How's Boots?*

I hope he's okay, and you can obviously take whatever time you need to take him into the vet today.

He's made it through the night, Tag tapped out. *Thanks to Opal. She also texted Deacon, and he got me an appointment just after nine.*

I'm calling Bryce to postpone our trip to Coral Canyon until next week.

You don't have to do that, Tag said. *I can go.*

No, we'll just wait a week. I know Boots won't be healed by then, but at least we won't have to leave him with Opal, Max, West, and the whole farm only two days in. It just feels like too much.

Tag knew what else she needed to say, but he'd worked with Gertrude Hammond long enough to know she wouldn't say it. She possessed a mighty stubborn streak, but Tag had a pretty good track record of saying something once and getting her to go along with him.

It was only what she was already thinking anyway and just didn't want to admit.

That'll give you some time to hire another farmhand, he said. *We can't take on four more horses, just the two of us, and you need someone here when we get back with those animals.*

Gerty started to type, but Tag lowered his phone

again. Several seconds later, he lifted his phone again. *Believe it or not, I've set up an interview for Thursday.*

Oh, yeah? Who is it? Someone we know?

Yes, Gerty said. *It's Steele Harris. He's been working with Hunter and Matt for a couple of years now, and I think he might be ready for more responsibility and less management.*

Tag read her message quickly, then read it again. *You think that or Hunter thinks that? Or Steele's daddy thinks that?*

I did get it from Travis, Gerty admitted. *Which is why I'm going to interview him. We don't have time to be babysitting here.*

No, they did not, and Tag sent her a thumbs-up emoji.

I want you to sit in on the interview, Gerty said. *It's here at the farm. Thursday at nine a.m.*

I'll be there, Tag said. He tucked his phone away again, and having silenced his alarm, he dozed for several more minutes. Then he had to move his arm as it started to tingle.

Opal moved too, and she sat all the way up, a long groan pulling from her. "It's so early," she said.

"Yes, it is." Tag watched as she got up and stumbled over to the door. She raised the lights and came back to the dogs. "Howdy, Max. Hey, boy."

The German shepherd licked her hand and whined, and Opal got up and went to the sink to wash her hands. Tag sat up and scrubbed his hands through his hair. He wanted a hot breakfast, a hot shower, and the ability to go back to bed.

He didn't think he'd get that until at least tonight, and even then, Tag would need to set an alarm to check on Boots often. *One thing at a time,* he told himself, just like the pastor had said at church yesterday.

God didn't expect him to know everything at once. He expected Tag to show an interest in learning what He had to teach, and once he'd learned one thing, He'd teach him another. Step by step. Line by line. One by one.

So he just needed to make it through the next hour, and that was breakfast, a shower, and getting the horses fed.

"I haven't seen this hour since I worked the ER," Opal said as she straightened. "It looks really good, Tag. I only put in four stitches, and I think it'll heal up just fine."

"How are his paws?"

"No damage on the pads at all," Opal said. "It's all up about the forearm. Scratches and whatnot that are pretty superficial." She reached for his hand, and he got to his feet as if she'd pulled him there. "You—we —slept in the barn together."

He smiled down at her and slid his free hand along her waist. "Scandalous. We laid on the blow-up couch all night."

"All night?" She scoffed. "Six hours is not all night."

"You've gotten a little...."

"Finish that sentence," she teased. "I dare you."

He chuckled and looked at the mess around them. The couch. The blankets. The first aid kits. The two dogs, both of whom looked at him.

"Hey, Boots." Tag dropped to the ground at the same time as someone opened the barn door behind him. His corgi looked at him with such trust in his eyes, and Tag experienced a ripping slash of guilt. "Hey, buddy. You're okay, aren't you?" He stroked his head, hoping the pup could forgive him.

"Opal," Gerty said with plenty of surprise in her voice. "What are you doing out here?"

"Trying to wake up," Opal said. "Although, I don't know why. I'm going to go back to bed."

"You slept out here?" Gerty said, and Tag looked over his shoulder to her. She put her hand on the back of the purple couch, looked at it, then Opal, and then finally Tag. She didn't have West in a sling attached to her chest or back, which meant Mike hadn't left for the office yet.

"Yes," Tag said. "We couldn't just leave Boots."

"*You* couldn't just leave him," Gerty said, and she trained her blue-eyed fire on her sister-in-law.

"Oh, don't look at me like that. That was one of the worst nights of my life, and I worked in an ER in

Burbank for years. I've had better rest on a cot in a crowded doctor's lounge, for crying out loud."

Tag chuckled, though he sincerely hoped last night wasn't one of the worst nights of her life. He hadn't slept much, no, but holding her in his arms? Tag would gladly do that again.

Boots started to get to his feet, and that drew Tag's attention away from Gerty and Opal. "Hey, buddy, you hurt yourself, okay? Don't put any weight on it."

His little dog didn't, and Tag wanted to pick him up and carry him everywhere until his leg had healed completely. But just because corgis were small didn't mean they were light, and Boots weighed thirty pounds. Not a lot for Tag, but he came in an awkward package, and Tag couldn't carry him all over the farm.

He licked Tag's face, which made him smile though he didn't usually let Boots lick him. "His tongue feels dry."

"Yeah, we should try to get him to eat and drink," Opal said. "And he obviously should be on cage rest until you get a real doctor to tell you how to manage him."

"You're a real doctor, Opal," Tag said as he stood. He bent and picked up Boots. "I'm gonna take him home and get us breakfast, take a shower, all that." He nodded to Gerty. "Nothing happened on the blow-up couch, boss, other than I learned that Opal snores."

"I do not," Opal said, and Tag laughed at the scandalized look on her face. "That was Max."

"And that she tried to blame it on me." Tag nodded to the barn and the couch. "Leave it all, you guys. I'll come back and clean it up when I feed the horses."

"My grandmother is already making cinnamon rolls," Gerty said as he reached the door. "They'll be ready by the time you and Boots are back from the vet. We want you to come by the house and tell us everything."

Tag's heart expanded to make room for these people in his life. They'd taken him in so easily, loved him so readily, made space for him without asking any questions. Mike knew how Tag had bounced from farm to farm, and about the relationship in Green River that had driven him here. He wasn't sure if Gerty did, and of course, Tag had only told Opal the good things so far. Or skimmed over the painful things, at the very least.

"Will there be hot chocolate?" he asked.

Gerty grinned and shook her head as if she couldn't believe he'd ask such a thing. "What do you think?"

"I think there better be," Tag said. "If you want me to give all the details about a vet visit."

"Tag," Opal said. "I want to go to the vet with you. What time is it?"

"Nine-ten," he said, shifting his corgi in his arms. "We have to leave about eight-forty to make that."

"Eight-forty," Opal repeated. "Dear Lord, when will I ever get to sleep again?"

Tag laughed as he left the barn, because he knew there'd be hot chocolate at the farmhouse to go with the cinnamon rolls, and if he knew Carrie at all, she'd also have a big pan of maple sausage links browned up and ready to go. Tag loved sausage the most out of all the breakfast meats, and Carrie would want him to have all of his favorites after a night like last night.

Boots just lay in his arms and let him carry him home. Inside the cabin, Tag put him on the couch and said, "Listen, bud, I'm gonna have to get out your crate, okay? You stay right there, and I'll get breakfast for you. Then you can have another rest while I shower."

His dog just looked at him, and Tag took that to mean, *Okay, thanks, Tag. I know you didn't mean to leave me outside for so long, and I'll just wait here for my breakfast.*

Tag pressed a fast kiss to Boots's head and then went into the kitchen. He started to fill a bowl with fresh, cold water from the tap, and he wasn't surprised to find Boots hobbling toward him before it reached the top.

He didn't put weight on his front right leg at all, and he hopped around in a pathetic way that tore at Tag's heart. "Here you go." He set the water bowl down and watched as Boots lapped at it eagerly.

While he did that, Tag got his food bowl filled and out, and he went into the back spare bedroom to find the dog crate. If he put Boots in it, he wouldn't be able to trot around the house at all, and that would only help him heal faster.

As he put the crate together, Boots crunched through his food while standing on three legs, and then Tag got him inside and locked the door. "You'll be okay, my friend. I'll be back for you in a couple of hours."

Now, he just had to shower and get as many chores done as he could before he had to leave for the vet. As he scrubbed last night down the drain, Tag leaned his head back and let the hot water run down his face.

Thank you, Jesus, he thought. *Thank you for guiding me to my dog. Thank you for Opal Hammond. Thank you for saving Boots.*

It sure felt good to be grateful, and after Tag got out of the shower, he took a moment he didn't have to perch on the edge of his bed and write in his journal the things that stood out the most about the past twelve hours.

"There you go, Mama," he whispered. Then he got dressed and got on with his day—after all, he had a lot to do today, and none of it was going to magically get done just because he was tired.

As he reached the barn and entered it, he got a text from Opal. *Gerty chewed me out for carrying the couch, but it so doesn't weigh more than a loaf of bread.*

Oh, and we need to set up a time for our first Christmas party planning committee meeting. Since Carrie is also on the committee, I was thinking today, while we have a brunch of cinnamon rolls and hot chocolate.

Tag wanted so much more than a party planning committee meeting with Opal. With Boots injured now, he wasn't sure when he could reasonably leave the farm again, but he still let his thumbs type out the very thing flowing through his heart.

Yeah, okay, he said. *And I want another date on the calendar too. Before I leave for Coral Canyon.*

He didn't wait for her to answer, because he'd already lost so much time today, and he'd lose even more taking Boots to the vet. But he couldn't wait to see Opal again in a more boyfriend-like capacity.

CHAPTER
Eight

OPAL CAME RUNNING out of the farmhouse, her coat flapping behind her as she'd only put in one arm. She tried unsuccessfully to get the other one as she hurried down the steps, but in the end, she abandoned the quest. Tag's truck would be warm anyhow.

She didn't believe for a moment he'd put Boots in the bed, and sure enough, she found the crate on the floor in the back of the king cab. "Hey," she said breathlessly. "Wow, I've done more running for you in the past twelve hours than I have in twelve months." She gave him a smile as she finally got her right arm into its sleeve and reached for her seatbelt.

"You ready?"

"Yes," she said. "Sorry I was late. I was just…sorry I was late."

"No, finish that," he said with plenty of teasing in his voice. "Why were you late?"

"Because." She held her head up high. "I don't have to feel bad because I love West."

"Yeah, that baby has you wrapped around all of his chubby fingers." Tag chuckled. "He's a cute baby, so I guess I can't blame you."

"He was answering the phone," Opal said with such joy running through her. "He'd call, and I'd make this ringing noise with my mouth, right? And then he'd pick up the phone and go, 'Eh-o,' and it's just the cutest thing in the *world*."

Opal sighed with such love, and West wasn't even her baby. She looked over to Tag. "Do you want kids, Tag?"

"Yeah, I wouldn't mind havin' kids," he said.

"You don't talk about your family much."

He gave her a look out of the corner of his eye. "I was—am—sort of this outsider in my family."

"What does that mean?" Opal truly hadn't heard him say much about his twin brothers, other than he had them, or his parents, other than they'd moved to Louisville after their sons had grown up and left home.

"I don't know," Tag said. "The twins always had each other, right? And I was quite a bit older than them, and I just always feel like I'm on the outside of whatever they're doing."

"And your parents?" Opal spoke in a soft, soothing voice, because she sometimes had to in order to get patients to talk. "They're still together?"

"Actually, no," he said. "Mama wanted to go back to Alabama after they moved to Louisville. Daddy didn't. They split up." He looked over to her. "They're in their mid-sixties. Doing good enough. I talk to my mama the most, but Daddy texts every now and then."

Opal looked out her window, her thoughts blurring by the same way the landscape did. Tag drove toward Ivory Peaks this time, as the vet was in another town just north of there. "I sometimes feel outside of my family too," she said. "The only girl, middle child, all of that."

"Mm."

"I'm looking to buy somewhere around here," she said next, not sure why she'd brought this up with him.

"You are?"

"Well, I can't live with my brother and his family forever," she said wistfully. "Even if I want to."

"Around here?"

"Yes." She looked over to him. "Does that make you happy?" She gave a light laugh and took his hand in hers. "I don't want to go too far. Gerty still needs help with West, and now that Jane's—" She cut herself off, but the damage had been done.

Tag wasn't a dumb cowboy, and he met her eyes. "She's gonna have a baby?"

"It's a secret," Opal said. "I'm sworn to secrecy."

"I'll be sure Boots doesn't tell anyone," he said dryly.

Opal laughed then, glad things between them could happen so easily. So carefree. "I haven't told anyone but Jane about buying someplace of my own," she said. "So it's another secret I need you to carry for me."

"At this rate, I won't be able to talk to anyone." He chuckled and brought her knuckles to his lips. "Thanks for coming with me."

"You betcha," she said. "And we didn't even have to bring West."

A couple of hours later, Tag pulled up to the farmhouse again. "I can smell the cinnamon out here," he said, grinning.

"Christmas party planning time," Opal announced as she got out of the truck. She led the way inside, and Tag brought up the rear with Boots in his crate.

"He's okay," Tag called as he entered the farmhouse. "No infection, but we got an antibiotic in case one flares up. New painkillers, which he has to be on for fourteen days, and he has to be on cage rest that long too."

"I killed it with the stitches," Opal said, grinning at Tag. He bent to set down the crate in the living room, and she faced Gerty and Carrie in the kitchen. Mike's truck wasn't here, so he'd gone to work in the city. West wasn't anywhere to be found, so Opal assumed he was down the hall in his crib, taking his morning nap.

She wished someone would put her to bed and tell her not to get up until she was good and ready, but sleep would have to wait, because the sight of Carrie's cream-cheese frosted cinnamon rolls had Opal's mouth watering.

The older woman smiled with such love, and Opal thought of her mother. She wasn't quite as old as Gerty's grandmother, but she had the capacity to open her heart to anyone and draw them right in. For some strange reason, Opal's eyes filled with tears.

"The vet replaced Opal's stitches with canine-strength thread, but that's all," Tag said. "He said it was well-cleaned and tended to. And he should heal up just fine. We've got an appointment in ten days to go in and have the stitches removed." He sighed as he pulled out a barstool and sank onto it. "Carrie, you're sent straight from heaven."

She laughed and swatted at his hand as he reached for one of the sausage links. He managed to take it, and Opal took the moment to blink her tears back where they belonged. She felt outside herself, perhaps from her restless night of sleep despite the strength and security of Tag's arms around her. Maybe from the constant thoughts of finding somewhere to live, or of when she could get dressed up and go out with Tag again, or when she should tell her parents of her plans.

Time to tell them, she thought, and she completely

missed the first cinnamon roll being served to Tag. He'd chosen the one right in the middle of the three-by-three grid, of course, and it was ooey and gooey and exactly what she knew him to love.

"All right," she said as she turned toward the bookcase in the kitchen. "I have sketched out a few ideas for the menu for our Christmas party." She sat down at the counter too and flipped open the binder. Carrie put a plate with a cinnamon roll on it in front of her, and Gerty poured steaming milk into mugs.

Everything about this country farmhouse spoke to Opal's soul, and she once again fought her emotions. Only by focusing on the words she'd typed up and printed could Opal get her tears to stay dormant. Thankfully, Gerty had more questions for Tag about Boots, and instead of starting the party planning for the Christmas shindig happening here in only three weeks, they chit-chatted about their plans to go to Coral Canyon next week.

"You can watch the dogs and West, right?" Gerty asked.

"Yes," Opal said, looking up from her binder.

"Steele is coming for an interview on Thursday." Gerty wore a brief look of worry. "I'm hoping to get him here by the weekend, and then we can take him through our minimal chores, and he can tend to the farm while we're gone." She sighed and picked up a knife to cut into her cinnamon roll. "If he can't, I'll ask my daddy to come, and Mike can do a little bit too."

"I can feed horses and cats and the chickens," Opal said.

"No, you can't," Tag said, shooting her a look. "You shouldn't even be here alone with West."

Opal blinked at him, half-irritated that he'd reminded her of her weakness and half-overjoyed that he was watching out for her. "It's not until next week. I'm feeling better and better by the minute."

"Grandpa can help too," Carrie said.

"We'll only be gone two days," Gerty said, watching Opal with an edge in her eyes too. "As long as everyone gets fed and watered, we'll be fine." She cut a bite of cinnamon roll and put it in her mouth. "I don't want to talk about it anymore."

Opal didn't want to talk about much of anything anymore, and she closed her binder and pulled her cinnamon roll and mug of warm milk closer. She stirred in two heaping spoonfuls of hot chocolate powder, and she let her spoon swirl around and around almost mindlessly.

"You're not going to start the meeting?" Tag asked playfully.

She gave him a small smile and shook her head. "No, I think I just want to enjoy this amazing food and then go take a nap."

"You never answered my text from earlier," Tag said just before he took a large bite of his sugary treat.

Opal glanced over to him, her mind suddenly blank. "What text?"

"Nothing," he mumbled. "We'll talk about it later."

Opal caught Gerty and her grandmother exchanging a glance, but she simply didn't have the energy to call them on it. Her and Tag's relationship wasn't a secret, and Opal's memory fired at her. He'd wanted another date with her, and she hadn't answered.

Yes, they could talk about that later, when there weren't any other eyes or ears around.

―――――

LATER THAT DAY, after Tag and Gerty had gone back out to the farm, and after Carrie had cleaned up her delicious brunch and gone back to the generational cabin, Opal lay on the couch in the farmhouse. She'd just gotten West down for his afternoon nap, and he lay on the floor only a few feet from her, Max curled up next to him on the dog bed.

Boots had likewise squished his eyes shut, and Opal was the only one still awake. "Time to send some texts."

She started with Tag, because right now, those would be the easiest messages to get out. *It's Monday today*, Opal said. *You're not going to Coral Canyon until next week. Again, I babysit my nephew during the day, and I throw feed to chickens twice a day, and I might have a date with the barn cats I'll have to move around, but I think I can reschedule with them.*

She tapped back to her texting app, where she had a family thread. It included Mike and Gerty, Easton and Allison, and Momma and Daddy. And Opal. The single one. The outlier. Tag's words about feeling on the outside of his family struck her heart like a gong. Even her pulse reverberated through her body.

They hadn't texted on the string in a couple of days, and Opal didn't always respond to every message her brothers or parents sent out. Allison and Gerty sometimes sent pictures of the kids, and Opal would long-hold and add a heart to those.

I have some news, she said, and once she got going, Opal's fingers could fly, fly, fly. *I have decided not to return to my job in Burbank. In fact, I quit several months ago; I'm not on sabbatical.*

She took a deep breath, hoping her father didn't call and imply she'd lied. She'd *started* on a sabbatical; she just hadn't continued it, and she hadn't told anyone otherwise.

I have decided to move to the Ivory Peaks area of Colorado. I don't know what I'll do, but there are hospitals and colleges here. Right now, I'm helping Gerty with her baby and spending my evenings with chickens, and I'm looking for a place of my own so Mike and Gerty can have their house back.

She sent that, then realized she'd told another small fib. Nothing she couldn't fix.

Actually, I'm hoping to be spending less evenings with chickens and more evenings with Taggart Crow. We finally went out over the weekend for the first time, and he's asked me on a second date.

She hit send on that and read back through her three messages. "Anything else?" she asked herself. She didn't think so, and she exhaled heavily as she let her cell fall to her chest. Exhaustion pulled through her from her night on the purple blow-up couch. It currently rested against the wall behind her, and Opal imagined herself there, wrapped up in Tag's arms.

Her phone beeped once, twice, three times in a row, and Opal didn't immediately lift her device to read the incoming messages. Mike would give her nothing but support. Easton and Allison too, because they lived all the way across the country, living almost completely different lives than everyone else.

Opal wasn't worried about her siblings or their spouses. No, Daddy was the one Opal feared hearing from, and Momma might even text something that seemed supportive but actually held a lot of questions.

Her phone rang, and Opal couldn't put off answering it. She'd literally just texted, and everyone knew she'd been put back on rib-rest, because Gerty had texted them after her appointment last week.

Daddy sat on the screen, and Opal swiped to answer the call. She tapped the speaker icon to get it to play through the speaker, and she set her phone on her chest as she said, "Hey, Daddy."

"Can you hear me?" he asked.

"Yes," she said with a smile, because he always

asked if she could hear him, as if he didn't trust cell-phones to work. "Can you hear me?"

"Yes," Daddy said. "Momma's on the call with me."

"Of course she is." Opal didn't mean to sound so belligerent. "Sorry, I didn't mean it like that."

No one said anything, and Opal certainly wasn't going to start. They'd called her. "Opal-baby," Daddy started, so he was going to tiptoe around her.

Opal couldn't have that. "Daddy, I'm not a little girl. You're not going to hurt my feelings."

"I'm surprised you quit your job," Daddy said. "You were—are—such an amazing doctor. You loved living in California."

"Yes, I know," Opal said. "You're right. That's all right."

"So...help us understand why you're moving to Ivory Peaks."

"Because," Opal said. "God told me to."

They couldn't very well argue with that, she knew, and she added, "I resisted Him for a long time, but Gerty's baby was the impetus that gave me enough courage to finally do it. And it turns out that I love that baby, and I love this farm, and I love being close to Mike and Gerty, and Jane and Cord, and I want to stay here."

A long pause filled the space between them, and then Momma said, "That all sounds right too."

"I'm happy here, Momma," Opal whispered. "I'll

find a nice place to live, and maybe I'll start thinking about some foundation or starting a business. You know, use that money you guys blessed me with. I still haven't done that."

"You're my absolute favorite daughter," Daddy said.

Opal smiled. "I'm your only daughter."

"We love you," Momma said. "We'll see you in a few weeks for Christmas."

"Yes," Opal said. "Love you guys, too."

The call ended, and Opal rolled onto her side and let her hand dangle over the edge of the couch. She rested her palm against baby West's belly, feeling him breathe in and then out, and Opal smiled to herself.

"You've made the right decision, Opal," she whispered. "You belong here in Ivory Peaks." Her eyes drifted closed, and she simply relaxed into the comfort and peace that God had led her here, and she'd listened.

She dozed until her phone buzzed, and when she checked it, she grinned all the wider when she saw Tag's text that said, *How about dinner at my place tomorrow night?*

That'll do, she told him, and she said out loud, "That'll do just fine."

CHAPTER
Nine

GERTRUDE HAMMOND SHRUGGED out of her backpack and set it on the backseat of the truck. When she turned, Mikey took her into his arms. "You call me if you need anything at all," he murmured before he kissed her.

Gerty loved being in his arms, loved being with him, loved how he loved her and took care of her. "My parents know you're coming, and they're expecting you and Tag for dinner."

"I'll stay in touch with them if things are slow," she said.

"The weather looks good the whole way," Mike said next, his lips falling down the length of her neck. Gerty shivered, and not only because the winter morning wind had just kicked up. "But keep in touch. Call me tonight." He pulled back and smiled at her. "Okay?"

"I'll call you tonight," she promised. "We'll be okay."

"The road can be windy, and you've got the trailer."

"I'll pull over if it's bad, and Tag's a more experienced driver than I am. He said he'd be happy to drive." Gerty knew she wasn't the best driver in the world, and Mike and her daddy sometimes teased her about it.

She had a horse trailer that would hold four equines, which was why she was only buying four of Bryce Young's horses instead of all five. She didn't want to rent an eight-stall trailer and drive it for twenty hours for that extra horse, though she did want it.

"I love you," she said to Mike, smiling at him.

"Love you too, baby." He backed up, and Gerty closed the back driver's side door. She got behind the wheel and made sure she had her coffee thermos, her sunglasses, her thread wallet, and her phone. With a charger.

"All set," she said, glancing up and out the windshield. Tag had already put his overnight bag in the back, and he'd run back inside to get coffee himself. As Gerty watched, he and Opal came out onto the front porch, and Gerty grinned at West on Opal's hip.

She'd already kissed her baby boy goodbye, and Gerty pulled back on the emotions flying through her. She loved being a mother way more than she'd thought she would, and everything about her blonde baby reminded her that God was a God of miracles.

Mike went up the steps and took West from Opal, said something, and went inside the house. Gerty ducked her head, because she didn't need to spy on Opal and Tag while they said goodbye. They wouldn't be gone for even forty-eight hours, but Opal and Tag had only been out a few times, and their relationship was still pretty new.

Gerty reached for her coffee and took a sip, startling as the passenger door opened. "Oh."

"Hey," Tag said. "Ready?"

"I am," she said, looking up again. Opal leaned against the pillar at the top of the steps, a smile on her face. She waved to Gerty, who smiled and waved back. Then she flipped the truck into drive and slowly eased around in a wide arc to get off the farm.

Gerty's nerves vibrated at her. She didn't normally need to say everything she thought, but Tag worked for her, and she wanted him to work for her for a very long time. She'd also been talking to Mike about Opal finding somewhere to live, but she wasn't ready to say anything about that yet.

Her skin felt like spiders were marching eight by eight up and down her arms and legs. She squirmed and cleared her throat.

"Just say what you want to say, Gerty," Tag drawled. "You're dancin' all over the place."

"You didn't kiss her goodbye," she said, shooting him a quick look. "Opal."

Tag's jaw tightened, and he pressed his lips into a flat line. "No," he finally said.

"Why not?" Gerty asked. "You two have been dating for a couple of weeks now. I didn't think—I mean—" Panic cut off her thoughts and her words. "She doesn't talk about you. To me." She shook her head. "She doesn't. And I don't ask, Tag. I really don't."

Tag exhaled and looked out his side window. "Do I have to talk about it?"

"No," Gerty said. "Sorry, Tag. Really." She watched him, and he seemed frustrated. Gerty hoped it was because of this conversation and not because of his relationship with Opal.

"Dinner with her parents tonight," she said lightly. "They know you two are dating."

"Yeah," he said. "Opal told them."

"It's going well?"

"Yes," he said, the word a bit more clipped. "I think it is." He swung his attention to Gerty. "She told me this would be okay. That she'd talked to her parents about us, and that they can't hound me to death tonight. She didn't warn me about *you*." The left corner of his mouth twitched up, and Gerty relaxed slightly.

"You're not really mad," she said.

"I'm just not talking about this for the next eight hours. Or even the next eight minutes."

"Give me eight seconds then," Gerty said. "Of what you're worried about."

"Eating dinner with your family," he said. "There. That's it. Five words."

"You've met Mike and Opal's parents before," she said.

"Different capacity," he said. "We've also never taken a trip together before." He reached for his coffee, and the conversation stalled as he took a long drink. "Maybe I'm a little nervous about that." A gust of wind shook the truck, and Gerty gripped the wheel and immediately checked her rearview mirror to make sure the trailer wasn't going to pull them off the road.

"And the wind is worrying me," he said.

"Me too," Gerty murmured. They'd hardly cut into the trip at all. Gerty hadn't even made it to the main highway that would take them north to the Wyoming border. "Would you drive?"

"Yeah," he said easily.

Gerty eased off to the shoulder and put the truck in park. "Thanks," she said. "I could do it, but—"

"I know you could," Tag said. He quickly unbuckled his seatbelt and switched places with her. "This doesn't mean you can question me relentlessly about Opal."

Gerty grinned at him and mimed zipping her lips. "No more questions about Opal."

"What you can do is talk about how I should avoid making a fool of myself at dinner tonight."

"What do you mean?"

"Oh, come on. Topics to avoid, things to bring up to impress Opal's daddy. Give me *something*."

Gerty grinned, because Tag was always so sure of himself. So calm and cool. So capable. "They're just people, Tag," she said. "What we really need to talk about is how Steele is going to fare with us at the farm."

Tag looked over to her, displaying his confidence as he kept driving without freaking out when another round of wind battered them from the west. "Steele is going to be great," he said.

"You've worked with him for two days."

"He's a quick learner," Tag said. "He doesn't say much, but neither do we." He grinned at Gerty. "He's going to be fine."

"Sometimes it's the quiet ones you have to be careful of," she said thoughtfully. Steele came with great recommendations, and of course Gerty had known Travis and Poppy—his parents—for decades now. She wasn't that much older than Steele, and she didn't know all of his struggles.

Uncle Matt had said he was "ready for a new challenge," and that a change of scenery would be good for him. Gerty wanted to help Steele, but she also needed a trustworthy employee she could count on to get the job done.

Don't second guess yourself, she thought, and she strengthened her shoulders and set her sights out the windshield. "Have you ever done something you didn't understand?" she asked. "Because God told you you should?"

Tag looked at her again. "Yes," he said slowly.

"That's how I feel about Steele," she said. "I don't know why he's supposed to be at the farm, but he is. I need you to be honest with him. Teach him. Correct him. Tell me how he's really doing." Nerves ran through Gerty again, much the way the wind whistled across the front of the truck. "Okay?"

"Yes, ma'am," Tag said. "Thanks for telling me."

Gerty nodded, the unrest inside her finally leaking out. They drove along in silence for a bit, and then Tag put on the radio. He had a nice singing voice, and Gerty even found herself humming along to a tune or two.

When they stopped for lunch, Gerty got out and stretched her arms above her head. Then she met Tag and together, they went into the little diner in a little town she didn't know the name of.

"I know what you can talk about with Opal's parents tonight," she said.

Tag picked up the menu and gave her a curious look. "Go on."

"Opal," she said. "And how amazing she was with Boots." She grinned. "Whenever I'm in a tight spot in the conversation, I always give someone a compliment

—and Mike's parents like hearing how amazing their son is."

"Yes, but you're married to him," Tag said. "I can't just spout off about how—how amazing Opal is. Then they'll think I'm in love with her or something."

"Oh, stop it. They will not."

"They will," he said.

"Okay, well, it was just a suggestion."

By the time Tag pulled up to Wes and Bree's house, the sun had set and the headlights had to carve their way through the darkness. Tag put the truck in park and exhaled out mightily. "We made it."

Gerty's legs ached along with her head, and she didn't answer as she slid from the truck. Winter here had already bitten in deep, though no snow lingered on the ground. She couldn't linger out here, and the front door opened anyway.

"You made it," Wes said, and Gerty put a smile on her face before she turned to face him.

"Hey." She laughed as she hurried up the sidewalk to hug him. He laughed too, and Gerty sure did love Mikey's daddy. "Oh, you're looking good," she said. "No cane tonight?"

"He should be using it," Bree said. "He's being naughty." She came down the steps and hugged Gerty too. "You made good time with the wind."

"Tag drove," she said.

"I'm eighty years old," Wes said. "I can't be naughty."

His wife just gave him a pointed look and then turned her attention to Tag coming up the sidewalk. He had Gerty's backpack with him, along with his overnight bag, and he gave everyone a smile. "Howdy."

"Taggart," Bree said, and Gerty fell to the side to watch this exchange. Perhaps she'd text Opal about it, but one look at Tag's face, and Gerty knew *he'd* be the one telling her about it.

"It's just Tag, ma'am." He put down the bags and extended his hand for her to shake. She stepped in and hugged him.

"It's great to see you again," she said. Bree could have sharp eyes when she wanted to, as could Wes, and Gerty saw and felt all the razors and knives as they both looked at him.

"Come on in," Wes said as he shook Tag's hand. "Supper's almost ready, right, sweetheart?" He cut a look over to his wife, and Bree nearly jumped out of her skin.

"Yes," she said. "Yes, dinner is ready. Why are we standing out in the cold?" She turned and bustled toward the front door, and Wes limped along behind her.

Gerty looked at Tag and reached for her backpack, but he simply nodded her up the sidewalk too. So she let him carry her bag inside, feeling a little bit like she was leading a lamb to the slaughter.

Then she reminded herself that Tag could handle

himself, and that included with Opal's parents. She hoped.

CHAPTER
Ten

TAG PUT his bag in the guest room Bree showed him to, and he stepped into the bathroom to wash up. He moved quickly and didn't waste any time, not even to text Opal and tell her that he'd arrived at her parents' house.

And yet, somehow, he was still the last to arrive back in the kitchen for dinner. He slipped into the last seat across from Gerty as she sat too. Their eyes met, and since he only worked for her, he didn't know what she was trying to say. Maybe nothing.

"It's nothing special," Bree said. "Meatloaf and poutine."

Tag had no idea what poutine was, but everything smelled delicious. With French fries and red meat on the table, he'd be happy enough.

"I'll say grace," Wes said. "And then Bree will teach you the ways of poutine." He grinned at his wife, who smiled back at him. Then Tag barely had time to duck his head in a bow before he started to pray.

"Lord, we're grateful Gerty and Tag arrived in Coral Canyon safely. Bless them to get their business done and get back to their loved ones without any issues. We're thankful for Thy bounty on our table tonight, and help us to watch out for those around us."

Tag didn't have many opportunities to serve those around him, and he felt the gentle rebuke of the Lord as Wes prayed. His circle was so small, but Tag could reach out and text others to see how they were doing, and he could ask if nearby farms and ranches had anything they needed.

Satisfied with those thoughts, he realized Wes had gone on with his prayer, and all he heard was, "...and we love Thee with all we have, and all we are, and all we hope to become. Amen."

"Amen," Tag said, his gaze flying to Wes. Before he could tell him what a beautiful thing it was to love God with all he had, and all he was, and all he hoped to become, Bree picked up a pair of tongs.

She clacked them together and said, "Okay, poutine. I grew up in Vermont, and my family would vacation in Canada sometimes. I fell in love with poutine there, and now, I impose it on my family for special occasions."

"You'll love it," Gerty said.

"Sometimes I make the gravy with meat, but today, it's just plain. I wasn't sure how you'd take it, Tag." She gave him a smile that he returned.

Then Bree tonged some French fries onto his plate. "So first, you take fries. Then, we're going to add some cheese." She nudged the bowl of little, miniature mozzarella cheese balls toward him. "As many as you want."

"These?" He reached for his fork and started to fish out a ball of cheese from the whey.

"Yes, those," Bree said. "The gravy will soften them, and it melts all together, and it's divine. Like a party in your mouth."

"Potatoes, cheese, and brown gravy," Gerty said. "It sounds simple, but it's so good." She took the tongs from Bree and took some fries for herself.

"My favorite is the elk version she makes," Wes said. "It's got meat in it, but we've got meatloaf tonight."

"My mama made a mean meatloaf," Tag said as Bree ladled brown gravy over his fries and cheese.

She smiled at Tag and nodded. "Try it."

"I can't wait to try it."

Gerty finished pouring gravy over her fries, and she said, "My mouth is watering. I really should make this at home instead of waiting to have it here." She stuck the dripping-with-gravy fry in her mouth and said, "West would love this."

"Of course he would," Bree said, not commenting

on Gerty talking with food in her mouth, and she smiled down the table to Wes.

"You're getting how many horses tomorrow?" Wes asked. He'd taken meatloaf, and he was the last to get any poutine.

"Just four," Gerty said.

"They'll be good for you," he said. "Bryce runs an amazing rescue operation."

"They're some of his permanent residents," Gerty said with a nod. "Not ones he can sell, and he's had them for years. He says it might break his heart, but he knows they need new pastures to roam."

"Mm," Wes said. "People are like that sometimes." He looked at Tag, and he could see where Opal got all of her dark genes. Her daddy had dark hair and eyes, as did her mother. She honestly had no chance to be anything but the gorgeous brunette she was.

"What do you mean?" he asked.

"Just look at Opal," Wes said. "She couldn't wait to get out of here, then she only stayed in California for a little bit, and now she's in Ivory Peaks."

Tag wasn't sure what he was supposed to say. He looked at Bree and then Gerty, and she seemed a tad nervous too.

"She's amazing with West," Gerty said.

Tag's throat couldn't swallow properly, but he still managed to say, "She makes the best oatmeal chocolate chip cookie in the world."

Wes stared at him for a beat, and then Gerty. "I— I'm not saying anything bad about her."

"Well...." Gerty drew in a breath. "Okay. But it sort of sounded like you're saying she'll get tired of Ivory Peaks and leave there eventually too."

"Oh, no," Wes said as he leaned back in his chair. "That's not what I meant. I just meant, sometimes people need to roam other pastures too. Opal's kind of like that, but she's loyal and true, and she always follows her heart."

"She does what's right," Bree said. "Is what he's trying to say."

"She does that too," Wes said. He smiled at Tag. "And she does make the best oatmeal chocolate chip cookies in the world."

That broke the tension, and Tag looked down at his poutine. "When I get back to the farm, I'm going to ask her if she knows how to make this." He grinned at Bree, who laughed. "Because if she does, and she's been holding out on me...we might have our first fight."

Everyone at the table erupted into laughter then, including Tag, and he couldn't wait to text Opal and tell her how well dinner had gone tonight.

———

"I'M TAG," he said as he stepped past Gerty to shake

Bryce Young's hand. "It's great to meet you. Gerty talks non-stop about how amazing your ranch is."

Bryce grinned and grinned, and he had a really good air about him. "She does?" He glanced over to her, and Gerty rolled her eyes. "Seems hard to believe."

"I'm not the saltiest woman on the planet," she said.

Bryce tipped his head back and laughed, and Tag got the impression that Bryce had called her exactly that in the past. Gerty did have some saltiness to her. But she ran an excellent farm, and she cared deeply about her animals, her family, and God.

Tag took in the grandeur of Bryce's ranch—named the Rising Sun Ranch—as the sun started to do that over the Teton Mountains in the distance. "This is a beautiful place," he murmured.

"Sure is." Bryce leaned against the railing of the deck where they stood. The roof of the house had been extended over the deck, so he wouldn't have to shovel it when the snows came. Everything Bryce had here Tag wanted.

"We work it hard," Bryce said. "Especially in the winter."

"There he is," a woman said, and Tag turned with everyone else to see a petite woman carrying a little boy on her hip. "He's busy with our friends already, baby. Just give him his morning hug, and then he'll have to get out to the stables."

Bryce chuckled as he crouched down. His wife—Codi, Tag had been told—set the little boy on his feet, and he ran-toddled toward Bryce, saying, "Daddy, Daddy, Daddy. Mor-ing hug. Mor-ing hug."

Bryce scooped up the child as they both laughed, and Tag had never seen such love so openly displayed. It permeated the air and expanded out and out and out until it filled the whole farm, then the sky, and it zoomed toward the towering mountains in the distance.

He cuddled the little boy close, Bryce's smile joyful. His eyes sat closed, and Tag couldn't look away from the pair of them. Then Bryce settled the child on his hip and said, "This is Momma and Daddy's friend, Gerty."

"How old is he now?" Gerty grinned at the boy, everything about her softening too.

"Eighteen months," Codi said as she smoothed down her boy's collar. "And West is…what? A year?"

"Next month," Gerty said.

"And Tag," Bryce said. "They're buying some of our horses." He grinned at his son. "This is Matthew."

"Matt," the boy said, his cute little-boy voice only telling Tag what he'd said but hadn't known until now —he wanted kids.

"That's right," Bryce said. "Matt. All right, go back to Momma. It's oatmeal day."

"O-meal-O-meal-O-meal," Matt sang as he got passed from one parent to another.

"Good to see you, Gerty," Codi said.

"Thanks for letting us disrupt your morning," Gerty said. "We just wanted to give the horses time to load up and get headed back to Ivory Peaks."

"Only Rooster will give you any trouble getting in the trailer," Bryce said. "We'll do him last, because he's a big sheep at heart." He grinned and looked up into the sky. He clapped his hands together and said right out loud, "Thank you, Lord, for this snowless day to move horses."

Then he started down the steps to the path that split the lawn and led to the gravel road beyond.

"All right, then," Tag said. "Let's move some horses."

"I'm feeling good," Gerty said, and they moved down the steps as Codi turned to go back inside the farmhouse with baby Matt.

Tag felt fine right now. Opal's parents had comfortable beds and hot coffee, and once they had the horses loaded up, he and Gerty would be back on the road toward home.

Home, Tag thought. Where was that for him?

Where am I supposed to be? he asked, and he wasn't sure if he was asking himself or God Above.

He loved Colorado, he knew that. He loved Gerty's farm, and Gerty's horses, and Gerty's family. The problem was, they all belonged to Gerty, not him.

He toyed with the idea of looking for his own piece of Colorado land in the heart of the Rocky Mountains as he helped Gerty and Bryce put the halters on the four horses they'd be loading and transporting that day.

Bryce handed him a thick lead rope and said, "Let's walk 'em around the trailer for a minute. Yours is Cinnamon, and he should go in first."

"Why are you selling these?" Tag asked as Cinnamon stood right next to Bryce, his nose down. "They sure seem to like you."

Bryce grinned at his red-coated horse. "They do. I've had them all for years now. I can't sell them to farms or ranches or into service. They were too malnourished when they came to me, or didn't rehabilitate fast enough. So we've kept 'em."

He sighed as he moved to hand a lead rope to Gerty. "This is Ontario Lake." The gray sure had a beautiful coat, and Tag noted how he moved right into Gerty's shoulder and no further. She didn't give the horse his way, and he shuffled back to give her the proper distance. These animals were well-trained already. Tag wouldn't be breaking them and rehabilitating them the way he had Gerty's other rescues.

They'd just have more horses on their farm.

"But Codi says we can't keep all of them. We need more stable and stall space for horses we can rehab and get back out there, living their best equine life. So I'm ripping my heart out—" He looked up. "You hear that, Lord? My heart is getting ripped right out of my chest down here. It's flopping and bleeding and this is awful for me."

Tag blinked at him in surprise. He'd never considered just yelling out to the Lord every thought that came into his head. He glanced over to Gerty, who didn't seem to think anything odd had happened at all.

Bryce took the remaining two lead ropes and started walking. "I know you guys will take good care of them. And it's time. So they—it's nice for them to have different pastures to roam, I think."

Tag followed Bryce, and they walked around the trailer a couple of times while he murmured secrets to the two equines plodding along with him. Then he said, "All right. Let's load 'em in. Tag, you're up first."

Tag had loaded plenty of horses in his life, and he got Cinnamon in the trailer without an issue. He looped the rope through the slats, as they'd secure him for the drive once they had all four horses on.

Gerty loaded Ontario Lake while Tag fell to Bryce's side. He took the lead rope for Ellie, a pretty bay with black markings. She went on next, and finally only Rooster and Bryce remained.

"All right, bud," he said. "They're all on, and you don't want to be left behind, do you?" He led him to the edge of the trailer, and Rooster even took the first step on. Then he balked and tried to go backward.

"Come on," Bryce said, pulling forward on the rope. "You can't stay here forever." Several tries later, all four hooves had made it up and into the trailer. Gerty set about securing the horses for the drive, while Tag helped get the lead ropes off and back to Bryce.

The back door finally got closed, and Gerty clapped her gloved hands together. She looked at Bryce, who wore a stone mask of determination. "I'll send you a bunch of pictures," she said.

"One hundred percent." He cleared his throat.

"You got the money from Mikey?"

"Yep."

Gerty grinned at him and stepped into his arms. "Cheer up, Bryce. You've been hoarding these horses to yourself for long enough. Now, you just get to make more friends."

He did relax into her embrace, and then quickly pulled out. "Thanks, Gerty. Drive safe." He shook hands with Tag, and he only had to look at Gerty to know she wanted him to drive. So he got behind the wheel, the pressure suddenly so much higher.

"Lord," he said once they'd all buckled and made it off Bryce's beautiful ranch. "We've got these amazing horses with us now, so please help us to get home safely."

"Amen," Gerty murmured. A few moments later, she started laughing quietly.

"What?" he asked.

"Bryce got to you with his praying-out-loud thing, didn't he?"

Tag grinned and shrugged slightly. "I mean, it's not a bad way to live, right?"

Gerty shook her head. "I suppose." Then she sighed and leaned her head back. "Ah, I can't wait to get home."

Tag thought of the farm, his cabin, Boots, and Opal —all waiting for him back in Ivory Peaks. "Me either," he said, deciding that home was not a place. It was a feeling where loved and cherished people and things existed.

And for now, that was his cabin, Gerty's farm, his work there, Boots...and Opal.

TAG WALKED SLOWLY from his cabin to the barn, though the gray morning light did everything in its power to urge him to go faster. Boots couldn't exactly go faster yet, and Tag wasn't even sure he should have the little dog out with him yet.

But it had been almost two weeks since the injury, and the poor corgi was going stir-crazy in his crate. So Tag had been bringing him to the morning feeding rounds and then taking him home no matter how forlorn he looked.

This morning, Max barked, which caused Tag to look up from the path in front of him. Boots answered him and picked up the pace. "Hey," Tag said. "Hey, hey, hey, calm down."

But Boots didn't know what that meant, and even if he had, he wouldn't have listened. The little dog trotted now, his limp less noticeable than before— heck, than yesterday—but still there. He made it to the stable first and went tearing around it, another yip coming from his throat.

Tag sighed and looked over to the farmhouse, but he didn't see Gerty or Mike or Max. Perhaps they'd simply let their dog out to use the bathroom, and the German shepherd had seen a pheasant or something. Max was fairly vocal, and he barked and talked at everything he saw or smelled.

Tag went past the chicken coops they used in warmer weather and around to the front of the stables. Their four new transplants to the farm had been settling in decently well. Tag took them all out every day and worked in the circle with them, because horses required a relationship filled with trust. Otherwise, they'd just as soon stay in their stalls whenever Tag wanted them to get out.

Divas, horses were, and Tag loved them so.

As he reached for the door to the stable, he heard a woman laughing. And not just any woman—Opal.

He frowned, because Opal didn't normally come out into the stable this early in the morning. Or at all, no matter the hour.

Tag's forward motion had him opening the door before he could truly comprehend the sound of Opal's joyous laughter. He stepped into the warmer interior of the stable and stopped at the sight of Steele and Opal in front of him.

She stood way too close to him, and everything surrounding Tag changed.

It wasn't wintertime, in a stable, in Colorado.

But summertime, in front of a feeding trough, on a ranch in Green River.

Opal didn't wear blue jeans and a heavy gray coat, but a pair of short cutoffs and a flowered blouse in pink, yellow, and white.

She laughed, her head tipping back, and the man standing with Talina leaned in and kissed her throat. She grabbed onto him, and his hands encircled her waist, and before Tag knew it, his girlfriend was kissing another man.

This time, he didn't stomp away with adrenaline pumping through his body like poison. Instead, he cleared his throat rather loudly and asked, "Opal, what the devil are you doing here?"

CHAPTER
Eleven

OPAL TURNED from the shelf where she'd been showing Steele where the gloves and other medical supplies were. "Hey," she said brightly when she saw Tag standing near the entrance.

Then, his tone of voice and what he'd asked rang in her ears. *What the devil are you doing here?*

She took a step toward him, but his face was a dark, dark mask of anger. "Tag?"

His gaze moved past her to Steele, who'd simply asked for help in getting a wrap for one of the horses. She'd only come in to get a leash for Max, who'd eaten all the fatty ends of the brisket Mike had smoked over the weekend. Off the counter.

So, then, of course, the dog needed to go out a lot more than usual. Since Gerty was working long hours on the farm, and Mike had fourteen-hour days including a commute and a life inside a busy high-rise, Opal had said she'd care for the dog.

But of course, Max only really obeyed Opal if she had food in her hand or she allowed him to do whatever he wanted. Since she simply wanted him to go out and take care of his business and then hurry back in, of course he'd caught wind of something and run off.

And she hadn't brought out a treat, because she, well, the truth was, she hadn't even thought of it. Max surely wouldn't want to be outside in such frigid temperatures, despite being covered in hair.

She knew they kept extra leashes, or at least a lead rope or something she could use like a leash, in the stable, and she'd come in here to find something before going back outside to find Max and tame him to her will.

Steele had asked for her help to find the wrap, which she'd done in two seconds flat. And he'd said, "Don't tell my momma about this. She says I wouldn't be able to find my own head if it wasn't attached to my body."

Opal recalled her mother saying something similar about Easton at some point in the past, and she'd laughed.

Tag made an angry noise that sputtered from his mouth, and then he turned and left the stable. Just like that.

Opal had never even seen him get upset before.

Maybe a little panicked when she'd been kicked by his horse, but never upset. Totally panicked over Boots, but not mad. Legit angry. She looked over to Steele, who kept his head down and said nothing.

She didn't know what to do, but something told her to go after Tag. So she did that, re-entering the wintry landscape she'd rather not. In fact, she just wanted to crawl back into bed until the clock had an eight as the first number.

"Max!" she yelled, looking for the dog as much as she scanned for Tag. "Tag?"

Boots came limp-trotting around the corner, and his little dog gave him away. Opal hurried toward the edge of the stable and right around it.

"Boots," Tag barked, but his dog had already started to follow him.

"Tag," she yelled.

He looked at her too, held her gaze for a long moment, and kept on going.

"I've lost Max," she called. That got his step to slow, and she could see his big, boxy, broad shoulders rise and then fall, as if he'd just had to inhale some patience into his system. Patience for dealing with her.

He turned back to Opal and with his eyes boring into hers, he whistled through his teeth. "Come on, Maximus!"

The German shepherd barked and came running from somewhere on her right. Opal managed to tear her gaze from the dark cowboy's, but it wasn't easy.

The classically marked shepherd appeared, his bushy tail held high as he ran toward Tag.

Not her. Tag.

"C'mon, you," he said to the German shepherd, and he turned his back on Opal and Boots again, clearly headed for his cabin. Which made no sense. He'd already left for the morning, and she knew he'd been bringing Boots out for the past couple of days just to "give him a little fresh air."

"Tag." Opal rushed after him. It had snowed a couple of times in the past week since Tag and Gerty had returned to the farm with four extra horses, but nothing had stuck for long. She'd been obsessively checking the weather to make sure her family could come for Christmas, and Mother Nature would be dumping the first major round of snow this weekend, and then it would be clear for the holidays.

"Tag, can you wait?" She picked up her pace and broke into a jog for the third time—for him.

"If you want to go out with Steele, go out with Steele," he said over his shoulder.

"I—what?" Opal's lungs ached with the cold searing them. It felt so strange that cold could burn, but it did as she took another breath, trying to riddle through what he'd said. She finally caught him, but she wouldn't be able to maintain his pace for long.

"What's wrong?" she asked.

"I will not—if you want to go out with Steele, go out with Steele."

"Why would I want to go out with Steele?" All those words in a row cost her too many seconds of not breathing, and she panted as she continued alongside him. He wasn't even winded, which so wasn't fair.

"Sure seemed like you wanted to back there," he said.

Opal stopped walking. Or running. Or trying to take steps too long for her legs. "Taggart, please stop for a second."

He took three more steps, putting quite a bit of distance between them with his long legs. "What?" With a withering look and a defiant sigh, he turned back to face her.

"I don't want to go out with Steele. He asked me to help him find a bandage for Marigold's leg, and I pointed it out to him. Case closed."

He shoved his hands deep into his leather jacket pockets. "You were standing really close to him."

Opal lifted her head high. "I was not."

"You laughed like he's the funniest man in the world."

She threw up her hands. "He said something funny. I laughed. It's not a crime." She took a few quick steps toward him and slid her hands up the zipper of his jacket. "Tag, this is nothing. Why does me talking to Steele upset you?"

"You were more than talking to him."

"I *wasn't*." Opal squinted at him, trying to see what he wasn't saying. "Why did you break-up with…your last girlfriend in Green River?" She couldn't remember the woman's name right now, but everything inside her told her this was important.

His jaw jumped, but Opal leaned in. "You said it ended badly. Why? How?"

"You want some hot chocolate?" He turned and started walking again. At least it wasn't the angry stomping he'd been doing a few moments ago.

"No," she called after him. "I only want hot chocolate if it comes with talking. *You* talking."

"I'll talk," he called over his shoulder, and Opal propelled herself after him again.

"It's far too early in the morning for this," she grumbled under her breath as she ran—for the fourth time—to catch him. It seemed the cold had sucked all the oxygen from their lungs, for they didn't speak on the trek back to his cabin.

He led the way up the steps to the porch and through the door, holding it for both dogs before Opal arrived. She met his eye, fired a fierce look at him she wasn't sure how he'd take, and continued past him into the warmth of his cabin.

She gave Max a death glare as the dog went to drink out of Boots's bowl, and she didn't quite know what to do with herself as Tag put Boots back in his crate and then started getting out milk, hot chocolate packets, mugs, and spoons.

Finally, he had nothing else to do to distract him, and he had to look at her. Then he turned away and said, "I was saving these." He opened the cupboard and grabbed something. When he plunked it on the counter, she saw the box of candy canes.

Her heartbeat bobbed against her breastbone. "You got candy canes for me?"

"I've never had them in hot chocolate, and you swear by them."

Opal reached for the box, and he let her take it. She opened it and pulled out one of the cheery red-and-white treats. "I love these."

"Never had much use for them myself," he said.

"This is not the kind of talking I want you to do," she said.

He turned to the microwave when it beeped and took out the milk he'd put in a few minutes ago. He poured it into two mugs and pushed one in front of her.

Tag came around the counter and sat down at the other end of it, with one barstool between them. Opal reached for a packet of hot chocolate powder and ripped it open. She poured it into her mug, then did it again with a second one. She used her candy cane to start mixing, knowing she'd get the extra-chocolatey flavor combined with mint in only a minute.

"Talina was a flirt," he said. "She cheated on me."

Opal's stirring motion stalled. She couldn't even get her eyes to move over to his. "That's crazy."

"What does that mean?"

"It means—that's crazy. Who would cheat on *you*?"

She managed to look at him then, this gentle giant of a man. He sat with his shoulders hunched forward as if he needed to protect himself. Head down. Eyes on his steaming milk, without any hot chocolate powder in it yet.

"With who?" Opal asked, her thoughts just spilling from her. "I mean, you're so, so amazing, and handsome, and wonderful. How could she ever want someone else?"

Silence descended on them then, amplifying and shouting her words back at her. Embarrassment climbed through her veins, and Opal sucked in a tight breath and held it in her lungs while she refocused on her hot drink.

"I just mean," she said when Tag didn't jump in with anything. "That I find it very odd that someone would want to cheat on you. It feels crazy to me, that's all."

"Well, thank you for sayin' so," he drawled. "But it happened, and maybe I jump—jumped to some conclusions of what was happening in the barn."

Opal slid off her stool and over to the next one. Tag usually put his arm around her first, or took her hand first, or leaned into her first. This morning, he sat like a statue, and Opal leaned her head against his arm.

"I don't want to go out with Steele," she said. "Not even a little bit. He said something funny about not being able to find anything, and it reminded me of something my momma used to say to Easton. That was *it*."

Tag nodded. "I hear you."

Opal took a moment to think about what he'd said. "But do you believe me?" she asked.

He started to nod really slowly, and he finally ducked his head and looked at her. "Yes, honeybear, I believe you."

Opal glowed under his attention. "Honeybear," she said. "That's a new one."

"I'm sorry I—I just saw something that wasn't there."

She'd learned to listen to what patients said—and what they didn't say—so she could ask questions to get to the root of their ailments. "What did you see?"

"The truth?"

"If you can't tell me the truth, I don't want to plan the Christmas party with you later today, and I don't want to go get breakfast burritos with you before church on Sunday."

Tag smiled, but it didn't stay long. "My mind blitzed out. I saw her flirting with another guy, and then him kissing her, and she was kissing him back, and...." He trailed off, his voice turning into a ghost of itself.

Opal said nothing, because Tag had gone, and he probably wouldn't hear her anyway.

"And I just walked away," Tag said, a hint of disgust moving into his voice now. "I didn't even say anything to her. I didn't bring it up with her later. Nothing." He scoffed, the sound similar to the angry one he'd made in the stable. "I just let her walk all over me. Over and over, and when I saw you...I just... blitzed."

Everything about him softened then, and he lifted his arm and curled it around her. "I'm sorry, Opal. Really."

"Do you trust me?"

"Yes," he whispered. "I do, which makes everything that just happened even more insane. I'm sorry."

"Accepted," she said. "Thank you for talking to me about this."

"I can be a right fool sometimes," he murmured.

"Stop it." She looked up at him. "Are you ever going to kiss me again?"

"Yes," he said.

"Right now?"

He met her gaze, and Opal could've bathed in the hot flames between them. They licked up her arms and down her neck, making everything heated between them. "Why haven't you kissed me since my birthday?"

"A coupla reasons," he said.

"Do tell."

"Do you want me to confess before or after I kiss you?"

Opal's nerves danced in pure anticipation. "Mm,

after." She tipped her head back slightly, and thankfully, Tag could read body cues.

He leaned down and matched his mouth to hers, uniting them in a way Opal had missed. She'd known she'd missed his touch, the stroke of his lips against hers, but she hadn't realized how much until this moment.

She hadn't realized how very dependent upon him she'd become. How important he'd become. How beautiful he was inside and out.

He pulled away first, just like he had beside the barn, weeks ago. "You make me nervous, Miss Opal," he whispered. He kissed her again, and oh, Opal could stay right here and do this all day.

But he once again ended the kiss before she was ready. She held so still, everything existing inside this tiny bubble of perfection. He moved his cheek to press against hers, which put his mouth right at her ear.

"And I don't normally kiss a woman as early as I kissed you. I just wanted to give us some more time to make sure *you* wanted to kiss *me* again."

"I did."

"A cowboy wants to make sure," he whispered. Then he lifted his head and reached for a hot chocolate packet. "Now, I saw you put two of these in your mug, and if you're gonna be doin' that all winter, I should probably buy some stock in Swiss Miss."

And just like she had earlier this morning, when

someone had said something funny, Opal tipped her head back and laughed.

CHAPTER
Twelve

TAG FINISHED CLEANING out the last stall in the stable, and he moved Dusty back into it, saying, "There you go, bud. You're all set for Christmas now." He smiled at Gerty's old horse, and then he turned to go back down the row.

They kept Rooster on the other end, because he was nosy. He liked to know who was coming in and out of his stable—for it *was* his. In fact, Rooster lifted his head over the gate and whiffed at Tag.

"Yeah, Merry Christmas to you too, Roost." He grinned at the big horse and stopped in front of him. "Now don't you be tellin' her I told you, but Gerty's got something special for you." He looked down the line of horses. "All y'all. So no funny business today. The rest of the Hammonds are coming in today."

In fact, Mike should be returning to the farm in the

next half-hour with his brother, his wife, and their daughter. They'd been entertaining Wes and Bree for a few days now, and Tag could admit he'd enjoyed the evening meals with Opal's parents.

"Big party tonight," he said. "Christmas in the morning. I'll bring out your stockings, okay?"

Rooster pressed the long bridge of his nose to Tag's shoulder, but he pushed right back. They played this game every now and then, but Tag always won. Rooster always acquiesced, as he should.

"When spring comes, you're going to be awed by the greenness of this place," Tag promised him. "It's a little muddy in the beginning, but you've never seen a summer like one in the Rocky Mountains." He grinned at the horse and ran his hand down Rooster's neck. "Merry Christmas Eve, my friend. I'll see you tonight."

With that, he left the horses to their afternoon. Gerty wasn't expecting him or Steele to do anything else for the day, except a quick evening feed. Steele had already gone back to the Harris Farm for the holidays, in fact, so Tag would do the evening feeding alone that night before he went home to his solitary cabin.

He'd helped Opal decorate the farmhouse with not just one Christmas tree, but two. He'd put one up in his cabin too, with a bit of her help, and he had a single stocking hanging from the bar of his island, because he didn't own a fireplace.

The dinners at the farmhouse had been festive for the past week or so, with garland, window clings of snowmen and cartoon Christmas trees and the Hammond stockings hung from the mantel. Gerty had gotten stockings for all the horses too, but she didn't want to put them up too early lest the equines got used to having treats hanging in giant socks on a daily basis.

Tag chuckled every time he thought about it.

Instead of going back to the cabin, he entered the farmhouse to the warmth of a good furnace and the scent of brown sugar and raising yeasty dough. Carrie didn't stand in the kitchen, where he'd found her so often in the past, but Opal came bustling down the hall, fixing the bright red belt encircling her waist.

She wasn't looking up, and Tag whistled as he took in the green-and-white plaid dress. It had bubbly sleeves along her shoulders that only went down a couple of inches from there. She'd cinched that festive belt around her waist to add some red, and the skirt then flared and fell to her knees.

"Wow, wow-ow-wee," he said, sauntering a little closer to her.

Opal smiled at him. "Oh, Tag, you're here."

"Yes, I am." He ran his hand along that belt and touched his lips to hers. "You're nervous."

"A little," she admitted.

"Why? Your parents have been here for a bit. It's literally just Easton and Allison."

"I know," she said, and then she blew out her breath. "I don't know why this gets me keyed up."

Tag knew why, and it had a lot to do with the binder she'd been using to plan this evening for her family. "Okay, well, do you have two minutes?"

"For what?" Opal eyed him suspiciously. "They're going to be here any minute, and I'll not have them walk in while we're kissing."

Tag chuckled and shook his head. "Come stand right here." He moved to her side and kept her facing the way she'd been walking already. "Look around this house and tell me what you see. What you feel."

"Tag."

"Two minutes," he said. "Just look around. See, feel, smell." He leaned closer, taking a deep breath of the scent of her hair, her skin, her dress. "Close your eyes now. Deep breath, and tell me what you see, feel, and smell."

Opal took that breath, everything slowing down in the room. "It smells like candied meat."

"That'll be the ham and the pulled pork," he murmured.

"And bread," she added. "I love the scent of a yeast dough before it bakes."

"Me too."

"I think there's still some lingering chocolate in the air from my morning baking," she said.

"Brown sugar," he said. "That's what I smelled when I came inside."

Opal took another deep breath. "I see the stockings, and West's toys, and that pretty Christmas tree with all the horse ornaments."

"And the horseshoes," he reminded her. "They glint in those pretty white lights."

"I see a wreath on the door, and West's fun clings, and the table all set for dinner." She turned into his chest. "My brother is going to drop his bags all over the place," Opal added. "He'll probably put his backpack on my pretty hollied plates."

"I'll guard the table," Tag told her. "You've only done two of the things."

Opal drew a breath and then exhaled it out like he was nothing but trouble. He smiled, because he liked her fire, her spunk, her stubbornness. "I feel...."

"Like you've been working hard for this night, and it's going to be perfect, no matter what?" Tag supplied. "Even if Easton puts his backpack on your holly berry plates, or West cries when he doesn't get exactly what he wants when he wants it, or if the bread gets a little too brown."

"Oh, please," Opal said as she wrapped her arms around him. "West never cries."

"That's because he always gets exactly what he wants," Tag quipped.

Opal giggled and buried her face in his chest, making him feel strong and desired. "Thank you, Tag."

"For what?"

"For making me slow down."

"It's not going to be perfect, honeybee," he said. "But it's going to be completely perfect at the same time."

"I'm not going to kiss you," she said. "Because I just caught a flash of movement outside, and that means they're here."

"Then you better go say hello," Tag said.

Opal squealed and headed for the front door in her sexy, shiny black heels. She pulled open the door and flowed right out onto the front porch. "You're here, you're here!"

Tag shook his head good-naturedly and made to follow her. Easton and Allison had a little girl named Violet, and he figured he could be useful in bringing in some suitcases. Mike and Gerty and Easton and Allison had gotten out of the truck, and the four of them clustered with Opal at the bottom of the steps. They all laughed and talked over one another, and for a breath, a mere slip, time stopped.

A hole opened up for him in the group. He could be the sixth person there, and when Wes and Bree exited the house and went down the steps, the group expanded for them too. They had room for him in their family, and Tag hadn't seen it until now.

"Opal's wrong," he whispered to himself. She wasn't an outlier in her family. She didn't sit on the outside of anything.

She was the glue that held them all together. She

bridged the gap from the oldest brother to the youngest, from her parents to her siblings, and she did it with grace, power, and beauty.

Tag felt himself falling in love with her, and with that came the terrifying sense of freefalling into an abyss. Of jumping out of an airplane without a parachute to save him. Of letting go of the past and stepping into an unknown future.

"Tag," someone called, and he pulled himself back to earth and anchored himself there. He hurried down the steps and to the back of the truck to get suitcases, but Opal intercepted him.

"Here he is," she said, hooking her arm through his. "Tag, this is my baby brother, Easton, and his wife, Allison. My momma just took Vi inside."

"So great to meet you," Tag said kindly. He shook Easton's hand, noting the khakis the man wore, with the pale yellow collared shirt. He wasn't cut from any of the same cloth as Tag, but he had a good smile.

Allison was likewise proper, with her flowered maxi dress. She had dirty blonde hair that parted right down the middle, and when he shook her hand too, she had a firm touch.

"Great to meet you," Easton said. "We've heard a lot about you."

"Is that so?" Tag asked.

"Opal texts about you all the time," Gerty said. "Spoiler alert."

"Just about Boots and Rooster and the fact that I

converted you to candy canes in your hot chocolate." She grinned at him. "Why are we standing outside in the cold?" She looked up into the blue, blue sky, which should've made them all feel warm.

But when it was this clear in the winter, that only brought sub-zero temperatures to go with the blinding light. Oh, and it meant a storm was rapidly approaching.

Tag did move to get the suitcases then, and he followed everyone into the house—where he found West looking at Violet like she was an alien invader in his house, and Easton had put his backpack on the corner of the table.

"At least he missed the plate," Tag murmured as he grabbed it and set it beside the door. Then he took the bags over to the kitchen door and set them out of the way. He'd take them with him when he went to his cabin, as Easton's family would be staying out in the trio of cabins this holiday season. Steele had taken the one next to Tag, which left one more on the end for them.

Tag had helped Opal get it aired out and heated for her brother, and he'd carry the bags out there for them too.

Behind him, West squealed in a less-than-delighted way, and that caused no less than all four Hammond women to lurch toward him as he ripped a toy away from his cousin. Tag wanted to burst out laughing, but he didn't want Bree, Opal, Gerty, or Allison to see him.

Thankfully, the door opened, and a metal tray started to enter ahead of Carrie. Tag lunged in that direction to help her, as he'd already spotted the beautifully decorated Christmas cookies. Sleds, stockings, snowflakes, and more.

"I got these," he said, taking the tray from her.

"Oh, Tag," Carrie said as she released the tray. She wore an earnest expression as her eyes darted around the kitchen and living room. "Kyle needs a hand getting out of the truck. He sprained his ankle this morning, and...."

"I'm on the way," he said. He slid the cookies onto the counter beside the fridge and then bustled outside to help Kyle. Their generational house didn't sit as far from the main farmhouse as the trio of cabins did, but they'd driven over tonight.

He met the older gentleman's eyes through the windshield, and Kyle wore a hint of resignation in his gaze. "Thank you, Tag," he said as he opened the door. "I thought Carrie was going to come back out, but you're better."

"Maybe Opal could look at your ankle," he said as he shored up the man's arm with his hand and shoulder. "Lean on me, Kyle. Can you put weight on it?"

"Yes." Kyle groaned. "A little, but not much." He slid from the truck, and Tag absorbed all of his weight until he could get his good foot down.

"Okay," Tag said a bit breathlessly. The wind kicked up and grabbed the brim of his cowboy hat. He let it fly off his head, because he didn't want to drop Kyle. "Here we go."

He helped Kyle the short distance to the steps and up into the house. "Let's get you to the purple couch." He spied it across the room, with only Mike on it, and both he and Opal seemed to notice Tag at the same time.

"What happened?" Opal asked, which drew everyone's attention where neither Tag nor Kyle wanted it.

"Nothing," Kyle said.

"He sprained his ankle this morning," Carrie said from the kitchen. Tag met Opal's eye, and they had a pretty significant conversation without him having to say anything. Since his accusation that she'd been flirting with Steele—and since finally kissing her again —Tag felt like he and Opal simply existed on a different plane than they had before.

He knew her better; she knew him.

"Let me look at it, Kyle," she said smoothly. "I can at least wrap it so it's stronger."

"Sit down," Mike said.

They got him to the couch, where Gerty sat next to him, West on her lap. "Gramps, you have to say something when something happens."

"I'm okay," he said, giving her a smile.

"Opal is a doctor," she said. "She could've helped you this morning."

"Let me have that baby," Bree said, and she took West from Gerty. Tag didn't need to hover, and he fell back to get out of the way. He stepped on a toy that squeaked, and he quickly lifted his boot as Violet giggled.

Max came over and nabbed the toy, and Tag scooped up the little girl. She was a pretty thing, with dark eyes and light hair, and he said, "Let's get you a cookie, should we?" He retreated to the kitchen and picked up one of the smallest cookies—a Santa hat. He broke off the tip of it with the puffy white ball and handed it to Violet.

Then he popped the rest of it into his mouth while Opal tended to Kyle's ankle. Activity went on around him, with Bree bringing West into the kitchen to get a cookie too. "And we better get these rolls formed and set for their final rise."

"I'll take the kids," Tag said. "We can play on the bouncy couch with Grandpa." He took West as Bree slid him into his other arm, and Tag headed for the other half of the couch where Kyle now sat with his ankle wrapped.

He settled down, feeling every eye on him as he did. "Wow, wow-ow-wee," Opal whispered as she stood with the first aid kit.

"You've used that way too much this month," he said to her.

"We have an announcement," Easton said. "Opal? Can we do announcements right now? I don't know what your plan is for tonight."

"It's—we're going to do some visiting, dinner,

games, and gifts." She shot a look at Tag. "You can do an announcement now." She seemed nervous, and Tag wished he could pull her onto his lap and comfort her too.

But Violet and West took up all of his current lap space, and the blow-up couch wasn't as stable as he'd like. Still, he managed to reach up and touch Opal's fingers on the hand that wasn't gripping the first aid kit like a shield.

"Sit down, honeydew."

She looked at him, then let herself fall back a step to perch on the arm of the couch. It moved a bit with her added weight, but didn't shift too violently as to buck them all off it.

Easton glowed with the light of the full moon. "Well, Allison and I are pleased to announce that we're going to have another baby next year." He beamed at his wife, and Tag could not imagine two people more opposite than himself.

Opal could be quite refined too, a side of her Tag only saw when they went out to dinner. Otherwise, she seemed far more down-to-earth than Easton or Allison.

"That's wonderful news," Bree said, rushing into the living room to congratulate her son and daughter-in-law.

"Super great," Mike said, laughing. He embraced his brother, and Wes engulfed them both with his impressive reach.

"Just great," Opal said almost under her breath. Then Tag took the first aid kit from her; their eyes met; he nodded at Allison as she stepped away from Gerty's light hug.

Opal propelled herself off the end of the couch and over to her sister-in-law, her voice absolutely gushing with rainbows and kittens as she said, "That's so wonderful, Alli. I'd love to come stay with you when you have the baby."

"Oh, I'd love that," Allison said. "We're due in April."

Tag marveled that Opal could stuff her jealousy away so quickly, and he suspected it was because she wasn't really jealous. He felt like that about the twins. He wasn't jealous of their friendship or the life they had.

He simply felt left out.

And that pinched inside a person's heart and soul in a way that words couldn't describe. So when Opal finished talking to Allison, she came back to the purple couch and picked up Violet. "Hey, you sweet thing." She pressed a kiss to the little girl's forehead and sat down between Kyle and Tag.

He didn't have to say anything, and Opal didn't need to explain. He knew exactly how she felt, and he reached over and took her hand in his. A quick squeeze, an acknowledging smile, and Tag felt more connected to her than he'd ever felt to anyone else.

"Merry Christmas Eve, honey-love," he

murmured, and Opal pressed into his kiss against her temple.

"Merry Christmas Eve, Taggart," she whispered back, and oh, how he loved his full name in her throaty whisper.

CHAPTER
Thirteen

TUCKER HAMMOND SCRAMBLED THE EGGS, trying to keep them tender and soft. Warm and cooked, but not overdone. He hated overdone scrambled eggs, and he'd been setting his alarm five minutes earlier so he could be the one at the stove in the mornings.

He loved his roommate, Tarr Olson, but the man overcooked his eggs.

"Morning," Tarr said in the moment Tucker deemed the eggs done enough, and he pulled the pan off the stove.

"Mornin'." Tucker put the pan on a potholder his twelve-year-old niece had crocheted him for his birthday, and he turned to get down plates from the cupboard. He watched Tarr settle at the bar, not the table, and he nudged the pan and rubber spatula closer to him. "I'm not serving you."

"Sausage and eggs." Tarr took in the breakfast food, glanced over to the full coffee pot, and then finally—finally—looked at Tuck. "You want an answer about the rodeo."

"Yes, sir," Tuck said. "I do." He turned his back on his best friend and the man he used to manage on the PRCA. They'd ridden the Montana Circuit, the Wilderness Circuit, the Mountain States Circuit, and the Texas Circuit. Tarr did well there, as he hailed from Texas, and Tuck was itching to get on the road again.

His gypsy soul didn't like all the sitting still, though he hardly had a moment to sit here on his family farm. Matt didn't hire cowboys needlessly, and everyone who lived and worked the farm had a full-time load to keep them busy—Tarr and Tuck included.

Seeing as how Tucker wasn't anywhere near the pro level of a rodeo champion, he couldn't just sign himself up for the first circuit he could, pack his bags, load his horse, and hit the road. He needed Tarr to want to get back in the saddle.

And so far, Tarr did not want to get back in the saddle.

Tarr sighed like Tucker was requiring a pint of blood instead of a decision about his career. "I like it here, Tucker." He slid a couple of links onto his plate alongside the eggs and reached for the saltshaker though he hadn't tasted the eggs. Tarr salted everything, and Tucker had gotten used to it.

"You liked it in Montana too," he said.

"I don't need the money." Tarr threw a pointed look to Tucker. "You don't either."

"Yeah, but the difference is, I'm going crazy." Tuck tipped the rest of the eggs onto his plate and snagged four sausage links. He rounded the semi-permanent island he'd installed himself and headed for the table. Then he could talk without Tarr staring at him, seeing straight into his soul.

"Bobbie Jo still won't go out with me. Melinda was a huge fail, and she still calls me several times a day." He yanked out a chair and sank into it. "A *day*, Tarr."

"Well, you shouldn't have kissed her on the first date." He carried joviality in his tone, and that only fueled Tuck's ire.

"I didn't," he said forcefully. He scooped up a big forkful of eggs and put them in his mouth. Tarr said nothing either, and that was his answer about joining the circuit for next year.

A no.

It seemed like all Tuck got—from anyone—was no.

He'd backed way off on Bobbie Jo since the Fourth of July, when Tarr had basically told him he was pathetic for how he acted around her. Embarrassment squirreled through him even now, months later.

"You'll want to join up as soon as you experience true snow," Tuck grumbled. "Winter ranching is no fun, brother."

Tarr chuckled then, because the weather had already turned. The leaves had turned and fallen.

Thanksgiving and Christmas were both gone, and it had snowed a few times, then melted—even the big storm last weekend had only left a few inches that hadn't stuck around. The New Year sat only two days from now, and Tuck needed a plan for it.

Something. Anything.

"Stuff that doesn't melt," Tuck said. "Like what we're gonna get this week."

The other cowboy sighed and came to sit at the table with Tuck. Their eyes met, and they had entire conversations in that single beat of time. Then Tuck speared a sausage link and bit off half of it. "I don't see you makin' any moves on Hattie."

"That's because I'm a gentleman, not thirteen years old." Tarr rolled his eyes.

"I'm sure that's why," Tuck said dryly. "And that it has nothing to do with her telling Clara and Lucy that she doesn't date cowboys."

"That was hearsay," Tarr said.

"She said it in line for the luncheon last month," Tuck said. "I even heard about it."

"From who?" Tarr gave him a wicked look, but Tucker could handle him. He'd been managing the cowboy's career for five years now, and he couldn't stand the thought of working this farm forever. Or even for another month. His very skin itched to get out there and do something.

What to do had always been Tucker's problem.

He loved his family. He did love this farm. He

simply didn't want to live here forever, work this same land forever, be trapped here forever. He disliked feeling like this and thinking like this, because it felt ungrateful to him, and Tucker really tried not to be ungrateful.

He'd even gone so far as to buy a gratitude journal, and he wrote one sentence in it every night before he went to bed. One thing he was grateful for. One thing he wanted to reflect on later, something he wanted to remember, something that meant something to him.

He glanced over to Tarr, who quirked his right eyebrow. "Fine," Tucker said. "I heard it from Molly."

"Molly." Tarr scoffed, though Molly ran Pony Power, and Hattie, Clara, and Lucy all worked within that program. Hattie worked with the horses, the way Gloria did, training them and attending the therapy appointments with the children. Clara and Lucy were counselors who worked in the cabins that ran along the north side of the pasture, before the family land took over, and then the cowboy cabins.

None of the counselors lived on-site, but Hattie did. In fact, Matt and Boone had just reorganized the cabin living situations, and now Hattie shared with Bobbie Jo.

In Tucker's over-imaginative mind, he saw himself and Tarr standing side-by-side on the porch of the cabin down the lane, waiting for their dates to answer the door. He'd hold Bobbie Jo's hand, and she'd forget all about that dentist boyfriend of hers in Oklahoma.

The fantasy evaporated as someone knocked on their front door. It started to swing open before either of them could move, and Boone Whettstein filled the doorway. "Boys," he said.

"What's up, Boone?" Tucker rose to his feet and stuck out his hand. This cabin was a bit bigger than the others, but he could still take a couple of steps and reach the door from the table.

"Morning." Boone had a big personality, with plenty of loud laughter and entertaining stories. This morning, he smiled, but it didn't quite hold the shine it usually did. "I'm just stopping by on my way off the farm. Matt wanted you two to come see him before you head out this morning."

"Sure." Tuck pulled his hand back. "You okay?"

"Yeah, yeah." Boone nodded and tucked his hands in his pockets. "I'm just going to sit with Gerty's baby while she goes to the doctor with Opal."

"Oh, does she have an appointment today?"

"Yep," Boone said, his smile growing in intensity. "Hopefully her last, but Gerty feels real responsible because she got hurt on her farm, and I'm not going to say no to a morning of playing Grandpa."

Tucker grinned and then chuckled. "I can't imagine why you would." Gerty and Mike had the cutest baby alive, and Tuck suddenly wanted to take the ten-mile trip south to their farm just to get off this one.

Outside, the wind howled, probably because the sun hadn't come up yet, and Boone reached up to tip his hat. "Just wanted you boys to know, and I forgot to text last night."

"We'll stop by," Tucker said, and Boone backed out of the doorway. Tucker closed the door behind him, sealing out the cold and wind. He sighed and turned around. "I can't believe this is where we're livin'." He hooked his thumb toward the closed door. "Did you see? It's still dark outside."

Tarr grinned and stood up. He collected their breakfast dishes, but Tuck was determined to be in a bad mood. He skulked over to the couch and sat down. "Now we have to meet with Matt. Boone's off the farm for the morning. You know what that means?"

Only the kitchen sink turning on answered him, and Tuck rolled his eyes. "It means we'll be on all the hardest jobs."

"They're all just jobs," Tarr said.

"Why can't I be mad?" Tuck asked.

"You can be."

"I just wish you'd get mad sometimes too."

Tarr hardly ever did. He was as even as even could be, and if he showed negative emotion, it was *neg-a-tive*. Otherwise, he did what he was assigned. He'd worked out hard for the rodeo. He trained relentlessly. He smiled all the time, and he had one of the most positive outlooks on life that Tuck had ever encountered.

Behind him, the dishes clanked loudly. He startled

and sat up. Looking over his shoulder, he found Tarr slamming his palm against the countertop. "I just can't *believe* we have to go to work in the dark."

Tucker blinked, not sure what was happening.

"And you know what? If Hattie doesn't want to date cowboys, that's her loss, you know?" He pointed to Tucker and then back to himself. "We're good men. We work hard." He gestured toward the front windows. "She'd be lucky to go out with one of us. And you know what else is totally ridiculous?"

Tuck cocked his head and rolled his eyes. "Okay, stop it."

"No, I won't." Tarr actually looked a little mad. "Who dates someone long-distance for months and months? Never flies out to see them? The fancy dentist can't come visit her? *That's* what I don't get."

Tucker smiled and shook his head. "Tarr, enough." He turned back around and sank into the couch. His best friend joined him, his smile sunny and shiny, and Tuck couldn't resist it. He grinned too, and the two of them burst out laughing.

As they sobered, Tarr looked at him. "Seriously, brother, I'm sorry about Bobbie Jo."

Tuck nodded. "Me too. And I'm sorry about Hattie."

Tarr's jaw twitched, but he shook his head. "Don't matter." He exhaled heavily as he got to his feet. He gazed down at Tuck. "Do you really think we'll stay here?"

"With all the glory of the sun, I hope not," Tuck said.

"Right," Tarr said. "So why would we want girl-friends? Do you think Bobbie Jo is going to run the circuit with us?"

No, Tuck did not think that. So he put his hand in Tarr's and let his best friend pull him to his feet. "Let's go see Matt."

"Don't worry, Tuck, the sun'll come up later today."

"Yeah, yeah," Tucker muttered as he followed Tarr out the front door. Another day in front of him. Another day at the farm. Another day trapped here in Ivory Peaks.

———

THE SUN DID INDEED RISE that day. Tuck did have to take a leadership role with the other cowboys, and he could admit that he enjoyed the variety. He still went back to the cabin and made himself a couple of sandwiches, grabbed the bag of potato chips from the counter beside the fridge, and filled his water bottle from the filtered spigot on the sink.

He left the cabin immediately, because he couldn't stand to be contained by four walls while he ate. He headed away from the cabins, went past the family bonfire pit, and crossed the road.

The seed shed sat over here, the only building on

this side, with field upon field stretching toward the pine trees, the fences that marked the boundary between this farm and the Harris' next door, and the highway.

Hardly anyone drove this way, so Tuck didn't hear any traffic, and he kept his eyes on the ground as he walked. Only gray existed on the farm right now. Gray in the sky. Gray on the ground. Gray in the fields. Heck, even the farmhouse had recently been freshly painted in its usual color—gray.

His boots made crunching noises against the dirt, and he could feel the snow in his bones. Oh, how he hated the snow.

He walked along the side of the shed, and it took him a couple of steps to realize there was more than just his footsteps filling the air with noise. It sounded like....

Tuck arrived at the corner of the shed and peered around it, half-expecting to see a hurt cat or a lost child.

He found Bobbie Jo Hanks, crying into her hands. Her shoulders shook, and she made high-pitched squeaks that tore at every piece of his heart. His feet had frozen, making it impossible for him to move, though he knew he should. She wouldn't want him to see her like this.

Then, his mouth betrayed him by asking, "Bobbie Jo?" Thankfully—and this was so going in his gratitude journal later that night—he didn't ask her if she was okay. She obviously wasn't.

She lowered the tissue and looked at him with those gorgeous forest green eyes. "Can I sit with you at lunch today?"

"Of course you can." He'd invited her to come eat with him behind this shed over the summer, and she'd told him—again—she didn't think her boyfriend would approve of it. She hadn't said that today.

He took the couple of steps to her and slid down the shed to sit beside her on the ground. "Sandwich?" He extended her one, and she took it.

"Thank you," she whispered.

"Are you hurt?" he asked. "Physically, I mean. Like, do I need to get a first aid kit?"

She shook her head, and Tuck nodded. "Okay, then." He didn't ask anything else, because the Lord shouted at him to *wait. Just wait.*

And though waiting and patience were not Tuck's strong suits, he prepared to do exactly that.

CHAPTER

Fourteen

BOBBIE JO HANKS couldn't believe she'd come to the seed shed. At the same time, she didn't want to be alone. Ironic, since she'd been living here in Ivory Peaks alone for the past several months.

She pulled the turkey and Swiss sandwich from the bag and took a bite. Tuck did the same thing. He set the bag of chips on the cold ground between them, and Bobbie Jo dipped her hand inside to get some of the ridged snacks.

This silence between them was comfortable, but foreign. Tuck didn't normally sit still or silent, something Bobbie Jo had actually admired about him. She'd admired a lot about him—appropriately, of course.

She could acknowledge that he had a handsome jawline without letting herself think too much of it. His sandy hair played differently with his dark eyes, and the man worked a farm relentlessly, so he definitely had muscles.

He got along with the other cowboys, and he knew his stuff around the ranch. She'd rounded up horses with him a few times, and he was always right where he needed to be to get the job done. His horse obviously trusted him explicitly, and they worked well together.

Yes, Bobbie Jo could tell a lot about a cowboy by the way he rode and worked with a horse.

The edges of her nose felt raw as her tears dried. Her face crackled with the salt, and she wished she'd gone home after Lawson's phone call.

"So, Lawson broke up with me over the phone," she said.

Tucker sucked in a breath and turned his head toward her swiftly. "He did what?"

Bobbie Jo shook her head, her emotions far too delicate to be having this conversation. Still, she'd chosen to come here, knowing Tuck would arrive with sandwiches. He did every single day; she'd seen him walking this way many times; he'd even invited her to eat with him once.

"I've known for a while that we weren't going to work out," she said. "It still—it's really weird how it still hurts." She sniffled and shook her head again. She looked up from her half-eaten sandwich and gazed at the cloudy sky. She identified with it, with the way the clouds were all one big mass of foaming, rolling, angry pressure.

"I'm really sorry it hurts." Tucker spoke kindly, softly, tenderly. He finally tore his eyes from her face, and some of the weight lifted from her shoulders. "I don't want you to hurt."

"Thank you, Tuck."

He finished his sandwich, and Bobbie Jo tucked the rest of hers back in the bag. She had no appetite left, and she simply leaned her head back against the shed while Tuck crunched his way through potato chips and then an apple.

Her thoughts seemed to have been suspended in gelatin. She didn't think anything; nothing entered or exited her mind. She may have even dozed, which was something Bobbie Jo never did.

Eventually, she came back to herself, realizing that the man beside her had gotten really quiet. A blip of panic moved through her at the thought of Tucker getting up and leaving her sitting there, and then his hand slid along hers.

She turned her hand over, and he took it into his. A scuffle along dirt, a cleared throat, and then Tuck's shoulder touched hers. Bobbie Jo sighed as she leaned into him, stealing his warmth and friendship and safety.

He wanted to be more than friends, Bobbie Jo knew. In soft, private, still moments like this, she could admit that if she hadn't been dating Lawson, she'd have definitely gone out with Tuck by now. The man was equal parts charm and good-looks, and he hadn't been shy about his crush on her.

He'd calmed down a lot in recent months, and Bobbie Jo wondered if she'd already had her chance with him.

Doesn't matter, she told herself. *You don't want to move from one relationship straight into another one anyway.*

Bobbie Jo had never had a lot of boyfriends, and just the fact that Tuck had shown interest had been surprising to her.

"Do you know why I came to Ivory Peaks?" she asked.

"Sure," he said quietly. "You'd just finished a degree in something no one gets a job in, and you needed a job."

True, but...also not true. "That's what I told everyone."

"Are you sayin' you lied to me, Miss Bobbie Jo?"

She opened her eyes as a smile graced her face. She turned toward Tuck, and oh, he sat close. So close, and it felt so good. She wasn't sure how she felt about this man, and she wasn't sure she should even be here with him.

What would he think of her now? Was she moving too fast?

The questions started piling on top of themselves then, and a keen sense of overwhelm descended on

Bobbie Jo. "Not exactly a lie," she said. "Just not the whole story."

"I see."

"I suppose you'd like the whole story."

"I suppose I would," he drawled.

Bobbie Jo laid her head against his bicep again, his fingers tightening in hers. Squeezing, almost encouraging her to go ahead and tell him. "I could've stayed in Oklahoma and found a job at a farm or ranch. I came here, because my family lost our ranch."

She paused to take a breath and to really examine how she felt about the losses she'd suffered in Oklahoma. "I'm sorry," Tuck murmured.

"I wanted to take it over," she said. "But it just didn't work out. I had this degree in metallurgical engineering—that's the study of metals and their uses—and you know what? I first started looking at this area because of a company called Hammond Manufacturing."

"You have got to be kidding."

"You do know what they do there, right?"

"I have no idea what they do there," he said. "But I bet my cousin hires metalluring engineers."

"Metallurgical."

"That sounds so…like something I'm allergic to." He chuckled. "Metalluring sounds so much prettier."

She grinned too, something she hadn't realized she could do so soon after such a horrific phone call. "Anyway, HMC wasn't hiring engineers at the time, but the website says they're constantly looking for good people. I put in my application, and I started looking for work in the area. Hunter Hammond hired me, just not for the company I was anticipating."

"Does Hunt know this?" Tuck asked.

"No," she said. "Unless he sees the applications that go through at HMC."

"Then no. That's all Mike. Probably not even him. He's got managers and department heads and stuff." Tucker squeezed her hand again. "Still, Bobbie Jo, why didn't you say something? Mike can pull your application and get you a job in like, two seconds flat." He looked at her again, and his gaze weighed so stinking much.

He wanted answers she didn't know how to give.

"I like it here," she said again. "This place reminds me of my family ranch, minus the mountains of course. And we had a lot more corn." She did smile then, and she let her eyes drift closed again. "I'm not really a city girl."

"You don't say," Tuck teased. Then he fell silent too, and they stayed that way, side-by-side, hands clasped together, until an alarm shattered their peace. "That's me." Tuck pulled his hand away and silenced his phone.

He folded his long legs under him and looked at her. Bobbie Jo might as well have been naked for how much he could see. "You'll be okay?"

"I have to get back to work too."

"Yeah, but what I meant was…you'll be okay?" He watched her, searching her face. "I'll bring you dinner tonight."

"Don't be ridiculous," she said. "People don't take dinner to people who've broken up with their loser, cheater boyfriends."

"He—wait, he cheated on you?"

"No," Bobbie Jo said miserably. "But it feels like it, and if I pretend he did, then I can dislike him more."

Tuck gave her half a smile, and it still made her pulse race. What that meant, she wasn't sure. She was almost embarrassed he affected her this way. "I've never liked him."

Bobbie Jo laughed, and Tuck got to his feet. He offered her his hand, and when she took it, snaps, crackles, and pops moved through her bloodstream. She stood too, and they looked at one another in the dull, flat light of the nearly New Year's day.

She had no idea what she'd say or do if Tuck asked her to dinner right now. He didn't ask, and instead, he finally said, "Dinner tonight. I'll bring you and Hattie something, okay?"

She wasn't going to argue with him. "Okay," she agreed. "No green peppers. Hattie's allergic to peppers."

"Good to know," he said as if he might actually be making her something with green peppers in it. He went around the corner first, and she followed him. "You have got to be kidding me," Tuck muttered.

Bobbie Jo looked up and peered past him to find Tarr and Matt coming their way. Her steps slowed, but both men had seen her. They'd clearly seen her and Tuck come around from the back of the shed together too, if Tarr's elevated eyebrows said anything.

"I'll see you later," Tuck murmured, and then he raised both hands. "Guys, come on. My alarm went off literally sixty seconds ago."

Matt looked at him and said, "We've got four cows in labor. We need everyone." He gestured to Bobbie Jo. "You too, Bobbie Jo. Let's go." If he found it weird to see her and Tuck emerging from behind a shed, he didn't show it.

Tarr sure did, and Tuck paused in front of his best friend, said something, and then brushed by him. Tarr didn't move. He stared at Bobbie Jo, and while she'd never thought the cowboy didn't like her, she did a little bit right now.

"Do I need to worry about you breakin' his heart?" Tarr asked after several long moments.

Bobbie Jo shook her head. "No, sir," she said.

Tarr Olson—tall, tough, millionaire Tarr Olson—nodded. "All right, then," he said. "Come on. We've got four cows in labor, and we need everyone."

———

"BOBBIE JO?"

Her name rang through her head, and Bobbie Jo

frowned as she rolled over. She just wanted to sleep. She'd had a terrible, no-good day, and though her stomach growled, she simply wanted to stay in bed.

"Bobbie Jo," Hattie, her cabinmate said, her voice much closer now. "Wake up. There's two of the hottest cowboys alive standing in our living room, holding food you said you wanted them to bring."

Bobbie Jo sat straight up, which did nothing to soothe the pounding in her head. "Tucker."

Hattie sat down on her bed, her deep brown eyes filled with concern. She'd only moved in a couple of weeks ago, but she and Bobbie Jo had hit it off. They'd become fast friends, and Bobbie Jo had really needed that.

She reached out and tucked Bobbie Jo's hair behind her ear, the way her mother might have done. "What's going on? Why did he bring dinner?" She glanced toward the open door and back to Bobbie Jo. "And Tarr Olson." Her face pinked up just saying his name, and Bobbie Jo managed to smile.

"I crashed his solitary lunch and bawled my eyes out about Lawson breaking up with me."

Hattie's eyes grew to the size of full moons by the end of the sentence. "There's—Lawson broke up with you?"

Bobbie Jo pushed her blanket off her legs as she nodded. She hadn't even bothered to change once she'd arrived home. She'd just collapsed into bed, and she sighed as she realized how dark it already was.

"So I guess he's not coming here for your birthday next month."

Bobbie Jo shook her head and stood, her hips feeling creaky. "No. Let's go see what the cowboys brought for dinner."

Hattie joined her, and as they crossed the small room, she whispered, "Do you think he actually cooks?"

"I mean, they live there together," Bobbie Jo whispered back. "And they haven't died yet, so." She shrugged and led the way out of the bedroom. She'd taken the one in the far corner, but it still only took four strides to arrive in the more public areas of the cabin.

Tucker and Tarr stood side by side, still in front of the door, the food they'd brought still in their hands. For some reason, that struck Bobbie Jo as funny. She grinned at them and gestured for them to come into the kitchen at the back of the house. "C'mon, boys," she said. "We won't bite."

Tarr exchanged a glance with Tuck, and then they stepped forward together. They'd clearly been home long enough to shower—both of them. She'd never seen cleaner clothes on either cowboy, unless they were going to church, and she eyed the pans and bags in their hands.

"What did you bring?" She looked from the covered casserole dish in Tuck's hands to his face. "And did you cook this?"

"I was in the birthing shed longer than you," he said as he slid the casserole dish onto the counter. "So, no. I enlisted the help of Cosette for this."

"She's a great cook," Tarr added as he put a plastic grocery bag of food on the counter. "She and Boone have us over sometimes."

"So you don't cook," Hattie said, not phrasing it as a question. Tarr's eyes flew to hers and locked there, and oh, the electricity in the room made the hair on Bobbie Jo's arms stand straight up.

"Tuck's better than me," Tarr said smoothly. "But we take turns in the kitchen." He flicked a look to Tuck. "Right, Tuck?"

"Right," he said easily. He pulled back the aluminum foil concealing the food inside. "It's chicken cordon bleu casserole—one of my favorites. She said it's not super warm, but it heats super fast in the oven or the microwave." He smiled at her, and wow, Bobbie Jo could sink into that. "Do you want me to put it in the oven?"

"I can—"

"I insist," he said with more force in his voice than he'd used with her in a long time. If he ever had.

Bobbie Jo's fiery personality reared up, and she felt sparkly and electric herself as she glared at him. He stared back, a silent battle of wills, and Bobbie Jo was too tired to try to win this fight.

"Just let him take care of it," Tarr said, breaking the tension between them before Bobbie Jo could concede.

"You ladies have worked real hard today, and some of us have had a lot to deal with." He nodded at Bobbie Jo, and she hadn't expected someone like him— someone so talented, so rich, and so handsome—to also be so kind.

"Thank you," she murmured. "The oven's great, Tuck. What else is there? I can get it ready while—"

"Nah," he said. "Why don't you two go sit down and rest? We'll get it all set up for you and then leave you alone." He gave her another smile as he moved around her and Hattie and went over to the stove.

"You're not going to stay and eat with us?" Hattie asked.

"No, ma'am," Tarr said in his rich baritone voice. "Cosette made all this for us too." He reached for Bobbie Jo and then Hattie, then he gestured for them to head into the living room and leave the kitchen to the cowboys. "Really, ladies. Just rest for a few minutes. We'll get you all served."

Bobbie Jo looked at Hattie, who stared back at her with wonder in her expression. It tingled through Bobbie Jo too, and then she said, "All right, then. We might as well let someone take care of us for once."

"Yeah," Hattie said, and they moved into the living room and sat on the couch. The two cowboys got to work behind them, and Bobbie Jo couldn't help turning to watch them over her shoulder.

Tarr pulled out a bagged salad and started looking for a bowl. Tuck washed a container of grape tomatoes and then peeled the plastic off one of mushrooms. He added them to the bowl Tarr found, and they seemed to move in perfect sync with each other.

"They're incredible," Hattie whispered, causing Bobbie Jo to stop staring. She hunkered down in the couch with her cabinmate as Hattie added, "Why didn't you tell me Lawson broke up with you?"

"I just hadn't gotten to it yet," she whispered.

"Are you going to go out with Tucker?"

Bobbie Jo had no idea what to say. How could she be having feelings for someone else so quickly? Had she been the one cheating on Lawson?

Guilt ripped through her, and she shook her head no.

"All right," Tuck said. "I think we're ready."

Bobbie Jo sprang to her feet and faced them. They had bread and butter on the counter, along with the salad, plates, utensils, and cups with ice. She had no idea how long she and Hattie had been huddling on the couch, but it hadn't felt like too long.

Gratitude overcame all her other emotions, and Bobbie Jo went around the couch and toward Tucker. "Thank you," she said again, her voice almost catching on itself as she spoke. She moved right into him, intending to sweep a kiss along his cheek.

To her everlasting surprise, he turned his head and her lips caught part of his. A noise of shock left her mouth; Tuck put his hand on her waist; their first kiss became undeniably horrendous and awkward.

Bobbie Jo ducked her head, pure humiliation filling her over and over and over. Her face burned. Her stomach boiled. Her heartbeat bobbed and weaved and tripped over itself.

Not only had she failed with another man, but this time, there had been witnesses. She wanted to say, "Excuse me," in the most diplomatic, queenly voice she could and act like nothing had happened.

Instead, she met Tucker's eyes for the briefest of moments, caught the disappointment there, and fled down the hall to her bedroom, despite his voice calling, "Bobbie Jo, wait."

CHAPTER

Fifteen

HUNTER HAMMOND OPENED THE FRIDGE, muttering, "Dip, dip, ah, there's the dip." He reached for the two square bowls—one with corn and bacon dip and one with triple onion dip—and picked them up.

"Dips," he said to his wife, Molly.

"They go on the sidebar," she said. "Where all the chips and crackers are." She shot him a look that told him he should know this, and Hunter simply picked up the glass bowls and moved over to the sidebar.

He and Molly had hosted a New Year's Eve party for the past few years, and he did know the dips, chips, crackers, and other finger foods went over here on this bar that stood along the wall that separated the kitchen from the hallway that led down to the bedrooms.

Molly had divided the main island into two halves:

one for the taco bar and one for the ice cream sundae bar. They'd decided to allow their two oldest children to invite their friends if they wanted to, and both Ryder and Lisa had a couple of people coming.

The Whettsteins and their children were coming, as well as all the cowboys and cowgirls who lived here on the ranch.

"Condiments," Jane said as she entered the kitchen from the front hallway, her husband right behind her. She started taking out containers of sour cream, salsa, hot sauce, and ranch dressing.

Cord carried a huge brown box with stretched-tight plastic wrap over it, and Molly said, "Right here, Cord. Thank you."

Hunter grinned at his brother-in-law and then the neat rows of hard taco shells beneath the plastic wrap. "You ready for this?"

"I suppose," Cord said, though he smiled. "We won't stay all the way until midnight. I'm far too old for that."

Hunter laughed and stepped out of the way so Molly and Jane could work at the counter. "I'm older than you, Cord."

"Still," he said.

"Stay as long as you want," Hunter said. "Leave whenever. That's the rule, right, sweetheart?"

"Yep," Molly said. "People can do whatever they want." She turned toward Hunter. "Oh, Hunt, honey, can you go hang all the streamers from the front

porch? Ryder and I got home late from driving practice, and I didn't have time."

"Where's Ryder?" Hunter asked, hoping he could
get some help with the pink, green, blue, and gold
streamers his wife wanted hung.

"He's doing the feeding in the family barn," Molly
said.

"Right." Hunter grabbed his coat from the front
closet on his way toward the porch, hoping his hands
wouldn't freeze without gloves. The farmhouse faced
south, which was a real blessing in the winter, but the
sun had already started to set.

As he stepped out onto the porch, laughter met his
ears and a black truck pulled in down the fence.
Perfect. Help.

He first focused on the two men coming up the
front steps. "Tucker," Hunter said. "Help me with the
streamers, would you?"

"Sure." He transferred the plastic grocery sacks in
his hands to Tarr's, and the other cowboy nodded as
he went by.

"What did you bring?" Hunter asked.

"Cookie bites and brownie bites for the sundae
bar," Tucker said. He hadn't been laughing—that had
been Tarr—and Hunter peered at his younger brother.

"What's wrong with you?"

Tuck averted his eyes. "Nothing's wrong with me."
He moved over to the table where Molly had laid the
streamers. "These?"

"Yeah." Hunter didn't move to pull over a chair so he could hang them from the hooks he'd installed into the ceiling of the roof many, many years ago. With his own father. A powerful shove barreled through his chest, because his parents didn't live in Ivory Peaks anymore.

They'd moved to Coral Canyon at the beginning of the summer, into a more accessible house, and they'd taken everything from the farmhouse here this past fall. The drive between Colorado and Wyoming wasn't pleasant in the winter, depending on the weather, and Momma and Daddy had chosen to stay in Coral Canyon with all of Daddy's brothers. They were ringing in the New Year together, and that thought made Hunt smile.

"Am I doing this?" Tuck asked, his dark eyes firing with displeasure. "Or are you helping?"

"I'm helping," Hunter said. "But only if you tell me what's eatin' at you."

"Thanks, *Daddy*." He rolled his eyes, and that was so unlike Tucker that Hunter once again froze.

Tuck pulled out the first streamer—a long, curly, shiny pink decoration that Hunt knew his girls would love. He looked over to Hunter, who stared back at him. "What?"

"What? You just bit my head off for no reason."

Tuck seemed to come to himself, and he ducked his head and hid his face behind his cowboy hat. "Sorry," he muttered. "I'm just not feeling very much like partying tonight."

"Why not? You and Tarr are always the life of the party." Hunter pulled over a chair and got on it. He took the streamer from Tucker and attached it to the hook.

"I just—I—Bobbie Jo broke up with her boyfriend, and we had this weird…thing the other night." Tucker handed him another streamer, and Hunt put the silver one with the pink one before getting down to move the chair.

"A weird thing," he said, recalling his brother's crush on the blonde cowgirl who worked this farm too. Tuck had asked her out relentlessly, teased her about her boyfriend in Oklahoma being fake, and more. "And she's going to be at the party."

"Yeah," Tuck said as he lifted up a blue streamer.

"Howdy, boys."

Hunt looked down at Mike and Gerty as they came up the steps, with their baby boy in Mike's arms and Gerty's filled with an oversized aluminum foil tray. "Howdy, Hammonds," he said cheerfully.

West screeched, which startled everyone, and he flapped his arms in apparent joy.

"Yes, you tell 'im," Mike said with a giant smile. "Say 'hello' to Uncle Hunter."

"Eh-o," West said, performing his trick on command.

Hunter grinned and grinned, and he said, "Hello. Who's there?" back to the little boy.

"Weh—Weh," he said, and Hunter chuckled.

"He's smart."

"And he knows it," Gerty said. "Opal plays with him all day long, teaching him all kinds of things. So we obviously can't take any credit." She nodded past Hunter and Tuck. "I have to take this in before I drop it." She left, but Mike stayed out on the porch while Hunter hung another couple of streamers.

"Opal must be coming with Tag," Hunter said casually.

"Yeah." Mike turned and looked out toward the parking area as the rumble of an engine came onto the farm. It wasn't Tag and Opal, but Matt and his family.

"How are we feeling about Opal and Tag?" Hunter asked. His fingers started to sting, and he kept working to get this job done.

"Tag's great," Mike said. "We've always loved Tag. Great worker. Great with horses. He's like part of the family."

"Sure," Hunter said. "Sounds like Cord. Doesn't mean you like Tag and Opal together."

"I do," Mike said. "Listen, are Keith and Lindsay coming tonight?"

"Yeah," Hunter said as Matt led the way up the steps. "Keith's coming tonight, right?"

"Yep," Matt said. "A little later, though. They're

having dinner at Blackhorse Bay with Lindsay's uncle and father. Then they'll head this way."

"How's the wedding planning coming?" Hunter asked.

Gloria perked right up. "Amazing. It's going to be spectacular." She guided her teenagers past Hunter and Mike and into the house.

"Where are they getting married?" Mike asked.

"Blackhorse Bay," Hunter said. "They're planning to buy into it once they're married."

"I heard she was selling her place," Mike said as Cord came outside.

"Going okay?" he asked.

"Almost done," Hunter said.

"Who's selling their place?" Cord asked.

"Lindsay," Hunter said. "Keith's fiancée. It's too far from Blackhorse Bay. Matt said they're looking for something closer to that."

"And they're north of here, right?" Cord asked.

"Yeah," Hunter said, noting the interest in Cord's voice. He wore it plainly on his face too. "About forty minutes...why? Are you and Jane looking for a farm?"

"Sure," Cord said. "Why not?"

"Because you own a busy mechanic shop," Mike said.

"You have a farm and you work eighty hours a week in the city," Cord shot back, grinning at Mike.

"It's Gerty's farm."

"Maybe this'll be Jane's farm."

Hunter laughed, as did Mike and Tucker, so they all knew it wouldn't be Jane's farm. No, if she and Cord bought a farm, it would be Cord's farm.

"We're already twenty minutes north of here," Cord said. "At the shop. Sounds like it wouldn't be a bad commute from the farm to the shop, at least."

"Something to look into," Hunter said.

"I'm going to ask him about it too," Mike said. "For Opal."

"Opal?" Hunter, Cord, and Tuck asked at the same time. Hunter chuckled again. "That's even more surprising than Jane, Mikey."

"She's looking for somewhere," he said. "And if she and Tag...." He didn't finish, but Tag was a cowboy through and through, and perhaps he wanted his own farm too.

Hunter got off the chair, the streamers done. "All right," he said. "Let's go see what else my wife needs done."

More people had arrived while he'd been out front hanging streamers, and the farmhouse held light, warmth, and chatter as he walked down the hallway to the overly large great room in the back. It housed the kitchen, dining area, and living room—and now at least twenty people. With more coming.

Hunter loved entertaining friends and family, so it didn't bother him one bit to find Tarr standing with Bobbie Jo and Hattie, and Boone laughing loudly with his brother, and Cord joining Mission and Gerty over by the sidebar.

Ryder had come in, and he loitered in the living room with Matt's and Boone's teens. The doorbell rang, and both him and Lisa shouted, "I'll get it!"

So it would be their friends. Hunter let them battle it out as they ran for the door, and instead, he took a folding chair over by the back door. This way, he could see whoever entered from the front door or the back, and he grinned at Ryder's friends as they came into the great room.

Tag and Opal arrived next, and she stopped just inside the room and scanned left and right. She held Tag's hand, and he seemed like he'd been hit with a wall of icy water too. They sure looked good together, and about then, Molly held up both hands and yelled for everyone to quiet down.

Opal quickly moved over to the island and put down the brown grocery sack. She extracted bottles of caramel and chocolate topping while everyone quieted. Then she fell back to Tag's side, and he pressed a kiss to her cheek.

Cute. They obviously liked one another, and they'd been dating for about a month is all.

"All right," Molly called into the house. "It's a taco bar and an ice cream sundae bar. We have plenty of chairs and seats for everyone, and we're going to eat first, and then we've got some games in the basement.

The pool table is down there too, and Lisa—" She cut off as the doorbell rang again.

Lisa squawked and headed that way. Molly continued as if she hadn't been interrupted. "Lisa has a balloon to pop every hour, on the hour, and we'll do whatever activity is written on the slip of paper inside."

"Can I pop the balloons, Mama?" Clay asked.

She bent down and picked him up, and Hunter's heart swelled with love at the sight of his wife holding their six-year-old. "Lisa is in charge of the balloons, buddy." She looked around, her soft gaze sharpening. "That goes for everyone. Ryder? Mason? *Lisa* gets to decide who pops the balloons every hour."

"Yeah, sure, Mama," Ryder said, but the boy did need to be told, and Hunter would not be surprised at all if he had to get after his son later that evening for tormenting his sister.

"Come and go," Molly said. "We're going to have a prayer first, and I've asked my husband to say it."

She hadn't, but Hunter got to his feet anyway. He grinned at everyone as he moved to Molly's side and took Clay from her. "Welcome, everyone," he said just as Britt and Lars slipped into the room. Britt brightened when she saw Opal, and she hugged her tightly.

"Thanks so much for coming to celebrate the New Year with us." He glanced to the back door as it opened and Travis walked in with Poppy and their two kids. Steele had left the Hammond Family Farm, and he worked at Gerty's place now. Hunter hadn't heard anything negative, and he hoped the young man was doing okay there.

"Hunter," Molly prompted.

"Right." He shifted Clay in his arms. "I'll say grace, and then the fun can begin." He met Tucker's eyes, noting that he stood clear across the room with Mike, Mission, and Cord instead of over by Tarr and the girls.

His heart hurt for his brother, and he said a silent prayer as he bowed his head and then started to pray vocally.

CHAPTER
Sixteen

OPAL SET West in his highchair and strapped him in before sliding the tray into place. The little boy immediately started slapping it with his palms and yelling something in Baby only he understood.

"I'm getting it," she told him as she turned back to the kitchen to get his lunch. He'd be one year old soon, and Opal often fed him some of whatever she was eating, but he needed far more fruits and vegetables than what Opal had in her diet.

"You'll be a one-year-old soon," she told him as she picked up the mixture of sweet potatoes and creamy peanut butter. She spread a little on a half a wheat cracker and put it on his tray. West drooled as he went after it, and he got it in his fingers easily enough.

Everything he touched went into his mouth, and

he blinked rapidly for a moment as he first tasted the baby-food-peanut-butter concoction.

"It's good, right?" she asked him with a grin. "Okay, now say Opal. O-Pal. Ope. Al." She'd been trying to get him to say her name, but he wasn't interested. He could babble out Mama and Dada, and he loved answering the phone.

He made plenty of other noises with his mouth, including barking for a dog and "ow, ow," for a cat. He buzzed and blew and babbled to himself all day long, and Opal loved him dearly.

"I'm planning a great party for you," she told him. "We'll be live-streaming it for Grandma and Grandpa up in Coral Canyon, but Auntie Jane and Uncle Cord are confirmed to come."

Opal smiled at West and kept talking to him while she fed him the rest of his lunch. The sun shone outside today, but that didn't mean the air held any warmth, and Opal bundled up West and then herself before she took him out the front door.

She liked to get out whenever she could, and West loved being able to see his momma before Opal brought him back for his afternoon nap. She'd been cleared to lift heavier objects after her last appointment just before New Year's, but she'd been advised to take it easy, especially if she felt any pain at all.

So she went down one step at a time and held West's chubby hand as he descended the steps the same way. When he hit the sidewalk in front of the farmhouse, he squealed and started running.

He'd been mobile for a couple of weeks now, and it took all of Opal's patience and willpower not to pick him up. He could fall at any moment, and she told herself everyone deserved a chance to learn.

She drew in a deep breath though it stung the inside of her nose, and she looked up into the clear sky. "Thank you, Lord," she said aloud. "For this beautiful place. For my amazing brother and his equally amazing wife, who let me live with them."

West went the wrong way, and Opal paused her prayer to say, "West, baby, this way." He turned back to her, unconvinced he couldn't run toward the wilds of the ranch instead of toward the barns and stables. Opal extended her hand toward him. "Come on. This way."

He decided she was right, and he came back her way. They meandered toward the barn on the cleared road, as it had snowed again, and this time, it hadn't melted all the way. Opal tucked her hands in her coat pockets, her thoughts wandering away from her gratitude and worries back to West's birthday party.

Then back to her tasks at-hand. As they neared the barn, she said, "I need to find my own place, don't You think? I'd like my own space to take care of. I'd like some privacy."

Opal had lived alone for a few years while she finished her residency in California, and she did need to feel responsible for her own space again. But she couldn't imagine living an hour from Gerty and Mike and West—and Tag.

Apparently, Keith's fiancée had a farm she wanted to sell before she got married. She and Keith were looking for somewhere closer to where they'd both work, and Mike had suggested Opal look at the hobby farm.

She'd looked it up online and nothing more. It sat an hour from this farm, and Opal didn't want to be that far away. And she didn't necessarily want a hobby farm. A nice house in a small town would be enough. Most of the lots provided enough space for a big lawn and a vegetable garden, as Opal was keen to try her hand at growing carrots, peas, and cabbages this summer.

But she didn't need to have eighty acres the way Gerty did, and she didn't even want it. She'd started looking at houses in Ivory Peaks, Cherry Creek, Willow Springs, or Glendale. They were all within a half-hour of Gerty and Mike, and if Opal could find somewhere in the middle, she could be that close to Jane and Cord too.

"Of course," she murmured while keeping an eye on West while he toddled over to a pile of snow. "Jane's considering moving too."

They still lived in the gated community about halfway between the farm and downtown, as that was where Hunter had lived with his family for all the years he ran HMC as the CEO. But Cord's shop was in Cherry Creek, so they wouldn't go too far from that.

"I just need to figure out where I fit," Opal said. "Where I belong."

Gerty opened the barn doors then, for she knew to come outside if it wasn't raining or snowing to see her son, and she dropped into a crouch as she said, "Hey, baby."

West squealed and ran toward her, exclaiming how excited he was to see his momma without using English words. Gerty scooped him up into her arms, gave him several fluttery kisses all over his face, and stood.

"I'm going to leave the rest of the day to Tag and Steele," she said to Opal. "So you're off the hook for this afternoon's babysitting too."

"Okay," Opal said easily. "I think I'm going to do some drive-bys of a few places. Just to see the curb appeal, you know?"

Gerty's joviality disappeared. "You are?"

"Yeah." Opal tried to smile at her, but Gerty wasn't receiving it. In fact, she dropped her gaze to West, completely avoiding Opal's gaze. "It's a pretty day, and I need to run to the grocery store anyway."

"What are you doing for dinner? Are you and Tag going out?"

Opal shook her head. "Staying here. He's going to build a fire in his backyard, and he claims he has a way to blow the heat back toward the porch, where we're going to put the purple couch and eat dinner and watch a movie on his computer."

It wasn't the most romantic thing Opal could imagine, but she'd been on plenty of dates to fancy restaurants and big-city events. She didn't need that anymore; she wanted someone who thought of her and what she wanted, and Tag knew she loved the flickering flames of a fire—but he didn't have a fireplace indoors.

"Ah, that's why I saw him carting that blow-up thing past the walking circle earlier." Gerty grinned. "Okay, we'll talk later then."

"Okay." Opal stepped into her and gave both her and West a squishy hug. He protested in his baby voice, and Opal smiled as she stepped away.

She did spend some time that afternoon driving past houses, but nothing lit a bulb in her heart, mind, or soul, and she returned to the farm with everything she needed to make pistachio crisps.

She barely had time to do that and get ready for her date, and she would've been late climbing the steps to Tag's front porch if Gerty hadn't finished the last batch for her. As it was, she arrived armed with the treats she'd promised Tag, and she wondered how she'd have done it if she'd babysat West as she'd planned on.

Didn't matter. She'd made it, and she raised her hand to knock.

"Come in," Tag called from inside, and Opal did that without second-guessing herself.

"Oh, it smells good in here," she said as she entered.

"Did you walk?"

"Yeah," she said.

"Honey, it's too cold to walk in the dark."

Opal handed him the plastic container of crisps and started to shed her coat. Tag took it from her and draped it over the back of his couch. He smiled at her and easily put one hand on her lower back and drew her close, then closer.

"Mm, you smell nice."

"Sugar and spice," she managed to say before he stole her words with his kiss. "Mm."

"You hungry?" he whispered.

"Yes," she said. "I ate crackers and peanut butter for lunch." Hours and hours ago.

"I think everything is pretty close," he said. "Do you want to bring your coat outside?"

"Am I going to need it?"

"I stocked the couch with blankets," he said, his gaze sliding down to her feet. "You got the memo about warm boots."

Opal looked at the black, fur-lined boots on her feet too. "Let's try it without a coat."

He took her hand and said, "Come on, Boots. You can come outside too." Tag led her outside, and Opal expected to be punched in the lungs with the cold the way she had been when she'd first left the farmhouse.

But, somehow, Tag had delivered on his promise. The back porch wasn't huge, and it sat only four steps above the yard, where she'd climbed eight or nine steps to get to the front porch. A glorious, flickering fire sat a few feet from the bottom of the steps, so Tag could still go down and maneuver around it.

The heat rose up, and he'd attached something Opal couldn't identify to extend the roof over the back porch. It caught the heat, and cycled it back toward the purple couch, where a black-and-copper blanket waited alongside a cow print one.

On the other side of the back door, Tag had set up a simple folding table, and he'd already laid down a stack of potholders, plates, silverware, and serving utensils.

"Have a seat, honeybear," he said. "I'll get dinner for you." He went down to the fire while Opal pulled the thick, silky-furry checkered blanket over her lap. She wore a black sweater, so her arms weren't bare, and she was still shocked she didn't need a coat.

Tag brought up one Dutch oven, and then a second, and Opal simply enjoyed the slow evening where he took care of her. "All right," he said a few minutes later. "Barbecue chicken and Dutch oven potatoes."

Opal blinked away from the dancing fire and focused

on the plate Tag held out for her. Everything steamed and the scent of tangy barbecue sauce mixed with melted cheese and salt. She swallowed the sudden saliva in her mouth. "Wow," she said. "Tag, this looks amazing."

"My daddy taught me to cook in a Dutch oven." He returned to the table to fix himself a plate. "I'm better over fire than I am in the kitchen."

"Why have I never known this?" She looked up at him as he took his place on the blow-up couch. It bounced with his extra weight, and she reached for his plate so he could pull the other blanket up and around his legs and hips.

He took his plate back with a smile and asked, "Do you want me to say a prayer?"

They had not prayed over other meals together, unless they were with a big group. Opal suddenly felt shy, like she couldn't speak the innermost feelings of her heart in front of him. Or that if he did, something would shift in their relationship.

"Yes," she whispered anyway.

"Okay." Tag balanced his food on a pile of his blanket and removed his cowboy hat. He pressed it against his chest as he lowered his head in respect to God. "Lord."

He didn't say anything else, and Opal absolutely felt everything between them shift. Tag's emotions swirled with the heat waves being cycled onto the porch, and Opal wanted to reach out and touch him, absorb some of what he felt so she'd know what it was.

She did, sliding her fingers along his arm and to his hand. He dropped it from his cowboy hat and continued with, "We're really thankful to be together tonight."

He paused again, and Opal wanted to say, "Amen," to that. She was grateful and glad to be with Tag in such a simple environment. She'd liked other men before. She'd dated them for a lot longer than she'd been seeing Tag.

But something about their relationship felt old, too, like they'd known one another for a lot longer than they had. As Opal waited in this serene space for Tag to continue his prayer, she definitely liked Tag more than anyone else she'd ever dated.

She liked him a lot.

A lot, a lot.

She liked him so much it started to feel like...love.

"Thank you for a clear day," Tag said next, his voice about half the volume it had been before. "Bless us to have a good dinner tonight, and bless Opal to find a house she'll be really happy in for a long time. Bless everyone on this farm with what they need to be healthy and happy, especially Kyle as he continues to recover from his latest cold. Help us to take care of each other and those around us who need it. Amen."

"Amen," Opal murmured, and she pulled her

hand away from his. He reset his hat and wouldn't look at her.

She picked up the fork on her plate and went for the potatoes first. They held a smokiness that only came from bacon, and her taste buds started rejoicing before she'd even taken a bite. When she did get the food in her mouth, she moaned at its deliciousness.

Tag chuckled, but he didn't ask if she liked it. She obviously did.

"Have you always gone to church, Tag?" she asked.

"Mostly," he said. "My parents were pretty active growing up. My mama praises Jesus for everything." He grinned at her. "I know you grew up religious."

"Yeah," she said, getting another forkful of food as she looked at the tips of the flames down below. "I feel like I've come and gone in my faith."

"Come and gone?" He spoke in a calm, easy voice, without any judgment at all.

"Yeah," she said. "Don't you have, I don't know, seasons? Times when you're really faithful, and you go to church every week, and you're reading the scriptures, and you're trying to serve others. And other times, where you're...not."

"I suppose so, yeah," he drawled.

"I barely went to church when I was in medical school," Opal said. "There was no time." She let her memories of what felt like a long time ago stream through her. "I was constantly tired. I didn't pray, didn't study, didn't read anything for my soul."

She looked over to him. "In some ways, I thought I was freer." She went back to her dinner, wondering why she'd started thinking about this tonight. Why she'd asked him this. "Every now and then, I'd get these little pinches from heaven. A reminder that I wasn't alone, and that Jesus wanted me to come back."

"Did you?" he asked.

She shook her head. "Slowly. Finally, God shouted at me to leave my job and come here." She gave him a sly smile. "Not sure if you know, but I can be pretty stubborn, and I resisted Him for a while. Months, actually."

"And yet, here you are."

"Here I am." She finally tried the chicken, which made her mouth sing and her heart happy. "This is *so* good, Tag."

"Thank you." He let a beat go by. "So you finally listened?"

"Yes," she said. "And now, God is telling me I need my own place, but there's nothing out there for me. It's confusing." She let out a little sigh, but she wanted tonight to be perfect. "What about you?" she asked, trying to perk up her voice. "Do you want your own place someday? Your own horses? A boarding stable? A farm?"

Tag didn't answer right away, and Opal ate a

couple of bites of chicken before she looked over to him. "Ah, I see the answer on your face." The firelight flickered against his fine features, making Tag twice as handsome as he already was.

"I think about it," he said.

"Lindsay Lewis is selling her hobby farm," she said. "Might be of interest to you."

"Hobby farms don't make much money," Tag said. "We're not all married to CEOs and billionaires."

Opal jerked her head up, her heart suddenly pounding, pounding, pounding. "Billionaires?"

"Or whatever," Tag said. "I'm just saying, Gerty doesn't need the farm to make any money. They're already really rich."

"Mm." Opal found a piece of bacon to go with her last bite of potatoes, and she filled her mouth with it, so she wouldn't blurt out that she was a billionaire too. But the food got swallowed, and Tag still hadn't moved the conversation to something else.

"Tag, do you know anything about, uh, Mike's, uh —my family background?"

He looked at her, interest streaming through his eyes now. "What do you mean?"

"My daddy ran HMC for decades," she said. "It's called *Hammond* Manufacturing Company."

"Yeah," he said slowly. "Are you asking me if I know you're rich?" He chuckled. "Yes, Opal, I know your family is rich."

"Not just my family," she said, her nerves tromping all through her body. "Uh, when we turn twenty-one, we get a, ahem, pretty hefty inheritance. We're charged to do something good with it. Most of us set up foundations that do things. Charitable things."

She was glad she'd eaten before she'd started talking about this, because she'd never had to explain it out loud to anyone before. "I haven't done anything with my money," she said. "It's another thing I put away, put on the backburner, for medical school and becoming a doctor."

She sighed, and Tag reached over and took her empty plate. He stacked it on top of his and leaned over to put it on the table. He could just barely reach it, and he pushed them so they slid onto the table.

"And now," Opal said as Tag settled against her side again. He lifted his arm, and she sank way into his side due to the cushy, air-couch. She certainly wasn't complaining about that, and she liked the way he pulled their blankets this way and that until they were both covered and fixed.

"Now, God won't tell me what to do with my money," she said. "Or where to live. And I love West with my whole heart, but he's not my baby. And all I'm doing is taking care of him." She stared out past the fire now, wishing she could see into the dark. Wishing it didn't represent her life so perfectly right now.

"I don't understand why I spent so long becoming a doctor if that's not what I'm meant to do. But God has been very clear on that. I'm supposed to be here."

"There are clinics and hospitals here," Tag said gently.

Clinics rang through Opal's head. "Yes," she said slowly. Perhaps she could open and run a free medical clinic. Completely free, for the good, hardworking people in these smaller towns outside of the city.

"I feel like I need my own place, so I'm working on that. Then, I'm going to figure out if I should just be the favorite aunt to all my nieces and nephews, or if I should start something with my money, or what."

Tag ran his fingers up and down her arm, and Opal looked up at him. "Don't you want to know how much money I have?"

"Does it matter?" he asked.

"It might."

He shook his head. "Not to me. It's obvious you have money."

"Why? Because I don't have a job?"

"And haven't for a year," he added.

Opal smiled and stretched up to kiss him. Tag took his time with her, and oh, Opal definitely felt the ground disappear beneath her. She floated on the purple blow-up couch, every stroke of Tag's mouth against hers making her fall more and more—and more—in love with him.

So wherever she ended up, she needed it to be

close to him, and she decided she'd double-down on her prayers in the hopes that God would finally give her a little hint about the next step to take in her life.

CHAPTER

Seventeen

GERTY PACED IN THE KITCHEN, irritated that Mike continued to eat his Lucky Charms as if he didn't have a care in the world. "We have to talk to her *today*," she said. "She's going to put an offer in on that place in Willow Springs."

"We're talking to her this morning," Mike said without looking up from his phone. He put his spoon back in the bowl and started texting, which meant someone from work had messaged him. Gerty tried to be patient with him, because he'd taken today and tomorrow off at her request.

Today, so they could talk to Opal, and tomorrow for their son's first birthday.

She turned away from her husband and looked through the living room to the hall. Opal did not appear. West played on the living room floor, still in his pajamas. Gerty had given him mashed bananas and toast for breakfast and cleaned him up before plunking him down on the ground with his toys.

She'd asked Steele and Tag to tend to the farm that day, and she felt very blessed to be able to take time off, though she sometimes grew restless when she didn't have enough to do. Truth be told, she could be West's mom full-time and love her life, as there was always something changing when it came to her son.

"When is she going to get up?" Gerty complained.

"She's a night-owl, baby," Mike said. "You know what time she gets up." He grinned at her and lifted his bowl to drink the milk out of it. "You're here every morning when she finally gets up."

"How are you so calm?"

"Because we're not asking her to donate a kidney?" He quirked his eyebrows at her. "Why are you freaking out?"

"Because," Gerty said with plenty of frustration in her voice. "We should've talked to her about this a month ago. Then she wouldn't have wasted time looking for places."

"We'll be lucky if she says yes," Mike said. "Do you have your hopes up?"

"I know this is the right thing to do," Gerty said firmly. "She'll know it too."

"Who'll know what?"

Gerty spun toward Opal's voice. She'd come into the living room, and she dropped to the ground beside

West. "Morning, baby." She gave him a kiss and smiled up to Gerty and Mike. "Double day off."

"Triple," Mike said. "You're not working today either." He got up and took his bowl into the kitchen, leaving Gerty to face Opal alone. Before she could begin, he returned to her side, and Gerty leaned into him to hopefully steal some of his strength.

"Opal, we want to talk to you about something."

Opal looked up from West, her smile fading away when she saw the two of them standing side-by-side. She got to her feet, and still wearing her pajamas, she folded her arms. "About what?"

Gerty looked at Mike, but he simply looked back at her.

"I'm moving out," Opal said. "I swear, I am. I'm going to get that place in Willow Springs, I think. I already have another appointment to walk through it again tomorrow, just to be sure."

She wore defiance in her gaze that almost made Gerty laugh. "I know I've lived here too long. I'm sorry. I'll be leaving soon—I can leave right now if I need to. I can stay with Jane or get a hotel."

Gerty started shaking her head about the time Opal apologized. "No," she barked out. "It's not that."

"It kind of is that," Mike said.

Opal looked between them, her dark eyes trying to find the answers she needed. "What?"

"We know you want to move out," Gerty said, everything she'd rehearsed now gone. "We agree that it's best for everyone, but we don't want you to take that place in Willow Springs."

Opal's eyebrows bent down. "You don't?"

Gerty shook her head and took a step toward her best friend in the world. "No," she said. "If it's so perfect, why do you need to go see it for the *third* time to be sure?" She ignored West as he screeched at one of his toys. "We want to give you five acres right here on the farm. You can build the exact house you want and have room for your vegetable garden and that big back lawn you want for your future kids and dogs and cats."

The words out, now Gerty just felt hollow from where they'd been caged inside her.

Opal stared at her and then switched her gaze to Mike. "Five acres?"

"It's not as much as you think."

"Yes, it is," Opal said. "Who's going to mow that much grass?" She shook her head. "No, thank you."

"Opal." A bolt of fear struck Gerty. "Is that a 'no, thank you' to the acreage or the offer itself?"

Opal fixed her cool gaze on her now. "I'm not sure."

"Why don't you want to live here? It's close to us. Close to West. Jane and Cord will find something closer to us out here." She swallowed, not sure she should say the next thing. But Opal and Tag had been dating for almost two months now, and by all accounts, they were getting along really well.

"Close to Tag," Gerty said, lifting her chin, almost daring Opal to say she wasn't considering Tag while she'd been looking for a place to call her own.

"Okay, let's go there," Opal said with a bite of acid in her tone.

"Here we go," Mike said. He sank onto the couch with a sigh. "You guys sit down. We're not in combat."

Opal turned and walked over to her blow-up couch and sat. Gerty took the spot next to Mike, and she let him take her hand in his and work her fingers out of the fist they'd curled into. Maybe she was a little bit too tense.

"Let's say Tag and I get married," Opal said. "And I take you up on your five-acre gift. Is that going to be enough for Tag?"

Gerty caught on quick, and she threw Mike a worried look. "I don't know. That's something you'll have to ask Tag."

"I think he wants his own place someday," Opal said.

"Sissy, you can't predict every step before you take it," Mike said quietly.

"I'm not trying to do that," Opal barked at him.

"You like your plans," Mike said. "That's all I'm saying."

"Everyone likes to have a plan for where they're going to live," Opal said.

"Okay." Gerty held up one hand. "Sweetie, this isn't us attacking you. We want you close. *I* want you here. I know you love West, and I know you think you're in the way, but you're not."

"I need my own space," Opal mumbled as she looked down at her hands. "There's something about being self-reliant and having something to take care of that human beings need."

"We agree," Gerty said quickly. "If you want to take some time to think about it, that's fine. If you decide to buy that hideous place in Willow Springs, I will swallow my ire and support you." She grinned at Opal as she looked up. "Okay?"

"You will not," Opal said with a dry laugh. "You'll be so salty, and you'll stomp around the house and bang closed cabinets in the morning just to wake me up."

"You're right." Gerty laughed too. "That's totally what I'll do." She sobered, and Opal's gaze turned intense again. "Just think about it. If you only want an acre, that's fine. We can identify some great places, and this place is eighty-two acres. We can spare a few for you."

"Might as well make it a whole Hammond compound," Mike said. "Call Jane up and give her five acres too."

Gerty whipped her head toward Mike to see if he was joking. He was, but.... "That's not a bad idea," she said.

"Are you kidding?" Mike asked.

"No," Gerty said thoughtfully. "Why can't this

farm be a Hammond Family compound? We're at capacity for horses, and we grow plenty to feed them. If we lost ten acres, it wouldn't be a big deal. We'd just buy what we need in the winter."

With three Hammonds living here, that was six *billion* dollars worth of hay and feed they could afford.

"Baby, it's your farm," he said. "Tell me what you want me to do, and I'll do it."

Gerty looked back to Opal. "I want you to tell your sister to think about it. Really think about it. And then take the offer."

Mike sighed as if she'd asked him to drink fruit punch. The man hated the stuff, and he made this seem like the same kind of torture. "Sissy, just think about it. Really think about it, okay? Pray over it. Talk to Tag, and Momma and Daddy." He squeezed Gerty's hand. "We're sure you'll get to where we are in knowing that this is the right thing."

Opal wouldn't give in easily, Gerty knew that. "I'll think about it," she said. "And *if* I decide it's a good idea, I will be *purchasing* five acres from you." She scooted to the edge of the wobbly couch and stood up. "Now, I promised my hot boyfriend I'd make brunch at his place. It's the only reason I'm up so dang early this morning."

"It's eight-fifteen," Mike said as she headed for the hallway, presumably to get dressed.

"Don't remind me," Opal said over her shoulder as she disappeared into the depths of the farmhouse.

Gerty looked at Mike, and Mike looked back at Gerty. "All things considering," he said. "That went really well."

"Yeah." Gerty chewed her bottom lip for a moment, then forced herself to stop. She leaned into Mike's chest. "What do you think she'll do?"

"With Opal, she always does what she thinks is right." He touched his mouth to the side of her jaw. "Once she leaves, we'll have the farmhouse to ourselves."

Gerty smiled at his flirtatious tone. "Yes, we will," she said. "I have to admit, I am looking forward to it just being us again."

"Me too." Mike gently turned her head and kissed her. "West is gonna be one tomorrow. Are you thinkin' you want another baby?"

Gerty had thought no such thing, so she couldn't say she had. "I don't know," she said. "I love the farm, Mike, but...I love being a mom too."

"You could hire more help," he murmured. "Only work part-time on the farm. Have more babies."

She grinned against his lips. "I think we have time to have more babies."

"Yeah, we do, but he's just so dang cute."

Gerty looked at their son, and he was the most adorable thing in the world. Especially when he looked up at her, his brown eyes so wide and so innocent. "Ma-Ma-Ma-Ma," he said almost in a whine. He held a block to his ear. "Eh-o. Eh-o."

"He's calling you," Gerty said to Mike. "Call Daddy."

"Dad, Dad, Dad," West said.

Mike took a breath and let it all out. Then, because he was the best daddy in the world, he made the sound of a ringing phone. West's whole face lit up, and he lifted the block again. "Eh-o?"

"Hello," Mike said. "Is West there?"

"Weh, Weh, Weh," he babbled, and he toddled away to get another toy. Gerty sighed and leaned against Mike again, so glad to have him home today, really glad they had found a way to make their busy lives work, and beyond glad that she was his and he was hers—and that they'd finally spoken to Opal.

Now, she just had to wait and see what Opal would decide.

Help her to see how perfect it would be, Gerty prayed, because she wasn't above trying to get the Lord on her side.

———

"OKAY," she said the next day. "Are you streaming, baby?"

"Yep." Mikey held up his phone, moving it slowly and steadily. "We're live."

Gerty grinned and picked up the birthday cake her grandmother had made. It had a single flaming candle in it, shaped like the number one. "All right," she said. "Here we go."

Opal had just finished snapping on West's bib, and she moved out of the way as Gerty walked slowly around the kitchen island and toward his highchair. "Happy birthday to you," she started to sing, glad when everyone else joined in.

It was a small party; her parents and half-siblings had come. Her uncle Matt and Aunt Gloria, though their girls were off doing something at the high school that night. Her grandparents, of course. Mike, Tag, Steele, and Opal. Cord and Jane.

So maybe not that small. But Mikey's parents couldn't be there, because it was a long drive for a five-minute thing where West would get help blowing out his candle and then mash his face into the chocolate cake. A long drive in the winter, where the wind blew against the glass, angry it could not get to the flame and snuff it out.

The song finished as Gerty set the cake—a miniature of the one Grams had made for everyone else—in front of West. He stared at it with wonder, and Gerty's heart filled with love time and again. And then again.

In that moment, Gerty realized how God felt about her. About all of His children. She'd thought she'd fail at being a mother, that she wasn't nurturing enough, that she couldn't tolerate crying over silly things. And she really couldn't. But that didn't mean she didn't love West completely—and exactly how he needed to be loved.

"You blow it out, baby." She bent down and looked right at him. He looked back at her with complete trust in those big eyes. "Momma will help you, okay?"

He started to reach for the flame, and Gerty held up her hand to protect him from it. "No, you don't touch it, West. You blow on it. Watch." She gave a quick puff of air, and the flame went right out. West flinched backward.

A thin stream of smoke lifted from the candle, and Gerty giggled as Opal handed her the lighter again. "Okay," she said. "Your turn." She relit the candle and smiled at her son. Maybe she did want another baby.

Most days, though, Gerty could barely operate under the guilt of leaving West with Opal while she tended to chickens, horses, fences, and fields. How would she deal with walking out on two children every single day?

So maybe she wasn't ready for another baby.

"Blow on it," she coached gently.

West leaned toward it, and at least he didn't try to grab the moving, dancing, flickering entity. He opened his mouth and did what Gerty had done, but not enough air came out. So Gerty extinguished the flame for him and clapped her hands. "Happy birthday, baby."

Everyone else cheered, and Mikey brought over the phone. "Look, Westy," he said. "Say hi to Grandma and Grandpa." He held the phone for West, who took it in his chubby hand. It weighed more than one of his toy blocks, but he managed to lift it right up to his nose.

"Eh-o," he said, his favorite thing to do.

"Hello," Wes and Bree said on the other end of the call. "Is this West? The birthday boy?" Bree sniffled, and Gerty's emotions got yanked left and right too.

"Weh," he said. "Ma-Ma." He almost threw the phone as he pointed it at Gerty. "Dad-Daddy."

"Let's have some cake," Gerty's daddy said, and because his voice always seemed to carry more than others, it helped Gerty pull on the reins of her runaway feelings.

"I'll take them," Opal said as she took the phone from West before he could drop it. "Time for cake, Westy."

Gerty pulled out the chair right next to West and sat down. Daddy brought her some cake, and she smiled gratefully up at him. "Thank you, Dad." He leaned down and pressed a kiss to her forehead.

"Love you, Gerty-girl." He beamed at West like no brighter star had ever shown. "And you, little man. I love you too." He kissed West as he growled playfully, and West giggled and shrieked out laughter.

Mikey sat down with them, and Gerty met her mom's eyes. "Would you take our picture?" She wanted to remember this version of her family forever. Her, Mike, and West, on his first birthday. She had no idea what life would bring her, if they'd stay on this farm forever, or if they'd be blessed with more children.

But she wanted this moment to live on. So she leaned into West in his high chair on one side while Mikey did the same on the other, and her mother took their family picture. She handed Gerty her phone back with, "You guys are my favorite family."

Gerty looked at the picture while Mikey encouraged West to dig into his cake with his bare hands, and as she looked at herself—so pale and blonde and light, she smiled. Mikey was her opposite, with all dark hair, the sexy beard, and those shining-from-within eyes the color of good, rich earth.

And right between them, smiling like the charmer he was, sat West. With Mikey's brown eyes, but Gerty's blonde hair, he bridged the gap between both of them. Tears filled her eyes, and she blinked them back as she stuck her phone in her back pocket.

"Send me that picture, love," Mikey said. "Would you?"

She met his eyes, and she knew he'd just seen everything brewing and boiling inside her. Alarm crossed his face for just a moment, and then it smoothed away into a soft smile. "Not so nurturing, huh?"

She just shook her head and smiled. Then she picked up her cake and took a bite while she took in the rest of those she loved in the farmhouse. Tag touched his lips to Opal's in a quick kiss, and for some reason, that startled Gerty.

"They're getting along," she said across West's tray to Mikey.

He looked over to where Opal stood laughing in Tag's arms. Neither of them had cake yet, as Daddy was still cutting and serving up slices. "Yeah," Mikey said. "Seems so."

"I'm glad," Gerty said as a sense of supreme satisfaction streamed through her. "Opal needs someone like him in her life."

"Maybe he needs someone like her."

Gerty studied Tag for a moment. She'd liked him from the moment he'd walked into Mike's office here at the farmhouse for his initial interview. "Yeah," she said slowly. "Maybe they both need each other."

"Guess we'll see how it works out," Mike said just as West yelled.

Gerty looked at him, because it wasn't one of his usual happy yells. He wore a wild look in his eyes as he grabbed a fistful of cake and shoved the whole thing into his mouth. Gerty blinked and then burst out laughing.

"You get that cake, buddy," Mikey said between his chuckles. And West did exactly that.

CHAPTER
Eighteen

TAG STOOD on the outside of the ring, watching Steele as he worked with Cinnamon. "Keep the flag lower," he coached. Cinnamon was well-trained, but he didn't like the flag. Tag hadn't thought he'd find himself in the outdoor ring at the beginning of February, working with one of the horses he and Gerty had brought back from Coral Canyon.

And he wasn't in the circle. Steele was. Tag was training Steele on how to work with horses, using horses who could use some exercise, wouldn't give Steele a problem, and who did need to be oriented to how they did things here in Colorado.

Steele didn't look at him, because that lesson had already been learned. *Don't look away from the fifteen-hundred pound animal in the ring with you.*

"He doesn't need the flag," Tag said. "You've got it

in case something spooks him, but you're trying to get him to read your body cues. Follow your voice commands."

"Got it," Steele said, his voice deep and rumbly. One could construe it as grumpy or growly, but Tag had learned that was just how Steele operated. He didn't say much to begin with, but he liked getting together for breakfast sandwiches in the evening, and he never missed a morning of stopping by for coffee.

He claimed he couldn't make the stuff to save his life, and Tag had enjoyed getting to know him in the few minutes before their days got away from them. Steele had trouble keeping track of things, like his keys, his phone, and his wallet. Tag had been to his cabin many times in the past couple of months, and the man didn't have much to have lying around.

He did his dishes every day, and Tag hadn't detected any foul odors. He'd talked about getting his own dog, which Tag had encouraged him to do. If Tag wasn't seeing Opal in the evening, he and Steele might get together and watch TV or play cards.

But Tag saw Opal most evenings. He either came to the farmhouse and hung out there, or he took her to dinner in one of the neighboring towns. More often than not, Opal came to his cabin bearing her blow-up couch, a smile, and questions about his day.

He'd teased her that he had his own couch, but he never complained about cuddling into her on the cushy thing he'd given her for her birthday. The air-filled furniture sort of mashed them together, and Tag really enjoyed holding her close and blaming the couch for making her sit practically on top of him.

Tonight, though, Opal was meeting with a builder, as she'd decided to move forward with plans to construct a house right here on the farm. Gerty and Mike were selling her three acres of land near the epicenter of the farm, where their farmhouse and personal lawn stood.

Tag cleared his mind of all that had happened in the past couple of weeks. Opal couldn't stop talking about having a house to herself, and he wasn't going to burst any of her happiness balloons. He wasn't so sure she'd be the kind of joyful she thought she'd be living literally down the lane from Mike and Gerty.

And him.

He'd worried immediately about what might happen between them if they broke up. Would she leave then? Would he be expected to get another job?

And what if they ended up together? Would he move from his cabin to her house and live on this farm too? Continue to work it? What if he wanted to purchase a place of his own?

Then Gerty and Mike would have an extra house on their land, and Opal would own it and those three acres.

It all felt really messy to Tag, and his thoughts

ended up going round and round in circles whenever he let himself linger on the topic. He felt like he'd boarded one of those trains that encircled a Christmas tree, and he couldn't get off.

Cinnamon huffed, and Tag got himself off the crazy train. He couldn't let his mind wander like that while working with horses. Or Steele.

"What doesn't he like?" Tag asked. Boots barked, and that also spiked Tag's adrenaline.

Steele glanced over to him. "I'm not sure. I didn't do anything differently."

Tag hunkered down into his collar as the wind swished by him. A raindrop struck his forehead, and a slight whistle irritated his ears.

Cinnamon huffed and tossed his head, which further alerted Tag to his distress. "Come on out," he said to Steele. "Maybe it's the weather." Animals, particularly horses as they were prey animals, were far more attuned to their environment, and they could sense things in the weather humans couldn't.

Steele climbed the fence and came over it as Cinnamon whinnied. Tag's pulse, which had been slow and even to match Cinnamon's, suddenly skyrocketed. "It's the whistling," Tag said, everything lining up suddenly. "A storm. Let's get him inside, and let's do it fast." He got off the fence and added, "Let's go, Boots."

"Okay," Steele said, and he jogged over to the gate

to go back inside and get Cinnamon. The horse pranced left and right, pacing and nervous.

Tag looked up into the sky, which held clouds in every shade of gray God had ever created. In any other situation, he might've taken a moment to experience the beauty of the earth in all her glory. From sunrises and sunsets to angry thunderheads, Tag loved it all.

Another raindrop landed on his bare hand, and then one struck his face. The wind gusted, and a chill ran down his spine. Steele had just brought Cinnamon out of the ring, and Tag stopped standing around and went to close the gate.

The rain started in earnest as they went from the training ring to the stable, and he and Steele ducked inside before they got truly soaked. Thankfully. Cinnamon had a stall about in the middle, and a couple of other horses seemed agitated by the change in weather as well.

With everyone inside, Tag turned back to pull the door closed, but the wind grabbed it and yanked it away from him. It hit the outside of the barn with a terrifyingly loud, sharp bang, and Tag flinched as he swore.

More than one equine made some sort of noise, from a huff to a blow to a whinny. Both Boots and Max barked. None of them sounded happy, and Tag wasn't either. He had to go back out into the rain, and he did that just as another horrible noise filled the air.

It sounded like a series of gunshots being fired. Every nanosecond another one sounded, and they crowded on top of one another. Tag saw the hail in the next moment, and it pummeled him as he took the three steps out to get the flapping door. He hauled it closed successfully this time and latched it.

However, now he and Steele were trapped inside the barn with nine horses where the noise only grew and grew and grew as the hail continued to berate the roof. Max whined as he hurried toward the main room of the barn, but Boots stayed with Tag.

He bent down to pat his corgi. "We're okay, boy. It's just a storm, and heaven knows we've lived through a lot of those." He smiled at his dog and straightened to the horses.

"Hey, Dusty," Tag said quietly as he went by the horse's stall. "You're okay, Ontario." He stroked the gray's nose. "It's gonna be fine, Marigold. You're all right." She stuck her head over the gate and pushed his shoulder. "I know," he said. "It's just a little hail though, and it doesn't last long."

His ears felt like they'd been attacked, because the metal roof took every pelt of hail and amplified it.

"Sounds like they're huge," Steele called from down the row. He had to yell to be heard above the noise of the weather. The scent of dust and straw filled the barn, and Tag didn't hate it. It spoke to him of a good day's work, of living and working outside and with the animals who'd always soothed his soul.

"There you are, Congo," he said to the next horse down. "It's almost over." He gave the horse a neck pat and moved on. "Ah, you made it back inside, Cinnamon." Tag leaned his head against the red's long nose. "Thanks for warning us, or we might still be out there, getting beaten on."

He smiled and paused in front of the next stall, which belonged to Silver. "You're not nervous at all, are you?" He grinned at the calmest horse Gerty owned and looked over to where Florence lived.

Of course, she wasn't there. She was still skittish at best, and as Tag moved closer to her stall, he caught the horse tossing her head, obviously agitated. "Come on, Flo," he said to the black beauty. "It's fine. It's just a little hail." He didn't try to reach into the stall to touch the horse. "You came from Calgary, girl. You've been around snow and hail before."

Maybe not in a good way, and since they hadn't even owned Florence for a year yet, Tag found her to be the most unpredictable. Next to her, they'd placed Ellie, one of the horses they'd acquired from Bryce, because she was sweet as pie, and her energy seemed to help calm both Florence on her left and Rooster on her right.

Sure enough, Rooster huffed and flapped his lips, and that caused Flo to whinny like she was getting ripped up into the sky and would be carried away in the funnel of a tornado.

Tag couldn't comfort her, and in fact, she made him

more nervous. So he moved down and stroked both hands down the sides of Ellie's neck. "Tell them to calm down, would you?" She snuffled at his jacket pocket, where he sometimes kept treats. "None today," he said.

Rooster came to the gate as Tag looked his way. "You're okay, Roost," he said. "It's just a little hail." It seemed to have slowed and lightened already, and Tag had hope that he and Steele wouldn't be trapped in here for much longer.

His phone vibrated, and he pulled it out of his jacket pocket. Opal's name sat there, and surprise darted through him when he realized she was calling, not texting. His brain caught up to his eyes, and he swiped on the call.

"Hey," he said as he lifted the phone to his ear.

"Is there power at the farm?" she asked.

Tag looked up to the lights blazing in the barn. "Yeah. Where are you?" A popping noise came through the line, and Tag didn't like the sound of it.

"I pulled over on the side of the road," she said, her voice a bit breathless and definitely tinged with fear. "There's a hailstorm, and I can't see anything."

"We just went through the hail," he said. "Steele and I barely made it into the barn with Cinnamon."

"I was on my way to meet with the general contractor, but I think I might just cancel. I checked the weather, and it's supposed to start snowing and not stop until morning."

"I looked earlier," he said. "It wasn't supposed to start snowing until nine or ten."

"Well, it's four-ten," Opal said matter-of-factly.

Tag smiled to himself. "It sure is, honeybear."

"Don't tease me, Tag." She sighed, and he could just picture her pushing her hair back as she tried to see the solution to her current problem. "I swear, it's like every time I decide to take a step forward, something pushes me back two. Or three."

He frowned as he sank onto a stool. "What do you mean?" He watched Boots circle next to Max and lie down. Steele moved about the barn, putting away lead ropes and doing some general tidying up.

"I mean, I'd finally decided to buy the acreage from Mike, right? And the banker I need to sign my forms is out of town until next week. On vacation in Mexico, if you can believe that. And now that I'm on the way to go over plans for the house, I can't get there. It's just so irritating and frustrating."

"I'm sorry, sweetheart," he murmured. He pressed his eyes closed and tried to hear the Lord whispering to him what he should say. He'd definitely had help from On High with Opal in the past, and he needed it again. "I don't think it means you shouldn't be doing what you're doing."

"No?" she asked, her voice a touch higher than normal. "It feels like it." She sniffled, and Tag hated that she was crying on the side of the road somewhere, alone. A roar sounded in his ears, and he simply wanted to be with her to shore her up and help her feel better.

"Life can just be life sometimes," he said. "It's wintertime, and everyone wants to escape. Heck, if I could be in Cancun right now, I would be." He smiled as he said it, because he much preferred mountains to beaches, but he would take some warmer weather about now.

He thought of his brothers in Texas, and he bet they weren't dealing with loud-mouthed hail and nervous horses and crying girlfriends.

"Honeybee," he whispered. "Let's talk about Valentine's Day, okay?"

"Okay," Opal said, and Tag's heart got wrung out at her agonized tone.

"I got a reservation at this great place your cousin told me about."

"Which cousin?" Her voice sounded stronger now, and Tag ducked his head as Steele came to sit beside him. Pinging still sounded on the roof, though it had quieted quite a bit. It was probably turning to rain now, but Tag didn't want to go out in that any more than he did hail.

"Hunter," Tag said, employing his Southern accent. "He said he was allowed to tell two people about it, because they're doing a special menu, and they're not open to everyone."

"Sounds interesting," Opal said.

And expensive, but Tag didn't say so. "I'm told

they'll have all of your favorites."

"By whom?" Opal asked, her voice now guarded instead of emotional.

"Gerty," he said with a smile. "Don't you trust me, Opal?"

"I do," she said.

"Yeah, I'm convinced." He laughed and looked over to the indoor chicken coops. None of the birds seemed worried about the hail or rain or the agitation of the horses. "It's going to be a great night. It's over in Littleton, so a bit of a drive, and I've been told I need to tell you to dress nicely."

"Define that, please," she said.

"I'm wearing a jacket," he said. "Or we can't get into dinner."

"So sequins-dress-nicely."

"I guess," Tag said. "I've never been out with anyone who wore sequins."

"Oh, I bet you have," Opal said.

"When?" Tag challenged, as Opal had known him for less than a year, and he'd lived his whole life.

"A prom date," Opal said. "Most prom dresses have sequins."

Tag glanced at Steele, who cut him a look out of the corner of his eye too. "I never went to prom," he said.

A small smile touched Steele's face, and he shook his head. "Me either," he murmured while Opal said, "You're kidding."

"Didn't see the point," Tag said.

"Didn't see the point?" Opal repeated, her tone much more scandalized. "Taggart, the point is you would've made someone's whole year."

His face grew a bit warmer. "Is that what I'm doing for you this Valentine's Day?" He half-turned away from Steele, wishing he could flirt in private. "Making your whole year?"

"I—why are you whispering?" Opal asked.

"Because I'm not alone." Tag's embarrassment grew, and he realized he'd been hunkered down and hunched over. He drew his shoulders back and lifted his head. "It's almost passed here, honeybee. I'm sure you'll be able to get to your appointment in no time."

"I'm worried I won't be able to get back to the farm."

"You could stay with Jane," he suggested.

"I'll call her."

Tag put his hand in his pocket and drew out his notebook. "Okay, sweetheart. I have to go, because we'll have to get out and check a few things before we head home."

"Okay," she said. "Thank you, Taggart, for talking to me until I calmed."

"Anytime, honey." He hung up, and he pulled the pen out of the coil at the top of the notebook.

"Anytime, honey," Steele mimicking, his voice just as slow and twangy as Tag's had been. He chuckled, but not in a mean way. "No wonder she's smitten with you."

Tag flipped open his notebook. "Is that what she is?" He found his place and read the sentences he'd put there earlier. *Worried about Opal buying land here and building a house, but I'm having a hard time articulating why.*

Need to call Flint and Sawyer. Their birthday is coming up soon. Set an alarm for it.

"Seems like it," Steele grumbled. "I don't know how you do it. I can't talk to women."

Tag was going to write about the hail and his call with Opal, not sure why it needed to go into the notebook. But he'd stopped trying to figure out what got jotted down and what didn't. When he felt like writing something down, he did it, no questions asked.

He looked over to Steele. "They make you nervous?"

"Oh, yeah," he said.

"Why's that?" Tag asked. "You're a good-looking man. You work hard. Anyone would be lucky to go out with you."

Steele looked up from his phone, which he texted on. Tag had never seen him actually speak to anyone on it, but surely he called his momma from time to time. Something else Tag needed to do.

"You mean that?" he asked.

"Of course I mean that," Tag said.

Steele's face colored, and he dropped his attention back to his device again. "Thank you, Tag," he murmured.

"If I knew any women, I'd set you up." Tag looked at his notebook and started writing. *Hailed today, and it scared the horses—and me. Been a while since I've been caught in a hailstorm. So loud on the roof.*

Opal called, scared and pulled over on the side of the road. I know I shouldn't be glad about that, but it was nice to see her be less-than-perfect.

We talked about Valentine's Day, and I'm so nervous about our date. She'll be gone tonight, so I'm going to watch those dancing tutorials again.

Satisfied with his thoughts, he flipped the notebook closed and replaced the pen in the coils. Back it went into his pocket, and he got to his feet. "I think it's just rain now."

"I'll come do the evening feeding tonight," Steele said.

"I can help too," Tag said. "Opal's off the farm."

"Take the night to yourself then," Steele said. "If I need help, I'll text you."

Tag wasn't going to argue with that, so he simply nodded. They went out the front door of the barn, because the back one couldn't be locked from the outside. That meant Tag had to walk around the barn in the rain. It wasn't exactly pouring, and the drops felt thicker than regular water as they landed on the brim of his hat, his shoulders, and his boots.

"Slush," Steele said with disgust. "There's slush falling from the sky."

"Gonna be snow soon enough," Tag said. "I'll text

Gerty with where we are when I get to my cabin. Do you want to come over for dinner? Pizza night."

"Sure," Steele said.

"Max, go to the farmhouse," Tag said. The shepherd looked at him, and Tag nodded over to the house. "Go on. They'll let you in."

Max whined and barked, but he ran toward the kitchen entrance on the side of the house. He barked and barked, and he'd definitely get let in that way.

Tag walked with Steele and Boots back to his cabin in silence, and as Tag went up his steps, Steele finally added, "See you in an hour."

"Yep." Tag followed Boots into his cabin and closed the door against the weather behind him. He sighed in the silence of his house, in the way he felt so safe here, in how different his life here was from other places he'd been.

"Dear Jesus," he whispered into the silence. "I don't know why it makes me nervous to have Opal build a house here. But I want her to be happy, so please, bless her that her path toward this house will be open and clear."

His furnace blew, and Tag found he didn't need to ask God for more. So he shed his jacket in the kitchen and hung it by the back door to dry. Then he went down the hall to shower away the cold, the noise, the worry, believing that no matter what came next, he had God on his side, and he'd be able to cope.

"With God...and Opal?" he murmured to himself,

and that alone told him how intertwined he'd allowed his life to become with hers. How much he *wanted* his life to be intertwined with hers. And how much rode on the upcoming Valentine's Day dinner and the building of Opal's house.

CHAPTER
Nineteen

OPAL ARRIVED BACK at the farmhouse thirty minutes later than she'd anticipated. "Come on, baby," she said to West in the back seat. He couldn't unbuckle himself, though, and Opal had to duck back there and get him out of his seat. She usually let him toddle his way toward the front door at his own pace, but today, she grabbed his diaper bag and him and hurried to the house.

"Auntie Opal needs to get ready," she said as she kicked the door closed behind her and dropped his bag.

"Ope, Ope," he sang merrily. Her heart turned to melted butter every time he said her name, and she took him down the hall to her bedroom.

"It's Valentine's Day, bud, and I have a special date with Tag." She smiled at him as she set him on the floor. She hadn't been out painting a house or working out, though one might consider attending a toddler event at the library on Valentine's Day quite the workout. She didn't need to shower. She simply needed to get her hair up, her makeup on, and her dress donned.

She started with her hair as West sang to himself.

"I'm here," Gerty called, and Opal jumped to her feet. Two steps from her dressing table, she opened the door.

"Momma's home," she told West. "Go find her, Westy."

"Mama!" The little boy clambered to his feet and went running past Opal and into the hallway. She left her door open and listened to their reunion, West babbling away in a language only he understood and Gerty acting like she knew what he'd said.

Opal finished her hair and continued with her makeup. She already had dark features, so she didn't do much to enhance them. She did put on her deep, dark red lipstick, and then she stuck her head out into the hall. "Gerty," she called. "Can you help with my dress?"

"Coming," Gerty called, and her footsteps came quickly.

Opal had already stepped into her slip, and when Gerty arrived, she picked up the black dress with shiny, sparkling sequins she'd found for this date. She'd paid an astronomical amount to have it shipped here in only two days, and she'd been extremely lucky and blessed that the dress fit well enough to avoid alterations.

"My goodness," Gerty said. "Where are you guys going?"

"I don't know," Opal said. "Tag wouldn't say. He only said I had to wear a dress."

"I have never seen a dress like this before." Gerty barely wore dresses to church, so that didn't surprise Opal at all.

"It's an Anna Thom," Opal said. "They only make one of each dress."

"What?" Gerty's fingers stilled as Opal pulled the thick strap up and over her left shoulder. The dress possessed a certain weight that made Opal feel luxurious and powerful at the same time.

"You order it and send in your measurements," she said, meeting her cousin's eye in the mirror. "They make it and ship it. They only sell each dress once."

"I'm afraid to ask, but how much does this cost?"

Opal put on her other strap and settled the dress over her chest, tugging it this way and then that to get it in place. She'd use body tape to make sure it didn't gape in the wrong way during her date, but since she'd sent in her measurements, the dress fit remarkably well.

"A lot," Opal said. "And I paid extra to get it here in time."

"You and your brother," Gerty said as she started

to zip her into the dress. "It's like you don't even understand regular people."

Opal drew in a sharp breath. "I understand regular people."

Gerty finished with the zipper and stood behind Opal. She had four or five inches on her, and she hugged her from behind. "Sometimes," she said. "But no one I've ever known would be able to buy a dress they only make one of."

Opal supposed that was true. "I don't do this all the time," she said, suddenly feeling small.

"I didn't mean to criticize you," Gerty said.

Opal leaned her head back against her best friend's shoulder. "I know. It's silly when I think about it."

"Here they are," Mike said, and Gerty moved away from Opal. "What's—oh, I see." He swept his gaze down to the hem—asymmetrical and ruffled fabric with feathers and fourteen-carat gold thread—and back to Opal. "You look like a million bucks."

Opal smiled as she turned and faced him. "Not quite," she said, throwing Gerty a knowing look. "It's okay? It's not too much for Valentine's Day?"

"You're going to Velvet," Mike said as he passed West to Gerty. "So absolutely not. I've heard that place requires things like this."

"Velvet," Opal repeated. "Tag hadn't said the name of it before."

"Hunter told him about it," Mike said. "Me too,

but Gerty and I are going to enjoy our time alone here at home."

Guilt ripped through Opal. "I'm going to be moving out really soon."

"Opal," Gerty said as she rolled her eyes. "It's not you." She left the bedroom saying, "Let's go get dinner, Westy. Then you can go to bed early, so Mommy and Daddy can have a peaceful evening."

Opal met her older brother's eyes. "You're not a problem," Mike said. "I didn't mean anything by it."

"Now that Mister Hanks is back," she said. "The paperwork went through, and I'm waiting on plans for the house. I just have to pick those, and Jeremy said they'd start as soon as that happens, since I've already funded."

Mike nodded, his smile kind and calm. "Are you excited?"

"Yes," she said.

"Okay," he said. "Then focus on tonight. This is a big deal for you—Valentine's Day."

Opal's pulse rippled through her veins. "I'm not as much of a holiday fiend as I used to be."

"No?" Mike grinned at her. "It's okay if they're important to you."

"I know," she said. "But I don't judge entire relationships on birthdays and holidays anymore." She once had, that was true. "Or gifts. I know there's more to life than those things. And someone can give amazing presents and still be all wrong for me."

"Sounds like you're speaking from some experience, Sissy."

"A little," Opal admitted. She turned back to her reflection. A sigh filled her whole body. "I love this dress."

"Yeah, Tag's gonna love it too," Mike said. "Should I make him come in and take pictures by the fireplace?" He laughed, but Opal actually considered it. He'd never gone to prom, and everyone should have to suffer through their parents making them take awkward pictures before they could finally escape the house.

Mike left her bedroom, and Opal adorned her earlobes with a special pair of earrings and draped a matching necklace around her throat. She'd not stepped into her shoes yet when the doorbell rang.

"That's Tag," she gasped. She hurried to get into her heels, and she took one last look at herself in the mirror. Yes, she'd spent almost six figures to buy and get this dress here specifically for this date, a number she'd never tell to anyone. "They don't need to know," she whispered. "It's my money."

And she had plenty more where that came from.

"Opal?" Gerty came into the room and stopped again. "Oh, you are so gorgeous." Her blue eyes sparkled like sapphires—a color Opal had considered for her dress. "Tag is dressed up nicely too. Come on." She reached for Opal, and Opal let her take her hand

and lead her out to meet Tag for their Valentine's Day date.

Her nerves kept her smile on her face, and Gerty seemed to melt out of the way when she reached the living room. Then, all Opal could see was Taggart Crow. He'd dressed in black from head to toe as well, with a hint of a pale pink shirt at his throat, with a deep-not-overly-bright fuchsia tie knotted there.

He held his midnight cowboy hat, and he'd shaved his beard into perfection. Tag stared at her, his face slack with disbelief, and then his trademark crooked smile appeared. "The stars have nothing on you, honeybee."

Opal stepped toward him, and she eased into his arms like she'd sink into a hot bath. Everything about being with him felt right, even the way he kissed her right there in front of Gerty and Mike.

"You are the most beautiful woman in the world," he whispered. "How did I get so lucky?"

"You're a god in a cowboy hat," she whispered back.

"Not yet." He pulled away a little and settled his cowboy hat back on his head. "There. You ready? You need anything?"

She held up her phone. "Could you carry this for me?"

"Yes, ma'am," he said, and Opal gave him a coy smile. Then, she watched the ground at her feet as she left the farmhouse.

"Ope, Ope, Ope!" West cried, and she turned back to the darling boy.

Gerty held him despite his efforts to break free. "She's leaving, baby. It's okay. She'll be back."

"Ope!" West actually had tears in his eyes, and Opal's heart tore from the top down. She hurried over to him, mindful of the drive ahead and the distance they had to go to get to the restaurant.

"Westy," she said as she drew closer. "Give me a kiss and then I have to go." She swept a kiss along his cheek, feeling so loved when he held her head in a hug. "You be good for your momma and daddy tonight, okay?"

"Ope," he said in a much quieter voice.

"West." She grinned at him as she pulled back, and this time, she managed to make it out of the house without incident. She held Tag's hand as they went down the steps, and she allowed him to help her into his truck.

He drove off the farm, and Opal's adrenaline finally started to wane. "Mike told me we're going to Velvet," she said, not sure she should keep talking.

"Yep," Tag said.

"I've never been," she said casually. "Have you?"

He looked over to her, clearly onto her game. "No," he said. He could've added any number of things, like, "It's not really my style," or "It's out of my price range, honeybee."

But he didn't say anything more.

Opal opened her mouth, and it felt like someone had stuffed a pair of socks down her throat. She could barely swallow, and breathing? Forget about it. She panicked and shifted in her seat, trying to get past these feelings to the other side.

Don't say it.

The words rang through her ears, throat, and mind, and Opal swallowed her offer to pay for dinner that night. She took in a breath of air, glad the episode had passed quickly. "My funding is done," she said. "I'm expecting plans for the house in the next couple of weeks."

"That's great, Opal," Tag said, his voice barely louder than the quiet radio playing in the background.

"Would you—would you look at the proposals with me and help me choose?"

He glanced over to her and took her hand in his. "Yes," he said simply.

Warmth filled Opal, and she relaxed into the seat behind her. Finally. "I think I might move out while the house is built."

"Yeah?"

"Yeah," she said. "Mike and Gerty keep saying it's fine if I'm there, but I don't know. I have this feeling it's not okay."

"Where will you go?"

"I've been looking at a couple of places," she said. "For rent. Houses for rent. My house is going to take at least six months to build. Probably longer."

"At least you won't be moving in the winter," he said.

"I have so much stuff in storage in California," she said, her mood dropping at the thought of having to go there and get it. "Maybe I'll just buy all new everything."

Tag chuckled and squeezed her hand. "Spoken like a true Hammond."

Opal opened her mouth to protest, or at least defend herself. Then she remembered what she'd spent on this dress, and she started to laugh. "I suppose so," she said through her giggles.

She leaned back and watched the night flow by. "I feel so much more in control of my life," she said.

"I'm glad."

Looking over to him, she wondered if God would cut off her vocal cords again if she tried to ask the question dancing through her mind. She decided to open her mouth and try, and this time, she easily asked, "What about you? How are you feeling?"

"I'm fine," he drawled.

"You know what I mean," she said.

"I'm not looking for a house or a farm," he said. His voice had taken on a black note, and Opal wanted to backtrack quickly.

"I meant about us," she said. "About your life in general. Not where you live." In truth, she wanted to know all of it, but she didn't want anything to ruin tonight.

"I feel great about us, honey-love," he said. "I love my life at the farm, and I'm not sure I need anything different."

Opal grinned at him. "That's great. I'm glad."

Tag nodded, but Opal saw how tight his jaw remained. When they arrived at Velvet, the words spelled out in gold lights, Opal waited for him to come help her from the truck. As she found her footing, he wrapped her up tightly and held her.

She smiled against his chest, the feelings of love rising within her. "I'm worried I'm not enough to hold your attention," he murmured.

Opal pulled back. "What? That's ridiculous."

"Nevertheless." Tag gave her that sexy smile, and Opal just wanted to reassure him that he was the only man who'd held her interest for longer than a date or two in years. In her heels, she only had to tip up a few inches to kiss him, and she did exactly that.

An inferno roared to life between them, and surely he felt that. Every kiss with him felt like the first time, and Opal simply didn't believe that was only on her end. He certainly kissed her back with a sense of urgency and passion.

"You're mine," she whispered against his lips. "Okay?"

"Yes, ma'am," he murmured back. "But I actually got you a giant teddy bear that's holding a heart that says, 'Be mine.'" He touched his lips to hers again, and

Opal wanted more, more, more. "So can you be mine too?"

"Yes," she whispered. "But I'm going to need to see the bear."

Tag chuckled, and Opal smiled way down in her soul. "You're mine," he said, pulling her as close as she could get. "Bear or no bear."

"Mm, okay," she said, and she joyfully received his kiss once again. She wanted to believe she'd found her Prince Charming, and for tonight, on this gloriously clear, bright, and perfect Valentine's Day, she wasn't going to bring up anything that made Tag's jaw tighten like it had in the truck earlier.

And she'd figure out what that belonged to when she wasn't wearing a ninety-thousand dollar dress and when she wasn't standing outside the nicest, most expensive restaurant in the state of Colorado.

Oh, yes, she would, whether Tag wanted to talk about it or not.

CHAPTER
Twenty

TAG HAD NEVER EATEN such good food. He'd never seen steak cooked to pure perfection. Opal had been moaning and exclaiming over everything that had been put on the table that night, including the black tuxedo cake sitting between them now.

"Tag," she said, and he looked up, the last of his cake melting in his mouth. "This has been the perfect day."

"Has it?"

"I mean, since you picked me up," she said. "Though I don't mind tending West."

He grinned at her. "You love that baby," he said. "Don't act like it's a chore for you to babysit him."

She grinned back at him. "Fine, I won't." She put her elbows on the table. "Tag."

"Go on, love."

"It's *honey*-love," she teased, but she sobered

quickly. "I don't want to get a job. I don't want to guest lecture at a college or university anywhere."

He knew Opal had been trying to figure out what she wanted her life to be, and he'd been silently at her side, listening to her talk when she felt like talking. "What are you thinking?" he asked.

Opal leaned away from the last few bites of cake. Everything about her sparkled, from the diamonds hanging from her ears and glinting from her collarbone. Her sequins had first blinded him at the farmhouse, then the physical diamonds, and then her pure inner radiance.

Tag knew now that he could love this woman, and on some level, he already did. But he honestly had no idea how to be her equal, and he wanted a husband-wife relationship that existed on even ground.

"I know it's going to be work," she said. "But hear me out."

"Have I ever not heard you out?"

She gave him a timid smile and glanced up as the waiter arrived to remove their dessert. "Dancing will be in the waterfall garden in about ten minutes."

"Thank you," Tag said.

Opal's face lit up. "Dancing?"

"In the waterfall garden," he echoed, half-wishing he and Opal could just escape the press of the public and find somewhere private to be.

"Do you dance?" she asked.

Tag nodded. "I've been taking online classes.

Well." He gave his shoulders a little shake. "Sort of. There are these tutorials on YouTube. I've been practicing with those."

Opal reached across the table and took both of his hands in hers. "Taggart, you are the sweetest man alive."

He glanced around the restaurant, which held table after table of men just like him. "I don't know about that, Opal."

"Well, I do." She squeezed her fingers around his. "I want to start a non-profit health clinic for farmers and ranchers." Her glow had returned, and Tag had seen this look in her eyes and parading across her face when she'd spoken of things she felt passionately about.

He waited for her to explain more, and when she didn't, he asked, "And?"

"And that's as far as I've gotten," she said. "I have a lot of other things going on, but once I'm settled in my own place, I'm going to need something to fill my day."

"Maybe you'll be married," he said. "With babies of your own."

Her eyebrows rose, and oh, he liked it when she challenged him silently.

"I'm just saying." He tried to shrug again, but he wasn't sure it came off right.

"What are you saying, exactly?"

"How long do you need to date someone before

you know you want to be with them forever?" he asked.

Opal's eyebrows went down and now she regarded him like he was a puzzle she needed to solve. "I don't know. I think that's different for every person."

"I'm not asking generally," he said. "I'm asking *you*. How long do *you* need to date me before you know you want to be with me forever?"

Opal looked like he'd picked up her fizzy lemonade and thrown it in her face. Splashed it down that gorgeous dress that had to cost more than he made in a year. "I don't know, Taggart," she whispered.

His full name had become a term of endearment when she said it, and Tag loved hearing it in her voice. "Okay," he said. "But just because I don't say everything I think doesn't mean I don't see you with West. It doesn't mean I don't know you want a baby of your own, and maybe you won't want to be tied to a clinic when you can be home with that baby."

On a farm with her family literally right next door. She might want to open and operate a non-profit clinic for farmers and ranchers, but Tag also knew Opal wanted to be a mother. Maybe more than anything.

"Maybe," she finally said.

"Ladies and gentlemen," a man with a cool, smooth voice said over the speaker system. "The waterfall garden is now open for dancing."

Tag looked at Opal and removed the napkin from his lap. "Can I have this dance?"

She smiled at him in a way that made his heart want to march to the top of the highest cliff and then fling itself off. He'd do anything for her, anything to make her laugh and smile, anything to make sure she could have every dream of hers realized.

If that wasn't love, Tag didn't know what was. But he'd never been in love before, and he didn't want to move too fast. *Plus, you're not telling her you love her on Valentine's Day. Too cliché.*

"Yes, please." Opal put her hand in his and stood, her dress settling in all the right places easily. She grinned at him with those dark red lips he couldn't wait to kiss later, and they moved into the waterfall garden, where a whole new world opened up before him.

"Oh, there's an actual waterfall," he said. "Indoors." He'd never seen that before, and he couldn't look away from the three-story tall waterfall, the sound of which created a soothing harmony to accompany the twinkling music being played by a live band in the corner.

Potted plants and trellises with vines dotted the dancefloor and created separate areas inside the large space. Tag wanted to find a dark corner, but Opal pointed to his left and said, "Tag, look at those lilacs."

"How'd they get this stuff to grow here?" he wondered aloud as he went up a couple of steps and across a bridge—that ran over water from the water-fall—to the part of the room that housed the lilacs Opal liked.

He took her into his arms easily, the scent of lilacs and sugar surrounding him only to get replaced by the soft, sexy quality of Opal's perfume, her skin, her hair. Tag let his eyes drift closed, and suddenly, the rest of his senses came to high alert.

He felt the shape of Opal in his arms, in his life, in his heart. He hadn't realized a hole exactly her height, her size, her shape, had existed in his life until he'd met her. He hadn't realized how incomplete he'd been until tonight, and he wanted to keep her at his side forever.

So he just needed to figure out how to believe he was worthy to be with her. Worthy to be a Hammond. Worthy to be the simple cowboy he was and still be the man at Opal's side.

And that seemed to need the hand of God, so as Tag swayed back and forth with Opal, gently leading her around the lilac-rimmed patio, he prayed for the divine help he needed to become who she needed him to be.

————

FEBRUARY MELTED INTO MARCH, literally. Around the farm, everything turned to mud and mush, and Tag caught sight of Opal sitting on her bright purple couch outside of the farmhouse some afternoons. The really sunny ones.

She set up a low, waist-high fence and let West run wild while she laid back, her feet on one of the arm rests and her head on the cushions, and read. Whenever the one-year-old would squawk, she'd look over to him, and Tag found them both down on the ground, examining an earthworm once.

He could admit he loved watching her with West. She adored him, obviously, and she took immaculate care of him.

The ground had been broken for her house and the cement foundation poured. It sat curing right now, and as the sunshine continued throughout March, Tag's workload expanded. He watched the weather religiously, because Mother Nature could surprise them with a late spring snowstorm at any time—and often did. She was fickle and unpredictable in March and April, that was for certain.

One day about mid-March, Tag had finished riding the whole ranch to check the fences. He'd made notes about what needed to be fixed or replaced before planting, which they'd do in another four or six weeks.

He and Steele still worked with the horses every day too, of course. Rooster and the others had settled in just fine. He'd moved the chicken coop back outside, and the barn was almost back to where it would be until winter descended over the land again.

Right now, he grabbed his mail from the farmhouse and joined the dogs outside again. "Got it,
guys," he said. Then he, Boots, and Max made the
walk over to his cabin. Inside, Tag sighed, glad to be
home after a long day of work.

He didn't get much mail, because he didn't pay
rent or utilities here. Every now and then, his mom
would send something through the postal system, but
he usually got coupon books or advertisements.

Today, he had a soft, silky envelope with his name
printed on it in fancy cursive. The return address said
Lewis at the top, and Tag's mind misfired. "What's
this?" he asked himself as he flipped over the ivory
envelope and ran his thumb under the flap.

Just as he pulled out the wedding announcement,
he remembered. "Oh, duh," he said. "Keith and Lindsay." The two of them stood in the field, facing one
another. They both wore smiles of complete love and
joy as Keith had his head bent toward Lindsay, his
eyes closed, and she beamed up at him with hers
open.

Wow, Tag thought, the word not coming out of his
mouth. That was what love looked like, and Tag's
throat closed in on itself. He wanted this picture in his
life, but he wanted to be the one standing in the field
with the woman he loved.

With Opal.

"You don't love her," he muttered to himself.
They'd only been dating for a few months, and he

wasn't going to be the one to lose his heart this time. Even as he pulled back on his feelings, he felt them slipping further from him.

He turned to the fridge and put the wedding announcement up, glancing at the dates. Their wedding would happen in another month or so, and Tag already had it on his calendar. He wouldn't miss it, because he wanted to witness that love and joy first-hand.

He wanted to call Opal and see her that night, but she'd left the farm already for an evening with Cord and Jane. When she wasn't spending time with her family or tending to West, Opal had been meeting with her general contractor, subcontractors, and now, a new business consultant about what she needed to do to start a non-profit medical clinic in the state of Colorado.

All of it made Tag tired—and Opal busier than ever. He didn't get to see her nearly as much as he had in the winter, and a vein of frustration sprouted and started to grow. He tamped it down again and again as he made himself a roast beef sandwich and tater tots for dinner.

By the time he sat down on his couch, with Boots next to him and Max curled at his feet, Tag had lost the battle against his loneliness. He wanted Opal here, and the TV was a poor substitute for the woman.

He thought of Valentine's Day, and how stunningly magical their evening together had been. Her dress.

That meal. Holding her in his arms. Kissing her good-night until it felt like his lips were bruised.

It almost felt like that night had happened to someone else. "It's been a month," he said. "She won't be busy like this forever. Calm down."

He calmed enough to eat, but once he finished, he really had nothing interesting to hold his attention. He got up and rinsed his plate, set it in the dishwasher, and avoided looking at Keith and Lindsay's obvious bliss.

"Come on, guys," he said to the dogs. "Can't stay in tonight." He wasn't sure why or how this mood had come over him, but he hoped the great outdoors would give him more space to think, better air to breathe, and a chance for his toxic feelings to dissipate and disappear.

He left through the back door instead of the front, and he walked along the tree line behind the cabins. Boots and Max trotted around, sniffing everything and marking their territory. Max barked once, his way of letting the world know he existed.

Tag smiled at the shepherd, surprised he hadn't stayed at the farmhouse. But Gerty and Mike hadn't been there either, and Tag decided to do a loop that went past the farmhouse, so he could drop off their dog on his way back.

The river bubbled about a half-mile away, and while Tag stepped in some muddy spots along the way, he didn't mind the walk. The sun had gone behind the mountains, but it wasn't quite dark yet, and he allowed himself to breathe fully.

"It's okay to miss her," he told himself, feeling that powerfully for a moment. "It's also okay that she's out there, doing what she wants to do."

His phone rang, and Tag tugged it free of his pocket. Mike's name sat there, and Tag swiped on the call. "Hey, Mikey."

"Hey, Tag." The man sounded generally upbeat, so nothing too wrong could be happening. "Listen, Gerty and I are at the Cinemax, and they're having their annual buy-one-get-one ticket sale. She wondered if you wanted some tickets?"

"Sure," Tag said. "Are they doing a year expiration again?"

"Uh…yeah. Yep."

Tag could just hear the nod in Mike's voice, and it made him smile. "A year."

"Okay," Tag said. "Get me six."

"Six?" Mike asked, and Tag heard Gerty repeat it.

"Doesn't seem like enough," Gerty said, her voice quieter than Mike's.

"It's every other month," Tag said. "I don't get off the farm to the Cinemax that much as it is. I think that sounds generous."

"Oh, six tickets gets him twelve tickets," Gerty said.

Tag just let them talk for a moment, and he wondered why twelve tickets was somehow acceptable when six wasn't. Did they think he'd be going alone once a month?

"Okay," Mike said. "Thanks, Tag."

"Yep." He ended the call, and he didn't even have the phone back in his pocket before it rang again. This time, his brother's name sat there, and surprise filled Tag.

"Sawyer," he said after he'd answered the call. "What's up?"

"Taggart!" The cowboy on the other end of the line could drawl—and laugh, which Sawyer did next. "How are you, brother?"

"Good," Taggart said, turning left along a dirt path that sat between two dormant fields. He'd plant them this year after a year of soil rest, and he suddenly remembered he needed to meet with Keith to go over his planting plan. "Getting ready for planting. Getting the farm cleaned up from winter. Pretty standard stuff." He walked away from the mountains now, but the shadows they cast draped over the land in front of him.

I love it here, he thought. Out loud, he asked, "You? How are you and Flint?"

"That's why I'm calling, actually," Sawyer said, and he sobered quite a bit.

Tag tilted his head, something in his brother's tone he didn't like. "Yeah? Trouble?"

"No, not trouble, exactly," Sawyer said. "We want

to come up there for your birthday. Could you house us?"

Tag didn't know what to say for a moment. Then, a sense of being cared for, of someone thinking about him, of him not being the lone wolf, the odd man out, the last one to know everything, filled him. "Yeah," he said. "Of course."

"Do you want us to come?" Sawyer asked. "I know May's a busy time on any ranch, especially one in spring and moving into summer. It would be a weekend or three days. And we can help you work in the morning and evening or whatever."

"Of course I want you to come," Tag said. "I'll talk to Gerty and Mike. We've got Steele now. I might not have to work at all." He swallowed, because he hadn't even told the twins about Opal. "And you can meet my girlfriend."

Sawyer let a beat of silence go by, and then he said, "Hoo, boy, you have been holdin' out on us!" in his party-boy voice.

Tag laughed this time, because Sawyer always made having a girlfriend into a big deal. Tag supposed it was, but at the same time, it wasn't. He made it back to the main dirt road that would lead him to the farm-house—and now past Opal's house too—as he grinned and grinned.

Sawyer told Flint about Tag's girlfriend, and he listened to the two of them tease him for a couple of minutes. "All right, all right," he said. "Do either of you animals have girlfriends?"

"Nope," Sawyer said.

"No wonder you think it's a marvel or a wonder," Tag said dryly. "Believe it or not, I've been out with women before."

"Yeah, but after Talina," Sawyer said, once again bringing the mood back to level.

"Yeah," Tag said and nothing else. Ahead of him, Boots trotted along with Max, and then both dogs looked to their left. Tag followed their gaze too, but he couldn't see anything.

Max barked and broke into a run, with Boots hot on his heels. Tag's adrenaline kicked up a notch, especially as he made it past a copse of trees and Opal's SUV came into view. She'd parked in front of her foundation, but he couldn't see her anywhere.

Then a cry filled the air, and Tag dang near dropped his phone. "I have to go," he said, remembering he was on a call.

"Tag—"

"I'll call you back," he barked, and he didn't bother hanging up before he broke into a jog too. He knew that sound, and with Opal's car in front of him, he felt certain she needed help.

Right now.

CHAPTER
Twenty-One

OPAL YELPED as she tried to get to her feet for the third time. This time, her right foot slid even further right, causing her to fall into the splits. Oh, she couldn't do the splits, and certainly not in the mud.

Max barked again, and Opal looked up to find the dog. Perhaps she could grab onto him and get herself up. She pulled her legs together, beyond trying to stay clean. Her clothes held about as much mud as the entire plot of land she planned to use for her vegetable garden. Her house wouldn't be done, but Opal could raise peas, carrots, and corn without it.

"Opal?" Tag called, and her heart sank right down into the earth. Of course he'd be the one to find her. She wasn't even supposed to be here tonight, but Jane hadn't been feeling well after a spaghetti-and-meatball lunch had caused some acid reflux.

She and Cord had canceled dinner, which was

okay with Opal. She'd come back to the farm after getting a hamburger from The Burger Babe, a restaurant her daddy had helped fund and start through the foundation at HMC when he'd been the CEO.

Then, she'd collected her garden map from her purse and come to the house. The foundation would be done curing in a week or so, and then the framing would begin. Opal had chosen an open layout on the main floor, with a master suite and a small connected room that could be a nursery, and then turned into an office once the kids moved either to the upstairs bedrooms or the basement ones.

She couldn't wait to see it, to go through every choice for flooring, paint colors, curtains, furniture, and more. And she wanted to start doing something with the land she'd purchased from Gerty and Mike, thus, her visit to the garden tonight.

"Opal?"

"I'm in the garden," she called as Tag came into view. She lifted one muddy hand over her head and waved. Tag saw her and slowed. He kept coming, but not quite at a run.

"Holy smokes," he said as he got to the edge of the garden closest to her. Max and Boots stopped there as well. "I—I don't even know what to do." He grinned at her, but Opal didn't feel like smiling.

"I was just doing some garden prep," she said as calmly as she could.

Tag tipped his head back and laughed, and Opal supposed she deserved that.

"Come help me, cowboy." She made a noise of dissatisfaction, and Tag sobered.

"You look like you've been sucked into the ground." He looked down at his boots, his jeans, his jacket. He hadn't changed after work, because he had mud streaked along his thighs too.

"You haven't showered yet," she said. "I just need a hand. It's so slippery out here."

"All right," he said dubiously. He stepped out into the mud, and it wasn't as deep or as wet on the edges. He took four strides to reach her, and he planted his feet side-by-side and reached for her. "Up you go."

She put her disgustingly dirty hands in his, mud squishing out between her fingers as she gripped his. "Okay," she said, but she felt powerless to get her feet under her.

Tag lifted her by his sheer strength, which sent streams of embarrassment through Opal as she rose from the muck with horribly humiliating squelching sounds filling the air. Oh, and his grunting as he bore her full weight. Yeah, that wasn't embarrassing or anything.

She got one foot on the ground, and she threw her arms around Tag as she struggled to get the other one under her. "Okay," she said, but Tag started to topple.

"Okay?" he asked, his voice strained.

"Okay," she said, moving further into his chest. His

left foot moved out, and Opal's went between his, making her now unsteady again.

"Not okay," he said as he wrapped both of his arms around her.

"I'm sliding," she said with plenty of panic in her voice.

"Join the club." Tag dropped to one knee, and that meant Opal couldn't stay standing either. She couldn't pull Tag down with her, so she released him and started to fall backward. But he had ahold of her, and that only brought him forward over her.

She landed hard on her backside, another cry flying from her mouth, Tag's eyes met hers for the briefest of moments before he finally got the memo and let go of her. His hands landed in the mud at her sides as his right leg finally yielded and bent at the knee.

Both of them breathed in and out, in and out, hard. He looked at her, an indecipherable look on his face. "This mud is cold," he said.

For some reason, Opal found that funny, and she started to laugh. "Yeah, it's no picnic," she said through her giggles. Her lower jaw shuddered, and she hadn't realized how chilled she'd become.

"The sun's down," she said.

"And we can't stay out here much longer," Tag said. "Or we'll be stumbling back to the farmhouse in the pitch dark."

Opal grinned at him. "You've got a little mud

here." She reached up and wiped her messy hands along his cheekbone and down into his beard.

Pure shock entered his expression. "You have got to be kidding me."

She laughed, then shrieked when Tag lifted his completely muddy hand too. "Taggart Crow, don't you dare."

"Don't *I* dare?" He grinned wickedly at her, his hand still raised. But instead of him smearing the muck through her hair, he leaned forward and kissed her. Opal got a little grit on her lips, along with the taste of earth, but she didn't mind so much. Not when it was Tag doing the kissing.

He pulled away with a laugh bubbling out of his mouth. "We really can't stay out here like this." He put one hand on her shoulder to steady himself. Behind him, Max barked. Tag looked at the dog and back to Opal. "Maybe we should just scoot to the edge. It's drier over there."

"I am not mud-scooting in front of you."

His eyes danced with delight. "Embarrassed?"

"Thoroughly."

"Oh, come on, Opal," he said good-naturedly. "You've got to have something you don't excel at."

"Prepping vegetable garden plots," Opal said. "Check."

"I'll take it."

She thought she saw something strained on Tag's face for a moment, but then he dropped his gaze to the dirt. "I'm just gonna...." He leaned into her, and she braced herself against his weight as he used her to get to his feet.

He offered her his hand again, but Opal wasn't so sure she should take it. "Come on, honey-sweets," he said. "At the very least, I can pull you toward the edge."

How mortifying, she thought. In the end, she had no other choice. Trying to get to her feet in front of him and falling again would be worse. So she put her hand in his and let him pull her up again.

They stayed upright this time, and he said, "Let's just shuffle over toward the dogs." He went backward, and Opal took tiny, mincing steps forward. After what felt like a long journey, Tag stepped up a bit, pulled Opal with him, and she stood on drier ground.

Max barked and looked up at both of them, then ran around them in a circle, and barked again.

"Yes, yes," Opal said, almost scolding the dog. "We're out." She looked down at her clothes—a nice pair of navy blue pants and a blouse that would never be white again. It had splashy flowers on it, but they wouldn't look the same against a dingy background.

In that moment, she realized she'd lost a shoe. And she'd driven. Her hands flew to her pockets, and thankfully, she felt the hard plastic of the key fob. "I can't get in my car like this," she said.

"You can't go in the farmhouse like that," Tag teased.

She didn't want to tell him she'd lost a shoe, but she didn't see any other way around it. "I lost a shoe."

Tag looked down at her feet, and in the quickly fading light, he made a noise somewhere between a scoff and a laugh. He looked up again, and Opal met his eyes. "We better get going." He took her hand, dried and wet mud and all, and they started back toward the dirt road.

Opal limped along, doing her best not to cry out whenever she stepped on something less than pleasant. Thankfully, the road was just hard-packed dirt, with some smaller loose pebbles. Her socked foot also had a layer of mud, and she managed to keep up with Tag.

"Are you...?" She didn't know how to bring up the questions in her mind.

"Am I what?" Tag looked over to her.

"Never mind," she said. He'd already admitted he thought she was perfect, and she didn't want to talk about any of that tonight.

"You need a good pair of garden boots for gardening, honey," he said.

"Noted," she said.

"I'll get you some," he said. "Because I know you're not going to quit on that garden." He wore joviality in his tone, and it made Opal smile. "Now, you're going to be mad at me, but it'll only last five minutes."

Her heartbeat swooped through her body like a bird riding a strong wind current. "Mad at you?"

"The outdoor water isn't on at the farmhouse yet," he said. "But we've got it in the barn."

It took Opal several seconds to connect the dots. "You're going to make me go to the barn to be hosed off like an animal?"

"Honey, would you like to deal with Gerty when she sees mud all over her house?" He looked at her like she was some sort of swamp monster. "You're *dripping* with the stuff."

Opal held her head high, but she could admit it was hard, because the mud weighed a lot. "Fine," she said. "Hose me down like a cow."

Tag chuckled, but Opal just wanted to be in a hot shower, then her pjs, so she could bask in her own humiliation. "You're not a cow." He pressed a gritty kiss to her temple. "And bonus, you can spray me down too, and I have a much longer walk to a hot shower than you do."

"There's no way you can walk through the dark, soaking wet, to your cabin," Opal said. "Just come shower at the house."

"And put on what after?"

"Mike has clothes," she said airily.

"Why aren't you at Jane's?" he asked, and Opal recognized him dodging her suggestion.

"She wasn't feeling well."

"That's too bad."

Opal let him lead her past the brightly lit farmhouse and toward the barn. Shivering, she said,

"Maybe you can stay and watch a movie with me after we shower."

"And maybe your brother will slit my throat when he walks in, sees me wearing his clothes and cuddling with his younger sister."

Opal grinned into the night, glad Tag had come along. She hadn't even realized how quickly the sun set, though it was still March. The days had been getting longer, but she'd been foolish to think daylight hours lasted as long as they did in the summer.

"Mike has never had a say in who I date," she said. "And he and Gerty wouldn't want you walking home in the dark soaking wet."

"This feels like an unwinnable situation," he said.

Opal laughed. "Oh, Taggart, honey, don't you know I always win?"

He chuckled and said, "Yes, Opal-honey, I do know that."

In the barn, he led her down to the end where the wash stall was. "I'll go first," he said. "Then you won't be wet for as long." He stepped into the stall and nodded to the hose. "Go on now."

Opal only hesitated for a moment, and then she took the hose off the wall. She looked at it for a moment, sure she wasn't about to spray down her boyfriend with cold water on a March night.

"Do it," he said, gritting his teeth. He closed his eyes, and Opal wanted to close hers. Instead, she pressed the handle on the nozzle on the hose, and the water came out. She stepped back as the water pressure bucked against her hand, and the water sprayed all over—left and right—until she could control the hose and get it on Tag's lower half. He stuck his hands out in front of him to rinse those, and after only about ten seconds, he said, "Good enough."

He took a few steps toward her and took the hose. "Your turn."

Opal took his place, and Tag didn't waste a moment before turning the hose on her. She'd barely turned, in fact, and she yelped as he said, "I'm sorry. I'm sorry, Opal-honey."

She gritted her teeth and went into a happy place. Somewhere where she didn't feel the icy shards of water as it blasted her skin and clothes. Before she knew it, Tag said, "Good enough," and the water stopped. "Let's get inside."

He took her hand again, and while the water dripping from her fingers and chin wasn't completely clear, it was far better than before. She had to run every third step to keep up with him, and her teeth chattered by the time Tag hurried her up the steps to the small kitchen entrance deck.

"Everything off," he said.

"What?"

"I'll grab you a towel from the laundry room," he said. "You're dripping muddy water. I won't look." With that, he ducked inside, and Opal stared after him.

Then, she stepped out of her remaining shoe—not even a sneaker—her pants, and had just lifted her sopping blouse over her head when Tag said, "I have my eyes closed."

She glanced over and all she saw was a towel. She grabbed it and wrapped it around herself, then quickly stepped into the warmer house. "I-I-I'm going to shower," she said through shaking emotions and chattering cold.

Tag didn't speak, and Opal hurried through the kitchen and living room to the hallway. She flipped on the water in the bathroom and dropped the towel. The farmhouse had great hot water, and only second later, Opal stepped into the stream of it.

A sigh sank through her body, and she rinsed her hair and body until the water ran clear. Then she soaped up and washed, brushed her teeth, and got dressed in her warmest pjs and fluffiest socks.

Then she grabbed a blanket from the hall closet and towed it with her down the hall to the living room, where she found Tag sitting on the couch, texting.

"So you did shower here," she said.

He looked up, his smile gracing that handsome face. "I did." He indicated the kitchen exit. "I put our clothes in the washer, but I was waiting to start it."

Opal didn't head in that direction. "Okay." She joined him on the couch and pulled the blanket over her legs as she leaned into his chest. "I guess you're staying?"

"I texted Mike and Gerty about using their shower, so I feel less like I might get in trouble if I stay."

Opal smiled at him. "You smell good."

"Mm, so do you." He touched his mouth to hers, and Opal sure could get used to nights like this, mud and all. "Opal, I've missed you these past couple of weeks."

"Mm, I miss you too."

"How's the clinic coming?"

Opal leaned back into his chest and pulled the blanket up to her chin. After tucking her arms in, Tag re-tucked it, and Opal closed her eyes. "I actually have a site now."

"Do you?" His voice pitched up.

Opal nodded. "It's a little south and a little east of here," she said. "There's a hospital in Caster Falls, and small clinics out this way, but nothing in Maplewood. There's a big piece of commercial land, and I've talked to the realtor about it."

Tag didn't respond right away, and then he asked, "And?" in his blunt but positive way.

"But my daddy says I should do everything through a business or a foundation, and I don't have anything like that. So I've been talking to him about getting that all set up. I can't buy the land until that's done."

"Does that take a long time?"

"Shouldn't," Opal said. "I don't want to talk anymore tonight. Can you just hold me, and we'll pretend to watch something on TV?"

Tag's body behind hers relaxed, and she hadn't realized how tight he'd been until then. "Yeah, all right." He used the remote control and switched on the TV. "Opal, can we talk about something serious next time we have a minute?"

Now everything inside her tensed. "Yeah," she said anyway. "Of course we can."

"Okay," he whispered, and then he slid down behind her, wrapping her more fully in his arms.

"Oooh, Mike isn't going to be happy about this," she teased in a whisper.

Tag didn't laugh. Not even a chuckle. Instead, he kissed her right behind her ear, and Opal started shivering all over again—for an entirely different reason. She wasn't sure what "serious thing" he wanted to talk about, but she sure hoped it wasn't too serious, and that they'd be able to find their way through whatever maze they found themselves in.

She really needed that, because as she kissed him, Opal felt herself falling, falling, falling in love with the gorgeous cowboy—and she didn't want to stop.

CHAPTER
Twenty-Two

KEITH WHETTSTEIN CAME in from his fiancée's stables and called, "Everything is good to go, Linds."

The scent of maple and bacon hung in the air, and Keith reached down to get off his boots. That done, he continued through the utility room and into the kitchen. His gorgeous almost-bride stood at the stove, her hair already twisted up into a topknot. As he watched, a little awe-struck she was about to be his wife, she lifted a pan and flipped off the flame under it.

"Breakfast is done," she called.

"Okay," he said, and she turned toward him.

"Oh, you're right there."

Keith gave her a warm smile. "You didn't need to make breakfast on moving day."

"We have to eat, don't we?" She gave him a smile. "Besides, we don't have to be out for a few more hours, and I wanted to use my gas range one more time."

"I'll get you a new range when we get back from our honeymoon." Keith let her set down the pan of bacon before he took her into his arms. "Tomorrow," he whispered into her hair. "We'll be married and on our way to Florida."

"I can't believe it," she murmured back.

"You still want to marry me?"

"Of course." Lindsay beamed up at him and stretched forward to kiss him.

He could waste hours doing this exact thing, but he didn't let himself carry on for too long. "Great," he said. "Because I can't wait to marry you."

"Let's eat." She stepped out of his embrace and picked up a plate. Lindsay handed it to him and then took the second one for herself. Neither of them seemed to have much to say while they ate the bacon, eggs, and pancakes she'd put together while he'd done her farm chores.

Leaving Twilight Fields was going to be harder than he'd anticipated—and this wasn't even his place. He watched her swipe the last bite of her pancake through her syrup and put it in her mouth.

"Derrick and I went by the new place last night," he said. "Everything is ready for the animals."

Lindsay met his eye. "You texted me that."

Yes, he had. He nodded, not sure why he'd said it

out loud too. "Maybe I'm just trying to reassure both of us that we want to move over to the new place."

"I sold this farm," she said. "We have to move even if we don't want to."

"But we want to." Keith picked up her plate and stacked it on his. "Because it'll be *our* place, and we'll be living there together." He actually couldn't wait for that; he was tired of going to bed alone, and tired of dealing with three other men in his cabin.

"Right," she agreed. "I can't wait."

"You'll be there alone tonight, but that's it."

"I'll be fine," she said. "I have Hamlet."

Keith nodded and moved into the kitchen to clean up breakfast. Lindsay said, "I'm going to go finish in the bedroom and bathroom, and then we can start loading."

"My dad and Lars will be here in thirty minutes."

"I'll be ready."

Twenty minutes later, Keith had the kitchen clean and boxed up, labeled, and waiting with the other things that needed to be taken out. Only a couple of minutes later, the front door opened, and his daddy called, "We're here."

Keith went out into the living room, relief flowing through him. "Hey," he said, glad when his uncle's broad shoulders came through the door next. Then Lars, his sister's husband, and Hunter Hammond.

"Thanks for coming to help," he said, easing into his father's arms. "Everything is pretty much ready to get loaded." He stepped back and looked at the couch and love seat. The coffee table, the entertainment center, the TV—with cords and remote taped to the back of it—and all the boxes they'd packed, labeled, and stacked against the wall.

"There's a lot." Keith reached to hug Uncle Boone and then Lars. Finally, Hunter grinned as he shook his hand and pulled him into his chest.

"Ryder's outside," he said. "He was talking to Molly for a sec."

"My kids are around back," Uncle Boone said. "We won't have a problem with any of this."

"You got the truck?" Keith asked his father.

"Parked out front, the ramp down and ready."

Gratitude flowed up through Keith and out the top of his head. "Thank you, everyone."

"Hey." Lindsay grinned as she went by him. "Thanks for coming to help." She hugged Keith's daddy too, and the front door opened, and more people entered. His cousins, his mom, Ryder, and Mission Redbay—one of Keith's best friends from the Hammond Family Farm.

"All right," Keith said. He drew in a deep breath. "Hon, do you want them to...? Where do you want them to start?"

"I think the bigger furniture items," she said. "We've got everything in here. A big bed and dresser in the master. My dining room table and chairs. A few bookshelves and cabinets." She exchanged a glance with Keith. "It's a lot."

"We've got a twenty-four-foot truck," Dad said. "And a few pick-ups."

"Let's get the house done," Keith said. "Then we'll work on the animals." The enormity of moving her horses, chickens, the big mama pig…. If he let himself dwell on it for too long, he just wanted to sag to the ground and give up.

He couldn't do that, so he went with Hunter down the hall to the master bedroom. Together, they got the mattress and box springs out, then returned for the headboard and frame. Item by item, and with strong, willing men, the house emptied and the truck filled.

"I'm ordering lunch," Lindsay said. "Then people can eat whenever at the other house."

"Okay," Keith said. He wiped his forehead with the back of his hand. "It's hot today."

"Good weather for the wedding tomorrow." She gave him a quick smile, and they got back to work.

An hour later, Keith pulled up to the house and property he and Lindsay had purchased. The place they'd start their new life together. It was only twenty-two acres instead of over eighty. The barns and stables and other outbuildings Lindsay needed for her animals stood ready for them, and while the house needed some work, it would be a safe haven and sanctuary for them right from the beginning.

Keith could paint walls and install new appliances.

He could rip out carpet and put down newer, better flooring. Lindsay could sew and hang curtains and stain a deck and fix up the barn the way she wanted it.

They'd work hard here, and for the first time, Keith didn't get overwhelmed by that prospect.

The truck got emptied almost as fast as they'd filled it, and they all loaded up again and started the drive back to Twilight Fields to get the second half of the farm loaded and moved.

Animal feed, supplies, equipment. The chicken cages filled the back of Uncle Boone's truck, and Lindsay loaded her horses into her trailer and sent Lars on his way with them.

"You guys have been working hard," Dad said.

"I'm already abusing you," Keith said as he lifted a saddle in each hand. "The last thing we wanted was to not be ready for you."

Dad grinned at him. "I'm so proud of you, son."

"Yeah?" Keith hesitated before leaving the barn. "Why's that?"

"Because you wanted something different for your life, and you went out and found it. Worked for it."

Keith had done that, but he didn't think he'd done anything special. "Lots of people do that, Dad."

"And many more don't," he said.

Gloria came into the barn and found them standing there. "Everything okay?"

"Yeah," Dad said, turning toward her. "Just telling Keith how amazing he is."

"He's taking it well," she quipped. They chuckled together, and even Keith laughed.

He wasn't sure how, but after he put the saddles in the truck, it seemed they'd gotten everything. He and Lindsay walked through it all again, and she nodded. He texted his father to go, and they'd be behind them in her truck.

Lindsay wandered over to the fence separating the epicenter of the farm from the fields beyond, and she put her foot up on the bottom rung. He'd approached her in this same position before, in another place, at another time.

He gave her a few moments to herself, and he didn't have to wonder or ask what she was thinking or feeling. She'd told him everything while they'd been planning this move, this wedding, all of it. He'd laid on her couch and held her while she talked, while she wept, while they made their plans together.

He loved her so deeply, and he couldn't wait to continue to get to know her. He approached and eased to her side. She looked over at him, and he put his arm around her and drew her close. "This is such a beautiful place," he murmured.

"I'm going to miss it."

"Me too."

The wind tried to converse with them too, but Keith couldn't tell what it wanted to say. Lindsay said, "I'm going to love our new place."

"Me too."

"Let's go," she said. "Shadow and Sunshine are going to love the new pasture."

"They sure are." Keith placed a kiss on her forehead. "I love you, Linds."

"I love you too, Keith." She smiled at him, a measure of light and happiness chasing away the melancholy that had descended on them for a minute there.

"Let's go finish today, and then tomorrow is our day." He led her toward the truck and opened the driver's door for her. She got behind the wheel, and Keith wasn't surprised to find her wiping her eyes before she put the truck in gear.

"Here we go," she said, and the truck started down the lane and off the farm she'd bought for herself—for her fresh start—several years ago.

Keith thought about what his dad had said. He hadn't been happy at the Hammond's farm for months before he'd left. Then, he'd struck out at a different place, trying to find new people, new friends, new opportunities.

And now, he had them. A pretty woman at his side. The chance to buy into Blackhorse Bay. A mini-farm of his own.

"God is good," he said quietly.

"That He is," Lindsay said. "That He is."

CHAPTER
Twenty-Three

CORD BEHR GUIDED his beautiful wife down the aisle to where their sister-in-law sat. Jane sighed as she sat beside Molly, and she looked at Cord. "I'll save you a spot, baby."

"Thanks." He swept his lips across her silken hair, then turned and headed back the way he'd come. Keith had asked him to be a groomsman, and Cord couldn't say no to that. He didn't even want to.

He joined up with Mission and Travis, and the three of them re-entered the big administration building at Blackhorse Bay. Lindsay and Keith were getting married outside on the balcony, which had been decorated with flowers, ribbons, and other frilly things to the point of perfection.

Inside, Mission led them down a hall and into a room, where Keith stood in front of his father with his hand out. Matt Whettstein worked on his cufflink, and Cord took the cowboy hat Boone gave him.

"To keep?" he asked.

"Yep," Boone said. The idea of getting a free cowboy hat would've once made Cord weep in gratitude. Now, he still felt the same feelings, but he'd grown more used to the abundance in his life. He tried to list at least three things each evening that he was grateful for, because he never wanted to get to a place where he thought he was smarter than God. Where he thought he deserved the good things he enjoyed in his life.

He always wanted the Lord to know how incredibly grateful he was, through good times and bad. *Like Jane's pregnancy*, he thought.

She had just over three months left until she'd deliver their son, and Cord couldn't wait—and not only because he wanted to be a father so badly. But because her pregnancy had not been easy for her. She'd been sick every day, on some level, since the very beginning, and he needed her to be done with the pain. The exhaustion. The throwing up.

But every night, Cord thanked Jesus for the baby. For the fact that Jane had held onto her pregnancy, and that they got to be parents together.

Cord switched out his current cowboy hat and replaced it with the matching one he and the other groomsmen would wear as they walked down the aisle. Keith finished getting dressed; he called everyone over to him; Cord hugged him tight and said, "You're going to love being married."

"My daddy's got something to say," Keith said, ever the picture of calmness and coolness. The only time Cord had ever seen him without the classic, stoic look on his face was when he'd left the farm they'd both been working for years.

Another hard thing Cord understood. While he'd left the Hammond Family Farm for an even bigger dream—opening and running his own mechanic shop —it had still been incredibly difficult.

"Thanks for being here for Keith," Matt said. He'd been the best boss a man could have, and Cord loved him with the deepest part of his heart. "He's waited a while for this day, and it means a lot to him —and me—to see him surrounded by such good men."

Matt cleared his throat. "I never dreamed I'd be standing here with so many of you. See, I left Montana with exactly two people, and I didn't think I'd ever let anyone else in again. But the Hammonds broke down the door, and all of you walked right in like you belonged in my life and my children's lives. And you know what? You do."

He gave them all a smile that shook a little bit. Cord ducked his head, his own emotions beginning to swell. "We love you," Matt said. "We've enjoyed working with each of you over the years, and while so many of you have moved on to something else—and we find ourselves moving on too—we will always be family." His voice broke on the last word.

Cord looked up then, and Boone took a tiny step forward. "Amen to everything my brother said," Boone boomed. "Now, it's time to get this man married." He grinned and clapped his hand on Keith's shoulder.

Keith smiled too, and he hugged his father hard while Boone herded everyone into the line where they belonged. From what Cord understood, Lindsay didn't have a lot of family, so Cord had no idea what the bridesmaid situation would be.

He stood back a few people, and he moved into the hall when everyone else did. Matt and Boone headed out to the wedding, and then Cord looked over to the woman standing beside him. "I'm Cord Behr," he said.

"Alicia," she said. "I'm one of Lindsay's neighbors. Well, I was. Out by Twilight Fields."

"Sure," Cord said. "We're, uh, my wife and I bought her farm. So we'll be neighbors soon enough."

Alicia's eyes brightened and sharpened at the same time. "Oh, *you* bought it."

"Yeah," Cord said, glancing up to Travis. He knew Cord and Jane had purchased Twilight Fields from Lindsay, but Cord wasn't sure who else did. They hadn't exactly broadcasted that fact.

But Cord wanted more land than the suburban home where he and Jane had been living since their wedding last year. He wanted horses and the ability to have more dogs, and Jane said she could take care of some chickens and a couple of barn cats.

Twilight Fields would be too big for them, but Cord reasoned he didn't have to plant it all or fill every stall with horses. He could get a few dairy cows too, and then he and Jane would have fresh milk, butter, cream, and eggs.

He could still run his mechanic shop, and they'd be a little further from her family farm, but still plenty close enough to see them anytime they wanted.

"I can't wait to welcome you and your wife to the area," Alicia said.

"He owns the new mechanic shop Dave goes to," another woman said. Alicia turned and looked at the woman behind her, as did Cord. She smiled. "Right, Cord?"

"Yes, ma'am," he said. "If you're talking about Dave Kidman."

"I am." She touched her chest. "I'm Beth, his wife. He says you're the best."

"I try," Cord said, accepting the compliment far easier than he had others. Jane had been telling him to be kind and gracious, but he didn't have to be self-depreciating. He couldn't wait to tell her he'd finally done it.

"And your wife is due with your first baby soon," Beth said.

"That's right," Cord said. "It's a little freaky how much you know."

Beth laughed lightly. "That's all I know."

He grinned at her. "That's about all we are," he said. "We'll be moving in slowly over the next month or so. We don't have to be out of our place, and Jane works with me at the shop."

The line started moving then, ending their conversation. Cord offered his arm to Alicia, and she linked her hand through his elbow. They walked down the aisle with everyone watching them, and Cord's skin started to itch. He reminded himself no one really cared about him, and once they'd circled around the altar, he got to go back to his saved seat.

Jane smiled at him. "You're so handsome," she murmured as she leaned into his bicep.

"Met some of our new neighbors," he whispered back.

"Oh?" Jane's face brightened, and Cord sincerely hoped she'd be happy in a more rural environment. They'd been over it several times, and she claimed she'd be perfectly happy, because she got to talk to customers at the shop six days a week.

The shop was for him, the farm was for him, and Cord just wanted Jane to have something she loved, adored, and craved.

That's what your son will be, he told himself as the music changed. Cord twisted to find the bride waiting at the end of the aisle, and he quickly got to his feet so he could help Jane up too. She took a few extra seconds, then stood at his side with her hand resting maternally on her belly.

He loved feeling his baby move inside her, and the first time he'd been able to...Cord still got a little misty-eyed when he thought about it. Or maybe that was the way Lindsay shone like the sun, moon, and the stars as she smiled down the aisle at Keith.

He too wore a sort of silver-gold radiance that Cord had decided only brides and grooms could achieve on their wedding day.

She walked with her brother on one side of her and her daddy on the other, and Cord knew there were stories there. Probably long, dusty roads too, that all three of them had trod to get to this point.

Jane slipped her fingers into Cord's, and he squeezed. Not too long ago, this had been them, and he couldn't wait for the next fourteen months, and then the next.

Lindsay's dress looked like it had been made with white palm fronds, the tops of which had been sewn together at the waist. They hung down in layers of feathery leaves, with the top half covered in lace and jewels in equal measure.

"She's so beautiful," Jane whispered, and Cord could agree with that. She moved one step at a time, advancing fairly slowly toward Keith. When she reached the first row, she paused to kiss Gloria's cheek, and she hugged Matt. Then her daddy passed her to Keith, who took her easily into his arms and pressed his cheek against hers.

Derrick and his dad sat in the two reserved seats up front, and the whole audience retook their seats as the pastor came forward and stood behind the altar.

"What a joyous occasion which has brought us all together," the man said. He spoke with a quiet power that reached into Cord's chest and struck right against his heart. The man reminded Cord of Gray Hammond, who could whip a man with words barely spoken louder than a whisper.

He and Elise had made the drive from Coral Canyon for Keith's wedding, as Keith had grown up on their family farm and was like another son for them. Having Jane's parents here was one reason she and Cord weren't moving immediately to their new farm.

His shop was another—spring was an incredibly busy time as farmers and ranchers got their machines and equipment out of storage from the winter. Spring planting sat only a couple of weeks away, and the bigger operations had already started, taking a chance that a late freeze wouldn't strike them this year.

Cord had no plans to plant on the new farm—other than a few rows of corn and maybe some pumpkins. But those could go in the ground weeks from now and still be okay. He didn't own any horses, nor chickens, and they really only needed to move their personal belongings from the house in the gated community to the more rural one that actually sat closer to the mechanic shop.

"Ladies and gentlemen, we gather here today under this vast, open sky, surrounded by the beauty of nature, to celebrate the union of Keith Whettstein and Lindsay Lewis in marriage. As we stand here, let us be reminded of the enduring spirit of the cowboy: a spirit of courage, resilience, and integrity—a spirit that Keith and Lindsay embody in their love for one another."

Cord had never had much use for cowboys until he'd become one—and then, the cowboy way had literally saved him. Thankfully, air continued to flow through his nose and into his lungs, despite the storm of emotions inside him.

"In the journey of marriage, much like the life of a cowboy, there will be long trails, sunrises, and sunsets. There will be storms to weather and clear skies to cherish. Marriage, like the land we stand on, requires nurturing and respect. It requires the hard work of tending and the joy of harvesting."

Jane leaned her head against Cord's arm, and he reached over with his other hand and covered hers, covered their baby. She looked up at him, and so much was said without a single word being spoken.

"A bit of advice, if I may," the pastor continued. "Not just to Keith and Lindsay, but to everyone here." He spread his arms wide. "Let your love for others be as steadfast as the mountains around us. Let your commitment to each other be as enduring as the ground beneath your feet. Remember that we're all wounded in some way. We all have need of the Master Healer. We all need to be loved, cared for, and guided."

"Amen," Cord whispered. So many people hid so much beneath the surface. It was impossible to tell if they were suffering greatly or not, and he never wanted to add more to someone's plate when they were already carrying a heavy load.

"Now, let's get these two married," the pastor said. "I believe Lindsay has something to say to Keith."

"You do?" Keith asked, and that elicited a few chuckles.

She nodded, and she turned back to her brother, who handed her a single index card.

"You need a card for it?" Keith teased, and Cord found himself laughing with most of the other cowboys. Everyone who worked for Blackhorse Bay had come to this wedding, which meant a lot of cowboys and their dates.

Lindsay only smiled at him, and then she glanced at her card. "I want to face all of my challenges with you by my side, Mister Whettstein. I want us to be able to speak with honesty to each other, and I want to build a sanctuary away from the world with you."

She lowered the card. "I know it might not be easy, but I believe that with God guiding us, we can do it. I'm so glad you brought that horse to me last year, and I know God orchestrated that storm to keep you with me long enough to make you think you couldn't live without me."

"I can't," he whispered, and a few people went, "Aww."

Cord did it internally, because his dang emotions threatened to choke him again.

"I don't have a card prepared," Keith said. "I didn't know I needed to say anything."

"You don't." Lindsay handed the card back to Derrick without looking at him, and she took both of Keith's hands in hers. "I just wanted to say that."

He searched her face, the silence becoming strained. Cord started praying mighty hard that Keith would know what to do and say in this moment. It was the man's wedding day, after all, and he didn't particularly like being in the spotlight either.

"I'll just say this," Keith said. "I left the job I had before I came to Blackhorse Bay, because God told me I should. I fought Him real hard on it, too. Just ask my daddy." He grinned over to his father, then quickly sobered. "I wanted a chance to meet more people—and that really meant women."

Lindsay giggled and ducked her head.

"I wasn't having much luck there either," Keith said. "But I put my head down, and I worked. I kept praying. I didn't give up on God—and you know what? He didn't give up on me, even when I thought He had. I've learned since then that God doesn't give up on us at all, not a single one of us. You needed me that night, and I needed you in my life permanently."

He drew in a breath big enough to lift his shoulders and expand his chest. "I love you with all I have, and as I grow and change and mature, I'm sure how much I love you will too—and I can't wait for it."

Keith nodded like that was that, and both he and Lindsay turned to face the pastor. He said all the right words in the right place, ending with, "I now pronounce you husband and wife. You may kiss your bride."

Cowboys started hooting and hollering before Keith could even face Lindsay again. Cord brought his hands together as Travis whistled through his teeth. Keith pulled Lindsay to him and kissed her, and then they faced the crowd.

"Everyone kiss the one you love!" Keith yelled, and Cord wasn't going to second-guess that.

He pulled Jane into his chest, met her eye, and said in a voice that might've been considered growly to those who didn't know him, "I love you, Jane Behr."

"I love you too, Cord," she said back, just as seriously.

And then he kissed her. After all, he'd been told to, and Cord tried to follow all the rules at any wedding he attended. Fine, all the rules all the time, in anything —and kissing Jane still brought a roar of fire with it that reminded Cord just how much he loved his wife.

CHAPTER

Twenty-Four

OPAL LEANED in to see her father's spreadsheet more clearly. "I think I see what you mean, Daddy," she said when she spotted the numbers he'd put together for her. Sighing, she leaned back. "It's a lot to get started."

"It always is," he said. "But once you have things going, it won't be that bad." He took the spreadsheet away and smiled at her over the video call. "You'll be able to apply for grants for salaries, supplies, all of it. They usually want some statements, that kind of thing. But we can turn in these projections, and some companies take those."

The idea of having to hunt down grants and go through the application process made Opal feel like she'd just worked a sixteen-hour shift in the emergency room. "I don't know, Daddy."

"What don't you know, sugar?"

"This feels like a lot of work." She looked away from the computer, from the camera, from her father, who'd always guided her so effortlessly. Who had such a good business mind that thought in ways Opal's didn't.

Give her a broken bone or someone complaining of shortness of breath, and Opal knew what to do. She at least knew what questions to ask. Business…it just felt different, and Opal didn't know how to navigate the terrain.

"You can hire a foundation manager," Daddy said. "And a grant writer. That'll be all that person does— research grants, apply for them, manage the status, follow-up. All of it."

"I suppose that's true," Opal said, seeing another line for payroll inside the foundation. "And then I— what? Sit back and oversee?"

"Yes," Daddy said simply. "Being the CEO isn't about doing everything. It's about knowing what needs to be done and getting the best person or department to do that thing."

"So it's a lot of management."

"It's a lot of management," Daddy agreed. "You managed the ER, sugar. You knew which doctors were where, with which patients, and who needed what. This is going to be exactly like that, but in a non-emergent situation."

Opal met her father's eyes again. "You might be right."

"You're thinking about it as running a foundation."

"Yes," she said slowly. "That's what it is."

"No, it's running the ER," he said. "Which you did for a full year, without fail."

"But Daddy, I didn't love running the ER." A tremor ran through her chest. "Remember how I took a sabbatical and then quit? And I didn't even tell anyone I quit, because it was something I'd worked so hard for, for so long."

Opal let the humiliation run through her. She reached up and wiped her right eye, which had started to leak the tiniest of tears. "I've spent a decade of my life in the medical field," she said. "And it's all I know how to do. But what if I'm meant to do something else?"

"You're a mighty fine doctor, Opal," Daddy said quietly. "But if you don't want to do that anymore, I promise you, you're the only one who thinks the past decade of your life has been a waste."

She sniffled as she studied her hands, then the carpet in her bedroom. "You and Momma--?"

"Your mother and I are nothing but proud of you, Opal. You went after what you wanted, and you worked hard to get it. Then, when it made no sense to leave it all behind, you did exactly that, because God told you to. So you're brilliant, and hard-working, and faithful. Momma and I can't ask for anything more than that."

She nodded, taking in his compliments and

feeding on them in a way she hadn't realized she needed. "Letting you down is my biggest fear, Daddy."

"Well, you never have," he said. "Opal, sugar, look at me."

Opal swallowed and tried to get her eyes to stop leaking. She needed courage—and humility—to look her father in the eye, but after several seconds of his patient silence, she managed it.

She started crying even harder at the pure compassion and love shining in his face.

"You are my daughter, and I love you endlessly," he whispered. "There is nothing you could do that would make me *stop* loving you. So if you decide to start a medical foundation—which I think is a stellar idea and needed in that area—great. If you decide you don't want to do this, and you want to be Mike and Gerty's nanny forever, also great. They need you. They love you. There's absolutely no shame in *anything* you're doing or have done."

Opal nodded while tears streamed down her face. "Thank you, Daddy."

"Take a think about it," he said, his brilliant smile lighting his face. He'd aged steadily in the past five years, but Opal could still see his spirit. She could still see his devotion to his family, to Momma, to living his life the way God wanted him to.

"Ask God what He wants you to do." Daddy clicked around on his side of the screen. "These projections will still be here if or when you're ready for them." His eyes came back to hers. "How's the house coming?"

"Good." She drew in a breath and covered her face with her hands. She wiped her tears away and came up with a smile for her father. "They've got it framed, and it looks so big."

He chuckled. "You'll fill it right up."

"Everything I own is in California," she said. "And I certainly don't see how I can fill five bedrooms when I came from a one-bedroom apartment."

"I believe in your shopping ability," Daddy quipped.

That got Opal to giggle, and she didn't want to get going into full-blown manic laughter. So she curbed herself and said, "I love you, Daddy. Thank you so much for your advice and work on this for me."

"Oh, he loves it," Momma called from somewhere. He looked over his shoulder, and Opal grinned as her mother came into the frame.

"Hey, Momma. We're done."

"Good, because it's time for Daddy's walk."

"Oh, you're walking him these days?"

"Him and Creamie," Momma said as she sat on Daddy's lap. "If they don't get out every day, they're beasts."

"She's the beast if she doesn't get outside every day," Daddy said, smiling at Momma.

"Well, I'll let you guys take your walk. Give

Creamie a hug from me." She'd only met her parents' dog a few times, but she was a sweet little pup who kept her parents company, and that meant Opal loved her too.

The video call ended with *I love you's* and *we'll talk soon's*, and Opal finally clicked *end* and sat back from her computer. "What do I want?" she asked the empty room, the silence, herself, and God.

Could she even have what she wanted? And if not, why not?

"Because you're not married," she muttered. She really wanted to take care of babies all day, every day. Gerty's and Mike's sure. Even Jane's and Cord's. But really, what she wanted more than anything was to be a mother to her own babies.

Since she had no idea when that would happen, the medical foundation seemed like a good idea, but she wasn't sure how long she'd be able to maintain it. "It feels like a short-term solution to my issues," she muttered to herself.

Her phone buzzed and chimed, and Opal reached for it, a measure of exhaustion behind both of her eyes.

Meet Spencer Alexander Hammond! her sister-in-law had sent. Immediately following that, the cutest picture of a sleeping newborn with a shock of the Hammond dark hair arrived.

Opal fell in love with the baby immediately, and her tears reared up again. *I love him,* she sent, the first to respond on the group text. With nimble fingers, she quickly tapped over to a private string with Easton and Allison.

I know your mother is there, Alli, but let me know when she leaves, and I'll be on the first plane to Raleigh.

And Opal would be. As she got to her feet to go meet Tag for dinner, the sweetest feeling descended on her.

Being a mother is a most noble calling.

She put her hand against the doorjamb and paused, her emotions overcoming her once again. "And there are many ways to be a mother," she whispered. She could get joy from West, from Allison's new boy, from Jane's who was coming, from any number of ways to take care of others who needed her.

Satisfied she wouldn't break down in tears in front of anyone, she finally left her bedroom. Something had settled inside her with her father's words, and she entered the kitchen, ready to leave it again.

"Headed out?" Gerty asked from the stovetop. "Or are you eating with us?"

"Headed out," she said. "Where's West and Mikey?"

"Oh, Mikey got something for him." Gerty carried the eyeroll in her voice. "A baby pig. West squealed as loud as it did." She giggled then, and Opal would've liked to have seen that.

The back door opened before she could pull it in, and Carrie and Kyle started to enter. Opal fell back a step to give them room, and she said a quick hello-and-goodbye, and left.

Outside, the farm had come to life with the intro-duction of spring rain and sunshine. The grass had greened nicely; the chickens had been moved back outside; Tag and Steele had been planting alfalfa for a couple of days now.

The farm wasn't huge, but they weren't in a hurry either. Keith had approved their planting plan, and Tag had been like a little boy on Christmas morning when that had happened. Opal smiled to herself as she took in the horses in the pasture across the dirt lane, and she wandered over to the chickens.

She'd kept them alive all winter, and she took a moment to speak to each one as she went by. "I'll get your eggs tomorrow," she said. "Okay? So be good layers."

"There you are," Tag said from behind her, and Opal turned toward him.

Her whole future opened up at the sight of him, and she smiled widely. "Here I am. I'm not late, am I?"

He still wore his work gloves, so she definitely wasn't late. "Nope." He pulled his fingers out of the gloves. "I've still got one horse in the ring, and Steele's finishing up with a field right now. We've got to get everything put away for the night, and then I need to shower."

Opal eased herself into his arms, though he said, "I'm sweaty and gross."

"Mm, I like it." She kissed him, glad when he returned the gesture.

A growl emanated from his throat. "You smell fantastic."

She'd just gotten new body wash in the scent of apples and blossoms, but she didn't tell him that. Number one, he'd only broken their kiss for the few seconds it took to tell her that, and she didn't want to stop kissing him to talk.

Eventually, the warbling of the chickens entered her awareness, and Opal remembered Tag had chores to finish still. She could kiss him later.

"Your place?" she asked. "My couch? The stars?"

"Yes to all of it," he whispered. "I need at least an hour until I'm back to my place."

"I'll go get dinner," she said.

"We've got a while until the stars come out," he said. "If you don't mind. Otherwise, wait for me, and we can go together."

"I just want you, me, and the stars tonight," she murmured. She kissed him again, keeping it slow and easy and short. "I'll go get something, and we can eat in your backyard."

His eyes met hers, and Opal wasn't sure what she saw in the blazing depths of them. Something intense and strong. Something meaningful. "Tag," she whispered. "Allison had her baby, and I'll probably go to North Carolina for a few weeks."

"Okay," he whispered back, drawing her closer.

She laid her cheek against his chest. "I miss you already."

"That's because you like me so much," he said.

Opal smiled right there in the shade of the barn, her eyes closed, and the scent of Tag all around her. "I think you'll miss me too."

"Mm, I can admit to that, I guess."

"You guess?"

"I'll miss you," he said. "Because I like you so much, Opal-honey."

She smiled at the pet name. "When do you know if your like is starting to turn into love?"

"I think about the time you realize you can't live without someone or something," he said. "Like potatoes. Can't live without them, so I love 'em."

Opal burst out laughing, and with Tag's voice joining hers, they made a great harmony and melody. She hung onto his shoulders and looked at him. "I think I'm getting close with you, cowboy."

That intensity came roaring back into his expression, and Opal realized what it was now: love, desire, hope.

"Can't live without me, huh?"

"Maybe," she said coyly. She pushed him back a step. "Now, go finish your chores so we can have a date tonight at a decent hour."

"You're the one who started kissing me," he said. "For the record."

"I got it on the official record," she said, and he

chuckled as he walked away, toward the back corner of the barn and around it, where the walking circles for equines were.

Opal sighed into the golden evening, as this was her perfect hour. She loved everything about a Colorado springtime in the evening, when the sun was still up and casting it's treasure over the mountains.

Her phone chimed, and she checked it. Allison had said, *My mom will be here until May 5. You're welcome any time after that.*

Great, Opal said. *I'll be there on the sixth.*

And now she had to go get dinner and book a flight, so she didn't linger next to the chicken coop any longer. After all, she had a magical star-watching date to get set up with a man she might-possibly almost already be in love with.

CHAPTER
Twenty-Five

TAG SHOWERED, shaved, and dressed while thinking about Opal and what she'd said. *When do you know if your like is starting to turn into love?*

He'd made a joke about it, but he couldn't stop thinking about it. He'd grown very fond of Opal. Did that mean he loved her?

He'd started envisioning a future with her, that was for certain. The building of her house frustrated him as much as it excited her. She'd been working on her foundation more and more too, and he knew she'd had a call with her daddy this evening to go over numbers. Numbers for what, he didn't know.

Tag was just a simple cowboy, after all. He knew how to make sure he had enough money in his bank account for what he had to pay for, and that was about it.

When Opal still hadn't arrived with dinner, he

went into the spare bedroom to make sure it was ready for the twins. They'd be here in a couple-three weeks, and they were staying with him. He'd cleared it with Gerty and Steele to have the whole weekend off, and the last person he needed to prep for Flint and Sawyer's arrival was Opal.

He needed to talk to her about a lot of things, actually. He'd still never had that "serious conversation," and not because she hadn't asked. But because he hadn't been able to find the words yet.

He'd been hoping and praying and working to get himself to a place where he felt like he stood on even ground with Opal, and he figured if he could get that done, he wouldn't need to bring anything up with her. "What's she gonna do about it anyway?" he muttered to himself.

She couldn't change who she was, or how much money her family had. He didn't even want her to. No, what he wanted to change was himself.

"Knock, knock," she called from out in the main part of the cabin, and Tag turned away from the made-and-ready beds in the spare bedroom. He kept a computer in here too, but he hardly used it for much more than personal banking a couple of times each month. Everything else he could do from his phone.

"Coming," he called. "C'mon in, honey-love."

Boots darted into the room, pure doggy happiness on his face. He ran around Tag's legs and right back out the door, clearly saying, *Come on! Opal's here!*

Tag chuckled and said, "I know, buddy." He went down the hall and found Opal peeling back the lid on a long, aluminum foil container that looked like it could feed a dozen people.

"Whatcha got there?" he asked as the first tang of barbecue sauce hit his nose.

"Ribs, potato salad, mashed potatoes, cole slaw, and cornbread." Opal looked up, clearly pleased with herself. "With honey butter."

"Mm." Tag moved into the kitchen and wrapped both arms around her. "And you."

"And me," she said, smiling up at him. "Purple couch is out back, with some blankets, though it's not too cold yet."

"We'll need 'em," he said. "Sun's down, and that means the temp's falling fast." He refrained from looking at the thermometer he'd hung just outside the window above the sink. He liked knowing what he was going into before he did it, especially in the winter.

"Fields are done for the summer," he said. "Planted and ready to go."

"That's great, Taggart."

He warmed with the use of his full name. Opal wasn't volunteering a lot of info right now, and she seemed more reserved than usual. Tag quickly got down a pair of plates and grabbed out some forks.

"You want to eat outside?"

"Yes," she said simply, taking a plate from him.

They took their fill, and Opal grabbed a bottle of peach sweet tea before she went outside. He followed with a bottle of pink lemonade, thrilled to see that blow-up purple couch.

He'd had no idea what Opal would do with it when he'd bought it, but she'd literally been carrying it everywhere, plopping it down, and lying on it. Now, it made him smile as she settled onto one end of it and balanced her plate on the other side while she pulled a blanket over her legs.

Tag waited until she got settled, and then he sat down too. She took his plate; he pulled the blanket over; she handed his plate back to him. The way they helped one another, moved in tandem, wasn't lost on Tag. For maybe the first time, he felt part of a real couple—one-half of a whole that knew the other person so well, they could choregraph their movements, predict their thoughts, be one together.

"Should be real clear tonight," he said as he scooped up a bite of potato salad. "Lots of stars."

"I hope so," she said. "I love the stars."

As she'd told him previously, and why he'd planned this date specifically for this night. It was a new moon, which meant there'd be no light pollution from anything on the ground or in the sky. It would be dark, dark, dark if they got too far from the cabin or farm, and the stars would be the only thing giving light to the earth.

"Allison had her baby," Opal said. "This morning. They named him Spencer."

Tag looked over to her, the pureness of her voice striking against his heartstrings and making them vibrate. "That's great news."

"Her mom's there," she said. "Or will be tomorrow. I think they're coming from Alabama or something like that."

"Georgia," he said gently. "I talked to her at Christmas, and her family is in Georgia."

"Ah, Georgia." Opal gave him a fast smile. "I suppose you know every family from Alabama, is that it?"

He chuckled and shook his head. "No, honey, I sure don't."

"Oh, don't do that sexy drawl on me."

"You like it," he shot back. "So when are you going to see the baby?"

"Who says I'm going to go? It's clear across the country."

"Right," he said. "So when are you going?"

"Her mom's going to be there for a couple of weeks," she said casually. "So I'll go after that."

"Mm." Tag didn't mention his birthday, though he'd told the twins they could meet Opal. He wasn't going to change her plans to go see her new nephew. He'd seen her with one of those already, and no man should stand in Opal Hammond's way when it came to her and babies.

"How was your call with your Daddy?" he asked.

"It was…good." Opal blew out her breath. "I'm not sure I got the answers I wanted, but I got some answers."

"That's good then."

"Yeah," she said. She fell silent again, and Tag wasn't sure if he should press her for more information about the answers she'd gotten or not. She sometimes just told him, talking and talking until she realized she'd started repeating herself.

He didn't mind that either, because he liked learning what was in her head, what was important to her, what she wanted in her life.

They finished eating, and Tag simply dropped his plate to the grass beside the couch, where Boots happily trotted over and started licking it.

"Come lay with me, honey," he whispered, and Opal looked away from the nearly dark sky. She shifted, letting the blow-up couch slide her into his side. He lifted his left leg up onto the couch. That allowed him to settle into the very corner of the couch, and Opal laid against his chest while he adjusted the blanket over both of them.

He drew in a deep breath of her appley skin and hair, closed his eyes, and exhaled it all out. The dirtiness of the day, the busyness of planting, the worry about him and Opal. It all just left, leaving him open for something better to come into his mind and heart.

"I'm not sure about the foundation now," Opal said.

"Oh?"

"It feels like a short-term solution to me wanting to feel important," she said. "I'm not sure I want to run it long-term."

"Mm." Tag didn't know what to say, and it felt like Opal just needed a sounding board. So he'd let her talk, and he wouldn't offer advice unless she asked him a question. "You're important to me," he murmured.

She snuggled closer. "I know, Taggart."

"Is it not enough?"

She froze, every muscle tensed against him. "What do you mean?"

"Is being important to me not enough for you?" he asked. "I know you're used to being the head honcho, the one calling all the shots. You're used to being important in important ways, to important things."

She didn't say anything for a moment, and Tag wished he'd kept his big mouth shut. "And now I'm here," she said.

"And you're important here too," he said. "To Gerty and Mike. To that cute baby you care for every day. To me."

She nodded against his chest. "Yes, I know."

He wanted to ask—*so is it not enough*? again, but he willed his voice to stay dormant.

"There are other ways to make a difference without

starting a foundation and running a free medical clinic."

"I agree," he said. "It would be amazing to be sure, but you're right. There are other ways to make a difference."

Another bout of silence covered them. Then Opal said, "The stars are out, sweetheart. No more talking," to which he murmured, "No problem, my honey-love."

———

"DING-DONG!" someone yelled, and Tag spun from the kitchen sink where he'd been washing his hands.

Flint and Sawyer practically tripped over one another as they entered his cabin, and all three of them laughed as they congregated at the end of the couch.

"You made it," Tag said.

"We made it," Flint agreed. "Barely. Sawyer's forgotten how to use the GPS."

"I have not," Sawyer argued over the top of him. "It was so wonky in that rental."

"You said you'd text when you landed," Tag said.

"We did, bro," Flint said as he started glancing around.

"Maybe I was out in the field still," Tag said, trying to remember where he'd been about ninety minutes ago, when his brothers had surely landed.

"I don't smell dinner," Sawyer said.

"That's because it's lunchtime." Flint elbowed his brother. "You ate on the plane besides."

"I'm hungry," Sawyer complained, and since he'd been born second and the smaller of the twins, he often teased Flint about taking all his nutrients in the womb.

"Let's go to lunch," Tag said. "There's a great burger place only about twenty minutes away."

"You're done with work?" Flint asked.

"Yep, done for the whole weekend." Tag grinned at them. "So we can go hiking or camping. We can go into the city. Whatever you want."

"Where's Opal?" Sawyer actually looked down the hallway, like Tag would be hiding her back there.

His stomach cinched. "Oh, uh, she had to go out of town."

"Out of town?" Flint asked as Sawyer said, "Dude, did you invent a girlfriend?"

"No." Tag shot his youngest brother a glare. "She's real. Her brother had a baby."

"Dude, boys don't have babies." Sawyer grinned at him like he was the funniest man alive.

Tag rolled his eyes, though everything with the twins was a party. "Her brother's wife had a baby, and Opal went to help for a couple of weeks."

"A couple of weeks?" Sawyer asked. "That's a long time."

So Tag didn't mention that the little boy was

almost a month old now. "She loves babies," was all he said. "She'll be back next week. Thursday."

"Convenient," Flint said.

"Do you want to see a picture?" Tag glared at him and reached for his phone on the counter.

"Yes," Flint said with a nod. "Yes, we want to see a picture."

"And not an old one, dude. Have her text you one right now." They both crowded into Tag, and he wanted to shove them back.

Instead, he let their travel stench and their hot breath waft over him while he texted Opal. *Hey, honey. My brothers are here, and they think you don't exist. Can you send me a picture real quick?*

Then, realizing how pathetic and maybe even creepy that sounded, his thumbs flew to get a second message sent. *This isn't creepy or a joke. The twins came for my birthday, and I originally told them they could meet you, but obviously they can't.*

"Let's take a selfie," he said. "Stay where you are." Because they already hovered around him, all Tag had to do was reach out with his phone and snap the photo.

See? He attached the photo to the text and sent it too. *They're waiting right on top of me, just so you know.*

Not that she'd send a scandalous picture, but the message did get Flint to fall back a pace. Then two. "Nice place," he said.

Sawyer continued to watch Tag's phone, and Tag

rolled his eyes again and handed it to his brother. "She's real, you idiot." Sawyer only grinned at him, then went back to the phone.

"It's not the biggest, nicest place," Tag said. "But I like it. It's home."

Flint nodded, his smile bright and bold as he faced Tag. "You look good, brother. Happy birthday."

"Tomorrow," Tag said. "My birthday's tomorrow."

Flint grabbed him in a hug. "I know when your birthday is, Taggart." He pounded him on the back. "Colorado is nice. Cooler. Big mountains."

"Yeah," Tag said. "I like it here."

"So you're going to stay?" Sawyer asked, finally able to tear himself from the messages, which Opal still had not answered.

"Yeah," Tag said slowly. "I don't see any reason why I'd leave. They pay me well here. It's a good-sized farm for us to run. I love Gerty and Mike."

"And Opal," Sawyer teased.

Tag simply looked at him, not denying it yet not confirming anything either. Sawyer sobered, his eyes going wide. "Oh, boy. Are you in love with her, Tag?"

"Could be," Tag said, seeing no reason to deny it. "She's building a house here. I'm here, and I want to stay. We've been together about six months now. Give or take. I've known her for longer than that. It's...it's a real thing, guys."

The twins both stared at him, and Tag swore it was

the first time either of them had ever seen him as an adult. A real, grown man.

"I told you this was serious," Flint said. "I just had a feeling."

"Then you need to get serious about Sarah," Sawyer said. "You're so flirty with her."

"*I'm* flirty with her?" Flint scoffed. "You haven't had a second date in a decade, Sawyer."

Tag grinned as the twins bickered back and forth about their own love lives. Or the lack thereof. His phone buzzed on the counter, and he took the few steps to it. He didn't interrupt the twinly conversation in the living room, but instead, stepped outside to take Opal's call.

"Hey, honey," he drawled.

"It's your birthday?" she demanded. "When? Today?"

Pure adrenaline shot through his veins, making his vision go white for a moment. He forgot where he stood, and why there were voices behind him in his cabin.

"Tag?" a woman asked, and he looked at the phone in his hand. "Taggart?"

Oh, Opal was *not* happy, and the way she said his full name now was *not* a term of endearment.

CHAPTER
Twenty-Six

OPAL WALKED across her brother's deck, the view from this place absolutely magical. And she'd thought the mountains couldn't be beat. Well, the beach might do it.

She wondered if Tag was ever going to say anything.

She wondered if she could just go back inside and take baby Spencer out of his swing and hug him close to get this pinching in her chest to subside.

"I'm going to hang up," she said.

"Don't hang up," Tag growled.

"Then say something."

"It's my birthday tomorrow," he said.

Pure defeat trampled through Opal. "Why—Why didn't you tell me?"

"You knew it was in May," he said quietly.

"You—I…did."

"You were so excited about Spencer," Tag said. "And I'm what? Going to make you stay here on this muddy farm to celebrate with me?" She could just see him shaking his head. "My brothers were already planning to come. It's fine."

"You didn't tell me they were coming."

"I didn't see the point," he said.

"Tag."

"Opal, the twins are here, and I don't want to discuss this with you over the phone."

Her eyebrows went up, but part of her liked that he wasn't just lying down on this. He'd given her whatever she wanted as they'd gotten to know one another, and she found him strong yet soft at the same time. She supposed there was a time for everything—for him to take the lead and for him to let her have the reins.

"Okay," she said, hating how haughty her voice came out. "But I want you to tell me everything when we sit down to talk. You said you had something serious to talk to me about, and you've said nothing of it."

"Maybe I don't need to say anything now," he said. "Maybe I worked through things on my own."

Opal didn't like that, but she didn't know what to say. Her heart wailed quietly, and she decided to let her true thoughts out. "I don't want you to work through it on your own. We're together, and I want us to work through things together."

"You don't even know what it was."

Frustration filled her. "Exactly."

"Tag," someone said on his end of the line, and he said, "Yeah, give me another sec."

Opal didn't want to keep him from his brothers. She knew he didn't get to see them very often. "What are you doing for your birthday?" she asked, her voice a touch higher than normal.

"We haven't decided yet," Tag said coolly. "We might go hiking or camping. Something. It'll be— totally lame without you, Opal."

"Will you tell me about the serious thing even if you've already solved it?"

He heaved a sigh but said, "If you want me to."

"I do," she said.

"Then we'll talk next Friday," he said. "When we go out as planned."

Opal hated having hard conversations, but she reminded herself that she didn't have to call in a doctor and tell them he wasn't good enough to stay in the ER. Or reprimand someone for a mistake that could've cost someone's life.

"I haven't gotten my picture of you and that baby today," Tag said, a flirty undercurrent in his gruff voice.

Opal's heartbeat pulsed. "I'll send you one," she said. "To show your brothers."

"Opal-honey," he said. "I miss you like crazy."

And there was that softness she loved. "See you

soon, Taggart." She ended the call, and she sighed as her hand dropped back to her side, taking her phone with her. The breeze played with her hair, and she loved the scent of the sea and the flowers perfuming the air here.

The sliding door opened, and Opal turned to see who'd come outside. Allison stood there as Violet toddled by, and she held up an apple. Opal smiled at the little girl. "You hungry, sweetheart?"

"Op-ple," Violet said. "Ap-ple."

She took it from the little girl. "Yes," she said. "I'll cut it up for you." She looked at Allison and put the best smile she could on her face.

"Everything okay?" Alli asked.

Opal remembered the way she'd gasped, scoffed, and then practically thrown Spencer to her before she'd stormed outside to call Tag. "Yes," she said anyway. "I just needed to make a call really quick." She smiled at Violet. "Who's ready for lunch?"

She was very good at stuffing away her emotions until she could deal with them. In the ER, she focused on the job and didn't let anything distract her. She could do the same here, and then she'd text and call Tag that evening, when she had more time to examine how she felt and what she hoped to achieve with him.

———

A COUPLE OF HOURS LATER, she smiled at Alli as she went down the hall toward the master. "Time for naps, Missy," she said to Violet. "Brother and Mama are napping. We are too."

Violet said something in her two-year-old voice, but Opal didn't catch it. She sat with Spencer in the living room, gently pushing herself back and forth with her toe, providing just enough movement to lull herself to sleep. Well, any other day she'd been here, she would've fallen asleep.

This afternoon, Opal's mind zigged and zagged from one topic to another.

Should she change her flight and go home early?

And why? So she could confront Tag earlier? What would she even say?

She thought about the little notebook he wrote in, and she wondered if he'd ever said something about her. And if so, what? Bad things? Good? The innermost workings of his mind?

She'd asked him about the notebook in the past, and he'd said he put all kinds of things in it. "Things I'm thinking about, lists of groceries, reminders to myself."

"Notes from church," she'd said, because that was when she'd seen him writing in it.

"Yes," he'd said, and she could still see the sly look on his face. "You spied on me."

She'd laughed and fallen into his arms. "You

pulled it out right in front of me. That can't be considered spying."

Now, she wanted to see what he wrote in that little notebook, and she wanted to see anything he may have written about her. "What could he be working through?" she whispered to Spencer, and the precious three-week-old didn't so much as stir.

Opal leaned over and touched her lips to the baby's forehead and whispered, "I think I'm going to go home earlier, Spencer. I'll miss you so much."

Gerty had been taking West out on the farm with her, and Mike had taken a few days off work to help with his son. Gerty's mom had come one day, Opal knew that, and she suddenly wanted to get back to Ivory Peaks.

She wanted to do that spying Tag had accused her of, and she wanted to do it now. She wanted to stand in his cabin and look around, just to absorb his space and see what she could feel coming from him.

"Is he going to break up with me?" she whispered, her chest suddenly collapsing in on itself. "Why would he?" She let the silence into her mind and heart then, trying to hear something, anything, from God.

"I need to know what I'm walking into," she whispered. "Please, Jesus, prepare me fully to return to Colorado." She closed her eyes and continued to rock. Other days, she'd have fallen asleep by now, pure bliss and happiness filling her.

Tag's one text had changed so much, and Opal's

chin wobbled a little bit as she fought against her emotions. "He's not going to break up with you," she told herself. Her memories of their relationship were all so good, with star-filled nights, and lying together on that purple couch, and the kisses they'd shared.

He'd said he had something serious to talk to her about, but she hadn't dwelt on it too much. She trusted Tag to talk to her, tell her what bothered him and what didn't, and—

"It's your money," she whispered, the pure magic of Valentine's Day running through her mind. So much made sense then, and Opal knew her thought about her money was right. Tag had mentioned it then, and Opal could see the price tag of her dress. Anyone with eyes could've seen it, even without knowing the numbers, and Tag wasn't a stupid man.

Oh, and she wanted a few acres of her brother's land? No problem. Let me write you a check. Oh, and hire a general contractor and start building within the week.

Yes, money could open doors and do things for people, and Opal hadn't held back from using its power. Tag had seen all of that, and she'd bet everything she had that he'd written something about her money—and his…lack of money?—in his notebook.

"He's not poor," Opal whispered to herself, and it didn't matter to her if he was. But her money probably scared him. "Maybe," she said. She wasn't exactly sure what he felt about it, because he hadn't said so.

What had he said on Valentine's Day? *I'm worried I'm not enough to hold your attention.*

As if she needed him to be more than who he was. "Maybe that's it," she mused. No matter what, it was something, or he wouldn't have said he'd worked through everything on his own.

A fact and a statement she hated. She didn't want him suffering on his own, trying to find exits he maybe didn't need to find. "I wish I'd pressed the issue with him," she muttered.

Or maybe she didn't. Tag hadn't been super keen to let her lecture him or back him into a corner today. Frustration and loneliness filled her, and Opal honestly didn't know what to do. She wanted to call Tag again, but she didn't want to interrupt his time with his brothers.

"Time you didn't even know he needed." She heard the bitterness in her own voice, and she felt the way her throat closed in around her windpipe.

Then, as if God had flipped on a light switch, her thoughts changed. She shifted baby Spencer a little bit so she could reach her phone, and then she started texting with one hand. She had people she could ask about this. Her momma. Molly, who'd married a billionaire, and Cord who had too.

"Jane," she whispered. Surely a man marrying a female billionaire would be harder than a woman doing it, and the revelations coming to Opal made her heartbeat quake with every pulse. She quickly sent

Jane quite a blunt text, hoping her cousin was on her phone right this moment.

"Please don't let my money be the reason Tag and I can't be together," she prayed. "Dear God, I will give up every penny to be with him. Help me to know what to say, or not say, and to let him have the voice he wants to have."

Jane responded to her question about whether Cord had had an issue with her money with the worst answer possible: *It was a thing, yes. Why? Is Tag upset?*

Opal wasn't sure if Tag was upset, and that was worse than knowing the answer to her cousin's question. But in an attempt for her to be more prepared for the conversation, she texted Jane back. *I don't know if he's upset or not. But it's a conversation we need to have. How did you handle it with Cord?*

And then she kept praying that when she finally got to Tag, she'd know what to say and what not to say, what to do and what not to do. Because she'd put off meeting and dating a man like him for far too long, and she didn't want to lose him. She couldn't add him —and the family she wanted—to her list of things she'd lost or delayed because of her previous life choices.

She simply couldn't.

CHAPTER
Twenty-Seven

MISSION REDBAY LEANED against a fence post a safe distance from the homestead, watching. He chewed his spearmint gum, an addiction better than others he'd had in the past, and wondered what ran through Opal Hammond's pretty little head.

"Can't think like that," he muttered to himself. She'd been dating another cowboy for half a year now, and Mission honestly expected to hear news of a proposal, engagement, and another wedding any day now.

He'd had a Rocky-Mountain-sized crush on the gorgeous brunette since the day he'd met her. He'd never gone to Coral Canyon with the Hammonds, but Opal and her family had come to Ivory Peaks and the Hammond Family Farm plenty.

Okay, maybe not *plenty*, but enough for Mission to seriously entertain the idea of going out with Opal.

But she'd flit in, flirt, and fly back to her big-wig doctor job in Burbank, and Mission rarely acted on his opportunities.

That fact made his eyebrows draw down—as did the way Molly Hammond met Opal on the porch of the homestead with a bottle of Diet Coke, a hug, and the hand gesture toward the table and chairs on the end closest to Mission.

Great. That meant he'd spend the rest of his break watching. Wondering what might've been had he been brave enough to make a real move in his relationship with Opal. Wishing she wasn't currently dating Taggart Crow.

Watching, wondering, wishing. Mission had wasted so much of his life doing those things.

Since Cord—a man Mission's age—had found his happily-ever-after with Jane, Mission had been trying to get outside the three Ws. He'd been out with more women in the past year than the previous decade, and no one seemed to fit.

No one from church. No one from town. No one on either of the dating apps he'd joined.

"Maybe you're too picky," he mused under his breath. Travis had originally asked him that, and Mission had denied it immediately. But would it kill him to go out with a blonde-haired woman?

One longing look at Opal said *yes*. Screamed it, actually. He much preferred brunettes, and he'd spend a lifetime telling himself that wasn't a crime.

Molly and Opal sat far enough away that Mission couldn't overhear them. He wouldn't want to know what they were talking about anyway, and he could guess better than most.

After all, he'd heard Opal was building a house out at Gerty and Mike's. He'd heard she was making this area her permanent home. He'd heard she and Tag were "getting serious," whatever that meant. And he'd heard all of those things simply by keeping his head down and doing his job here on the farm.

It helped that he ate dinner with Boone Whettstein and his family at least three times a week. Boone was Gerty's daddy, and he knew everything happening at her farm.

Mission almost wished he *didn't* know.

Opal didn't look happy, which also made Mission's heartbeat throb through his veins strangely. He lifted his bottle of water to his mouth in a slow, calculated way, so as to not draw any attention to himself. Nothing more than the waving of the tree branches in the slight wind on the farm today.

His phone buzzed in his back pocket, but his lunch break couldn't be over yet. Things on the farm definitely varied, something Mission enjoyed, so he pulled his device out, praying, "I just want to stay here a bit longer, Lord."

He wasn't entertaining inappropriate thoughts about Opal. He just liked looking at her so much, and apparently, he liked torturing himself with thoughts of his own stupidity in not asking her out over fifteen months ago, when she'd first come to Ivory Peaks.

His phone bore a message not from Matt or Boone, but from Rachelle, a gorgeous woman he'd met, believe it or not, at the bank a couple of weeks ago.

She'd been waiting to see the same loan officer as Mission, and he'd flirted successfully enough to get her number. They'd exchanged a few texts, but nothing too substantial. He hadn't officially asked her out yet, and everything inside him told him to get the job done before she started dating someone almost exactly like him.

Especially with Rachelle's message. *Hey, cowboy.*

Oh, so flirty, and Mission smiled at his device.

I've been thinking about you.

Always nice to hear, Mission thought.

And I won a couple of tickets to a ballet in the city. It comes with dinner at The Margarita, and I want to go with you. Any chance cowboys like you can suffer through a ballet if a steak dinner is attached?

Mission started typing quickly, not even considering his options, the way he usually did. *My sister danced ballet growing up*, he said. *I've seen The Nutcracker and other productions en pointe more times than I care to admit.*

He sent that one and kept on going. *So tell me when it is, and if I can get off the farm at all, I'd love to go with you.*

Rachelle sent a thumbs-up emoji and followed that with, *It's not until next month.*

Maybe we should go out before then, Mission sent. *Restaurants around here aren't The Margarita, but they keep a man alive from time to time.*

I'd love to, Rachelle said, and a glow started in Mission's chest.

Great, he said. *Are you available this weekend?* It was only Tuesday, and Mission could go earlier, as he didn't work in the evenings, usually. The farm had been planted, and now they were dealing with fence repair, machinery issues, and rebuilding the decks on a few of the cabins in the community where Mission lived.

I sure am, Rachelle said. *Friday or Saturday.*

Let's do Friday, he said. *Tell me what you like, and I'll get a reservation.*

About the only thing I don't like is sushi, she said. Mission half-scoffed and half-laughed.

"Good," he typed as he spoke. "Sushi shouldn't be consumed this far inland, and I'd be worried if you loved it."

He continued flirting with Rachelle until he had to get back to work, and then he returned his attention to the porch at the homestead. Opal and Molly had vacated it at some point, and Mission lamented the fact that he hadn't been able to see Opal leave. Why, he wasn't sure. He had zero chance with her, and he needed to get past this crush. Quickly.

"And you've got a date with someone else," he told himself. "And you're excited about it." And he was. So he pushed away from the fence post, turned over to the stables, and went to get the horses ready for their walking and riding lessons.

CHAPTER
Twenty-Eight

TAG ENTERED the barn and found Steele taking Rooster out of the stall. "Gonna take him today?"

"He's been good out in the fields," Steele said. "So yeah." He flashed a smile at Tag and added, "Oh, and Gerty's having a welcome-home dinner for Opal tonight."

Tag, who'd started to move toward the tack room so he could get out the other horses who needed to be worked today, stopped completely. "What? It's Tuesday, and Opal's not back until Thursday."

"She's coming in early," Steele said. "I guess. I don't know. That's just what Gerty said this morning when I was at the farmhouse." He took Rooster down the aisle and out the door, all while Tag stood stockstill, trying to understand what he'd heard.

And who he'd heard it from. "Steele," he scoffed.

"I have to hear about my girlfriend's early return to town from *Steele*." Jealousy and anger combined inside him in a way he didn't enjoy and didn't want. He pulled out his notebook and flipped to his spot in it.

Opal came home early without telling me. This upsets me, and I'm not sure why.

I know she doesn't like Steele, and it's not like she told him.

But it still hurts to find out from him, as if he's more important than me.

He looked up from his scribbling, glad he had this outlet to bleed out the negative emotions when he felt them.

Does she think I won't find out?

Does she think I'm going to appreciate being the last to know?

What does she have planned?

The last question in black pen and Tag's handwriting stared back at him, demanding an answer. Opal was smart and savvy, rich and powerful. She could have almost anything she wanted, and almost anything planned too. Simply being in another state wouldn't stop her.

"You spoke your mind with her last week," he reminded himself. "You can do the same thing when you see her." He didn't need to be the one in charge all the time, but he wanted his feelings to matter too. He wanted to be her equal in every way, and while that might never happen, he wanted *her* to know that he had merit too.

He flipped back several pages and started reading through some of his lists, his thoughts, his demons. Yes, he'd talked about Opal in here, and he didn't feel bad about it. He wasn't a robot, and his feelings *were* valid.

For a moment, he flashed back to his relationship with Talina, and how he'd bent over backward and done everything she'd told him, everything she wanted, every single thing in his life had been dictated by her. He didn't want a relationship like that.

He went back to his empty pages and started writing again. *My feelings matter too. I want a relation-ship of give and take.*

Compromise is fine, as long as I have a voice.

As long as I don't disappear.

Tag paused, then flipped the notebook closed. "I don't want to disappear again," he said. He'd done that once, and it wasn't the life or type of relationship he wanted to have. It had taken him months to come back to himself, to realize his worth, and to remember he was a valued human being, a son of the Almighty God, and worthy of being recognized as such.

"I won't go back to anyone like Talina," he told himself firmly, and then he tucked his notebook away and got to work.

About noon, he got a text from Opal that said, *I just landed in Denver, and I'll be back on the farm tonight. I know you have your leatherworking class tonight, but maybe we can move our date up to tomorrow night?*

Tag read and re-read the text, wondering how aggressive to be. He'd calmed down since that morning, since he'd written out his feelings and then put in a good half-day of work.

I can skip my class, he said.

No, it's okay, Opal said. *I'm meeting Molly and Jane for a late lunch, and Gerty's doing a party tonight. It's dumb, but I couldn't say no.*

Tomorrow is fine then, he said.

Thank you, Tag, Opal said, and he wasn't sure what to do with her gratitude.

He'd been planning to take her out on Thursday when she was supposed to originally return, and he quickly tapped to get to the text confirmation of his reservation. He opened the link and found the option to modify the reservation.

"Please let them have time tomorrow," he said aloud, wondering who wouldn't have space for two on a Wednesday night. Still, he needed all the pieces to be in place if he was to open his soul and let Opal see all the darkest parts of himself.

Thankfully, the restaurant had space tomorrow night, and he changed the reservation with a few taps of his fingertips. He texted Opal to let her know what time and where, because it influenced what she wore when they went out.

Thank you, she said again. *I'll see you tomorrow.*

He suddenly wanted to call her, to make sure she knew everything between them was fine, that nothing had changed. "But that's just your side," he said. "You didn't tell her about your birthday, and *she* thinks something about that."

Regret laced through him then, and he pulled out the notebook again. After writing down a few thoughts, he put it away and went back to the baler in front of him. He could fix a few things, but this might need to be taken in.

Cord Behr would know exactly what to do to get it to work, and it wasn't like Gerty couldn't afford to keep her machines in tip-top shape. Not only that, but Cord had married Opal's cousin, and he might know a thing or two about how it felt to marry such a beautiful, powerful, rich woman.

His decision made, Tag pulled out his phone and dialed the mechanic shop, praying that Jane had already left for her lunch with Opal. Sure enough, Cord answered with, "Behr's." He almost barked it, and somehow that made Tag smile.

"Hey, Cord," he said, immediately wondering how to turn the conversation toward personal things. He'd eaten plenty of meals with this man, enjoyed some holidays with him, and surely Tag could ask him a few questions. "It's Tag out at Gerty's place, and I've got a baler that I can't get to hold the twine right."

"I can look at it," he said. "When can you bring it in?"

"Whenever," Tag said. "Today, even."

"I've got a truck here this afternoon I have to get through," he said. "But yeah, bring it by."

"Great," Tag said. "Have you had lunch? I could bring you something to eat."

"I'm not going to say no to lunch," he said. "We packed food from home, but it wasn't my favorite last night, so I won't feel bad if I don't eat it."

Tag chuckled. "Fair enough. Steak sandwich from Mo's?"

"All day long," Cord said with a smile in his voice now. "And if you tell my wife I said I didn't want to eat her leftovers, I will deny it until the day I die."

Tag burst out laughing then, and he promised Cord he wouldn't say a word to Jane about the leftovers. Then he backed his truck up to the baler, hooked it up, and headed to the shop, praying he'd get answers to more than one question this afternoon.

———

"HOWDY, TAG." Cord stuck out his hand and Tag put his in it to shake. "Baler problems?"

"It's not like we need it right this second, but I've been goin' through things," he said, feeling a little foolish now that he'd arrived at the technician shop. He told himself Cord didn't know why he'd really come, and perhaps he just wanted lunch with another human being—and to get some expert eyes on the baler.

He lifted the white paper bag. "Sandwiches here."

Cord finished drying his hands, which he'd obviously just washed. "Let's eat first. Sound okay?"

"Sure," Tag said, letting his eyes sweep the bays where Cord worked. "You're done with the truck?"

"Found the problem right after you called," he said. "I sometimes just need to step away, and the answers come." He flashed another rare smile in Tag's direction. "We can eat in the office. It's the cleanest place."

Tag followed Cord into the smaller space, and he took the chair opposite the desk while Cord sank into the one behind it with a sigh. "Been busy lately."

"I can't even imagine," Tag said. "Planting, fertilizing, everyone getting things out from last year." He opened the bag and pulled out the first sandwich. It was labeled with a four, which was his.

"Mm, yep." Cord took the second sandwich Tag produced from the bag. "Thanks, Tag."

He smiled, but it felt so tight across his mouth. He ducked his head more than he needed to in order to focus on unwrapping his turkey, provolone, and avocado sandwich, sure Cord would be able to read him like an open book.

He suddenly felt like he didn't know Cord at all. He was at least a decade older than Tag, and he never called attention to himself at meals and parties. He spoke and participated, obviously, but he wasn't the life of the party.

Sometimes, Tag had gotten the feeling Cord would rather be at home than out, but he'd cleaned up and come all the same. Tag could definitely relate to that, and he dared to look up at the man as he lifted his first half-sandwich.

"What's on your mind?" Cord asked. He'd already bitten into his gravy-laden steak sandwich, and he took another bite while watching Tag.

Thankfully, Tag had already put his sandwich in motion, so he took a bite as he shook his head slightly. Cord picked up a napkin from the thick stack of them in the middle of the table and wiped his face.

They both ate, the silence about to burst Tag at the seams. He finally swallowed all the meat and cheese, and he wished he'd gotten drinks.

"I've got Coke and water," Cord said. "Maybe some ginger ale in there, leftover from when Jane was sick."

"Coke would be great," Tag said. He took the can from Cord, who wasn't going to ask Tag again. He could simply see that in the man's expression. Still, he popped the top on the Coke and took a fizzy gulp of it.

As he exhaled, he decided he'd come here to have this conversation. It wasn't going to be the first hard one he'd had, and it certainly wouldn't be the last. Especially with the way his date with Opal loomed on the horizon.

"Okay, fine," he said. "I'm feeling a little...I don't even know how to say it."

"Is this a farm thing?" Cord asked. "A life thing? You're unsettled working for someone else? Want a place of your own?" He ducked his head and lifted his sandwich. "Or an Opal thing?"

"Opal," scraped out of Tag's throat. "Or maybe a life thing. Or a farm thing. Maybe it's all wrapped together." He sighed and rolled his neck from side to side. "It feels knotted. Complicated."

Cord had taken another bite of his lunch, and he nodded in an overly enunciated way, obviously his nonverbal way of saying, *Go on. Keep talking.*

"She's just so—so perfect," Tag said like that was a bad thing to be. "She's smart. She has all this money, and she's talking of starting a foundation that'll fund a non-profit clinic. She wants a place of her own, so she buys land from her brother, hires a builder, and bam, the house is well on its way to completion."

He took a breath, but so many more words had started piling up. They choked him as they stacked down his throat, and Tag's only option was to keep talking. "And it's just so easy for her, you know? Nothing is hard for a Hammond. She has so much money, it's like she doesn't even understand what other people have to go through."

Cord said nothing, but he nodded again; took another bite of his sandwich. Tag had only had the one, and he didn't think he could stuff anything into his mouth until everything he needed to say came out.

"Then, she's not sure about the foundation or the clinic, and let me tell you, she doesn't really want those things. I know what she wants, and she does too, but it's like she's afraid to admit it."

As Tag spoke, he realized he was afraid too. So he said, "And I am too, because what if I'm not enough for her? I don't own any land. Or a farm. Or anything. And we'll...what? Get married, and I'll move into *her* house, on *her* land, and cater to *her*?"

He actually didn't mind all of those things. He'd do them a thousand times over. "I feel like I'm losing myself again," he said. "Where do I fit? Am I really that important to her? And how long could that possibly last? Until she has the babies she wants?"

He shook his head. "It's complicated," he muttered again, and then he stuffed his mouth with more meat and cheese.

Cord slid the end of his messy sandwich into his mouth and picked up another napkin. He cleaned up without saying anything, and Tag just wanted to toss his turkey and avocado at the wall and stalk out. He could obviously never come back here again, and he'd need to somehow make sure that Cord never said anything of this conversation to Jane.

He swallowed and looked at Cord. "I want to

matter too. It might be stupid or selfish or whatever, but it's how I feel."

"How you feel is valid," Cord finally said, dropping the napkin into a pile with the others he'd used. "And completely normal for being with someone like Opal."

"Did you feel like this with Jane?"

"Absolutely," Cord said. "Every day." He leaned back in his chair and folded his arms. "It wasn't an easy road for me, bein' with Jane. Her daddy didn't like me for her—in fact, he forbade me from dating her when we were younger." A smile came to his face that Tag did not comprehend.

"But we grew up. We matured, and Jane's very stubborn. She knows what she wants, and she's not afraid to go after it. I think Opal's a little like that."

Tag scoffed. "A little, sure. Must be a Hammond trait."

"It's not a bad thing," Cord said gently—as gently as he'd ever said anything, at least. "Jane has to talk everything out. She requires me to say things I might not normally say, because she *wants* my opinion. She *wants* me to have a voice. I'd be shocked if Opal will require you to be a puppet." He raised his eyes. "Yeah?"

Tag couldn't argue with him. "I think that's about right," he admitted.

"Then you better start talkin' to her," Cord said. "I don't know what's going on, obviously. But Jane didn't have a lunch date with her cousin this morning, and then she suddenly did. She'd had a serious look on her face after the call too, and she told me, 'It's important, baby. I have to go.' So she went."

Tag hung his head in shame, because he didn't want to cause any trouble or heartache for Opal.

"Don't do that," Cord said next, this time in his barky voice.

Tag looked up. "Do what?"

"Cower down like that." Cord leaned forward and put his arms on his desk. "You know what you want, Tag. I think anyone with eyes can see you're in love with her." He pointed one thick finger at Tag. "And that she's in love with you. So whatever dance you two are doing, it just needs to be spelled out."

"I didn't tell her about my birthday," he said. "Or my brothers coming, because I didn't want to interrupt her trip to see the new baby."

"Good intentions," Cord murmured.

"She's mad about it."

"Mm hm." Cord leaned away again, and some of the tension in the office alleviated with his new position. "So you apologize for that. Make sure she knows why you did it. And then, Tag, buddy, you have got to tell her everything else. It's not going to just go away, and she can't fix a problem she doesn't know exists."

"All right," Tag said, and as he stuffed the last bite of his lunch in his mouth, a bell rang.

"Customers call," Cord said, getting to his feet. "We good here?"

Tag nodded and spoke around his food. "Yeah. Yep. All good."

"I'll look at the baler." With that, Cord left the office, left Tag to ponder all he'd said, left him praying that when faced with the woman he loved instead of Cord, he actually could say what he needed to say in order to feel like he and Opal were equals.

CHAPTER
Twenty-Nine

TUCKER REFUSED to open his eyes even as the sunlight beyond his closed blinds continued to brighten. He simply couldn't believe he was still waking up in this cabin instead of the trailer he used to share with Tarr.

"I've got to get out of here," he muttered to himself as he rolled over and swung his legs off the side of the bed. He took a moment to stretch his arms above his head, and the unhappiness he experienced here pulled through him strongly as his muscles warmed.

Tuck reached for his phone and tapped to dial his daddy. He'd know what to do, because he always had. Whenever Tucker needed advice, he talked to his father. And at this point, he couldn't talk to Tarr. The man simply was not interested in re-entering the rodeo.

"Morning, Tuck," Daddy said, no wasted syllables

with a cowboy drawl. His father had earned and used a law degree for years before he'd retired from the family company to raise his kids on the farm where Tuck now lived.

He'd run the farm, and he'd worn the hat, but Daddy didn't talk with the accent many others living here at the Hammond Family Farm did—Tuck himself included. He'd learned quickly in the rodeo that a cowboy accent got the attention of the prettiest girls, and Tuck had enunciated his as much as possible.

"Hey, Daddy." He lay back down, a sigh pressing out of his mouth.

"What's with you?"

"I'm so unhappy here."

Daddy didn't say anything for a moment. "Nothing's changed?"

"No."

"Come to Coral Canyon for the summer."

Now Tucker let the idea roll through his head. Daddy hadn't suggested such a thing before. He'd advised him to stay and wait to see if anything changed. If Tarr would commit to summer training, and they could enter a few of the smaller rodeos as Tucker staged his comeback. If Bobbie Jo would come out of hiding and talk to Tucker again.

Rather, it was Tuck who'd tucked his tail and hid from the gorgeous strawberry blonde who'd infected his bloodstream from the moment he'd met her.

"Tarr's not going to go back into the rodeo," Tucker said. "So that's changed."

"He told you that?"

"Right to my face."

"And Bobbie Jo?" Daddy spoke in a soft voice now, and Tuck wasn't sure if he should be irritated or grateful. He could talk about women; he'd never had a problem with it before.

"I just don't know how to bridge the gap between us," Tucker said. He stared toward the blinds, wishing he'd opened them to the farm beyond. "I came on way too strong in the beginning. I tried to pull back, but I think I did too much damage. She knew how much I liked her, and she never allowed herself to like me back."

"I know, son."

"And then, when she broke up with Lawson, I became this super-eager puppy. *Again*." He closed his eyes and frowned. "I was really just trying to be nice by bringing her dinner. I totally didn't expect her to kiss me."

And it hadn't even been a true kiss. It'd been an accident, and Tuck hated that his name was associated with that word in Bobbie Jo's vocabulary at all.

An accident.

A mistake.

Both words she'd used in texts to him since. She'd run down the hall to her bedroom, and only her cabinmate, Hattie, had been allowed in. Tarr had rescued

Tucker from rushing after her and making a bigger fool of himself, and nothing had been the same since.

She didn't come eat with him in the shade of the seed shed. She'd gone home to Oklahoma for her birthday in January. Tuck hadn't bought her a gift, because he simply didn't know how to show up on her doorstep and hand it to her.

"It wasn't even a real kiss," he said. "Which I could understand if it was, if it was bad, if she regretted doing it the same day Lawson had broken up with her. Any of that."

"She's embarrassed too," Daddy said.

"We're adults," Tucker said. "Why can't we talk about it?"

"Maybe Hattie's right," he said. "And she's recovering from the relationship with Lawson, and she doesn't want to start something new too soon."

"It's been *forever*," Tucker complained, feeling very much like a fourteen-year-old instead of the almost-twenty-eight-year-old he was.

Daddy chuckled. "It only feels like it."

Tucker sighed out his frustration, wishing his unrest would go with it. "What would I do in Coral Canyon?"

"Any number of things," Daddy said, which meant he didn't have a specific answer. "Blaze and Jem Young run rodeo camps for kids, and they always need help. You can focus on your charity work for a few months without having to get up at dawn, move cattle and horses, or tend to fields and fences."

"Yeah," Tucker said. He could do any of those things. "I feel bad leaving Tarr here."

"And is Tarr suffering there?" Daddy asked. "Seems to me he's there by choice."

"He's in love with Hattie," Tucker said with another sigh. "They're still dating, even though she's leaving to go back to college in the fall."

"Maybe he'll go with her."

"Maybe."

"We can call Uncle Ames and see if he needs help at the academy. He always seems to. You can work on finding another cowboy to manage in the rodeo. The Walker boys are real into that, and Cole seems to need a new manager every few years. Not sure where he's at right now, but…we can find out."

And by "we," Daddy meant, "you." Tucker could find out. He'd give him all the contact numbers, but Daddy would expect Tucker to put in the legwork. And honestly, he wouldn't mind.

"Anything would be better than staying here," he said.

"Then get your affairs in order, and come up to Coral Canyon. Momma and I would love to have you. The house is plenty big enough, and the bedrooms are always ready."

That was Daddy-Speak for *Momma wants you to come home. She'd love to have you—and so would I.*

Tuck rolled onto his back. "So I just go talk to Hunter? Tell him I'm leaving?"

"And Matt," Daddy said. "He'll need to know, so he can replace you if necessary."

Tuck smiled softly. "I'm irreplaceable. Isn't that what you and Momma always told me?"

Daddy chuckled, and Tucker missed him so, so much. "That's right, son. You're irreplaceable, but Matt will have to try."

A bout of silence carried between them, until Tucker finally said, "I'm going to have to talk to Bobbie Jo about this, right?"

"You said it earlier," Daddy said. "You're an adult, and you can talk to her like an adult."

"So you wouldn't just sneak away in the night?"

"No, son, I would not."

Tucker wouldn't either, because he didn't want to slam the door completely on the idea of a relationship with Bobbie Jo. Pathetic, maybe. Delusional for sure. But the truth.

"Thanks, Daddy."

"Text or call your mother with when you're coming. She'll stock the house with food."

"I love you. Tell Momma I love her too."

"Will do. Love you, Tuck."

The call ended, and Tuck let the phone fall to the mattress. He was late to work, but he didn't get up. He had a lot on his mind weighing him down, and he needed a few more minutes to get things in order.

Then, he got up, showered, dressed, poured himself a cup of coffee, and stepped out onto the front porch. He could text Matt and Hunter in one go, and he did that as he stirred sugar and cream into his coffee. He took a sip, read over the text, and sent it.

Hey, guys, Tuck here. I have decided to go to Coral Canyon at the beginning of June. I'm sorry that's not much time to find someone to replace me, but it's a couple of weeks, at least.

Matt responded almost instantly. Is *Tarr going too?*

No, Tuck said. *Not that I know of. I haven't talked to him yet, so please don't say anything to anyone.* He didn't spell out that he'd like to tell Bobbie Jo himself too, but hopefully he wouldn't have to.

That's great, Tuck, Hunter said. *Momma and Daddy will love having you.*

Tuck knew that to be true too, and he closed his eyes as a prayer streamed through his mind. *Thank you, Lord, for the best parents on the planet.*

His momma *would* love to have him. She'd feed him and care for him and talk to him as much as he wanted. She'd leave him alone if he wanted her to as well, and Tuck suddenly couldn't wait to get to Coral Canyon and step into his mother's hug.

Bless me to have a few crucial conversations, he added to his prayer. *Help me not to make a fool of myself in front of Bobbie Jo again. Give her what she needs to be happy too, even if it's not me.*

Sadness pulled through him, but Tuck meant his

mental prayer. He did want Bobbie Jo to be happy; he simply wanted to be happy too. The fact was, he wasn't happy here, in this current situation, and something had to change.

Either the situation, or him, or where he was, and he'd decided to blow it all up. Now, he just had to tell everyone he cared about of his plans—and hope all the doors in his life stayed open.

———

A WEEK LATER, Tarr knew of Tuck's plans to go to Coral Canyon for the summer. Matt and Gloria knew, and they'd started interviewing for another horseman to help with the summer horseback riding lessons.

Everyone knew—except Bobbie Jo. Tuck would be shocked if she hadn't heard it from someone yet, but she hadn't said anything to him if she had. So, after he'd gotten up before his alarm and packed a few more boxes, he sat down at the kitchen table while Tarr scrambled eggs and made coffee, and he finally texted her.

I'd love to sit down with you for a few minutes, he said. Then he deleted it. That sounded so...corporate. He wanted to take her to dinner and lay everything out for her, but it felt like rubbing salt in a gash in his heart.

He sighed and looked over to his best friend. "I don't know what to say to her."

"Ask her to lunch," Tarr said. "Or dinner. Just ask her out."

"I'm leaving in eight days."

"Yeah, so lunch should be easy," he said.

Tuck looked back at his phone. "Ask her to lunch," he muttered. Like it was so easy. If it was, he'd have done it a week ago. Heck, five months ago, when she'd broken up with her boyfriend.

Bobbie Jo, he started. *I have something to tell you, and I'd like to do it in person. Can we go to lunch or dinner someday really soon? Like today, tonight, tomorrow?*

Without even reading over it again, he sent the text, then practically threw his phone away from him. "Done."

"Good job, Tuck." Tarr set a plate of toast and eggs in front of him. "You're going to miss me feeding you every morning."

Tuck looked up at him and rolled his eyes. "Yeah, those protein shakes you leave out on the counter are going to be really hard for me to get out myself."

Tarr laughed as he sat down kitty-corner to Tuck. "I really will miss you." He scooped up a bite of eggs. "And I have to get a new cabinmate, which I'm not looking forward to."

"You'd like it if it was Hattie." Tuck grinned at him and picked up a piece of toast.

"Yeah, well, me and Hattie...." He trailed off, that contemplative look Tuck had seen several times covering his expression. "We like each other, but the timing feels wrong."

"She's way too young for you, besides," Tuck said.

"Cord and Jane are eleven years apart."

"Yeah, but Jane wasn't twenty-two when they started dating."

"She's sweet, though." Tarr grinned, and Tuck simply shook his head. Across from him, near the wall where his phone had slid, his device vibrated against the blonde wood. "That's her." Tarr reached for the phone and picked it up. "You want me to read it?"

Tuck nodded and shoved half a slice of bread into his mouth.

"Your message was great," Tarr said, and his approval meant a lot to Tucker. "She said she's got a video interview at lunchtime today, but her evening is free tonight." Tarr didn't move his head a single centimeter. Only his eyes came to meet Tuck's.

He nodded, and Tarr returned his gaze to the phone and started typing. Tuck trusted him to say the right things, and when he finished, he set the phone next to Tuck's plate. "Tonight at six-thirty." He gave Tuck a kind smile that said so much. "You got your date with her, man."

"Yeah." Tuck didn't feel happy about it though. "Now I just have to figure out what to say that won't sink me for good."

Tarr nodded. "Maybe it just hasn't been the right time for you guys either. Maybe you'll go to Coral

Canyon and find your calling in life, and you'll be ready to take on someone like Bobbie Jo."

"Did she say what her interview was for?"

"No," Tarr said. "So, see? One thing you can talk about tonight that isn't you leaving town." He gave Tuck a great big cowboy-won-the-rodeo smile. The one he reserved for pretty women and huge crowds paying his prize money. "It's going to be fine, Tuck. More than fine. Great. The best conversation you've had with Bobbie Jo yet."

Tuck wasn't in a place where he could agree, so he just said, "If you say so," and hoped Tarr's prediction would make it to God's ears—and that the Lord would make it come true.

CHAPTER

Thirty

BOBBIE JO LEFT her bedroom decked out in denim from head to toe. Out in the living room, Hattie sat with Tarr at their tiny kitchen table, their heads bent over something on one of their phones.

"Is this too much?" she asked, drawing both of their gazes.

Hattie got to her feet, her smile already in place, while Tarr just leaned back and looked at her. "Absolutely perfect," Hattie said. "Are you wearing the red boots with the white stars?"

"Yes," Bobbie Jo said. "I just—they're out here in the closet." She indicated the coat closet behind the couch. "It's okay? I don't look like I'm trying too hard?"

"You're wearing jeans from head to toe," Hattie said. "It's fine."

Bobbie Jo didn't want to talk about her fears, her

humiliation, and her insecurities in front of Tucker's best friend. She didn't know what, if anything, Tarr told Tuck. She glanced at him, an idea occurring to her. "He didn't say what it was about tonight, but he texted to say we're going to Rockets, and that place is nice."

"It's casual-nice," Tarr said. "You look great, Bobbie Jo. Tuck'll be thrilled to see you in denim. It's his favorite fabric." He got up and picked up the empty plates from the table. "Hattie, let's give her some privacy."

Hattie didn't move from in front of Bobbie Jo. "You're okay?" She wore worry as easily as she did mascara, and Bobbie Jo loved her for it.

"I'm okay," she whispered. "It's Tucker, Hattie." He wasn't going to hurt her—at least not physically. She had no idea what he had to tell her, but she'd been on and off the farm in the past couple of weeks as she looked for another job.

Something had to give in her life, and Bobbie Jo had decided that maybe if she didn't live on the farm with Tucker, they could start a relationship. She still wasn't entirely sure she was ready to start dating again, but if she was, she wanted it to be with Tucker Hammond.

"Yeah." Hattie moved in and hugged her. "It's Tucker." She gave her a soft smile as she pulled away, and then she followed Tarr to the back door, laced her fingers through his, and together, they slipped outside.

Bobbie Jo drew a deep breath and turned in a full circle. "A date with Tucker," she murmured to herself. He hadn't specifically said it was a date, but he'd named a time well after work, when he'd have finished and showered, and he was taking her to a steakhouse on the outskirts of the city.

They could go anywhere in a fifteen-minute radius and get burgers, tacos, French fries, or pizza. But he wanted to drive forty minutes, eat with her, and drive her back. Her lips buzzed at the very possibility of kissing him that night, and Bobbie Jo started lecturing herself as she opened the coat closet to get out the star-studded boots.

"You will not kiss him tonight," she said sternly. "The last time you thought you'd do that and be all friendly caused this huge rift." Really, it was her inability to talk to Tuck, to get past her humiliation and fears, to start another relationship when so much was still bleeding and raw from Oklahoma.

Several knocks sounded on the door as she sat on the couch, and Bobbie Jo's pulse went into a complete tizzy. "Come in," she called anyway, and then she bent to get the boots on.

"Hey," Tucker said from behind her, and Bobbie Jo glanced at him without making eye contact.

"Hey, I'm just putting my boots on. Two seconds." She zipped up the sides of the ankle boots on the left, then the right, and she got to her feet. "Ready."

He hadn't come down and around the couch, and

she met his eyes with the piece of furniture between them. He was seriously what Hattie had called him months ago—the hottest cowboy alive—and Bobbie Jo's mouth turned to sand.

"Aren't you a pretty picture?" He grinned at her, flirting so easy for him. He wore a black and silver plaid shirt with short sleeves, blue jeans, and the darkest black cowboy hat a man could find.

"Thank you," she said. "It's new." She moved away from the couch and cocked her hip, planting one palm there. "It's a dress."

"I see that." Tuck moved toward her, and for a moment, it felt like it might be the easiest thing in the world for him to gather her into his arms and hold her tight. A hello hug.

Bobbie Jo ached for that, as she didn't get many hugs. Zero around here, in fact. He stuttered his step, something anxious in his gaze. Then he plowed forward and put his arms around her. "It's so good to see you," he murmured.

Bobbie Jo sighed and allowed herself to relax into the circle of his safe embrace. "You too."

"I mean, I see you around," he said. "But it's not the same."

It wasn't, but Bobbie Jo didn't need to verbally agree with him. "You've got a reservation?" she asked.

"Yes." But Tucker didn't move immediately. He held her for several more moments, and Bobbie Jo closed her eyes and simply melted away into the scent of his skin, his cologne, his fabric softener. "We better go."

"Yes." She cleared her throat and stepped back as he did, and they separated far easier than they'd come together. "Let me just grab my phone and wallet." They waited for her on the counter, so she took two steps and had them.

He took her hand and led her out the front door much the same way Tarr had led Hattie out the back. Bobbie Jo pulled the cabin door closed behind her and tucked her hair against the breeze trying to undo the curls she'd put in after her own post-work shower.

"Who'd you interview with today?" Tuck asked as he opened the passenger door of his truck for her.

"You'll never believe it," she said. "But HMC. Development and Research Department." She pushed herself up and onto the seat and grinned at him. "I think it went well too."

"That's fantastic, Bobbie Jo." He closed her door, his handsome smile etched in place, and rounded the truck to the driver's seat.

"It's at least a three-interview process," she said. "And this was my first one, so I've got a ways to go."

"No one will be better qualified than you," he said. He did seem more reserved tonight than she'd seen him in the past, and that caused her voice to dry right up.

Tuck drove them out of the cabin community and around the homestead to the main road. Then right off the farm and toward the city. The radio warbled on low, country music filling the silence between them.

The drive started out comfortable, but by the time Bobbie Jo realized Tuck had cleared his throat three or four times, the mood shifted. She glanced over to him. "You can just tell me."

He looked at her too, the highway they drove not busy right now. "I was hoping you'd have some of those fried mac and cheese balls you like before I do."

"Okay," she said. "But I can see you're quietly freaking out."

He grinned. "You can see that, huh?"

"You've cleared your throat a million times."

He chuckled, the sound deep and rich and delicious. "Sounds like you can *hear* it then, not see it."

"Tomato, tamahto," she said, a flash of irritation stealing through her. "It might be better for both of us if you just tell me."

"All right." But Tuck didn't blurt out the innermost thoughts of his heart. He shifted in his seat. He gripped the steering wheel. He even adjusted the radio up and then turned it right back down.

"Bobbie Jo," he said. "I'm really unhappy at the farm. It's not where I want to be. I came there for Tarr, to help him heal, with the expectation that we'd rejoin the rodeo as soon as he was cleared to do so."

"Yes," she said, because she knew all of this.

"It's been a year. Tarr's been cleared for months. He doesn't want to go back into the rodeo, and I don't want to be at the farm. So…." He looked over to her, a death grip on the wheel and the truck barreling forward at sixty-five miles-per-hour. Without watching the road, he said, "So I'm leaving. I'm going to Coral Canyon for the summer. I'll stay with my parents. I'll make a new plan for my life from there."

Bobbie Jo heard the words. She felt them punch the air right out of her lungs, leaving her gasping and desperate for a proper breath. She couldn't look at him while she did that, so she quickly switched her gaze over to the side window.

"You're leaving," she whispered. This wasn't a first date that would turn into a second. Part of her felt nothing but relief, but another part only wallowed in sadness, in regret. "When?"

"Next weekend," he said. "Sunday morning."

She whipped her attention back to him, fire blazing through her now. "Next weekend?"

"Yes." He'd refocused on the road, and he didn't look at her. "I gave my two-weeks notice last week, and I've been packing a few boxes every morning and every evening." He faced his own side window for a moment. "Heck, I could probably leave tomorrow morning. It's not like I own a whole bunch."

"I just—wow."

"Are you surprised?"

"Yes," she said. "Yes, I'm surprised."

"Why?" he asked. "You knew I didn't want to work my family farm for my whole life. I manage rodeo careers. It's what I'm good at. It's what I love doing. I'd love to stay with Tarr, but he doesn't want the career. So I'm gonna find someone else who needs a good manager, and I'm going to get back in the ring."

Bobbie Jo started nodding about halfway through his mini-speech, her gaze stuck out the windshield at the landscape blurring by. "I know, Tucker," she said quietly. "I'm sorry you're not happy at the farm."

"It's not like you are either," he said.

She gave him a glare. "I'm fine where I am."

"Yeah, which is why you've been applying to jobs all over the city."

"The reason I came here was to get a job."

"You've been at the farm for over a year too."

"It was…." Bobbie Jo choked on the words coming to mind. "Easy," she said. "I'm familiar with the work there. It was convenient. It was comfortable." And yes, Tuck had been there. She'd never said as much, but Tuck was a huge reason why Bobbie Jo had stayed at the farm. And now, it looked like they'd both been looking for other opportunities.

None of hers would take her to Wyoming, though, nor around the western US and Canada on the rodeo circuit.

"Easy, convenient, and comfortable," Tuck said. "Why are you leaving, then?"

"Because no one grows in an easy, convenient, comfortable environment," she said. "I feel stagnant.

Stale. I'm not moving forward, and I'm not moving backward. I'm just…suspended in air, desperate for someone to pull me back to solid ground."

Tuck reached over and threaded his fingers through hers. Oh, it felt so good to hold his hand. "I'd pull you back down, Bobbie Jo."

What he didn't say shouted through the cab of the truck: *If you'd let me.*

"I'm sure you would," she whispered. More houses and buildings started dotting the highway, and they'd be at the restaurant very soon. "Listen, Tuck," Bobbie Jo said. "I didn't mean to kiss you that day. You know that, right?"

"Of course," he said easily, like he hadn't given her blunder a second thought. But she knew Tucker better than that.

"I just—I've felt so guilty, because I had *just* broken up with Lawson, and I wasn't ready to start another relationship right away, and I didn't want you to think I'd taken advantage of you."

"I know I've had a crush on you since minute one," he said. "Everyone knows that." The last three words came in a tone of darkness, and Bobbie Jo wished she could erase it. "I didn't mean to put any pressure on you at all. It was a lot of flirting and fun and jokes. You know *that*, right?"

"Yes," she said. "And just so everything is out between us before we get there, I've wanted to go out with you for a while too. A long time, actually. I wished things between us weren't just flirting and fun and jokes. But I didn't know how to do that with you." She looked away from the golden evening light bathing everything in her line of sight. "I still don't."

"Not everything tonight is a flirting joke," he said. "This is a real conversation."

She leaned her head back against the rest and smiled at her partial reflection in the glass. "Yeah," she said. "It's been nice, too."

"I agree." He kept driving, and Bobbie Jo kept thinking about what she could say to him to get him to stay on the farm. But the truth was, she might not even be there for much longer. *You'll be in town, though,* she thought.

He pulled into the parking lot at Rockets, and Bobbie Jo's time ran low. He parked; he dropped to the ground and came around to open her door for her; he filled the doorway, all smiles and gentlemanly cowboy vibes, and he reached for her hand.

Bobbie Jo gave it to him again, marveling at how wonderful skin-to-skin contact could be, and she slid into his arms. "I wish you weren't leaving," she said. "And I just need to make sure it's not because of me."

"Well, it's partly because of you," Tuck said. "I'm not going to lie about that. My feelings for you haven't really changed—I've just hidden them better. But it's like Tarr said this morning, maybe it's just not the right time for us."

"Do you think you'll come back to the farm ever?"

"My family is here," he said. "Of course I'll be back in the area from time to time."

"But not permanently."

"Permanently is not in my plan right now, no." He gazed at her with sadness and pure male desire. "I do wish things had been different when we'd first met. You know that, right?"

She nodded, letting her eyelids fall closed. "I won't long-distance date again, so I won't suggest that."

He chuckled, and she leaned her cheek against his chest to feel the vibrations of it. "Yeah, the last time didn't work out so well for you."

"Maybe God will bring us together again," she whispered.

"Maybe." Tuck drew a deep breath, and Bobbie Jo lifted her head. He looked toward the restaurant and back to her. "I would really like to kiss you once before I leave. Just to have that with me."

Her eyebrows went up. "Tucker Hammond, are you being a flirt right now?"

"No, ma'am." He didn't even smile, and Bobbie Jo's slipped from her face too. "Distance can make the heart grow fonder, right? And if I know what I'm missing, maybe I'll come back faster. Sooner."

He didn't seem to be joking or poking fun at her. Bobbie Jo did want to kiss him. So she slid her hands up his arms to his shoulders, then to cradle his face. "All right," she whispered.

Tuck had never truly hesitated with her until that

moment, and he looked at her for what felt like a good, long while but was probably only a second or two. Then he cupped the back of her head in one of his big, strong hands, and lowered his mouth to kiss her.

Bobbie Jo had had several boyfriends over the years, but none of them had ever, *ever* kissed her the way Tucker Hammond did.

So she kissed him with everything she had, hoping to give him a really good memory…that would hopefully bring him back to her someday.

CHAPTER
Thirty-One

OPAL HAD everything set for her date with Tag by noon, and she'd sorted her seeds for this afternoon's planting last night. So she took her tote out to the garden, her feet clad in a simple pair of running shoes instead of the garden boots Tag had said she needed.

The garden had dried, at least, and she'd been able to get in a few rows of corn and carrots and peas before she'd left for Raleigh. She'd taken in the neatly weeded rows last night after she'd returned to the farm close to dusk, and she'd known exactly who'd been there taking care of her garden in her absence.

Taggart.

Opal sighed as she got out the rake and hoe she needed to put in a row of pumpkins and then one of potato hills. She'd read all about how to space them and how much to water them while she'd rocked with Spencer and Violet out of town, and she got right to work. She pulled dirt this way and that, quickly realizing that building a hill for her pumpkins was harder than the videos she'd watched online made it look.

Still, she was determined to get this done today, so she could feel like she'd done something useful that day. Then she'd shower and prep herself for her date with Tag, who would be early over late.

Opal went over the things she wanted to tell him as she worked the earth, and she was so glad for good women in her life to help her. Both Molly and Jane had calmed her so much yesterday, and they'd given her some really great advice.

Let him talk, Jane had said. *He wants a voice, Opal. Let him have it.*

Make him apologize for not telling you about his birthday, Molly had said. *But don't punish him for it. If he owns it as a mistake, then you just forgive him and kiss him and tell him you love him.*

She'd grinned through that last sentence, and Opal had tried to stay straight-faced for as long as possible. When she'd broken, it had been into tears, not grins, and both Jane and Molly had been right there to wrap her up in hugs and tell her it was okay to admit she loved Tag.

Opal still hadn't said the words out loud yet, because she wanted to taste them as they left her mouth. She wanted to watch Tag's face when he heard them, and she wanted him to kiss her the way a man who loved a woman back would kiss her. So she couldn't admit to herself that she loved Tag quite yet.

She simply wanted to see him, and it had taken all of her willpower to stay out of his space today. Going to the city this morning had helped, and now she worked on the opposite side of the farm from him, pretty much guaranteeing she wouldn't run into him until she was ready.

Sweat ran down the side of her face while she bent over to lovingly press the pumpkin seeds into the mound she'd managed to make. Three went around in a triangular formation, and Opal moved down to do another one. With four mounds done—and a dozen pumpkin plants in the ground—she went to get the hose.

The property had water on it already, but it came in the form of a spigot sticking up and out of the ground. She had to pump the handle a few times to get any water to come out, and then it gushed and gushed.

And gushed, right over her shoes, making them a muddy mess of sneakers. Opal stared at it for a moment, feeling helpless and dirty and hot and like crying. Then she simply trained the hose on her feet and let the ice-cold water flow over her shoes until they were clean.

Then, she walked in squelching socks and shoes back to the garden. She took one step out into the soil before she realized she'd basically just come in from the ocean. And now that she was wet, the sand would stick to literally everything that had even a single water molecule on it.

Dirt acted the same way, and Opal had already committed to taking the first step. So out she went, her feet hot now as the water warmed under the heat of the afternoon sun. With every move she made, more and more dirt stuck to her shoes, and ankles, and even up her leg.

She felt like she had mud bricks on her feet as she walked, and by the time she reached the end of the row, she simply kicked off her shoes and left them there. She stared at them, getting more and more upset with every passing second.

Squeezing the hose hard, she tipped her head back and yelled out her irritation with her lack of gardening skills. "Why can't anything just be easy?" she griped. Of course, she knew plenty of things in her life were easy, but right now, it felt like everything had been tied up into a giant ball of rubber bands, and she'd never find the way out.

The sound of chuckling met her ears, further igniting her ire. She turned, expecting to find Mikey standing there with baby West on his hip or his hand in his son's.

Instead, she found Tag.

Her pulse leaped and raced and froze all in the same breath, leaving her gasping and unable to make a move in any direction.

"Hey, there," he drawled, stepping out into her

garden. He avoided the muddy and wet spots where she'd watered her precious pumpkins as he came closer. "I was hoping to catch you a little earlier."

Opal stood there, the hose at her side, filling the garden with more water, and thus, more mud. She even felt herself sinking into it a little bit.

"I brought you something," Tag said as he lifted a bright blue pair of garden boots. "But you beat me to the planting." He glanced at the pumpkin mound as he went by it. "Seems like you've lost your shoes."

Opal's eyes filled with tears, and she still didn't know what to say.

His eyes came back to hers. "Opal, honey, I'm really sorry I didn't tell you about the twins coming for my birthday—or even when my birthday was."

She sniffled, determined not to cry again tonight. She was far too old for such things, and she certainly didn't want Tag to see her erratic emotions.

He set down the boots about a pace from her and held up the other item in his hands. "I got you this too. So you can bring it out here, tend to your garden, and then take a rest in the shade."

The picture on the front showed a bright green inflatable chair, and Opal lost the battle against her tears. They flowed down her face, and she figured they could join the muddy mess that was her feet, her garden, and her life.

"Oh, my sweet honeybear," Tag whispered. He took a couple of side steps, took the hose and tossed it away to the already-planted rows, and set down the inflatable chair. "I'm in love with you, Opal Hammond, and it's just a little mud."

"The boots," she said through her tears as he gathered her close to his heart.

"And a little plastic," he said. "Plastic boots, plastic chair. It all cleans up nicely."

She put her arms around him and held on, everything catching up to her at once. "You weeded my garden."

"Someone had to," he whispered. "And you were off loving that baby." He ran his hands up and down her back, soothing her. "Sawyer and Flint helped. They can't wait to meet you."

"I can't wait to meet them either," she said, sniffling as she once again fought for control. "I'm sorry I got upset, Tag. It's just, I would've liked to have been here to celebrate your birthday with you."

"It's just an arbitrary day, honey. We can celebrate it anytime."

She pushed gently against his chest. "It would've meant something to me," she said. "And you—"

"I know," he said roughly. "I'm sorry. I said I was sorry. I should've told you. I just didn't want to disrupt your plans to go to Raleigh. I know how important that was to you."

Opal studied his face, and she didn't see anything to mistrust. "Tell me about the serious thing you wanted to talk about a month or two ago."

His jaw jumped, and he fell back another step. "I've worked through some of it already."

"Did you write about it in your notebook?" She didn't see it anywhere on him, but he had to have it. He always had it.

"Yes," he said simply.

"Will you show me?" She tried to ask gently, but she wasn't sure it came across that way to Tag.

His eyes stormed with danger, and then he blinked, and it all went out. "I can show you," he said. "But you'd be the first to ever see what I write in that notebook."

Opal knew what that meant, and her memories flowed through her now in a fast, furious way. "You said you loved me."

Tag allowed a slow, Southern smile to come to his face. "You're just getting to that, huh?"

Opal wanted to hear him say it again. "Taggart."

"Oh, honeybee, you can't say my name like that." He reached out and grabbed onto her front belt loops and pulled her closer. "It makes me fall even more in love with you when you do." His lips skated across her jaw and down the column of her neck.

"I'm sincerely sorry, honey. Please forgive me."

"You're forgiven," she murmured. "Now, could we get out of the mud to continue this conversation?"

He stepped back, cupped her hand in his, and led her past her gardening, picking up the gifts he'd brought for her as he went. "I'm assuming you'll want to shower," he said. "Get ready for tonight."

"Yes," she said.

He reached the edge of the garden and stepped out of it. "I'll get your chair set up for you, and I'll be back at the farmhouse to get you at six-thirty."

She turned back toward the pumpkin mounds. "Oh, my shoes...."

"Honey, they're a lost cause." He grinned at her and handed her the boots. "Put those on for now. We can rinse them out at the farmhouse."

Opal pulled on the bright blue boots, unsurprised that they fit perfectly. Of course. Tag knew her well enough to know her shoe size, and he'd bought the cutest boots in the best color. "These have flowers on them," she said.

"You like flowers," he said.

"I like you," she said.

"Mm, you only like me?"

Opal hadn't envisioned this scenario, with the two of them standing near a construction site while she proclaimed her love for the cowboy. But life was all about making adjustments, living in an imperfect world, and doing the best she could.

"Okay," she said, leaning into his chest. "I more than like you, Taggart. I'm in love with you too."

He made the tiniest noise of surprise, and then he growled as he leaned down and claimed her lips in a fierce, urgent, and delicious kiss.

CHAPTER
Thirty-Two

TAG'S NERVES frayed with every passing moment where Opal read the things in his notebook. He'd taken her back to the farmhouse, and they'd separated for a few hours. Well, kind of. Opal had brought her lime-green chair to the edge of the barn and sat in it to watch him finish his afternoon work with the horses.

He'd gone back to his house to shower, and Opal had been sitting on his front porch in the green chair. So he hadn't even gone to the farmhouse to pick her up properly. She didn't care, and honestly, Tag didn't either.

Now, they sat at a pizza parlor, with Opal in blue jeans and an oversized sweatshirt with the word "cozy" on it, his notebook in front of her.

"It's just—"

"A reminder to call the twins," she said, lightly touching the page. "Thoughts from sermons. Things about the horses, your life, my life." She turned the page, and Tag wanted to rip the notebook away from her.

"If I write it down, it doesn't get to fester inside me," he said quietly. "It's nothing bad. The thoughts are super raw. I scribble them down, so they don't infect me for too long."

Opal said nothing, and Tag knew where she was in the timeline: the part where Tag had started struggling with her building a house, starting a non-profit clinic, and being worthy to be her boyfriend.

"This is agony for me," he said, his voice dark and dangerous. He didn't try to sweeten it up, and he had no interest in ordering dessert pizza. So he waved away the waitress while Opal continued to study his innermost demons.

Opal closed the notebook and pushed it away from her. She wore coolness in her eyes that made Tag wonder if his apologies and gifts and declarations of love would ever be enough.

"Did you finish it?" he asked.

"No." She reached for her glass of soda and took the last, watery sip. "I didn't need to."

"Opal—"

"Taggart, I don't want this to be a thing between us, so I just need to talk for a minute." She held up one hand, her dark eyes blazing at him. Blazing with life, with compassion, with something else he couldn't quite name. "Then, I will give you all the time you need to talk to me too. I want to know what you think. I *need* to know. I can't make adjustments if you keep everything to yourself, if you spill all your secrets to ink and paper."

"Sometimes, it helps," he said. "And then those things don't need to be said out loud. Sometimes, it's not you that needs to adjust, but me."

Opal reached across the table and took both of his hands in hers, and there came that smile that put him more at ease. "Tag, there are a couple of things I can't change about myself, even if I wanted to. Maybe three. Do you want to know what they are?"

"Yes, ma'am."

"One, I love babies, and I want to be a mother more than anything."

Tag allowed a small smile to come to his face. "That doesn't need to change, honeybear."

"Two, I have a lot of money. I'd like to spend it on pumpkin seeds, and inflatable furniture, and horses for you and me, because I'm going to learn to ride one day if it's the last thing I do."

Tag dropped his chin and laughed. When he raised his eyes to Opal's again, he saw the seriousness there. "I know my money bothers you," she said quietly. "I don't know how to change that, Taggart. I would give up every penny just to be with you."

No better words had ever been spoken, and Tag squeezed her hands. "I would never ask you to do that."

"You're on equal ground with me," she said, her tone increasing in urgency. "Money is just money. It doesn't buy me what I want most—love and family. Only you can give me those things, baby, and I only want them *with* you."

Tag's emotions surged, making his nose hot and his eyes burn. "You're a good woman, Opal."

"I know you'll still struggle with it," she said, and she nodded to the notebook. "You can tell your notebook, but I'm going to ask you to please tell me too. It might not change how things go, but we should be able to face things like this together, not separately. You don't have to do anything by yourself anymore."

"Except get up before dawn in the winter and make sure your coffee is nice and hot."

Opal grinned at him. "Definitely that."

He leaned across the table, half-standing in the booth, and touched his lips to hers. "I love you, Opal."

"Mm, I love you too, Tag."

He settled back in his seat, feeling warm and full and calm. "What's the third thing?" he asked.

"I just said it." Opal picked up the last piece of Alfredo Hawaiian pizza, her favorite. "I'm in love with you, and I don't know how to stop doing that."

"I don't want you to stop doing that."

"Then you have to talk to me," she said. "About everything." She looked at him with a measure of challenge in her expression, and Tag wanted to wipe it away completely.

"Okay," he said. "But you might regret requesting that."

"I doubt it." She took a bite of the pizza, a moan coming from her mouth. "Now, eating this last piece of pizza; I'll probably regret that."

Tag picked up his notebook and tucked it away in its safe spot. No, he hadn't wanted to show it to her. He'd fought with himself all afternoon about it. Part of him had wanted to burn it, lie to her and tell her he'd lost it, something—anything—to get out of showing it to her.

And then, in the still, small way the Lord spoke to him, Tag had been gently reminded that honesty was the best policy. That he could trust Opal. That God would be with him in all things, even something as simple as letting Opal see the writings in the notebook.

So he'd brought it. He'd shown it to her.

"I have a couple of things," he said.

Opal nodded, nothing playful in her gaze now. "I'd love to hear them."

"I'm worried about living on Mike and Gerty's land," he said. "What if I want my own farm someday? Like the way Cord did."

"Then we start looking for a farm for us," she said simply.

"What if I feel really guilty about using your money to buy said farm?"

"We'll work through it together," Opal said.

Tag ducked his cowboy-hatted head again. "Opal, honey, what if you can't have babies?"

She sat quietly for a moment, until Tag dared to look up at her. "I trust God," she said. "And He knows I want babies more than anything. If we can't have any of our own, I know He'll provide a way for me to have them somehow."

Tag nodded, her faith and testimony beautiful. "Okay."

"Why are you worried about living near Mike and Gerty?"

"I don't know," Tag said, looking over to the door as it opened. "It's just been gnawing at me ever since you bought the acreage and started building that house."

"You looked at the plans. You chose."

"I know." He shook his head and focused on her again. "It's not anything I can articulate. That's why it goes in the notebook."

"You like working for them, don't you?"

"Yes," he said. "It's the best job I've ever had."

"And I'm helping with West," she said. "And they'll have more kids. And we will, and the house is a half-mile from theirs. We'll have our own space."

"So you're just assuming I'll move in with you." He wasn't asking, and he found Opal's double-blink quite cute.

"Yes," she said simply.

"Good." Tag slid to the end of the bench and

pulled his wallet out of his back pocket. "Because I can't wait to live there with you." He tossed some money on the table and extended his hand toward her. She took it, and he pulled her right into his chest. "And we can start making those babies," he whispered right in her ear.

Opal giggled and pushed against his chest. "Take me for a walk, cowboy."

"You got it, honeybear." He left the pizza parlor with Opal's hand in his, and that wasn't a bad way to be. Not a bad way at all. He wasn't sure how to articulate everything in his head to another person, especially if it was that other person making him stew and wonder and question things. Especially if it was Opal and maybe he didn't agree with her.

"I'll talk to you," he promised. "Okay? It might be really hard for me in the beginning, because I'm not used to that. I don't just say everything I'm thinking about."

"I don't need you to say everything you're thinking about," Opal said. Tag faced into the breeze and let it wash over his face. Beside him, Opal hunkered down into her sweatshirt. "Wow, it's chilly when the sun goes down still."

"Not quite summer yet," he said.

"I wouldn't mind hearing what you're thinking about," she said. "But I don't expect every thought you have to come out of your mouth. That actually sounds exhausting."

"To you and me both," he said dryly.

"But if it's something with me that's bothering you —like what we spend money on or me trying to take on a huge foundation that's way beyond what I really want my life to be, then yes. You absolutely need to tell me."

"What if you don't like what I think?"

"Tag, either you want to be on equal ground with me, or you want to say only what you think I want to hear. You can't have it both ways."

"Okay," he said. "Then I want to know how much that dress you wore on Valentine's Day was."

Opal didn't answer for a moment, and Tag looked over to her. "I know it's a lot," he said. "You can even ballpark it if you don't have the exact number."

"Tag, you won't like it."

"So either you have to tell me things I want to know too—the things I ask you about as I'm talking and telling you what you ask me to tell you—or you can hide things from me, keep secrets, and drive wedges between us. You don't get to have it both ways either, Opal."

"Okay," Opal said in a somewhat sassy voice. "It was ninety-one thousand dollars for the dress and the shipping to get it to me on time."

Tag stopped walking, because his limbs did not know how to move with that information. He stared at her. "Dear Lord, you're not joking."

Opal shook her head, no coy smile in sight.

"And see, I want to pull out my notebook and start scribbling," he said.

"About what?" she asked. "What would you write down?" She moved out of the way for a man walking his dog, but Tag couldn't get anything to work inside his body. His brain had turned into a blender, and all the things he knew and understood were suddenly shredded and mixed together into one big pile of slush.

"Taggart."

He blinked and came back to reality. He glanced left and right down the simple street in downtown Ivory Peaks. They'd been headed toward the park, and he managed to take a step in that direction without the ground shattering and swallowing him whole. "I'd be writing down that number," he said. "Trying to make sense of it. How much it is, what it could buy, all of it."

"It bought me an amazing dress, for an amazing night with an amazing cowboy," she said. "It was worth every penny."

"I just—I have no idea what that much money looks like," he said. "It's mind-boggling for me."

"So you'd be writing down the money."

"Yes," he said. "And then probably some thoughts about how unworthy I am to be on your arm in my forty-dollar jeans and years-old cowboy hat. And then I'd try to pull myself back up again by saying something about how I have value too, even though I'm not rich. Stuff like that."

They reached the end of the block, and Tag stepped out into the crosswalk to get over to the park. "You want to sit over here for a minute?"

"I guess," she said. "You know what this park needs? Inflatable couches. They're so much more comfortable than wooden benches."

Tag laughed, but his mind still lingered on the number *ninety-one thousand*. They found a bench not too much further down the path, and Tag crowded in close to Opal after she sat down.

"Tag, baby," she said. "You realize when we get married, you'll be rich too, right?"

"No," he said. "No way. I know you Hammonds, and you'll have something in place to protect that wealth."

"Mm, I don't think so," Opal said quietly. "None of my siblings or cousins have done that."

"What?" He swung his attention to her, completely disbelieving. "That can't be true."

She gave him a soft, somewhat sad smile. "More musings for your notebook."

"I—" Tag didn't know what to say. After a full minute, he found the right thing. "Honestly, I wish there would be some protections. A prenup or something. Because I don't want the responsibility of that much money. It's just...too much for me." He peered at her, even going so far as the take her chin in his hand. "You know that, right, Opal? I'm a really simple man."

"Not any simpler than Cord," she said. "Or Mike, or Easton."

He scoffed as he released her and looked away. "Please. Your brothers are mega-rich and super-smart." He practically spat the words as he added, "So are you."

"And so are you," she said just as poisonously.

"Minus the mega-rich part," he said. "And the scientific degrees and grant work, and the business degrees and military service." He shook his head. "Honestly, Mike should've kicked me to the curb months ago."

"Nah." Opal leaned her head against his shoulder and sighed. "He knows how much you mean to me. He knows how wonderful you are. How much Gerty trusts and relies on you. How good of a person you are. How—"

"Okay," Tag said, not needing the compliments or accolades. "I got it." He fumed silently for several beats of his heart, and then he finally started to calm down.

Opal waited through all of that, and then she waited some more. "I love you, Taggart Crow," she whispered. "Please tell me we can go back to the farm and cuddle on my new chair and watch the stars."

He got to his feet and pulled her up too. "Let's get back to the farm to watch the stars, honey-love." He pressed a kiss to her forehead. "I'm sorry, okay? I'm working on it."

"You're doing great," she said.

He took her back to his truck and opened her door for her. She got in, but he didn't back up and close the door. He crowded in close, his hand drifting across her thighs to her waist. "Opal, there's three things I can't really change about myself, even if I wanted to. Do you want to know what they are?"

"Yes," she whispered.

Tag grinned at her, and he leaned in close as he said, "One, I love you. Two, I love you, and three...."

He pressed his lips to hers and stole a kiss before he whispered, "I love you," for the third time.

CHAPTER
Thirty-Three

OPAL TOOK Mike's hand and stepped up into the house. Her house. Gerty, Tag, and Steele had already entered, and Opal had been last. She stopped as the others spread out throughout the space, and while it didn't have all the walls perfectly plastered and painted, nor any windows, doors, countertops, furniture, or fixtures, Opal felt the pure oxygen of it filling her lungs.

This was her house.

No, her home.

A home. Maybe the first one she'd ever lived in.

"Honey?"

She looked at Tag as he came back to her. "It's so bright in here," she said. "I love it."

He smiled and tucked her against his side. "It's bigger than it looks from the outside."

"There's not even a front door," she said. "You can see straight through the house, from front to back."

"Yeah, but it's deeper than it looks. That's all I meant."

The house wasn't a box, as Opal had lived in many of those and had rejected any plan that just had four corners. Therefore, her house faced the street with a flat front and a porch that ran the width of that—and around the south side, where she could sit in the winter and take in the golden sunshine.

The house ran diagonally south, creating a back-yard that had solid walls along two sides, the garden at the back, and a lane that she could drive on to park anything she wanted—a boat, a trailer, extra farm trucks.

"A nice big area for living," she said, taking the first steps into the house. "Where I'll spend most of the time with the kids—if we're not outside." She went all the way to the kitchen at the back. "Separate entrance for muddy cowboys." She beamed at Tag and nodded to the right. "Back door leading to our fabulous deck."

The kitchen literally had nothing it in but walls with outlets and wires sticking out of them. No appliances. No counters. No cupboards. But Opal could see it all, including herself scrambling eggs for Tag before he went to work on the farm, and cutting up apples into chunks for the cutest dark-haired boy, who had Tag's lopsided smile and affinity for writing down his

confusing thoughts, his fears, his worries, reminders
for himself—and how very much he loved Opal.

She felt warm from head to toe, and not only
because June had arrived, and the house had no air
conditioning yet.

"Still got a few months to go," she said.

"Only two or three," Tag said. "All the finishes go
in fast if they're scheduled."

She looked over to him. "Scheduled? I have to
schedule them?"

"Your contractor should know when your stuff is
coming," Tag said. "You want me to call him and get
the schedule?"

Relief painted through Opal. "Yes," she said. "I'd
love that."

They continued to walk through the house while
Gerty said she wanted a back deck like the one Opal
had, and Mike told her she could have whatever she
wanted. She tensed for a moment, but Tag didn't say
anything. It seemed so "Hammond" to just get whatever she wanted, and Opal hadn't been so sensitive to
such things before.

Outside, she and Tag meandered to the edge of her
garden, and such pride filled her. "I know I shouldn't
think I'm so amazing," she said. "But look at my
garden. There are peas and carrots and corn growing,
Taggart. They're *growing*."

He didn't laugh at her, but he did give her that
gorgeous smile. "It's pretty amazing, Opal." He

cleared his throat, and she looped her arm through his to let him know she was right here, right at his side. Not in front of him, not behind. Just at his side.

"I've been thinkin'," he said gruffly. "What does a wedding look like for Opal Hammond?"

Of course she'd been thinking about marrying Tag. She loved him, and he loved her. The next logical step was marriage, especially because she wanted a family.

"I don't know," she said, the wind very nearly whipping away her words.

"Oh, that's just not true." Tag dropped his hand from his pocket and took hers safely inside his. "Here's what I know: there will be a fabulous dress, and that might take some time to get. Gorgeous flowers everywhere, because you love the way they smell *and* the way they look. Your family surrounding you, the men in matching cowboy hats and ties."

"No," Opal finally said. "They won't need matching ties."

Tag chuckled and leaned over to kiss her. "What will I wear?"

"A gorgeous tuxedo," she whispered. "And a silver tie, to mimic the stars. A big, smiling cowboy hat and matching boots you've polished all the dirt from, though you've probably weeded my vegetable garden only an hour earlier."

She smiled up at him and touched her mouth to his. "And you'll have a pure white rose in your lapel that will signal how pure and amazing our love is."

"And your bouquet will only be silver and white," Tag whispered back, his lips catching on hers as he spoke, and then catching to kiss her properly. "The only color will come from the guests, from the flowers, and from the food."

"I'd like to serve dinner and have dancing."

"And this would take place…?"

Opal hesitated, because while she'd thought a lot about marrying Tag and being Tag's wife and living with Tag here, she had skipped over the actual event that got her there. A lot of women dreamt of their wedding day, and Opal could admit she'd thought of it a time or two. But she'd been so focused on other things, and she had quite a bit going on right now with the construction, and continuing to build her relationship with Tag, and still coming into the woman God wanted her to be.

"I don't know," Opal said. "I'll talk to Jane and Molly. There are some great reception centers in the city."

"Do you want to get married in the city?"

"I don't know," she said. "We could get married here or at my uncle's place. I suppose it depends on the time of year too. Outdoor weddings require certain weather, and if we do something indoors, then the weather is a non-issue."

"Honeybear, I'm pretty sure you'd like an indoor wedding over an outdoor one."

"You're right about that," she murmured. "And it's June already."

"Give me a timeline," Tag said gently. "Are we talking an autumnal wedding? A winter wedding? Am I waiting until next spring to move in with you?"

Opal took a moment to consider his questions. "Can I call my mom and talk to her about it?"

"Of course, honeybear."

"Traveling for them might be hard in the winter, but maybe they could just come down here and live with me while we plan the wedding." Opal honestly didn't know what her parents might do. She knew the roads between Ivory Peaks and Coral Canyon were cleared in the winter, but snowstorms were unpredictable, and she absolutely had to have her daddy walk her down the aisle.

"Taggart," she said.

"Mm?"

"I want something big and fancy for our wedding."

"And there it is." He laughed right out loud and turned into her. "You really hadn't thought of it until now?"

"Not entirely."

"Opes," Mikey called. "We're headed back to the farmhouse."

She turned toward her brother and his family and waved. "It looks good, right?"

Mikey grinned and grinned while Gerty nodded

and nodded. "Yeah," he called. "It's going to be amazing, Sissy."

"Come for dinner," Gerty said. "My grandma made corn and potato chowder, and you'll love it."

"We'll be there," Opal promised. Her family left, along with Steele, and she went back to Tag. "Will you hold me on the couch?"

And since he was the best boyfriend ever—and he had the rest of the afternoon off—he asked, "Where did you put it this time?"

————

"IT'S JUST ME," Opal called as she opened the door to Jane and Cord's new house, on their new farm. It had once belonged to Lindsay Lewis, but she'd sold it before she married Keith. They had their own place closer to where Keith worked, and Cord wanted a more rural life than a house in a gated community. "And I have cake samples."

"In the kitchen," Jane called, and Opal hurried through the living room, with its luxurious leather couches, and into the kitchen. Molly had already arrived, as had Gerty and Opal's momma. They'd left the farm a few minutes before Opal, and she'd had to stop for the cake samples too.

She went straight to the table and set down the tray that stretched her arms wide. "Okay, we've got eight flavors of cake to sample." She pulled a piece of paper out from underneath the overly large slices of cake, each one neatly situated in a plastic clam-shell container.

"Chocolate chocolate chip," she said, pointing to the corner container. "Vanilla bean, carrot, German chocolate, Chantilly white, strawberry cheesecake, chocolate mousse, and banana."

"You went with the fruits," Jane said as she joined Opal at the table. She handed her a cup of tea and said, "It's chamomile, with honey."

"Thank you, Janey." She leaned into her cousin, such love flowing through her. She smiled at her momma, who lifted her left hand.

"Has he proposed yet?"

Opal's gaze dropped to her left hand too, where no, she did not wear a diamond yet. She held up her naked finger so everyone could see. "Not yet."

"What's he waiting for?" Molly asked. "I swear, cowboys know how to take their sweet time."

"He probably just wants to get it perfect," Gerty said. "Tag is a good guy. He loves Opal, and since he knows it's going to be a winter wedding—"

"And that we're already planning it," Opal said.

"Right," Gerty said. "He's just trying to make it perfect."

"Do you know something we don't?" Momma asked, zeroing in on Gerty.

Her face colored up quickly, and she brushed her hair back. "No."

"Oh, I think she does," Jane said with a giggle.

"I don't," Gerty insisted. "I just know Tag, that's all."

"Forks," Molly said, getting to her feet. "Let's taste the cakes, and then I believe Opal has her dress choices narrowed down to three, and they sent her renderings with her in the dresses."

Opal bounced on the balls of her feet with giddiness. "All true. But I want cake chosen first." She took the fork Molly offered and started popping open the clamshells.

She already knew she didn't want any of the fruity ones. So the banana, carrot, and strawberry cheesecake were out. But she tasted them anyway, because the Paris Bakery made delectable cakes in any flavor.

They were all moist, and the frostings were all creamy and perfectly balanced in their sweetness compared to the cakes.

"No to the chocolate chocolate chip," she said, pushing the clamshell toward her mother. "You'll like that one."

"I know what you're going to pick," Momma said with a sly smile. She pulled the chocolate chocolate chip toward her and forked up a bite.

Opal took a bite of the vanilla bean, and she did love that one. She wanted white, white, and more white. The bakery could make the outside of any cake pure, snowy white, but Opal wanted the inside to match too.

She'd already tasted the Chantilly white, but she took another bite of it. Then another. And one more, only then realizing that the other four women had stopped tasting and were watching her.

"I think it's the Chantilly white," Jane said delicately.

"It's the winner," Opal said, licking the last of the frosting from her fork. "Now, who wants to see the dresses?" She started to reach for the dresses when Molly pushed the white cake toward her again.

"Wait, are you sure? What about the frosting on the very end?"

Opal looked down at it. The piece of cake had three layers, and they'd eaten about half of it. The thicker end, where the frosting did pile up, looked normal to Opal. "I suppose I should try it." She took her fork and swiped it through the frosting there, then put that in her mouth.

"It's so good," she said, going back for more. This time, she took a bigger bite of cake and frosting, and when she lifted her fork, something glittery and gold hung from it.

Opal froze, the breath in her lungs turning to absolute ice.

"Honeybear," came from behind her, and Opal sucked in a breath and spun to face Tag.

He wasn't standing where she thought he'd be, but he'd already dropped to both knees, right there in Jane's kitchen.

"Oh, dear Lord." Opal still held the fork with cake and a diamond, and she backed up, trying to assess the situation in only a moment. Of course she couldn't do that, but she did catalog that her female family had all scuttled into the kitchen, and both Momma and Molly had their phones up, likely recording.

Cord leaned in the doorway leading into the living room, as did Mikey, Hunter, and Daddy.

Opal's eyes filled with tears as her heartbeat paraded through her body. "Taggart," she gasped out.

"Let me have that, honey." He reached for the fork, and Opal practically dropped it. He took a handkerchief from Daddy, and cleaned the cake crumbs and frosting from the diamond. Tag gazed at it for a long, loving moment, and then his gaze came to hers.

His smile wobbled a little, and he said, "I wrote all this down in my notebook, and now I've forgotten it all."

Opal smiled back at him, the moment between them pure and priceless. "You can do it," she whispered.

"Honey, I'm in love with you," he said. "It's something I can't fight, and I can't change. I want you at my side for the rest of my life, and I want to be your biggest champion, your confidante, and your best friend."

He held up the ring, as if Opal hadn't seen the giant round rock. "Will you do me a great honor and marry me?"

"Yes," she whispered.

"Oh, we can't hear you in the back," Daddy called.

Opal didn't move her gaze from Tag's. He looked at her with so much hope and desire, and Opal lowered her hands from her pounding pulse and said, "Yes, I'll marry you."

"There you go," someone yelled as the applause and cheering filled the kitchen.

Tag's hands shook as he slipped the ring on her finger, and they both looked at it as he got to his feet. His hand slipped under hers, and while she heard the yelling, yeehawing, and congratulating, all she could see in that moment was her hand wearing that diamond, layered over his.

All she could smell was Taggart's cologne, and the leather that went everywhere with him, and the sweetness of frosting.

All she wanted sat right in front of her, and Opal finally felt like the woman who deserved it, could have it, and would take it.

She looked up at Tag, and said, "I love you."

"You're mine," he whispered, and then he kissed her. With every stroke of his lips against hers, Opal truly claimed him as her own while simultaneously giving herself completely to him.

CHAPTER
Thirty-Four

TAG CLIMBED the steps to Opal's porch, which had been finished last week. The front door blazed at him in a bright blue, and he smiled as he opened it. Inside, the house still had plenty to get done, but Opal had windows now, and appliances, and cupboards hung in the kitchen.

She needed her quartz countertops, and the walls needed to be painted the off-set color from the crown molding and baseboards. She needed the furnace and AC unit hooked up, and she needed to do the final walk-through with all the inspectors. But the house was getting closer and closer and closer.

Opal sat on her bright purple couch, which she'd positioned in front of the big bay window that looked north, back toward the farm. She'd kept as many trees as possible, so she couldn't see much, and he wondered what she was looking at as he sank onto the couch with her.

"That's a big sigh," Opal said without looking at him.

"Our new horse is a diva," he said. "She's going to take a while to break, but we'll get there. Steele's doing great with her." And Steele needed the practice with a horse who didn't already know the rules. And this new horse—a pretty black thing named Black Gold—had come to them wild, pure, a blank page for them to train and teach.

Honestly, that was Tag's favorite kind of horse, and he couldn't wait to see Black Gold come into herself. "She might be a good one for you to ride one day," he said quietly, because the unfinished house held a soft spirit today, and he didn't want to puncture it with his loud voice.

Opal shifted and lay down, putting her head in his lap and continuing to look outside. "Okay," she said. "I'm getting better. Molly even says so."

"I'm sure." He stroked her hair and thought of the first time she'd made it into the saddle during her first riding lesson, a couple of weeks ago. She went to her cousin's farm a few times a week for the lessons—and so they could go over wedding plans.

Tag's impatience reared, but he tamped it right back down. He and Opal were getting married at the beginning of November, because she wanted to be in this house together, with him, for the holidays. He wanted that desperately too.

"What's wrong, honeybear?"

"Just feeling like things are moving so slowly."

"The countertops are only a week behind," he said, stroking her hair.

"Let's just get married tonight," she said.

He didn't chuckle, though he knew Opal was kidding. "I would, honey, but I've got that leather-working class tonight."

She giggled for a moment, then fell back to silence.

"Jane's gonna have her baby in a few weeks."

"Yes," Opal said. "I can't wait."

"Have you heard on a name?"

"They're keeping it under wraps."

"Even from you?"

"Even from me."

Tag ran his fingers through her hair again. "Do you want me to get dinner?"

"Yes," she said. "Can we look at the stars tonight?"

Now that the thick of summer had arrived, the sun didn't set until quite late, and if Tag stayed up until it was truly dark enough to see the stars, it would be way past his bedtime. He'd be tired in the morning and all day long. But he said, "Sure thing, honeybear."

She sighed as she sat up, and Tag said, "That's a big sigh."

She gave him a weary smile. "I'm just tired from chasing West. He should be here soon, because he got a new trike, and we rode it here this morning, and he wants to do it again."

"So you'll be chipper for Westy, but not for me." Tag grinned at her. "I see how it is."

She slid into his side again. "Not at all, baby. I'm chipper for you." She touched her lips to his. "This is just one of many Opal-facets."

He breathed in the fruity scent of her hair. "I know you want this house done. It'll probably only be another two weeks. Four, tops. Way before we get married."

"You still want to marry me, even if you find me staring at nothing when you get home from work?"

"Opal-honey," he murmured. "I want to marry you *because* I find you staring at nothing when I get home from work."

"I have two wedding things for you tonight," she said as she sat up and pushed herself to the edge of the blow-up couch. "Are you game?"

"If I can get two things from you tonight," he teased.

Opal got to her feet and turned back to him. "Mister Crow, whatever do you mean?"

He grinned at her and draped his arm along the back of the couch. "They're surprises."

"So I have to agree before knowing what they are?"

"That's the definition of a surprise, yes."

She considered him for a moment, and he watched

his playful, vibrant Opal emerge from wherever she'd been keeping her. "All right," she drawled the way he would when trying to impress her. "Let me get my folder."

"Oh, it's folder-wedding stuff?"

Opal walked away without answering him. "Can I see the dress?" he asked.

"No," she called over her shoulder. "And don't you dare snoop through my phone."

Tag saw it sitting over on the other side of the couch, but he didn't reach for it. Opal returned in only a few seconds anyway, and she had a blue folder in her hand. "That's your facilities folder," he said.

"Yes." She sat on his lap, and he encircled her in his arms. "I want you to help me pick a venue. I have to book one, and I promised them both I'd call by tomorrow."

"All right," he drawled.

"And." She shuffled some pages in the folder, drawing Tag's attention. "I want your opinion on where you'd like to go for our honeymoon."

Ah, the honeymoon. "Baby Bear, I told you to pick," he said gently. They'd already had this conversation—twice, actually. She was funding it, and he felt like she should get to choose where she wanted to go. He'd happily go with, and he liked beaches, mountains, and foreign countries equally, as he didn't spend a lot of time visiting any of them.

"I've narrowed it to three destinations," she said. She speared him with a sassy-Opal look. "I would like your opinion."

"Yes, ma'am," he murmured.

Satisfied, she looked back at her folder. "Grand Cayman," she said, holding up a full-color printout of the whitest sand Tag had ever seen. Teal, blue, and deeper blue water. Glorious sunshine.

"Nice," he said, wanting to board a plane and go right now.

"It'll be nice to escape the colder weather for the beach in November," she said. "That's choice one. Number two." She exchanged the beach paradise for a picture of what looked like a Swiss village. "Germany," she said. "They have the cutest little towns and festivals. And we'll be there sort of during holiday season, and we can go to their Christmas markets."

"Mm," he said, liking the other one better. "I don't have a passport."

"You have time to get one," Opal said. "I called and checked. Twelve weeks."

"Okay." He gave her a smile. "Third?"

"Okay, hear me out on this."

"Have I ever not heard you out?"

She gave him a beautiful smile. "No, it's one of the things I love most about you." She held up a picture of a cruise ship. "Caribbean cruise," she said. "All the Saints. Saint Thomas. Saint Martin. Saint Lucia."

Bright blue skies. Endless food and drinks. Trapped on a ship with Opal for days and days.

"Into...." She whipped out another picture and covered the first one. "A Mediterranean cruise. Spain, Italy, Croatia, Greece."

"Wow," he said, truly surprised. "Gerty will approve this much time off?"

"It'll be a little over three weeks," Opal said, clearly unconcerned. "With travel and time zones and stuff."

"How long are these cruises?"

"Eight days, and then twelve days."

"Wow," he said again.

"I know *wow* means *no*," Opal said, tucking her papers back into her folder.

"It means I'm processing." He leaned in and nuzzled her neck. She tipped her head back and let him too, so she wasn't truly upset. "I want a beach thing," he murmured against the delicate skin of her neck. "So Grand Cayman or the cruises. That's my opinion."

"Cruises are fun," she said. "I think you'd love it."

"Then let's go cruising," he said. "I just want to be with you, Opal."

She leaned into his chest and said, "I just want to be with you too, Tag."

"Venues," he said. "Then surprises."

"I already know what venue you'll like best."

"Show me anyway."

So she took out the two venues, one of which boasted luxurious indoor gardens—which Opal would definitely choose—and the other which portrayed a down-to-earth country wedding—if cowboy billionaires were planning and paying for everything.

In this case, a cow*girl* billionaire.

"They're both great," he said. "And look, you can do a foliage option on the lodge."

She grinned at him. "I knew you'd like the lodge."

"It feels more like me," he admitted. "But the botanical gardens totally feels like you. I'm fine with either, as long as you're mine at the end of the night."

"I'm yours right now," she whispered, and Opal kissed him like her life depended on having her lips touching his.

He didn't mind that at all, and he still hadn't gotten to the surprises when the front door flew open, and an eighteen-month-old West yelled, "Ope! I here!"

———

TAG LOOKED over as gravel crunched under someone's feet. Opal came around the corner of the barn wearing a pair of black shorts and a tank top the color of pine trees. "You owe me two surprises," she said as she sauntered closer, her lime-green chair over her shoulder.

"Where's West?"

"Mikey had a headache and came home from work early. They're napping together."

He looked back into the ring where Steele worked with Black Gold. "You okay, bud? I can take thirty minutes away?"

Steele didn't look away from his equine. "Sure. Go."

Tag moved away from the circle and took the inflatable furniture from her. "Where do you want to go? I have thirty minutes."

"Somewhere shady," she said.

"Come with me." He led her past the barn, past the stables, and just when he thought she'd utter a word of complaint, he heard the river. Opal obviously heard it too, because she looked at him. Another thirty yards, and he moved along a footpath and between two trees to the most magical place on the farm.

"Here you go, madam." He set down her chair, grinning, and then sat in it. She settled onto his lap, a sigh slipping from between her lips.

"This is amazing," she said. "You've been holding out on me."

"The water doesn't run all the time," he said. "But we had a lot of snow this year."

"It's so serene."

"Mm hm."

"Get talking," she said.

He chuckled, but he hadn't really been holding out on her. They'd simply gotten interrupted the other day, and they were busy. "All right, first up: my whole family is coming to the wedding."

Opal pulled in a breath and jerked her attention to him. "You're kidding. Your daddy too?"

Tag smiled as he nodded. "Heard from him over the weekend. Said he wouldn't miss it."

Her grin matched his. "Oh, that's great news, Taggart." She hugged him about the head and kissed him quickly. "Are you happy?"

"Yeah," he drawled out. "Of course, the twins are now blaming me for the constant barrage of texts they're getting from my mama." He shook his head and watched the water go by. "I keep tellin' them I don't have it any better. She's already haranguing me about grandchildren."

Opal giggled and leaned into his neck. "I can't wait to meet her."

"Maybe we can take a trip before the wedding," he murmured, thinking that if he didn't say it too loud, he could pretend like he hadn't.

"That's a great idea." Opal raised her head to study him. "Is that the second surprise?"

"No, honey." He grinned at her. "For the second surprise, we have to go to the house."

Opal got right to her feet. "Let's go."

Tag collected her chair and they started the walk

back. He left the chair in the shade of the barn, and when Opal detoured toward the farmhouse, he squeezed her hand and nodded down the lane. "Your house, honey."

"My house?" She fell back to his side. "What could you possibly have done at my house?"

"It's a surprise," he said.

"I'm there every day, Tag."

"I'm aware." He bumped her with his hip. "But when you're with West, you don't see much further than your arm."

Opal sucked in a breath. "How dare you?" She then burst out laughing in the next moment. "So you're saying you trespassed onto my property when I was busy with West."

"That's what I'm saying." He sure enjoyed holding her hand as they walked down the dirt road, and Tag's version of happiness could be summed up in a summer afternoon with Opal at his side.

He led her around the back of the house to the basement entrance, ignoring her curious look. After opening the door for her, he gestured her inside. Then he followed her and said, "Last bedroom, honeybear."

She went into the bedroom first, and Tag closed the door behind them. The blinds had been pulled shut over the window, and he made no move to flip the switch. Even if he had, no lights would've come on, as the house had no electricity.

"What are you planning to do with this bedroom?" he asked.

Opal looked around at the bare walls, turning in a full circle before she focused on him again. "I don't know." She took a step toward him. "Taggart, there's no surprise here."

"I was thinkin'," he said. "Of maybe another piece of inflatable furniture."

"Well, if we have a lot of kids, I don't think that's going to work."

"But in the beginning," he continued. "But I'm thinkin' a mattress this time. A bed."

"A bed?"

"Then, you can come down here day or night, rain or shine, and lie down." He nodded to the floor. "And see the stars."

"See the—?" She craned her head back to look up, her voice cutting out like someone had pressed mute. She breathed out, the word, "Stars," coming with the air.

Tag got down on his knees and then lay flat on his back, stretching his arms up and behind his head. "Yep, there they are." He switched his gaze to hers. "Lay by me, honeylove."

Opal hastened to do that, and she curled into his side, one arm sliding over his torso, her fingers slipping into his belt loop on the opposite side. "Taggart," she whispered. "This is the best thing anyone's ever given me."

He laughed, because he'd paid someone to come paint the ceiling black and then use glow in the dark fluorescent paint to make the stars. "It's a little paint, honey."

"It's so much more than that."

"See Orion?" He lifted his free arm and pointed up. "The belt right there?"

"I see it," she whispered.

"So when you're feeling a little...down. Or off, or like things are moving too slow, you can come down here and see your stars." He pressed his lips to her forehead. "And you won't have to stare out the window at nothing."

"Mm." She laughed lightly too. "I do that sometimes, don't I?"

"Just a little bit," he whispered.

"I love this," Opal said.

"And I love you." He rolled toward her slightly, and she lifted her head to meet his kiss. She didn't say she loved him back—at least not in words. But he had the shape of her next to him and the stars above, and Tag couldn't wait until she was his and he was hers.

I love Opal and Tag - and that bright purple blow-up couch! I hope you do too. If so, **please leave a review for His Eighth Ride by scanning this code on your phone.**

You can read the first two chapters HIS NINTH PROMISE now! Just turn the page.

Sneak Peek! His Ninth Promise Chapter One

TUCKER HAMMOND COULDN'T STOP LAUGHING as he followed his older brother and uncle out of the farmhouse. Hunter and Uncle Wes had been sharing stories about their time as the CEO of the family company—Hammond Manufacturing Company. Hunt had run it for seventeen years, and Uncle Wes probably twenty-five.

And today, they were all heading into the city. Aunt Bree and Opal had some shopping and other wedding things to do; Tucker's only sister had just had her baby, and he was tagging along with Hunter and Uncle Wes to take lunch to everyone at Jane's house.

Tuck had come back to Ivory Peaks with his parents to see Jane and Cord's new son, and he'd been in town for less than twenty-four hours. Still, he'd thought of Bobbie Jo Hanks several times. If she hadn't gotten a new phone number, he could text her and find out if she had dinner plans.

For some reason, he hadn't. Tuck had been learning that just because he had a thought didn't mean he had to speak. Didn't mean he had to act on it.

No one had mentioned her. Not Hunt or Cord, nor Molly or Jane. So as Tuck left the homestead, he looked over to the stables, hoping to catch a glimpse of her. From this distance, she'd have to be literally walking toward him or crossing the pasture, and she wasn't doing either.

So he hitched his smile in place and listened as Hunt started a new story about staying late one night and accidentally asking three different people to order dinner in for those who'd had to work through the meal.

"You've never seen so much pizza," he said, his boisterous laugh filling the August sky. "Boxes and boxes of it."

"I could eat pizza for every meal," Tuck said.

"It's a favorite," Uncle Wes said. "But Jane requested the roast beef sandwich from Deli Harvest, so that's where we're going first."

"And then to Porky's, right?" Tuck asked. His mouth watered for the sloppy barbecue pulled pork sandwich, and he knew for a fact that Mike, Uncle Wes's son, Tucker's cousin, and the current CEO of HMC, had requested the same sandwich for his lunch.

"Right," Hunt said as he got in the passenger seat of Uncle Wes's truck. "You starving, little brother?"

Tuck grinned as he climbed into the backseat. "Always."

"Well, we've got a ways to go," Uncle Wes said, glancing in the rearview mirror. "Lunch pick-up, driving to Jane's, another drive, more food pick-up, and then to the high rise downtown."

"He literally just ate two bowls of cereal inside," Hunt said. "He's fine."

"I'm fine," Tuck agreed. He tuned out the conversation as the drive started. He turned to his phone instead, where he'd been communicating with another manager in the rodeo about a cowboy who might potentially need a manager.

He'd met with Cole Walker, but he'd been working with a great manager named Leon Peters for only a couple of years. Tuck wasn't going to try to poach the man away, and he'd enjoyed his summer working with Blaze and Jem Young in their youth rodeo program.

He wasn't sure what the next step for him was, but he had faith in God that something would open up for him. He wasn't sure if that opportunity would present itself in Coral Canyon, or here in Ivory Peaks, or somewhere else completely.

He was trying to be patient, be open to all things, and keep his nose clean and his head down.

Since his parents were going to be staying in Ivory

Peaks for a few months—until his cousin Opal married her fiancé Taggart Crow—Tuck would be here too. He'd moved into the generational house with his younger brother, because his old cabinmate had a new man living with him, so Tuck couldn't go back there.

He could've moved in with Hunter too, or even stayed with his parents, who were living in the fore-man's cabin out in the cowboy community, away from the homestead. He'd opted for staying with Deacon, because it *wasn't* with the other cowboys.

He didn't want to stay on the family farm, plain and simple, and if he integrated himself into the community out there, it would be harder for him to leave. Tuck had already gone through that once a few months ago, and he didn't want to do it again.

Plus, you didn't want to run into Bobbie Jo.

He dismissed the thought almost as instantly as it had come into his mind. It might be true, but Tuck didn't trust himself to be alone with Bobbie Jo. "Especially after kissing her the way you did," he muttered.

The reason he'd given everyone was that he missed his brother, which wasn't untrue. Tuck did miss Deacon, and he actually admired how stalwart and steady his brother was. He knew what he wanted, and he got up every day and worked toward that thing.

Tuck felt blown about in the wind, the way a dandelion seed did after a child made a wish on it and sent it off to come true.

He'd always been a dreamer, and his daddy has

spent the better part of the summer telling him it was okay to be who he was. That God had made him to be more spontaneous than Deacon, and that he could still make a good life for himself by dreaming and going after those dreams.

"We need help carrying everything," Hunt said, and Tuck pulled himself out of his head. He got out of the truck and went in with his family members to get the food they'd ordered for everyone out at Jane and Cord's new farm.

They'd moved completely onto the property now, and the house in the suburbs—where he'd lived with Jane before she and Cord tied the knot—had gone onto the market. Yes, she'd asked him if he'd wanted it. No, Tucker did not want a six-thousand-square-foot house in a neighborhood behind a gate.

What he really wanted was a big camper to tow around and live in while he moved from rodeo to rodeo with a really talented cowboy. He'd prayed and prayed for God to give him the talent in the saddle, but it simply hadn't happened yet. At this point, Tuck was pretty sure he wasn't going to be a rodeo champion.

He was great with a rope, and if he could find a partner with patience and deadly aim as the lead man, he might-could make a living in the rodeo. But so far, he hadn't been able to find that partner either.

Not since his last cowboy and best friend, Tarr, had retired officially.

He helped pick up the bags of food, and it all got put in the back of the truck with him. They then made the drive to Twilight Fields, the name of the farm Cord and Jane had bought. They hadn't renamed it, and a sense of shimmering sunshine and serenity passed over Tuck as Uncle Wes turned onto the dirt road that led toward seemingly only trees.

Tuck did like trees, and his mind wandered according to the rumbling of the tires. Maybe he could be a lumberjack or something. Did they travel and see different forests? What skills would he need, and would he have to go to college to get them?

Tuck did not like college or book learning very much.

"Tuck," Hunter said, and his loud voice startled Tucker.

"What?" he asked crossly. "I'm right here."

Hunter had already gotten out of the truck. "I've said your name three times." Hunter wore a frown that melted away as he slammed his door and pulled open Tuck's. "What are you thinkin' about?"

Tuck could absolutely not say *trees*. Not to his high-powered, super-CEO, older brother. "Nothing," he growled. "I'm coming." He twisted and reached for the bags of food he'd carried out of the restaurant.

Hunt watched him, but Tucker had been living with Daddy for the summer, and he knew how to withstand those dark-eyed looks that asked too many questions. He kept his head low, utilizing his cowboy hat to hide his eyes, as he went by.

Uncle Wes led the way inside, and everyone turned dark compared to his big personality. And right now, Tuck didn't mind living in the shadow of his magnetic uncle. He took the food into the kitchen so everyone at the farm would have something to eat, and then he skedaddled back to the living room, where the cutest baby in the whole wide world currently rested in a swing.

"Howdy, Clint," Tucker said as he moved toward the gently swinging infant. He was only a week old, and Tuck seriously didn't know how the little boy's head could fold into that ninety-degree angle.

"You can get him out," Jane said. "He needs to wake up now."

Tucker looked over to her, suddenly nervous though he'd held the baby already. "I can? Should I?"

"I'd love you forever if you'd hold him while I eat." She gave him a quick side-hug. "You guys are getting lunch somewhere else, right?"

"Yeah," Tucker said, looking back to the baby. They held such wonder for him, and he decided he could fumble around with Clint and learn how to deal with a newborn baby. So as Jane moved into the kitchen, Tucker moved over to the swing.

He switched it off and unclipped the safety belt around the pudgy baby. "All right, buddy," he said.

"Come see Uncle Tuck." He lifted the baby up, one hand sliding up behind his floppy head.

Clint made the cutest squeak and groan possible, and a shot of joy injected itself right into Tucker's heart. Then he cradled the baby against his chest and moved as slowly as he ever had—and that meant something for Tucker, who'd been hustling and bustling everywhere he went since the age of four.

The baby made a disgruntled noise, and Tuck went, "Shh, shh, shh." Then he remembered Jane wanted the baby to wake up. He honestly had no idea how to keep a baby awake, and he figured his sister knew that.

People talked and laughed in the other room, but Tuck ignored them. The noise of his family faded away, and all he could see and hear and smell was the perfect little boy in his arms. Tuck had never considered himself as a father, but the feelings running through him told him that perhaps Tuck should be looking for someone to call home, someone he could be a partner with throughout the whole of his life, and someone who could give him a perfect baby like Clint.

Of course, because his mind liked to torture his heart, an image of a pretty strawberry blonde came to the front of his thoughts. Bobbie Jo Hanks.

"Maybe I should just text her," he murmured to Clint. "What do you think, buddy? I mean, it's a text. She can ignore if she wants, right?"

Clint groaned again, and Tuck swore he heard the

baby give him permission to text Bobbie Jo. He could do it from the truck, as Uncle Wes drove them from the small town life an hour from the city to the high rise building where Mike worked in downtown Denver.

"Ready, Tuck?" Hunter asked.

Cord followed him, and he finished wiping his mouth as he did. "I'll take him, Tuck."

Tucker easily eased Cord's son into his arms, noting how soft and paternal Cord had become in a single moment. He gazed at Clint with such love, and Tuck's heart sang for this to be his life too.

These thoughts half-surprised him and half-irritated him. He'd been working for months to find a cowboy to manage. Getting back his contacts in the rodeo—and Blaze and Jem Young were still *huge* in that arena—and mapping out what he wanted the next few years of his life.

Fatherhood had been nowhere in the plan.

"Tucker," Hunter said, more wariness in his voice now.

"I'm coming," he said.

"You're really checked out today," Hunter said.

"He is?" Daddy asked.

Tucker threw a glare at his father, then one to Hunter. "I am not," he said. "Let's go."

"Waitin' on you," Hunter said with an over-exaggerated wave of his arm toward the front door. Tucker did his best not to stomp past everyone and out of the house, because he wasn't thirteen anymore.

He heard his father and Hunter start a conversation behind him, and he knew they were talking about him. Daddy would probably wait a while and then text, or he'd bring it up with Tucker the next time they were together.

Tuck rolled his eyes now, but he knew his daddy loved him, worried about him, and prayed over him constantly. So he didn't really mind talking to his father and spilling everything in his heart and mind.

He did his darndest to stay present, though he didn't care about the conversation happening in the front seat. He did care about getting his pulled pork sandwich, and he did care about getting up to Mike's office as quickly as possible to eat.

So he didn't have Hunter breathing down his back, Tuck stayed attentive through it all, and he carried his beloved sandwich and a huge cup of soda across the lobby and toward the elevator.

One more ride up a bunch of floors, then a walk down a long hall, and finally, *finally*, Tuck could eat. He was so anxious to get to the food—and to prove to Hunter that he didn't need to be prodded like an errant child—that the moment the elevator chimed its arrival, Tuck started toward it.

A voice he knew met his ears, and it took his eyes a moment to catch up to his memory. The prettiest woman in the world had her head tipped back as she laughed, and Tucker wanted to bathe in the sound of Bobbie Jo's voice.

Unfortunately, he'd been living in small-town Coral Canyon or Ivory Peaks for years, and he didn't frequent a lot of elevators. And double unfortunately, he'd already started moving onto the elevator.

He didn't realize that etiquette dictated that he should've waited for the people already on the elevator to get off, and Bobbie Jo did exactly that.

And since she wasn't looking directly at Tucker, she didn't see him.

Everything in the world turned into slow motion. He tried to stop, but his long legs were between steps. He instinctively lifted his hand to block her or shield himself or something. Truth be told, his brain couldn't work that fast.

Bobbie Jo looked at him, and he caught a hint of surprised recognition a mere nanosecond before he ran straight into her with his cola cup.

Which exploded.

Brown liquid shot out of the top, dislodging the lid and sending fizzy soda in all directions. Tucker even got a few drops straight to the face.

And in a triple move of unfortunate, most of his Diet Coke spilled down the front of Bobbie Jo's pristine white scientific lab coat.

Sneak Peek! His Ninth Promise Chapter Two

BOBBIE JO HANKS had a temper that fired like an automatic weapon when she got irritated. Or even when she just hadn't gotten enough sleep the night before.

And right now, as ice-cold cola seeped into her clothes and ran down her skin, a deadly combination of exhaustion and irritation made her go, "Tucker Hammond, what is wrong with you?"

Someone in the elevator had gasped. Someone else had cried out. Bobbie Jo took a step back, the brown puddle of liquid at her feet only adding to the nightmare unfolding in the elevator.

She held up both hands as if she'd dipped them in tar and looked at Tucker like he'd done the worst thing imaginable.

"I'm so sorry," he gushed. "I just got on, and I didn't—" He cut off, his face turning a deeper shade of red with every passing moment. "What are you doing here?"

So not the time for this conversation.

"Tucker," Hunter Hammond said. "Brother, you're in the way. Let's let everyone get off this car. Uncle Wes went to get security."

Tucker spun toward his older brother. "Security? Why?"

"They'll close this car down," Hunter said matter-of-factly. Then he turned toward someone, laughed loudly, and drew the man into his chest for a hug. "Howdy, Earnest. We're gonna need maintenance and janitorial."

"Oh, ropin' and ridin'," Tucker muttered under his breath, and it almost made Bobbie Jo smile.

The elevator car started to whine, and he did get out of the way then. That allowed the people behind Bobbie Jo to get off the elevator, and she looked help-lessly at Troy, a co-worker she'd been about to go to lunch with.

"I'll be at The Corner Bakery," he said. "I'll get you the soup and salad combo. Catch up to me when you're cleaned up." And off he went, leaving Bobbie Jo only a single step from leaving the elevator and getting her overdue meal.

Tucker stood in front of the doors so they couldn't close, and the high-pitched wail only bothered her more. She let out an exasperated sigh and looked over to the panel of buttons. She jabbed at the red one, the one she'd use if the elevator stalled or she needed help, and on the second try, she hit it.

A siren sounded, and Bobbie Jo cowered down as if fighter jets would soon be peppering the building with bullets.

"Great," Tucker yelled over the noise. "As if everyone wasn't already staring at us."

"Us?" She glared at him. "I think you mean me. You don't have cola all over you."

"Don't I?" He held up the ruined cup, which still dripped ominously with Diet Coke.

At least she assumed it was Diet Coke. She'd never known Tucker to drink anything else.

You might not know anything about him, she thought, and Bobbie Jo felt herself coming down out of the red zone. Thankfully, before either of them could say anything else, more people arrived.

A maintenance worker and a man with a mop, along with at least three of the men who stood at the front counter and took care of any problems with people coming and going in the lobby.

"Let's get you out of that puddle," the janitor said. "Maybe the showers, Mister Hammond?"

"Sure," Hunter and an older gentleman said. Bobbie Jo didn't know him, but he bore the same long, sloped nose as Tucker and Hunter, so she assumed they were related. They both laughed while Tucker stood there with a brown paper bag and his half-crushed cup.

Hunter gestured to the older man. "We're both Mister Hammond. We both ran HMC."

"Oh." Bobbie Jo didn't know what else to say. "I don't need a shower. I don't have other clothes here." She looked over to Tucker, but he'd handed his cup off and ducked his head.

"We'll find you something," Hunter said jovially. "Come on, Bobbie Jo." He guided her out of the elevator, and the maintenance worker stepped onto it and silenced the alarm. "We've got full facilities on this level, and I can get you something new to wear for today. Unless you've moved closer? I can send someone to your place and get you something. Or you can just jet home really quick."

Of course he could do any number of things. Hunter had unlimited resources, and she had no doubt he had any number of minions who would run to her apartment and get her precisely what she dictated to them.

She glanced over to Tucker, her heartbeat doing strange flips and flops in her chest. She really wished her old cabinmate had never called him the hottest cowboy in the country, because since she had, every time she looked at him, that was all she could think.

He'd cut his hair recently, if the clean-shaved look of his neck and up around his ears meant anything. He wore a cowboy hat indoors, which wasn't surprising, but only made her like him more. Blue jeans—standard for a cowboy. His shirt wasn't a polo or a button-up, but a plain old short-sleeved T-shirt, which meant he hadn't come in from the farm for lunch today.

The dark gray made him seem a bit more mysterious, as did the logo on the front—a B, J, and Y—as she had no idea what it meant.

He looked up at her, and their eyes met for a moment. Her whole world changed in that moment, and Bobbie Jo didn't know how or why or even which way was up anymore. She only knew that Tucker Hammond had walked right back into her life, spilled a lot of cold cola down the front of her body, and then stood there looking like the surface of the sun.

"Bobbie Jo?" Hunter asked, and when she slid her gaze to his, she found him looking over to Tuck.

"I don't live close," she said. "I really can just…get a new lab coat."

"Tuck here will get you something." Hunter grinned with all he had as he nudged Bobbie Jo toward the Cowboy Who Hadn't Moved.

"What?" he barked. "I don't know how to do that. I didn't run this place."

"Mike's expecting us," Hunt said. "We've got some business to discuss with him."

The other Mister Hammond looked at Hunter, obviously confused. "He won't—"

"He is *starving*," Hunt said over him. "He's been texting me for twenty minutes." He still wore a smile akin to a clown, and Bobbie Jo's ire skyrocketed again.

"*I'm* starving," Tucker said. "I don't know where

the shower facilities are, and I certainly don't have everyone in this building queueing up to get my autograph." He glared at Hunter. "You're embarrassing me."

Bobbie Jo's heart went out to Tucker, because he was a sweet, sweet man. Her lips tingled with the memory of kissing him. "I'm really okay," she said. "I'll just go get cleaned up in the restroom."

Hunter had fallen back a step, and he didn't say anything. The older man stood there too, obviously going to let someone else play this out.

Tucker said, "Me too. Let's go, Bobbie Jo. You two go on up without me. I know the way to Mike's office, at least." He stalked away from the situation, and Bobbie Jo decided not to dawdle.

She went after him, saying, "Tucker."

"Look, I'm really sorry," he said. "I just—my brother's been riding me all day, and I was just in a hurry to get upstairs and eat. I should've just waited to get on the elevator."

He had the longest legs ever, and Bobbie Jo jogged to catch up to him. "Hey," she said, her temper rising again. "Can you just *wait*?"

Tucker came to a complete stop now, and she nearly ran straight into his back. He turned, and if she hadn't stopped herself in time, his shoulder would've taken her out. "What?" he barked.

She blinked at him, trying to make the pieces of him line up. "I've never seen you in a bad mood."

He rolled his eyes. "Of course you have."

She actually smiled. "No, I don't think I have."

Tucker's square shoulders deflated. "Well, I guess there's a first time for everything." He dropped his chin, his right hand still gripping that brown bag. He looked up at her from beneath the brim of that sexy hat. "I really am sorry."

"Do you have the same phone number?" she asked.

He raised his head fully and stared openly at her. "Sure do," he said easily. Then he swallowed, so maybe it wasn't as easy to say as she'd assumed.

Bobbie Jo wanted him to ask her out. Words streamed through her head, things she could say if she had more courage, if she wanted to know what he was doing here, on a Wednesday afternoon, at her new place of employment.

But she wanted him to ask her out. Him to ask if he could text her or call her. Maybe suggest dinner, so she could kiss him before they even got inside the restaurant.

He said nothing.

Maybe their kiss almost three months ago hadn't meant as much to him as it had her. Maybe she wasn't a good kisser, and men like Tucker probably had plenty of women to compare her to.

"Where you livin' now?" he asked.

"I've got a place up in Aurora," she said. "It's a cute little blue house with three bedrooms. I share with two other girls." She swallowed, not sure why she'd started rambling about where she lived.

"Aurora," he said. "That's still a commute."

"Everything is a commute to HMC," she said. "Unless you have the last name Hammond and can live in the building next door." She quirked her left eyebrow at him, almost daring him to contradict her.

He graced her with a smile. "You're right about that."

"Did you sign another cowboy?"

"Not yet," he said. "I did summer rodeo camp work in Coral Canyon, with a couple of big-name cowboys. Blaze and Jem Young."

Her eyes dropped to his chest. "Is that what the BJY is?"

"Yes, ma'am."

Her fingers stuck together, and she pried them apart. The soda had started to dry, and she really should get into the bathroom, get cleaned up, and get to The Corner Bakery. Troy would have her food, and he'd demand to know the story behind her knowing the Hammonds.

When he didn't ask or offer anything else, Bobbie Jo took a breath. For a moment there, that single moment suspended in time with their eyes locked, she'd thought God had reunited them. That He'd brought Tucker back to the area specifically so they could have their second chance at something meaningful and lasting.

Maybe he's dating someone else.

The thought struck her like a ton of bricks being dropped on her head, and Bobbie Jo let out a frustrated breath. "Okay, well—"

"There you are, sweetheart."

Both she and Tucker turned toward the male voice, and she found another co-worker rushing toward her. Ben wore a semi-crazed, half-panicked look, and he lifted his arm as he approached her.

That was when the word *sweetheart* rang in her ears. "Ben—"

His arm landed around her shoulders, something he'd never done before. He tucked her into his side like he'd done it a thousand times, though. He grinned down at her like he was just so thrilled to see her.

"What—?"

"Who's this?" he asked, cutting her off. He definitely cooled as he looked at Tucker. "Is he that friend you said we might be able to double with?"

"What?" Bobbie Jo swung her attention to Tucker, who had both eyebrows sky-high now.

"Double with?" Tucker asked. He looked at Bobbie Jo. "He's your boyfriend?"

Bobbie Jo wanted to laugh, but her throat seemed to be full of sand with only a hint of saliva, and everything felt too thick.

Surely Tucker wouldn't buy that. Ben looked nothing like the type of man Bobbie Jo would ever, ever go out with. He wore *slacks*, for crying out loud.

Tucker was a smart cowboy; he'd figure it out. He'd make a joke, laugh about the ridiculousness of her and Ben, something.

But things were moving so fast, and neither of them had time to say anything before Ben said, "Yeah, I'm her boyfriend. Who are you?"

———

Ohhh, boy. Is Bobbie Jo going to go along with this ruse to protect her heart? Or will she make sure Tucker knows she's available? Preorder **HIS NINTH PROMISE** so you don't miss a moment of life in Ivory Peaks with the Hammond family!

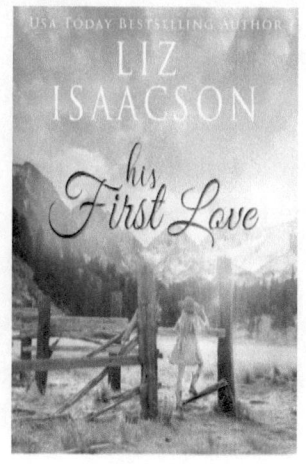

His First Love (Book 1): She broke up with him a decade ago. He's back in town after finishing a degree at MIT, ready to start his job at the family company. Can Hunter and Molly find their way through their pasts to build a future together?

His Second Chance (Book 2): They broke up over twenty years ago. She's lost everything when she shows up at the farm in Ivory Peaks where he works. Can Matt and Gloria heal from their pasts to find a future happily-ever-after with each other?

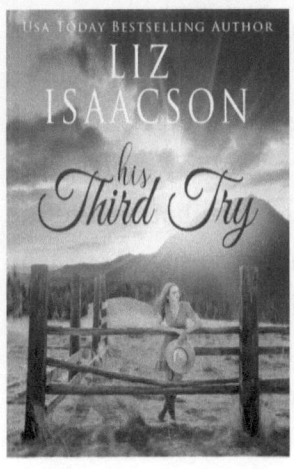

His Third Try (Book 3): He moved to Ivory Peaks with his daughter to start over after a devastating break-up. She's never had a meaningful relationship with a man, especially a cowboy. Can Boone and Cosette help each other heal enough to build a happily-ever-after...and a family?

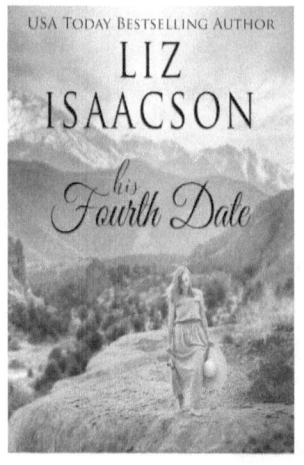

His Fourth Date (Book 4): Their relationship has been nothing but loose goats, a leaking roof, and her complete humiliation after he pays her mortgage so she won't lose her farm. Travis wants to go back in time and start over with Poppy, but he doesn't know how. Can a small town speed-dating event get their second chance off on the right foot?

His Fifth Kiss (Book 5): They once had a few summers together. Now, Michael Hammond is back in town after a devastating injury overseas. He's looking to reset and recover...not to fall in love. But with Gertrude Whettstein also back at the farm, can Gerty and Mike make their second chance romance into a happily-ever-after?

His Sixth Sweetheart (Book 6): She's had a crush on him for decades. He's finally in a place where he feels ready to date the boss's daughter. Can Cord and Jane take their relationship to the next level without getting burned?

His Seventh Stop (Book 7): He's a seasoned cowboy on a delivery mission. She's a resilient hobby farm owner braving the winter storm. Can Keith and Lindsay forge a bond in the heart of a tempest and find love in the calm that follows?

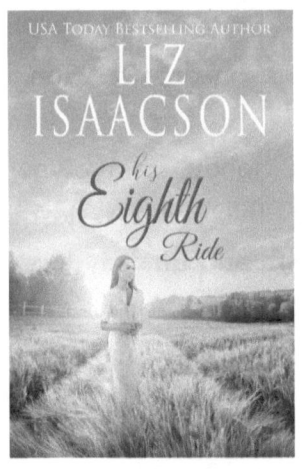

His Eighth Ride (Book 8): Tag has secretly admired Opal from afar. He even went so far as to ask her out, but the timing was all off, and now he's just awkward around his best friend's little sister. Can their unexpected reunion mend the fences between them and finally lead them to the forever love they've been waiting for?

His Ninth Promise (Book 9): At home on the Hammond Family Farm, where gypsy souls and rodeo dreams collide, Tucker's heart has been beating for Bobbie Jo. But with her heart set on a distant love and Tucker searching for something more, their paths seemed destined to cross but never converge. Can he stick it out for another ride if the promise is coming home to Bobbie Jo?

Her Cowboy Billionaire Birthday Wish (Book 1): All the maid at Whiskey Mountain Lodge wants for her birthday is a handsome cowboy billionaire. And Colton can make that wish come true—if only he hadn't escaped to Coral Canyon after being left at the altar...

Her Cowboy Billionaire Butler (Book 2): She broke up with him to date another man...who broke her heart. He's a former CEO with nothing to do who can't get her out of his head. Can Wes and Bree find a way toward happily-ever-after at Whiskey Mountain Lodge?

Her Cowboy Billionaire Best Friend's Brother (Book 3): She's best friends with the single dad cowboy's brother and has watched two friends find love with the sexy new cowboys in town. When Gray Hammond comes to Whiskey Mountain Lodge with his son, will Elise finally get her own happily-ever-after with one of the Hammond brothers?

Her Cowboy Billionaire Beast (Book 4): A cowboy billionaire beast, his new manager, and the Christmas traditions that soften his heart and bring them together.

Her Cowboy Billionaire Bad Boy (Book 5): A cowboy billionaire cop who's a stickler for rules, the woman he pulls over when he's not even on duty, and the personal mandates he has to break to keep her in his life...

Books in the Christmas in Coral Canyon Romance series

Her Cowboy Billionaire Best Friend (Book 1): Graham Whittaker returns to Coral Canyon a few days after Christmas—after the death of his father. He takes over the energy company his dad built from the ground up and buys a high-end lodge to live in—only a mile from the home of his once-best friend, Laney McAllister. They were best friends once, but Laney's always entertained feelings for him, and spending so much time with him while they make Christmas memories puts her heart in danger of getting broken again…

Her Cowboy Billionaire Boss (Book 2): Since the death of his wife a few years ago, Eli Whittaker has been running from one job to another, unable to find somewhere for him and his son to settle. Meg Palmer is Stockton's nanny, and she comes with her boss, Eli, to the lodge, her long-time crush on the man no different in Wyoming than it was on the beach. When she confesses her feelings for him and gets nothing in return, she's crushed, embarrassed, and unsure if she can stay in Coral Canyon for Christmas. Then Eli starts to show some feelings for her too...

Her Cowboy Billionaire Boyfriend (Book 3): Andrew Whittaker is the public face for the Whittaker Brothers' family energy company, and with his older brother's robot about to be announced, he needs a press secretary to help him get everything ready and tour the state to make the announcements. When he's hit by a protest sign being carried by the company's biggest opponent, Rebecca Collings, he learns with a few clicks that she has the background they need. He offers her the job of press secretary when she thought she was going to be arrested, and not only because the spark between them in so hot Andrew can't see straight.

Can Becca and Andrew work together and keep their relationship a secret? Or will hearts break in this classic romance retelling reminiscent of *Two Weeks Notice*?

Her Cowboy Billionaire Bodyguard (Book 4): Beau Whittaker has watched his brothers find love one by one, but every attempt he's made has ended in disaster. Lily Everett has been in the spotlight since childhood and has half a dozen platinum records with her two sisters. She's taking a break from the brutal music industry and hiding out in Wyoming while her ex-husband continues to cause trouble for her. When she hears of Beau Whittaker and what he offers his clients, she wants to meet him. Beau is instantly attracted to Lily, but he tried a relationship with his last client that left a scar that still hasn't healed...

Can Lily use the spirit of Christmas to discover what matters most? Will Beau open his heart to the possibility of love with someone so different from him?

Her Cowboy Billionaire Bull Rider (Book 5): Todd Christopherson has just retired from the professional rodeo circuit and returned to his hometown of Coral Canyon. Problem is, he's got no family there anymore, no land, and no job. Not that he needs a job--he's got plenty of money from his illustrious career riding bulls.

Then Todd gets thrown during a routine horseback ride up the canyon, and his only support as he recovers physically is the beautiful Violet Everett. She's no nurse, but she does the best she can for the handsome cowboy. **Will she lose her heart to the billionaire bull rider? Can Todd trust that God led him to Coral Canyon...and Vi?**

Her Cowboy Billionaire Bachelor (Book 6): Rose Everett isn't sure what to do with her life now that her country music career is on hold. After all, with both of her sisters in Coral Canyon, and one about to have a baby, they're not making albums anymore.

Liam Murphy has been working for Doctors Without Borders, but he's back in the US now, and looking to start a new clinic in Coral Canyon, where he spent his summers.

When Rose wins a date with Liam in a bachelor auction, their relationship blooms and grows quickly. **Can Liam and Rose find a solution to their problems that doesn't involve one of them leaving Coral Canyon with a broken heart?**

Her Cowboy Billionaire Blind Date (Book 7): Her sons want her to be happy, but she's too old to be set up on a blind date...isn't she?

Amanda Whittaker has been looking for a second chance at love since the death of her husband several years ago. Finley Barber is a cowboy in every sense of the word. Born and raised on a racehorse farm in Kentucky, he's since moved to Dog Valley and started his own breeding stable for champion horses. He hasn't dated in years, and everything about Amanda makes him nervous.

Will Amanda take the leap of faith required to be with Finn? Or will he become just another boyfriend who doesn't make the cut?

Her Cowboy Billionaire Best Man (Book 8): When Celia Abbott-Armstrong runs into a gorgeous cowboy at her best friend's wedding, she decides she's ready to start dating again.

But the cowboy is Zach Zuckerman, and the Zuckermans and Abbotts have been at war for generations.

Can Zach and Celia find a way to reconcile their family's differences so they can have a future together?

Tex (Book 1): He's back in town after a successful country music career. She owns a bordering farm to the family land he wants to buy...and she outbids him at the auction. Can Tex and Abigail rekindle their old flame, or will the issue of land ownership come between them?

Otis (Book 2): He's finished with his last album and looking for a soft place to fall after a devastating break-up. She runs the small town bookshop in Coral Canyon and needs a new boyfriend to get her old one out of her life for good. Can Georgia convince Otis to take another shot at real love when their first kiss was fake?

Morris (Book 3): Morris Young is just settling into his new life as the manager of Country Quad when he attends a wedding. He sees his ex-wife there—apparently Leighann is back in Coral Canyon—along with a little boy who can't be more or less than five years old... Could he be Morris's? And why is his heart hoping for that, and for a reconciliation with the woman who left him because he traveled too much?

Trace (Book 4): He's been accused of only dating celebrities. She's a simple line dance instructor in small town Coral Canyon, with a soft spot for kids...and cowboys. Trace could use some dance lessons to go along with his love lessons... Can he and Everly fall in love with the beat, or will she dance her way right out of his arms?

Blaze (Book 5): He's dark as night, a single dad, and a retired bull riding champion. With all his money, his rugged good looks, and his ability to say all the right things, Faith has no chance against Blaze Young's charms. But she's his complete opposite, and she just doesn't see how they can be together...

...so she ends things with him.

Gabe (Book 6): He's a father's rights advocate lawyer with a sweet little girl. She's fighting for her own daughter. Can Gabe and Hilde find happily-ever-after when they're at such odds with one another?

Jem (Book 7): He's still healing from his vices, and Jem has dedicated everything he has to his two kids. At least he's not mourning his divorce anymore, and in fact, he might be ready to move on. She's his former best friend, and once he breaks his wrist, his nurse. Can Sunny somehow rope this cowboy's heart?

Luke (Book 8): He swore off women when his ex told him he might not be their daughter's father. But a paternity test confirmed he is, and Luke Young has dedicated his life to his little girl and his brothers' band. There hasn't been time for a girlfriend anyway. He's tried here and there, and the women in small-town Coral Canyon are certainly interested in him.

But he's been thinking about his massage therapist for a while now. Can he ask Sterling out when all they've ever been is professional? Oh, and there's the fact that she's seen practically every inch of his body... Awkward, right?

Bryce (Book 9): Bryce Young has been broken and drifting for years. After giving up his son for adoption, he left Coral Canyon and hasn't returned...until now.

Harry (Book 10): He's a country music star who doesn't live in town. She's a Missing Persons Investigator with strong ties to her community... and she's not so sure about Harry's T-shirts... But Belle knows her heart sings whenever she sees Harry - if only that were more often.

About Liz

Liz Isaacson writes inspirational romance, usually set in Texas, or Wyoming, or anywhere else horses and cowboys exist. She lives in Utah, where she writes full-time, takes her two dogs to the park everyday, and eats a lot of veggies while writing. Find her on her website, along with all of her pen names, at authorelanajohnson.com